WHAT REMAINS

What Remains is dedicated to Joe,
my beloved husband.

Acknowledgments

With gratitude and friendship, I wish to acknowledge the following individuals for their gifts of research information, advice, and encouragement: Jay Evans, Peter Miller, Jennifer Robinson, Beverly K. Sewell, Dorothy N. Poole, Robin M. Carter, Nicholas P. Carter, Dorothy R. Carter, Nancy L. Poole, Tawny Kilborne, Lynette Walker, Kate Stine, Jeff Abbott, Joan Lowery Nixon, Geneva Fulgham, Tom W. Glaser, Debra Osterman, Anna Louise Bruner, Sarah Harris, Happy Dodson, Pam Matthews, and CoraLynn McCabe.

What Remains

by

R. Poole-Carter

Top Publications, Ltd.
Dallas, Texas

What Remains

A Top Publications Paperback

First Edition

Top Publications, Ltd.
12221 Merit Drive, Suite 750
Dallas, Texas 75251

ISBN 1-929976-16-X

Library of Congress Control Number 2002107037

Printed in Canada

CHAPTER ONE

It was Isabelle's turn to sit with the body. The room was mercifully cold. The chill masked the odor of decay, froze it midair between the coffin by the shuttered windows and the smoldering fire in the tiled hearth across the room. Isabelle stared into the ashes crumbling around a half-hidden heart of embers that glowed orange beneath black like a small, secret hell.

In one hand Isabelle held the last letter she had received from Forest Brodie, dated June of 1863, and in her other a letter she had written to Forest in May of 1864. She wondered what had happened to all the other letters she had written him before and after that date, and she wondered why this particular letter had been in his jacket on the day he died.

Isabelle's aunt, Delora Raveneaux, had found the letter while preparing Forest's remains for burial and returned it to her. A faded violet was pressed between its pages. In every letter to him she had included a pressed flower or leaf found in the woods bordering Halcyon, his family's estate, or on the grounds of Belle Ombre Plantation, where she lived with her aunt. Once she had sent him a lock of her pale golden-brown hair tied with stems of agrimony. Once she had sent magnolia seeds, red and bright as drops of fresh blood. Every seed, leaf, and petal held a memory of walks Isabelle and Forest had shared in the orchards and woods and along the banks of Lyre's Creek.

The few of his letters that had reached her—she knew he must have written more—contained bits of flowers she had never seen before, flowers he had found on marches and by camps and in battlefields in states far from west Louisiana. In life there had always been flowers between them, but there were no flowers now. She imagined his body lying within its oblong box, no longer so far from her. She was with him in the still, dark, oblong room, in the rambling, shadowy house, buried in the night.

Isabelle folded the letters together and slipped them into her skirt pocket. She had not wanted to read her own letter again, written a year and a half ago when she was full of hope and still believed that for Forest's homecoming she would wear a white veil, not a black one. His last letter she knew by heart:

"Beloved Isabelle, thoughts of you are all my strength. God forgive me, but it is you, not He, that sustains my heart. I can tell you nothing—not where we are nor where we've been nor what is to become of us. I can say I've been wounded and promoted in rank and wounded again. If this pattern continues, I may be a general by the end of the War—if there's anything left of me. But don't fret, my dear girl. The wounds are healing nicely and are not so bad that you'd notice them right off. As of tonight, you would still know my face as I know yours. If the worst comes tomorrow and my body and soul part company, I promise you this—I will hover still in this world and delay eternal rest if I might yet do you good. As always, your devoted Forest."

Isabelle slowly drew in her breath. Would she know his face now? Perhaps she might more easily recognize his apparition than his remains, if she believed in ghosts. But in all her longing for lost loved ones, her parents most especially, she had never seen a departed spirit. When Forest's corpse arrived, Aunt Delora had refused her even a glimpse of the body. "Remember him as he was, dear," she had said. "I won't have you haunted by what's become of him." If it had been anything but death—if he were lamed, disfigured, his mind lost in memories of the horrors he had seen—she vowed she would still have taken him to her heart.

Forest had never told her he hadn't wanted to go to war, but how could he not go and still be a man? If any young men had once wavered in their sense of duty, Isabelle's uncle, Charles Orvin Raveneaux was there to guide them; Colonel Raveneaux was the magnetic leader of the parish, drawing all the new recruits after him, as if they were no more than a gray line of metal filings. Pulling them toward destruction, Isabelle thought.

Forest had pleaded with her to marry him before he left, but she had hesitated, and like a good niece and ward, had let herself be guided by Aunt Delora. "Marry now in some hushed, rushed ceremony? Never! Why, this scuffle with the North will be over in a month at most," her aunt had said. "Then you shall have a *real* wedding." But when the month turned into years, Delora still stood by her advice: "Be thankful, my dear, that you're not raising Forest's baby in our time of adversity."

Rising from the bench before the hearth, she turned toward the coffin. Always Delora had tried to prepare her for this conclusion, never for the happy one. "Even when our men are with us, Isabelle, they're never quite with us. In war and in peace, we must learn to live within ourselves. We have no one else." But still Isabelle had hoped she would have Forest, hoped until word had reached them last evening that a body had arrived in town for the folks at Belle Ombre. Even as Delora comforted Isabelle, she maintained for a certainty that her own man, her husband, the masterful Colonel Raveneaux, would return unharmed. It seemed never to enter Delora's mind that the body would belong to anyone but Forest. And she had been right.

"But why send word to us?" Isabelle had asked. "Here, at Belle Ombre?"

"Why, everyone for miles around here knows Halcyon was burned to the ground ages ago," Delora had replied. "Old Mr. Brodie building that showy place near the pike—it was a bold invitation to those Yankee raiders. Thank heavens Belle Ombre is more privately situated. And, of course, word must have gotten around too that Forest's people are all dead and gone or moved off. It was only natural to send him to you, his beloved. Goes to show someone out there has some feelings. And now you know your precious letter was close to his heart when he died."

Langford, one of Delora's former slaves who had continued to work for her after the War, had spent half the previous night making the coffin from pine planks pried up from the attic floor. Then at dawn he had driven the buckboard to town to fetch the body home. The remains, salted and wrapped in a tarpaulin, had come south by train and then on by wagon to Verbena and St. Jerome's chapel. During the War and just after, the chapel had been a clearing house for the bodies of so many men from Verbena and the surrounding farms and plantations. But now, in November 1865, few Confederate soldiers, alive or dead, were still making the journey home.

Forest's coffin was supported by two small tables pushed together. A single candle in a brass holder flickered on the coffin lid. All around this small circle of yellow light, a vast shadow, many times the length and breadth of the coffin, filled the room.

Isabelle remembered how the room had looked before the War, bright with dozens of candles. Forest and his father, coming over for an evening from their own nearby plantation, had sat at one of the little tables playing cards with her uncles, Charles Orvin and Louis Raveneaux. Nearby, her aunts, Delora, Lydia Everett Raveneaux, and Lydie Vee Vasseur embroidered and chatted, while Great-Uncle Babcock Vasseur, his breath hot with brandy and cigar smoke, whispered old jokes to young Isabelle and her little cousin, Euphrasie. And the girls would giggle and blush and clap their hands to their ears.

Babcock Vasseur had married late in life, when most of his family had given up on the possibility. His wife, remarking that Louis had already brought a Lydia into the clan, took the name of Lydie Vee. No one since had called her otherwise, not even after Lydia Everett's death. Not long after, Louis Raveneaux passed over, following Isabelle's parents with yellow fever, and leaving his daughter, Euphrasie, an orphan like Isabelle herself. Fever, influenza, smallpox, cholera all came and went and came again through the years, taking casualties in a cruel war of Nature. And if that weren't enough, women died giving birth, and their sons grew up to butcher one another on battlefields.

Now when Isabelle held her breath, the back parlor was quiet as a grave. Then even as carefully as she moved, approaching the coffin, the rustle of her skirt and petticoats, the soft click of her footfalls, the throbbing of her pulse in her temples set up a cacophony that made her head whirl. She reached out for support, clutching the edge of the coffin lid and recoiling as a splinter of wood pierced the palm of her hand.

A thud of boots sounded in the hall, the door flew open, and suddenly the room was split in two by a lantern beam. Isabelle spun toward the noise and light. She gasped, her lungs filling with fetid air made even more noxious by a steaming cloud of odors of sweaty wool and spilled whiskey emanating from the overseer of Belle Ombre.

"Oh, Mr. Samson! You gave me quite a start."

Elroy Samson slammed the door with a rear kick, then took a step forward. Isabelle stood rigid, facing him, her back to the coffin.

"You and me needs to talk," snarled Samson.

"Really?" Isabelle swallowed hard. "I can't imagine what about. Plantation business is between you and my aunt—till Colonel Raveneaux returns, of course."

"And what makes you think he's coming back, missy?" Samson asked, slurring his words.

"Aunt Delora believes he will. She had a letter from him just last month," Isabelle replied, resolving not to be intimidated by Samson's rudeness.

"She's everlastingly getting letters and telling us all what to do. And she's still holding out on us—me and Faye and our boy—and her own kin, too. How long you want to go on being a poor relation?" Samson's heavy features loomed, distorted in the light of the lantern he held below his stubbly chin. "We live on crumbs while she's got a fortune stashed away, buried somewhere 'round here."

"Aunt Delora is more than generous to all of us. The War's taken its toll here same as everywhere else. You know that."

"I know that the other map of Belle Ombre is still missing. And an awful lot of finery and silver ain't been seen in this house since the War."

"Of course she can't have her nice things out on display when the Yankees are still paying us visits."

Samson squinted at her, and his upper lip curled over jagged teeth. "You know where that map is, don't you? You know she used it to mark her hidin' places. Don't deny it. I tell you, you been seen with that map. Radley told me so."

"And who told your son?"

"Your little cousin did."

"Euphrasie! A reliable source of information, indeed." Though nearly sixteen, Cousin Euphrasie was still as likely to invent stories and embellish facts as a six-year-old. Isabelle continued with restrained fury. "Mr. Samson, you are intruding upon my grief. Tomorrow morning we bury Forest Brodie. And as far as I'm concerned, he is the only treasure to be buried on this plantation. Now leave me and let me have what remains of my time with him in peace."

"But I ain't finished yet." Samson strode around her to the coffin and held his lantern high over it. "Don't it strike you odd—an elegant, refined lady like Miss Delora, laying out a putrefying corpse?"

"Aunt Delora's always taken charge of things. She's mistress of the plantation. And she wanted to spare me as much as possible."

"She didn't spare Beryl. She dragged her in to help out. Didn't ask Langford or one of the men."

"Would you have helped her?" Anger rose in her voice.

"I wasn't drunk enough."

"You're drunk now."

"Yeah." Samson set the lantern on the floor. "So now I mean to see just what Miss Delora's got in this here box. I bet you she's pulled some things from her hidey-holes 'round the house and tucked 'em in with the corpse."

"Why would you even imagine she'd do such a thing?"

"Oh, I seen her slap Beryl just t'other day for sniffing around, getting too close to Miss Delora's stash, I wager. Stands to reason she'd be looking for a safer hiding place. And this here is it." Samson struck his splayed hands down on the coffin lid. "You wanna have a look-see with me, missy? Just see if I ain't right."

"How dare you! Forest is in there, and there he'll stay—undisturbed. Do you understand me?" Isabelle cried, yanking his hands from the coffin lid.

Samson wheeled on her, gripped her arms, and shook her. His rancid breath choked her as he shoved his face down close to hers. "You don't know nothing, girl. Not hog shit!

'Cause all you know is what Miss Delora tells you."

Isabelle glared back at him, into the slits of his eyes, and fought to make her voice heard above the growl in his throat. "Get out! Get out or I'll scream 'til the whole house shakes. You wouldn't dare try this with all my kin looking on."

Samson snorted. "If I wanted to, girl, I could stop you screaming 'fore you ever got a peep out. You think on that." Slowly, he relaxed his grip on her arms, and she pulled free.

He retrieved the lantern and started toward the door. "Damn box lid's nailed shut anyway," he muttered, then turned back. "You want to see me gone, don't you, missy?"

Isabelle clenched her jaw and watched him without answering.

"Well, I tell you for sure, I ain't leaving Belle Ombre 'til I go in style. You want me out, you fetch me that treasure map real soon. You hear?"

"And if I can't find it?"

"Then maybe your horse goes lame or maybe your colored girl falls in the creek or—"

"I understand, Mr. Samson."

"Then I'll see that map tomorrow."

He left the door open behind him, and Isabelle heard the clomping sound of his boots receding down the hall and up the back stairs. Tomorrow, after Forest was buried, she would give Samson the map, though it would be as worthless to him as it had once been priceless to her.

Tears blurred her eyes. She blinked them away and strained to focus on a pale shape that had suddenly appeared, fluttering in the draughty doorway, strained to hear a thin voice whispering.

"Isabelle? Isabelle, Aunt Delora sent me to spell you for a while. But I didn't dare come in while that dreadful man was here."

It was Isabelle's cousin, Euphrasie, slipping in on bare feet and in her white flannel nightgown. Isabelle wondered if it had crossed Euphrasie's mind to fetch her some help while that dreadful man was here sputtering in her face.

"Do you want to go to supper, Cousin? Or I could ask Ardyce to bring you something on a tray? We could sit in here together, couldn't we?" Euphrasie obviously thought this was the best suggestion as she curled up on the bench before the hearth, tucking her feet beneath her gown. She patted the cushion beside her. "Come away from there, Isabelle, and sit by me. "

Isabelle moved away from the coffin and toward her cousin. "I'm not hungry, Euphrasie. And I don't want anyone to spell me—I can't sleep and I won't leave him 'til he's buried. You go on to bed."

"Oh, but I want to sit with you, Isabelle."

"All right. I'll make up the fire. You're shivering."

"Don't trouble yourself. Just ring for Ardyce. She'll fix it nice for us."

Isabelle shook her head as she added a log to the fire and prodded it with the poker. "Ardyce is at least as weary as everyone else."

"You should hear yourself," Euphrasie said with a shrug. "Before the War's been over a year, you'll be waiting on her."

"Maybe I'll just be working side by side with her."

Euphrasie fidgeted with her plait of straw-colored hair. "Well, I didn't stay to talk about Ardyce. I came to talk to you about him—over yonder." She nodded toward the coffin.

"And what have you to say about him?" Isabelle asked.

"This." Euphrasie leaned close to Isabelle, who had joined her on the bench. "I've seen Forest Brodie. I looked right at him."

Isabelle drew back from her cousin. "Oh, no,

Euphrasie. Why ever did you do such a thing? Does Aunt Delora know?"

"'Course not. I wouldn't dare tell her."

"You'd no right—no right to look on him. We lay out the dead when we must, when it's our duty. But this act was morbid, Euphrasie."

Isabelle's cousin was so often childlike and thoughtless; none of the family expected much from her, but Isabelle felt she must chide Euphrasie for her unwholesome curiosity.

Euphrasie crossed her hands upon her narrow breast and looked pleadingly at Isabelle. "Dear coz, you misunderstand me. I never, ever looked at his . . . his remains. Night before last, I saw Forest Brodie."

Isabelle felt a constriction in her chest. "That's impossible," she whispered. "He's been dead for nearly a month."

"Oh, don't you see, Isabelle? It was his ghost! I saw it with my own two eyes."

Those wide, pale eyes that loomed from Euphrasie's pinched face—when did they ever see beyond her fantasies? Isabelle wondered.

"This is wicked, Euphrasie. Forest is dead. His soul's in God's keeping."

"Don't believe it, Isabelle. Night before last his spirit walked on the veranda—limped, I'm sad to say. I saw him from the front parlor window. I know he was looking for you. I could feel it. He sort of drifted down the steps, out onto the lawn." She fluttered her fingertips through the air to illustrate spectral movement. "And then . . .Oh, then, Isabelle, he reached a hand upward, toward your bedroom window." Euphrasie gazed at her own wraithy arm outstretched. "It was the tenderest of gestures—enough to break your heart in two."

Euphrasie had such a gift for saying the wrong thing.

Isabelle pressed a hand against the letters in her skirt pocket and shut her eyes a moment before she spoke. "Cousin, you mustn't say a word about this to anyone. Do you understand?"

Euphrasie nodded.

"And I won't have you speaking of it to me again either. Forest will rest in peace."

"But, coz. . ."

"In my heart I know I have to release him. Don't make it harder for me with your stories. I just might find myself watching for him, too, hoping to catch a glimpse of him."

Euphrasie touched the tears on Isabelle's cheek. "As you wish," she said softly. "Oh, Isabelle, do you think anyone will ever love me the way Forest loved you?"

Isabelle didn't answer, but embraced her cousin. As a growing child, Euphrasie had reveled in the tales older women whispered to one another of dancing with their cavaliers, flirting among the veranda columns, receiving kisses, permitted or stolen. And she had begged to hear every detail of Isabelle's courtship. How difficult it must be, Isabelle thought, for her cousin now to look across the threshold from girlhood to womanhood and see no young man waiting, to have only fantasies, not prospects, nor memories of love.

They remained huddled together on the bench for a long while. Isabelle, resting her cheek on Euphrasie's crown of yellow hair, had given in to exhaustion when a sudden noise startled her from the brink of a dream.

A door slammed somewhere in the house. Muffled screaming followed, then a clattering sound, then silence. Euphrasie tensed in Isabelle's arms. Someone's running footsteps pounded down the hall, passing the back parlor door.

Isabelle held Euphrasie at arms' length and whispered, "Wait here. I'll go and see what's happened."

"Oh, no! I can't stay here alone with . . .with . . ."

Euphrasie shot a frightened glance toward the coffin.

"You may be better off here. I'll be back in a moment." Isabelle pulled her hands free of her cousin's clinging fingers and left her huddled on the bench.

"Leave the door open," Euphrasie called plaintively as Isabelle stepped into the hallway.

Light flickered from around the turn in the corridor, and bell-shaped shadows of ladies' skirts loomed on the opposite wall. The mingling of voices and moaning grew louder as Isabelle hurried toward the cluster of family and servants.

Near the back stairs, beneath the circular, railed airwell, the household formed a circle of its own. Great-Uncle Babcock Vasseur and his wife, Lydie Vee, stood rigid, hand in hand, their backs to Isabelle, whispering to one another. Next to them was Ardyce, the young woman Colonel Raveneaux had given to Isabelle as a slave when both girls were children. Ardyce wrapped a supporting arm around the old cook everyone called Auntie Pan, while Auntie Pan rocked and moaned in the embrace. Delora Raveneaux held high a candelabrum from the dining room set and admonished the others to be silent. Though Babcock Vasseur, as brother of Delora's late father and in the absence of Delora's husband, called himself "the man in charge," at her command he ceased his murmurings as quickly as did the others.

As Isabelle approached the group, Faye Samson, the overseer's wife, came scurrying from the front of the house and pushed past her.

"What's happening down here?" Faye cried in her shrill voice.

"There's been an accident," Delora announced, her gaze meeting Isabelle's, not Faye's, then traveling upward toward the airwell. It was a railed circular opening cut through the landings of the second and third floors for ventilation. The maids also used it to save themselves a few trips up and down stairs on wash day by tossing the dirty laundry over the railing so that it landed in a pile in the back hall.

At a nod from Delora, the circle opened. The reek of alcohol and an image of the grotesque assailed Isabelle's senses as she looked down. On the hardwood floor, directly below the airwell, the servant, Beryl, lay crumpled like a fallen rag doll. She was in her white shift, lying on her back, one arm twisted unnaturally, with her knees tossed over her shoulders and her feet above her head.

"Is she dead?" Faye asked stupidly.

Babcock harumphed loudly. "For heaven's sake, let's straighten her out," he said, and laboriously dropped his substantial bulk to one knee.

Delora brought the candlelight closer while Lydie Vee, taller, leaner, and a decade younger than her portly husband, assisted him in bringing Beryl's legs to the floor. Then Isabelle could see how one side of Beryl's coffee-brown face had struck the boards, and blood had run from her nose and pooled around her ear.

Auntie Pan groaned and clutched her sides. "Just look at that! Her head's smashed like a dropped melon." Ardyce led the cook aside, patting her and crooning to her.

Delora cleared her throat. "We'll lay the body out on the kitchen table for now. Tomorrow Langford can saw up that old chiffonier in her room to make her a coffin. Faye, where's that husband of yours? Fetch him and Radley to move the body."

"Yes, ma'am."

At that moment, Faye Samson's fifteen-year-old son, Radley, entered the hall from the kitchen door. "No need to fetch me, Ma. I'm right here."

"Where's your Pa?" Faye asked sharply.

Radley shrugged. "Ain't here."

Isabelle glanced up at the airwell railing. "I think Mr. Samson went upstairs some time ago," she said.

"Well, Radley," said Delora, ignoring Isabelle's comment, "Beryl's fallen through the airwell and died. Obviously, she was unsteady from drink. I'll have to ask you and Mr. Vasseur to carry her out."

"Yes, ma'am, Miss Delora."

Babcock hastily moved to take Beryl's feet, leaving Radley to lift her shoulders. As they hauled her up from the floor, her head dropped back and her bloodshot dead eyes stared accusingly at no one in particular.

Isabelle approached Ardyce and Auntie Pan. "Did you see this happen?" she asked. "Was Beryl leaning over the railing? Was anyone with her? The airwell's so narrow . . .I don't understand it . . .even if she were unsteady . . ."

"I didn't see nothing, miss, 'til I come out of the kitchen," Ardyce said softly. "And Auntie Pan was dozing in her chair when the clatter woke her."

"Two dead bodies at Belle Ombre," Auntie Pan quavered, "and things comes in threes." After this dark prediction, she sobbed heavily into the ragged shawl thrown around her old house dress.

"Take her to her bed," said Isabelle, "and you and I will talk later, Ardyce."

"You sure, miss?"

"Yes. Go on up."

Babcock had returned from the kitchen, wiping his hands on his white handkerchief. Radley had apparently chosen to stay with the corpse.

"Most distressing," Babcock muttered. "Lydie Vee, I'm heading back to the dining room for something to steady me."

"I'll come with you, dear." She took hold of his arm.

Then the couple paused before Isabelle.

"Dear girl," said Lydie Vee, "we're so sorry you had to see this—tonight of all nights. Come with us."

"By all means," Babcock added. "You must have a brandy." He laid a moist hand on her shoulder.

"Thank you both, but no. I must go back in a moment to sit with Forest."

Isabelle suddenly thought of Euphrasie, waiting for her in the back parlor. Shocked and confused by what she had seen in the hall, Isabelle was uncertain how long she had been away. A wave of dizziness swept over her, and she leaned against the corridor wall. Babcock's hand slipped downward from her shoulder and was quickly removed by Lydie Vee.

"We'll look in on you later, dear. Now come along, Babcock." Lydie Vee then guided her husband down the hall toward the front of the house.

Isabelle turned to Delora. Her aunt stood beneath the airwell, still gripping the heavy candelabrum in one delicate hand, giving instructions to Faye Samson.

"Get the oldest blanket you can find to cover her body. We've nothing nice to spare."

"And do you want me to stay here tonight?" Faye asked.

"No. You get her covered and then get on to your cabin," said Delora. "I don't want Elroy banging around this house in the middle of the night, looking for you—if he ever decides to come back from what he gets up to. And take Radley with you. You think I haven't noticed the pilfering that's been going on in my pantry?"

Faye's back stiffened. "Radley would never . . ."

"Spare me," Delora snapped.

Faye compressed her prim mouth before she spoke again. "What about this mess on the floor? Shall I call Ardyce?"

"It'll be here in the morning. That's soon enough to clean it up."

"Yes, ma'am." Faye retreated up the back stairs—to find an old blanket, Isabelle assumed.

Delora stood alone in the circle of candlelight, dressed in dove-gray and lace, her mass of auburn hair upswept with a silver comb. She was a buxom, short-waisted woman in her mid-thirties, not tall, not precisely beautiful, but imposing by virtue of her self-possession. The harshness about her mouth suddenly vanished along with the harsh tone she had used toward Faye; her voice and her face were smooth and sweet when she spoke to Isabelle.

"Isabelle, honey, what a dreadful sight for mourning eyes! I wish I could have spared you this, I truly do. You've borne more sorrow than any young girl ever should."

"I'm all right, Aunt Delora. Shaken, of course. But aren't you, too?"

Delora nodded with a sad smile.

"Did you see it happen? Did anyone?"

"We were all in the dining room," said Delora.

"Oh, and I left Euphrasie in the back parlor," Isabelle said.

"Oh, dear. Then I'll light your way there."

Delora stepped forward, the hem of her gown sweeping through the pool of Beryl's congealing blood and leaving dark streaks on the floorboards as she led Isabelle down the hall.

When they reached the back parlor, they found Euphrasie cowering beneath the hearth bench, tremulously singing "Old Folks at Home."

CHAPTER TWO

"Tonight, while the house slept, I paced the veranda, stopping now and again, my eyes searching the shadows on the lawn—as if the longing in these eyes of mine could draw you forth from among the trees and bring you to my side. There is no breeze tonight, almost no air, except the air we must drink—the fog rolling up from Lyre's Creek. I paced in my cotton gown, aching to run to you, even in such a state of disarray, trusting you would forgive me my impatience. My dearest, come back to me before I'm old and crippled and can run no more."

This was Paul Delahoussaye's favorite letter, written in August of 1861. Unlike some of the later correspondence, which was sometimes penciled on thin sheets, this letter was written on weighty, creamy paper, the fine script trailing across the page like sepia-colored lace. And even more unlike the other letters, it contained nothing ordinary, nothing matter-of-fact, for it had been written when passion was new—written on a hot, still summer night when a white cotton gown would cling to damp flesh. Paul wished the letter had been written to him.

But he was only the onlooker, who could touch the smooth paper, catch a whiff of musty gardenia, and read and re-read words he had not inspired.

Paul Delahoussaye was a young journalist who sold his stories primarily to Mr. Caulder, editor of the Laurel Dispatch in Missouri, and occasionally to small papers in Arkansas, Louisiana, and Texas. At the end of the War, Mr. Caulder assigned him to do a series of interviews with both Union and Confederate officers as they prepared to return home. That was how Paul had come into possession of the letters Isabelle Ross had written to her fiancé, Forest Brodie.

Paul had been sitting on a camp stool, his long legs cramped under him, taking notes on the adventures of a brash, twenty-four-year-old major. Holding forth about his exploits and boasting of the trophies he had taken from rebels he'd killed in Virginia and at Gettysbury, the major tossed various items out on his cot. A decorative flask, a revolver with someone's initials etched on the handle, a silver locket that held a girl's likeness, a gold watch fob and piece of chain (the watch itself had been destroyed by the major's bullet)—all were mementos of lives the major had ended. All were testaments, according to the major, of his superior prowess and courage.

Then abruptly, the major paused in his discourse and lifted from among the other items a packet of letters, tied with a blue-gray ribbon.

"I didn't take these off a rebel corpse," the major said. "Just found 'em lying on the ground after a battle. You know those rebs—dropping and losing things so they could run away faster."

"What kind of letters are they?" Paul asked.

"What kind do you think?" The major lifted one brow. "But I haven't bothered to read them. Here, you take them." The major pitched the bundle, and Paul, dropping his pencil, fumbled to catch it. "Maybe there's a story in them for you."

"Maybe so," Paul replied, gazing down at the first letter in the stack, at the gracefully slanted handwriting scrolled across heavy paper. "They're addressed in a lady's pretty hand."

"A lady's?" the major sneered. "A rebel's tart."

"They might be from a soldier's mother," said Paul, but

doubted it even as he spoke.

Fingering the frayed edge of the satin ribbon that bound the letters, he wondered if the writer had once worn that ribbon in her hair. Perhaps she had given it to her soldier as a parting token. Glancing up, Paul noticed the major eyeing him curiously, as if reconsidering his generosity. Quickly, he pocketed the letters with the satisfaction of having rescued them from a cad.

After Paul acquired the letters, he hesitated more than a week before reading them. He convinced himself first that their recipient, Forest Brodie, was most likely dead; therefore, Paul was not trespassing on the privacy of this young officer. The author of the letters, Isabelle Ross, was an orphan living with her aunt and uncle at Belle Ombre Plantation, apparently quite near the Brodie family's property. The two estates, Paul gathered, were divided by a tributary of the Sabine called Lyre's Creek. Isabelle's side of the correspondence indicated she and Forest were very much in love and hoped to marry after the War. In fact, once Paul had overcome his diffidence about reading her letters, he became intrigued with Isabelle's frankness of expression and depth of feeling for her fiancé. With a reporter's curiosity, Paul wished he could also read Forest's replies.   And with a romantic's sensibility, Paul imagined how he might answer Isabelle's emotion—if it were ever directed toward himself.

Paul had spent his war years sheltering in tents and less frequently in private homes, while reluctantly performing his duties as soldier, courier, and reporter. Now he sheltered in boarding houses and inns across the South, while willingly scribbling stories for his editor. Mr. Caulder was skeptical about the idea of a "war widow series," as he had called it, but had given Paul leave to return Miss Ross's letters and see for himself if there were anything out of the ordinary about the grieving women of Verbena, Louisiana and its environs. What he could not explain to Mr. Caulder was the effect that Isabelle Ross's letters had had on him.

In the Missouri farming community where he grew up, Paul's own experience with women had been limited and, for the most part, loveless. At the outbreak of hostilities between North and South, he had shuddered to see the eagerness with which some young women waved the men off to slaughter one another. Of course, the girls didn't understand in the beginning what war meant—no one who had not lived through a war, seen its devastation, could imagine the enormity of the next four years. But how many newspaper accounts did some ladies have to read before they would admit this was no gentlemen's duel? Paul had hung back from enlisting, until the grandparents who had raised him shamed him into a Confederate uniform. If only there had been a girl to write him letters, as Isabelle Ross had written to Forest Brodie.

On a damp November afternoon, Paul, suffering from a slight cold, arrived at Thorpe's Inn on the main road to Verbena. While the other guests, two of whom shared Paul's bed in a narrow upstairs room, crowded into the dining hall for the standard fare—beef, pork, boiled eggs, and cornbread—Paul savored a moment's quiet and thought of oysters on the half shell, fresh greens and summer squash, baked yams swimming in butter and brown sugar, and slices of juicy melon. Such delicacies were described in one of Miss Ross's early letters to her fiancé. But it was not long before her correspondence, though delicate in expression, reflected the uncertainty, depravation, and fear that were part of wartime.

Paul spread the letters out on the bed. Then he polished his spectacles on his sleeve before replacing them, simultaneously hooking the end pieces over his ears and smoothing his flax-colored hair back from his temples. Each time he read the letters he felt a step nearer to their author.

Yes, he thought, Forest Brodie must be dead. Isabelle's last letter, dated May of 1863, mentioned she had not received word from him for many months. Perhaps he had been wounded and died slowly, unable to write a final note. Paul wondered if Isabelle knew her fiancé was dead. Or would Paul, returning her letters, be the one to break the news to her of the strong and sad possibility?

Most of Isabelle's letters carried some news of the household in which she lived. She wrote in an intimate tone of people with whom Forest was obviously also well-acquainted. Paul guessed that she and Forest had made mutual attempts in their correspondence to shield each other from the brutal realities of war and the harshness of life in occupied territory; still he perceived hints of her concern and distress. "News travels so slowly to us at Belle Ombre," she wrote. "Word of Shiloh has just reached us. My brother-in-law is now with my sister Louise in Heaven. Oh, how I pray this letter reaches you and finds you safe on this earth."

Isabelle's tender words for Forest were surely balm to a lonely man's senses. And each of her letters contained a token, a reminder of times and places shared with her fiancé. There were pressed flowers, violets and wild orchids, "just like the ones we picked . . ." and she would mention a date and an occasion. One autumn she had sent a few magnolia seeds that were now faded to a dull red-brown, the color of dried blood. Paul held the smooth seeds in one palm and a lock of Isabelle's soft, fine hair in the other, hair the color of a walnut shell.

Might Forest Brodie not have taken that lock of hair from the folded letter and kept it elsewhere, perhaps in his breast pocket? Paul smoothed out a freshly laundered handkerchief and placed the golden-brown hair in the center of the white cloth. Refolding the handkerchief, he reassured himself that Isabelle would not miss the lock from among her letters. He tucked the handkerchief in his inside coat pocket.

Following the gentle slope of her handwriting, Paul pieced together in his mind a picture of Isabelle's life during the war years. Sifting through her words again, he felt almost as if he were reviewing memories he had—yet had not—shared with her.

"More slaves have run off," she wrote in an early letter. "But the one we really miss is Langford. He's worth twenty of the others, Aunt Delora says."

Later, she wrote: "Aunt Delora's letting more land to the tenant farmers—mostly grandpas and boys, those too old or too young to serve in the army. Somehow she always makes ends meet . . . A big family of Cajuns has settled in the southeast section, and we're glad to have them no matter what some folks say. They're working the land, and their brood of children is a delight. The young ones always find an excuse to come up to the big house on baking day, and of course, Auntie Pan and I give them treats. They laugh at my French, play in the yard, and climb the big magnolia as if there were no such thing as war."

Isabelle's descriptions of what to Paul seemed trivial goings-on made him feel close to her, comfortable, as if he might be at ease in her company. But her intimate words for Forest reminded Paul that he was the outsider.

"My dear Forest, I'm sure your people have written to you about how they had to move off to Shreveport after the fire. Your Aunt Agnes brought me some of your things that were saved to keep for your return. Your fishing tackle, your beetle and butterfly collection, and that barn owl you stuffed were all out in the shed and escaped the fire. I have them safe for you in our attic. You know my heart aches for you and your loss. But I don't doubt for a moment that one day you will rebuild Halcyon and make it more beautiful than ever . . . . Someday there will be a garden there as lush and fragrant as the one we walked in that evening when you first broke my wing. Oh, to walk with you again and feel once more the shelter of your arm around my shoulders . . ."

Paul imagined himself walking with Isabelle on the veranda or across the lawn. She would question him about how he had found her letters, then found her. And as they strolled together, he would offer her his arm.

"A few weeks ago there was a skirmish just northwest of here," she had written, "and some of the wounded were brought to Belle Ombre. Please know that I have devoted myself to their care with the same tenderness I would hope your nurses have shown you. Among our Cajun tenants there is an old *traiteuse* who's taught me ever so much about the dressing of wounds. And of course I spoon-fed the soldiers Auntie Pan's special broths, read to them, and wrote letters for those who were unable. One young corporal with eyes almost as blue as yours had lost his right hand and asked me to pen a message to his sweetheart in Galveston. He said if she'd still have him, he still had a hand to wear a wedding ring. I pray he'll be with her soon as I pray I'll be with you . . . Some of the soldiers have died here. Aunt Delora wrote to their families that now their brave boys are buried beyond her orchard."

How kind she is, how concerned for others, thought Paul, as he read once more familiar passages.

"The difficulties between Elroy and Faye Samson still upset our household on occasion. I pity their boy, Radley, caught in the cross-fire. He's been helpful around the house now that we have so few house servants. But Euphrasie does pester him so. She has no patience, and she's determined to have a beau, even when there's no one to pick from. So she traipses after Radley 'til Aunt Delora locks her up in her room . . ."

"Ardyce and I are closer than ever, tending the hogs and chickens and kitchen garden. I hope you won't disapprove of my saying this, but she and I could be sisters—we're so companionable, chatting away while we gather eggs or weed the garden. Her color doesn't lessen my love for her a bit, and I've never really felt I owned her, but our situation must make a terrible difference to her. Sometimes she looks so sad and so far away. When we win this war—well, I won't be disloyal, but I can't help wishing life were happier for all of us . . ."

Paul smiled at the possibility that Miss Ross might be someone who could sympathize with his own views, perhaps even approve of his surreptitious wartime activities with the Underground Railroad. He read on.

"You remember how we used to let the hogs run in the woods down by the creek and fatten themselves up on acorns. Well, we don't dare now for fear some people who don't belong around here will carry them off. Fortunately, Aunt Delora has plenty of ideas about how to keep what's hers. But old Priapus is mad as a rooster in an empty hen house when he can't get loose and chase his sows around the oak trees."

"Aunt Delora says she's given up trying to educate Euphrasie and asked me to do what I can with the girl. What to do, I don't know. When I mention arithmetic, Euphrasie just laughs and won't count past ten because that's all the fingers she has. History makes no impression upon her, and I often wonder if she knows yesterday from tomorrow. We've made a little progress with music. She won't sit still to practice the pianoforte herself, but she sings and capers when I play. She reads haltingly at best, but once she has a piece by heart, we hear it sing-song morning 'til night for days and days. That just drives Auntie Pan mad. Then yesterday Euphrasie danced around the kitchen, sprinkling flour all over her hair and dress, singing "I'm a Tiny Snowflake." What a mess and a waste of good white flour, too! Auntie Pan had to take a tonic and go to bed."

"Poor old Auntie Pan. Her joints are bad this winter

and she's been down with a cold. Ardyce and Faye and I are doing some of the cooking. But it's disheartening trying to put a nice meal together with so little to work with. I worry so about you and what kind of provisions you get. Is it nothing but sloosh? How are fighting men supposed to live on cornmeal and bacon grease? Right this minute, I wish I could fix you a big Tipsy Cake and a bowl of caramel pudding."

"Langford, who ran off two years ago, has come home, looking half-starved. You remember he belonged to Aunt Delora even before she married Uncle Charles Orvin. She's in hog heaven to have him back and won't hear of punishing him. She says now she can get Belle Ombre running again . . . Langford's an odd one. Mr. Samson was such a terror to him and many of the others in the old days, but drink's taken its toll, and the overseer doesn't have so much fight in him now. He's still mean, but Aunt Delora and Langford seem to get around him . . ."

"Letters from Uncle Charles Orvin have arrived more regularly these last six months, which is good news for all of us, especially Aunt Delora. He gives her the best advice—and Elroy Samson has to follow it—so life is flowing smoothly for now. But, of course, I still long for a letter from you. I hate to think how long it's been. I read your old letters again and again and cherish every word. Please God, you're safe and well . . ."

"There seems to have been some trouble up at Great-Uncle Babcock's place, up near the state line. He and Lydie Vee may come down to Belle Ombre before long. Aunt Delora says we'll just expect them when we see them and shouldn't fret, but naturally I do . . ."

Lydie Vee—an odd name, Paul thought, and one he was certain he had heard before, sometime during the War. Or had he simply read Isabelle's letters so many times that he imagined he knew her family?

Another note relayed: "The Vasseurs have arrived safely at last. They must be planning to stay awhile, Aunt Delora says, since Great-Uncle Babcock brought a trunkful of cigars. And Lydie Vee brought her calico cat, Carlotta—a welcome addition to our household."

Paul wondered if he might find Lydie Vee still with Isabelle Ross, if he found her at all at Belle Ombre. The innkeeper in Verbena had told him the house still stood, that folks lived there, but rarely came to town. He couldn't swear to the whereabouts of Miss Ross, and Paul couldn't ask him if she still paced the veranda at night, in a cotton gown.

Paul held again her last letter; as with her first one, he could recite the words, eyes closed. "I was mad with joy when Langford brought me your letter. And so touched! As you think of me each morning when you rise and dress in gray—the color of my eyes, you said—I, too, think of you in uniform with every gray dawn. And on every cold night this December I recall our meeting on the bridge over Lyre's Creek on another December night when you were as near to me as body is to soul. How I'm warmed by that memory!" Gray-eyed and fair-haired, Paul imagined Isabelle, but still her face was averted from him or only glimpsed, a little out of focus, by his mind's eye.

"The time and distance between us—the uncertainty—has made me bold in my affection," she wrote. "But please forgive my boldness, and when you hold this letter to your breast, dream with me as I would have you dream beside me, sharing my pillow when I call you husband."

Whatever had become of Forest Brodie—and Paul doubted he would envy the soldier his fate—Paul did envy him Isabelle's passion. Carefully, he refolded her letters, stacked them, and tied them with the blue-gray ribbon. The clatter of men's boots sounded on the stairs; dinner at Thorpe's Inn was over. Paul tucked the letters in his coat pocket and picked up his hat, preparing to leave for Belle Ombre. Perhaps word had already reached Isabelle Ross, confirming Forest's death. Perhaps he could not only return her letters, but, in addition, offer her some consolation.

Though Paul might not have invaded Forest's privacy, he knew quite well that he had invaded Isabelle's. Was he not intimate with her as a voyeur with the object of his obsession, gazing into her thoughts? Reading her letters, he felt as if he had opened her dressing gown and witnessed the beating of her heart.

CHAPTER THREE

Two days after Forest was laid to rest in the Raveneaux family plot and Beryl was buried near the old slave quarters, the clinging mist that had shrouded Belle Ombre for weeks lifted. The air became crisp and icy cold.

"Perfect weather for slaughter," Delora announced at breakfast. "It's always easier to hide hams than hogs."

So that morning Isabelle and Ardyce went to work, shivering in the yard behind the house, wearing old woolen dresses without hoops, stained aprons, and shawls knotted around their shoulders. Only their hands were warm as they poured more water into the steaming cast iron boiling pot. Nearby, Radley wrestled a bellowing hog into position, and Langford knocked it senseless and silent with one blow of an ax head.

"Mind your skirt, Miss Isabelle," said Langford as he pierced the hog's jugular vein, and blood flowed over the ground toward Isabelle's hem.

She stepped out of the way and waited with Ardyce until Langford was ready for help with scalding the hide.

"You sure you up to this?" Ardyce asked Isabelle.

"I'll be all right. Working helps take my mind off grieving." It was something to say, even if it weren't true; nothing yet had taken her mind off grieving.

The two young women were scraping the scalded hide of the third hog killed that morning when Captain Newell pulled his horse up short in front of them.

"Good morning, Miss Isabelle," he said, touching his hat without actually tipping it to her. "Looks like you girls are preparing some good eating for us this winter."

Isabelle knew the "us" referred to his occupying Yankee regiment, which had crowded Thorpe's Inn and taken over an abandoned mansion near Verbena. Luckily, Langford had already concealed the first hog carcass, and Newell could only see that they had slaughtered two hogs that morning. Isabelle glared at him.

"Not much genteel conversation out here, is there?" Captain Newell's horse snorted and tossed his head as if in agreement. "I'll ride on up to the house and pay my respects to Miss Delora."

With one fingertip, the captain smoothed his precise black moustache, then dug his heels in his horse's ribs and galloped out of sight around the side of the house.

"Respects, indeed," Isabelle muttered. "He ought to call her Mrs. Raveneaux. Did you ever hear her say he could call her Miss Delora?"

"Could be she don't have no more choice than the rest of folks 'bout some things," said Ardyce.

Isabelle's hands were chapped by cold wind and hot water; she rubbed them on her apron and examined her abraded knuckles. Auntie Pan would make her a salve from lard and herbs and things only Auntie Pan could put a name to.

"You wore out?" Ardyce asked.

"Maybe so. I haven't been sleeping too well." Isabelle resumed scraping the hide. "When we're done with this one, maybe we can turn the work over to Lydie Vee and Faye. They promised to come out for the cutting and sausage making. You know Faye—says she can't watch killing of any kind."

"She sure 'nough can butcher once a beast is strung up," said Ardyce. "And she don't really much mind wringing a hen's neck long as she's planning to cook it for her boy."

Isabelle nodded. "It's just as well Lydie Vee wasn't out here to greet the captain. For all the talk there was about her having Yankee sympathies, she sure doesn't have any use for that man."

Ardyce arched her back and braced it with her hands. "I don't reckon Miss Lydie Vee ever had much love for Yankees. She just has a real healthy dislike for slavery."

"Well, that's done with now."

"You think so?" Ardyce picked up her knife and sliced the hog's hind legs to expose the hamstrings. "You know I'd be lying if I said I'm sorry about how the War ended, but I am sorry for you, Miss Isabelle, about Mr. Forest. And I'm sick to death of that Captain Newell riding over Belle Ombre and taking what he wants. Miss Lydie Vee remarked just t'other day, the men left around here are a paltry lot, and we'd be better off without any of them."

"She said that? Meaning Uncle Babcock, too?"

"Don't you know it." Ardyce and Isabelle exchanged a brief smile of understanding.

"But she does take mighty good care of Uncle Babcock," said Isabelle.

"Oh, she keeps an eye on him—thank the Lord." Ardyce shuddered as if she were shaking off an unwelcome touch.

"If Uncle Charles Orvin had died in the War, things would be different now. Uncle Babcock would inherit, I suppose," Isabelle said thoughtfully, "and Lydie Vee would be mistress of Belle Ombre."

"That'd just 'bout kill Miss Delora's soul," Ardyce murmured.

"Surely this business Uncle Charles Orvin is tending to can't keep him away forever."

"Well, he don't seem too anxious to get himself home. But then he never did stop here much—even before the War."

Isabelle nodded, remembering her uncle's frequent hunting expeditions and extended business trips to New Orleans. Delora had had years of practice running Belle Ombre without him before he ever left to fight.

Together the young women worked the gambling stick behind the hog's tendons, and Isabelle called to Langford, "This one's ready to put on the pole."

Langford, with his polished mahogany-brown features, taut body, and sinewy arms, and Radley, with his slack, mottled face, squat build, and pudgy hands, together ran the supporting pole between the hog's legs and hoisted the carcass. Despite the cold, Radley's forehead was beaded with sweat as he struggled to lift his end of the pole into a forked support post. Quickly, Langford dropped his end in place and dove forward to catch Radley's end before the hog slipped down the pole.

Ardyce and Isabelle shook their heads, then turned to watch Captain Newell galloping away from the house. Under her breath Ardyce said, "One of these days we might ought to hang that tomfool Radley up and give his bacon to the captain."

"Aunt Delora wouldn't miss him. She thinks Radley's been stealing from the pantry."

"Oh, he don't have to. His mama makes sure he gets the choicest morsels."

Isabelle and Ardyce each filled a pitcher with hot water from the boiling pot. Langford and Radley had moved off to fetch the hidden carcass.

"Captain Newell didn't stay long this time," Isabelle remarked.

"Sure 'nough. Miss Delora knows how to make that man wait."

Through the years Isabelle had gathered a good deal of information from Ardyce about the convoluted relations of men and women. And although she didn't like to contemplate what the captain might be waiting to receive from her aunt, she did enjoy being taken into Ardyce's confidence.

Together the girls tossed hot water over the hog carcass and began scraping any missed spots on the hide.

"Speaking of good-for-nothing men, you heard tell anything about Mr. Samson?" Ardyce asked.

"Not a word," Isabelle replied. "Faye looked a little puffy in the face this morning, but she didn't have anything to say when Aunt Delora asked about him."

"Miss Faye's well rid of him—if he's gone for good. We all are."

"Still, it gives me a bad feeling somehow—his disappearing the night of Beryl's fall," said Isabelle. "A little while after I'd come to the back parlor to sit with Forest, Mr. Samson came stomping in, snarling at me. I sent him about his business, of course. But what business did he have up the back stairs? I'm sure that's where he went."

"Miss Isabelle." Ardyce sighed and shook her head. "Ain't you ever wondered where Beryl got her drink? If Mr. Samson went up to her room that night, it sure weren't the first time."

"Oh. But . . ."

"I reckon he left her drunk and dizzy," Ardyce added.

Isabelle took a deep breath and whispered, "If he left her—before she fell."

Ardyce met her gaze. "That man's done a heap of mischief in his time. I'd swear to that. But if he did in Beryl, what's anybody gonna do about it?"

"I could do something," said Isabelle.

"Well, you could pave a road with your good intentions, miss."

"I could talk to Captain Newell."

"Oh, now, hold on a minute. You think Miss Delora gonna stand for that?"

"The captain's supposed to keep law and order around here," Isabelle said, wishing she could believe he would. "There's no better place to start than locking up Elroy Samson."

Ardyce nodded. "Mr. Samson'd save us all a lot of grief if he'd just stay gone."

Turning back to her work, Ardyce cut around the hog's neck and hacked the throat through to the backbone. Isabelle turned away. Ever since the War began, when the girls were in their early teens, they had helped with the butchering. It was something that had to be done. Together, she and Ardyce—the poor relation and the slave—had also gardened, sewed, cooked, cleaned, and nursed the sick. But suddenly the mutilation of flesh, any flesh, sickened her.

"Let Langford finish the job, Ardyce. We've done enough."

Ardyce nodded. "I'm almost done twisting the head off."

At the grinding sound, Isabelle winced and shut her eyes, then opened them to catch a glimpse of a rider coming through the pecan orchard toward the yard.

"Ardyce, look. Someone's coming. He's not in uniform. I wonder why he's coming up the back way and not on the main drive."

A lanky young man, his coat flapping in the wind, cantered toward them on an even lankier sorrel horse. A few yards from Isabelle, the horse shied and violently shook his mane. The rider dismounted awkwardly as the horse side-stepped. Holding the reins tightly near the bit with one hand, the man doffed his hat with the other.

"Good afternoon, miss," he said, squinting through his spectacles at Isabelle.

Isabelle knew Ardyce had stepped back, a courtesy to white folks in conversation, but remained near in case she were needed. Both girls were wary of strangers; neither had been to town since the War broke out. But Isabelle had heard Aunt Delora and the Vasseurs discussing unscrupulous speculators—mostly Northerners—and land agents who practically stole estates from desperate planters. Isabelle waited for the young man to state his business.

But before he spoke, his horse snorted and stamped a hoof, splashing mud on Isabelle's skirt. "Sorry, miss," the man said hurriedly, "Pickwick can't abide the smell of blood."

Isabelle distanced herself from the hog carcasses, wiping her hands on her blood spattered apron, and the young man followed her.

Replacing his battered hat over pale, thinning hair, he said, "I'm looking for a place called Belle Ombre."

"Are you?" Isabelle replied noncommittally.

His tone and manner were respectful enough, and, though he didn't sound like a Yankee, neither did he sound like a near neighbor. Hadn't her aunt cautioned her that the unscrupulous strive to appear plausible?

"Well, yes," he said. "I've ridden 'round and 'round and I wonder if I'm anywhere close. My name is Paul Delahoussaye, and it's very important I find Belle Ombre. Could you help me, miss?"

Isabelle met his pleading look. Hesitantly, she said, "This is Belle Ombre."

His face brightened. "Oh, then I've arrived. I've come to see a lady."

The way he stared at her—she in her shabby, filthy clothes, her hair bedraggled, and for all she knew, a streak of hog's blood on her cheek—he couldn't think she was anyone's idea of a lady.

"Did you came to see Mrs. Raveneaux?" she asked.

His reply startled her. "Oh, no. Miss Isabelle Ross is the lady." He peered at her again, at the lock of hair falling loose from her hairpins. "You?" he said.

She took a quick breath and nodded.

"I've something of yours to return to you, Miss Ross."

"What could you have of mine?"

"Well, you see I'm a journalist, and I was interviewing a Union officer who happened to have found a packet of letters—your letters."

Isabelle's heart pounded. "Letters from Forest Brodie? The letters that never reached me?"

The young man hung his head, and his horse did likewise as if in imitation.

"Not letters from Forest Brodie," he said gently. "Letters to him, written by yourself, miss."

Isabelle said nothing.

"I looked at one of the letters to determine who they belonged to," he added. "I'm sorry to say I have no news of—"

Isabelle's hand fluttered to her flushed cheek as she spoke. "We've already had news, Mr. Delahoussaye. Perhaps we should go up to the house."

She glanced toward Ardyce, who came forward with Radley in tow. Langford remained some distance behind them, slicing into a hog carcass.

"Radley will see to your horse, sir," said Isabelle, and the boy took the reins. "This way, Mr. Delahoussaye."

Isabelle walked a little faster than the stranger, her mind racing ahead with the questions she would ask him when she was presentable. Until then, she was relieved he made no reference to her appearance or to her occupation.

Aunt Delora, impeccable in russet watered silk, waited for them in the front doorway as they mounted the steps of the veranda.

CHAPTER FOUR

Approaching Belle Ombre through the orchard, Paul's first glimpse had been of the ordinary, private side of the life it contained. He had seen a shabby kitchen out-building where cooking would be done in hot weather, a weedy vegetable garden fenced with sagging wire mesh, a spring house, a stable, a tool shed, a smokehouse, and nearby a black man and a tow-headed boy, butchering a hog. Riding closer, peering through his spectacles, he had also seen two graceful girls, one dark, one fair, participating in the grisly work.

Following the fair one to the front of the mansion, Paul viewed Belle Ombre's formal, public face of faded dignity. The Doric columns lining the veranda were weathered from white to gray, in places the brickwork crumbled, one window, presumably broken, was boarded up, and a deep gash marred the finish of the cypress wood door. Only the lady in the doorway was a still elegant reminder of grander days.

The woman fixed him with a piercing look as the girl beside him spoke softly, a gentle modulation in her voice. Paul would have liked to hear her read her letters aloud.

"Aunt Delora, this is Mr. Paul Delahoussaye. He has called to return some letters to me."

"Letters?" Paul thought he heard a note of alarm in the woman's utterance of that single word.

"Yes, Aunt. He's a journalist, and he's found some letters I sent to Forest—that were lost."

"Oh?" Isabelle Ross's aunt raised fine brows high above amber-colored eyes.

Isabelle seemed to take careful notice of her aunt's cool demeanor before she turned to Paul and spoke again. "Mr. Delahoussaye, may I introduce Mrs. Charles Orvin Raveneaux?"

Paul snatched his hat from his head and crushed it against his chest, murmuring, "It's an honor, ma'am."

Delora extended one white hand over which he quickly bowed. She was several inches shorter than her niece, with sloping shoulders and a heavily sloping bosom, but she held her head, weighted by a mass of auburn hair, as if it were lightly perched on a swan's neck.

"I'm sure my aunt will—" Isabelle began.

"Yes, of course, I'll take care of your caller," Delora finished for her. "You go on up, Isabelle, dear. We'll see you after a while in the front parlor. Will that suit you, Mr. Delahoussaye?"

"I don't want to put you ladies to any trouble." Paul looked to Isabelle, hoping she would stay, not wanting to lose her presence so soon after finding her. But she glanced away toward the staircase.

Of course she would want to be away from him, a strange man who'd come upon her while she was butchering a hog. If he had arrived while she sat at her embroidery frame, things might have begun differently. She would have offered him her hand as her aunt had done. Then he would have said, "Oh, please go on with your stitching, Miss Ross. Don't let me interrupt you." And she might allow him to watch her embroider red roses on white linen as he told of receiving her packet of letters. As things were, a gentleman could not refer to what she had been doing, nor could Paul even offer his handkerchief to wipe the blood and grime from her pale cheeks and brow. He stared at her. Gray-eyed and fair-haired she was, as he had pictured her. But now, despite her dirty face and old dress, the mystery of her features and form was dispelled as they came into clear focus and surpassed his imaginings.

Delora lightly tapped his arm, and he jumped sideways to avoid a collision with her hoops as she floated ahead of him through the front hall. Glancing back once more over his shoulder, he caught a glimpse of Isabelle, gathering the soiled hem of her skirt and racing up the broad stairs.

With a fluid motion, Delora parted the double doors of the parlor, closing them after Paul had passed into the room. Late afternoon sun at the long windows provided a hazy illumination, reflected distortedly in a beveled mirror and trapped in the cloudy glass of a half-full decanter and two used brandy snifters. Despite his head cold, Paul caught a whiff of tobacco smoke lingering in the air and felt more than smelled the pervasive damp, redolent as humus, that seeped upward from the foundation of the house. Stenciling of ivy and vine roses climbed over the walls. Ferns drooped over the edges of earthenware pots. Even the carving on the spinet suggested wisteria and creeper. Muted rose drapes and the moss green rugs, bordered with a floral design and tracked with muddy boot prints, completed Paul's impression of having been admitted to a secret garden—a garden recently vacated by another visitor.

A modest fire burned in the pink marble fireplace. Delora indicated Paul should sit in a ladder-back chair near the hearth to avail himself of some warmth. She arranged herself at a right angle to him, spreading the breadth of her russet gown over the faded green brocade sofa.

"It's been a day for callers," said Delora. "Captain Newell has already put in an appearance—smelled blood all the way to Verbena, I suppose, and came high-tailing out to look over the pork he plans to steal."

Paul was a little surprised by her frankness, but smiled politely as she continued confidently, as if anyone of sense

must agree with her. "That such a man ever made captain just
goes to show how many able men were lost to the North.
Have you met him?"

"No, ma'am. I haven't mixed much in town."

"Very wise, I'm sure. Newell's dull as a post," she said
with a light laugh. "And audacious. He always insists on the
best brandy when he calls. Though why he thinks I still have
any left after all the raiding during the War, I don't know."

After venting her annoyance with Captain Newell,
Delora's face and voice softened as if she now remembered she
were speaking to an unknown gentleman and must express an
interest in his business. "Now tell me again, Mr.—" she
paused, then drawled his name— "Delahoussaye, what brings
you to Belle Ombre?"

Paul sat straight on the edge of his chair and further
abused his battered felt hat. "Well, ma'am, as your niece said,
I've come into possession of some correspondence which I
thought she might like returned to her."

"Letters Isabelle wrote to Forest?"

"That's right, Mrs. Raveneaux."

"No letters from Forest that were never posted?"

"No, ma'am."

She watched him with interest as if his answers were
the most fascinating words she had heard all day.

"I see. Well, it was mighty kind of you to travel all the
way from. . ."

"Missouri."

"My, but you've come a long way, Mr. Delahoussaye.
Now let me think. Missouri. Isn't that where some folks had
trouble making up their minds?"

Paul had never before been so delicately questioned
about his politics. He wondered if she might become more
direct if he feigned innocence. He covered a cough, then said,
"I beg your pardon, ma'am?"

"Making up their minds," she said smoothly, "during the Late Unpleasantness?"

"Oh, I see, ma'am. Missouri stayed with the Union."

"Yes, I'm sure you're right, sir. But what I'm really wondering is where did you go?"

"Well, poor eyesight and a touch of pneumonia kept me from being much use as a sharp-shooter. I'm a journalist by profession and, and though I did a little fighting, I spent most of the War working as a correspondent and courier."

"For?"

"For the South, ma'am."

Delora relaxed against the sofa cushions, a smile flickering across her full lips. "Well, of course, kinfolk have always meant more to me than politics. But men must take a stand, mustn't they?" She didn't wait for an answer, but drawled his name again. "Delahoussaye. That's not a Missouri sort of surname, is it?"

"My father owned a general store in Shreveport. He died when I was a boy, and my maternal grandparents took me in."

"All the way to Missouri, with your dear mother, of course?"

"No, ma'am. My mother passed away when I was born."

"How very sad. May I offer you some brandy?"

From her concerned tone, Paul wondered if the drink were meant to fortify him after his loss, which had occurred some twenty-three years ago.

"That's very kind of you, Mrs. Raveneaux. But it needn't be your best brandy," he added with a half-smile.

"Better you and I should have it than Captain Newell." Delora moved aside the used glasses, reached for the decanter on the low table, and poured two fresh glasses. "There you are, Mr. Delahoussaye." As she handed him his snifter, she clinked the rim of her own against it.

Paul took a swallow, coughed, then swallowed more in an effort to calm the tickle in his throat.

"Don't tell me the brandy doesn't agree with you," said Delora.

"Oh, it's fine stuff. I'm just trying to get over a cold, ma'am."

"Then what luck you arrived today—slaughtering day. Our cook makes an excellent hog's hoof tea. Cures a cold like nothing else in this world."

"I wouldn't want to trouble her," Paul said between stifled coughs.

"Auntie Pan would be proud to brew you some. She's known for her remedies. And she may even have some on the stove right now, what with the chills and colds going around. She ministers to all our tenants. I'll see she fixes you some just as soon as Isabelle comes down."

Sudden determination silenced Paul's hacking. He slowly sipped the brandy and let it linger in his mouth.

Delora took a sip of brandy herself, then spoke. "So Forest Brodie's letters came into your possession, you say. You must have been very close to him if he entrusted Isabelle's correspondence to you before he. . ."

"Oh, I never actually met him, Mrs. Raveneaux."

"Then how. . .?"

"Well, ma'am, I don't want to bore you with all the details."

"Don't you worry about boring me," Delora replied. "I'm all attention. You just don't know how we *hunger* for news here, secluded as we are."

"Yes, ma'am. My editor, Mr. Caulder of the *Laurel Dispatch*, sent me out at the end of the War to do a series of interviews with officers, both northern and southern. A

Yankee major, who was bragging to me about his exploits, said he'd picked up a packet of letters left behind on a battlefield—Miss Ross's letters they turned out to be."

"Did he say which battlefield?" Delora asked abruptly.

"No, ma'am. He was a little vague about that. I gathered it was somewhere in Virginia or maybe Pennsylvania."

"When?" she asked even more sharply.

"I couldn't rightly say." But I could guess, Paul thought, since Isabelle's last letter was dated May of 1863.

Before speaking again, Delora set her face in a look of disdain that Paul hoped was meant for the absent Yankee major and not for himself. "And why did this . . . person . . . keep Isabelle's letters?"

"Seems the major was something of a collector of souvenirs," Paul answered.

Delora shuddered. "It's a violation to think such a man ever touched the paper Isabelle wrote on."

"Yes, ma'am." Paul continued with a slightly guilty conscience: "I took the liberty of perusing one of the letters to determine where it had come from, and then and there resolved to return the whole packet to the young lady who wrote them."

"And what a chivalrous gesture!" Delora said warmly. "You just don't know how much this means to all of us—after what we've been through."

"Miss Ross said you've received news of Forest Brodie." Paul gave the statement a questioning lilt.

"Indeed we have, Mr. Delahoussaye. Tragic news. Only a few days ago, Forest's remains were brought here and buried."

"Oh. I'm very sorry, ma'am."

"Thank you. Isabelle's borne up well, considering. She's my strong niece, not like . . ." Paul waited to hear her name Euphrasie, the fanciful cousin about whom Isabelle had written, but instead Delora said, "not like some others who break as easily as straw in a rough wind."

Half a dozen questions came to Paul's mind regarding Forest's death, and he searched for a delicate way to ask them.

"The War's been over a long time now, Mrs. Raveneaux," he began, tentatively.

"Has it? News travels so slowly to our part of the world—time almost stands still for us. Why, seems just yesterday we were gathered on the veranda, waving our best handkerchiefs, as our men rode away to glory."

Delora rose from the sofa and, with a graceful gesture of one hand, gave Paul permission to remain seated. She crossed to the window and gazed out. "There's never any sunlight on this lawn," she said softly. "It's all live oaks and shadows."

"Belle Ombre," Paul said half to himself.

"Yes. Beautiful shadows. Memories. Ghosts of things that were."

"Forgive me for asking, Mrs. Raveneaux, but are you a widow?"

"Me?" Delora turned away from the window and faced him. "No. I'm very fortunate. Colonel Raveneaux is only away, temporarily, on business in Washington—due back anytime now."

"Oh."

"Why, Mr. Delahoussaye, do I detect a note of disappointment?'

Paul choked momentarily on his last swallow of brandy.

"No, ma'am," he said, recovering. "I'm more than happy for your sake. It's just. . . well, you see, I persuaded Mr. Caulder to allow me to travel to Verbena by promising him I'd do a series of stories here on war widows."

"I see. Well, I'm thankful I can't oblige you as a story

subject. But perhaps Isabelle—"

"Surely her fiancé wasn't killed in the War," Paul blurted out. Sudden images flashed in his mind of long dead corpses disinterred from distant battlefield graves and transported to home states. Most were placed in wooden boxes or wrapped in heavy cloth, but some remains were sealed in cast iron coffins with small glass windows through which loved ones might view uncanny faces.

"He was killed not in the War," said Delora, "but certainly by the War."

"Ma'am?"

"Young Forest was made a colonel just before his capture—his regiment ran through officers in such a hurry. Then it seems he spent almost two years in a Northern prison camp. But when the War ended, he was too weak and sick to come home. He made his way with a few other wounded soldiers only as far as Mississippi. There a Christian family took him in and nursed him, but, sad to say, he died in their care a few weeks ago. Of course, I've sent them remuneration for their kindness in sending his remains home for burial."

"Miss Ross knows all this?" Paul asked.

"Most of it. It's eased her mind considerably to know why he didn't write for so long and to know he was in Christian hands when he died—even though the people weren't Catholic."

Delora crossed to the hearth and spread her hands toward the fire's warmth. She was as close to Paul as the circumference of her skirt allowed, and for a moment Paul thought he saw her hands tremble. She clasped them together, turning to face him.

"Forest had had a severe head wound and suffered terrible bouts of fever. The family who nursed him informed me he hardly knew who he was. He'd lost his reason. If he'd come home alive in body, but not in mind. . . Well, Isabelle is the sort of girl who'd keep her promise. She'd have spent the rest of her life taking care of him, even if he didn't know who she was. So you see things may be better as they are."

"Yes, I see."

"Isabelle was so very young when she promised herself."

"What will she do now?" Paul asked.

"Oh, she and my uncle's wife, Lydie Vee, talk some nonsense about her becoming a governess. But as her loving aunt, I can still hope that Romance may find her again—even in these sad times."

"You must be very happily married yourself."

"I understand my husband," she said. "Forest was such a handsome young man," she continued with feeling. "Tall, broad shouldered, curly dark hair, and eyes as blue and bright as sapphires. He went galloping off from here on a jet black stallion. Achilles in armor couldn't have looked finer than Forest in his gray uniform. That's how Isabelle can always remember him."

Though of course Delora had made no comparison between Paul and Forest, Paul felt a sudden twinge of inadequacy. He might be as tall as Forest had been, but he was lean and gangling, with thinning flaxen hair and pale eyes.

Delora resumed her place on the sofa.

"I assume, Mr. Delahoussaye, you are staying at Thorpe's Inn?"

"Yes, ma'am. They found me a few inches of bed space."

"I don't go to town myself, but I've heard the place is crawling with Captain Newell's minions."

Paul nodded agreement.

"So! You simply must stay here."

"But, Mrs. Raveneaux, I wouldn't want—"

"Now, now. I won't hear of your doing otherwise. I'll

send Langford to collect your things at the inn. The light's waning, but he'll make it back before it's very dark."

Paul wanted to stay at Belle Ombre far more than he wanted to return to Thorpe's Inn, and to his relief, Delora overcame every obstacle to accepting her hospitality. He could send a note with Langford, and the money to settle his bill at Thorpe's. Delora assured him Langford would bring him the change.

"Why, I could bet my life on Langford's honesty," she said. "And I've been wanting to send him to town in hopes he'd bring back a letter or two for me."

Then she excused herself to make the arrangements with her servant and to see what was keeping Isabelle.

Delora had no sooner stepped into the hall and closed the main parlor doors behind her than one of the double side doors in the room slid open. Paul turned to face a stout man with graying ginger sideburns, jutting wildly like wings on either side of his ruddy face. The man smiled, displaying prominent, yellowed teeth, and Paul was reminded of an illustration he'd once seen of a warthog.

"So you're the fellow from town," the man said genially, extending his right hand. "Babcock Vasseur." The great-uncle, Paul thought, recalling one of Isabelle's letters, who traveled with a trunkful of cigars.

"Paul Delahoussaye, sir."

Babcock's handshake was no more than a perfunctory clasp and release. Then he quickly sidled past Paul to the table on which rested brandy and glasses   and poured himself a generous snifterful, heedless that he had taken a used glass.

"The girl said we had a visitor," Babcock remarked.

Paul assumed the girl Babcock mentioned was a servant, perhaps the one who had been working with Isabelle. Briefly, he explained his reason for calling, adding that Mrs. Raveneaux had invited him to stay.

"Ah," said Babcock, after a long swallow of brandy. "My niece is mighty generous with her hospitality—when it suits her."

"Mrs. Raveneaux is your niece? And Miss Ross—"

"Oh, I'm everybody's uncle, or great-uncle. Delora's my dead brother's girl. And when her sister and brother-in-law died of fever, Delora took in their girl—Miss Ross, as you call her. Then after Raveneaux's brother and his wife died, she took in their little girl, Euphrasie. So I've got a houseful of nieces. And let me tell you, the two young ones are as sweet as a couple of August peaches."

Paul felt a knot of dislike twist inside of him as he watched Babcock smack his lips and down another drink. He hoped Delora's uncle did not always have access to her best brandy or her young wards.

Babcock chipped the foot of his glass as he set it roughly on the table. "If you're staying on around here, better watch your footing," he said, catching at the back of the sofa to keep his own balance. "Just a few days ago, one of our colored girls fell head over heels down the airwell. Think of that!"

"And died?" Paul asked.

"Don't you know it. Pity. She was a fine looking piece."

A tap sounded on the parlor door. Babcock nodded and winked at Paul, then backed into the adjoining dining room, sliding the side door shut after him. Quickly, Paul brushed a hand over his hair and straightened his tie, preparing to meet Isabelle again, this time to see her with her face washed, and perhaps to find her more receptive to his arrival at Belle Ombre. But instead of Isabelle, the young black woman who had been with her in the yard entered from the hall.

"Mrs. Raveneaux told me to bring you this, sir."

She held out a tray, and Paul took from it a steaming cup of murky liquid.

"What is it?" he asked.

"Auntie Pan's hog's hoof tea."

CHAPTER FIVE

Breathlessly, Isabelle had flown to her room and shed the layers of filthy work clothes and shabby undergarments, leaving them heaped like wilted petals on the floor. Thoughts spun in her mind. This man in her aunt's parlor had brought her letters. Perhaps he was a friend, a confidant to Forest; perhaps Forest had spoken to him of her. Naked she ran to the washstand, wrung out a cloth in cold water, and scrubbed her shivering flesh. She and Forest had been apart so long, it seemed sometimes he had only ever existed in her imagination. That he was dead and buried in the earth had given him a kind of final reality to her. But now Mr. Delahoussaye had come with his connections to the War, to lands and people beyond Belle Ombre, to Forest when he was alive and loved her. The old longing welled inside her, though she knew she must hide it away again even as she hid her body beneath the many layers of fresh garments.

As she turned to the dressing table mirror, fumbling with the tiny buttons at the throat of her shirtwaist, she was startled by the reflection of Euphrasie curled up on the edge of the bed.

"Euphrasie, how long have you been sitting there?"

"I don't know. I got lonesome." The girl shrugged and nestled more deeply into her crocheted shawl. Besides the shawl she wore only a dressing sacque and a pair of embroidered pantalets.

The cousins had adjoining bedrooms, and Isabelle saw

the door between them was left ajar. "I wish you'd knock instead of just appearing like a spook."

"Don't be cross, coz. I spied you from the window, out in the yard with a stranger. A man. Now, you can't keep all the goings-on to yourself. What's he doing here?"

"He's a journalist who acquired some letters I wrote to Forest."

"Oh, my word! Is he going to publish your letters in a newspaper?" Euphrasie leaned eagerly from the edge of the bed and had to catch hold of the counterpane to keep her balance.

"Heavens no! He's come to return them," Isabelle replied with a last brisk brush of her hair.

"Did he know Forest well?"

"That's something I hope to find out when I meet with him in the parlor."

"What's his name?"

"Mr. Paul Delahoussaye."

"Oh, that's my favorite name." Euphrasie sighed.

Isabelle shot a glance at her cousin. "Since when?'

"Since now. Is he very handsome?"

Isabelle finished tucking her hair into a brown net snood before she answered. "Oh, I suppose he's fair to middling. We've seen so few young men since the War."

Euphrasie quivered with barely suppressed excitement. "From the peek I got from the window, I'd guess he looks better than Radley."

"A stump looks better than Radley."

Delora tapped once and entered from the hall.

"Our guest is having some hog's hoof tea for his head cold," she announced. "He seems a nice young gentleman, and I've invited him to stay a spell with us. Langford's on the way to town now to collect his things."

"He's staying here, Aunt? Which room will he have?" asked Euphrasie.

"Never you mind." Delora glanced dismissively in Euphrasie's direction, then turned back to Isabelle. "Spin 'round, sugar. Your hem's caught up in your petticoat ruffle at the back. There now, that's got it."

Delora proceeded to share with Isabelle the information she had gleaned from conversation with Paul.

"So Mr. Delahoussaye never actually met Forest?" Isabelle felt a pang of disappointment.

"No, I'm sorry to say. But the young man's been out and about, traveling around the country, and may provide us with much news and useful tidbits about what's happening beyond Verbena," said Delora. "We'll just lead him gently through some parlor talk and suppertime conversation. You know what I mean."

"Yes, Aunt."

"Did Mr. Delahoussaye read Isabelle's letters?" Euphrasie asked.

"Certainly not," Delora replied with authority. "In my brief conversation with him, I quickly sensed Mr. Delahoussaye is a man of discretion and most polite reticence—qualities we've seen little of in recent years."

"But how could he not read them? They must be exciting letters," Euphrasie persisted, "knowing how Isabelle and Forest felt for each other." Her eyes widened at her own suggestive remark.

"You know no such thing," said Delora. "And Isabelle would not write anything unseemly." She gave Isabelle's cheeks a quick pinch. "You look charming, my dear. I'm glad you chose your dove gray."

"There's little choosing to do among the few dresses any of us have," said Euphrasie, with a little pout.

"But at least the rest of us make ourselves presentable in what we have before the sun goes down," Delora snapped, jerking the stopper from a bottle of lilac water.

"You're always fussing at me."

"Euphrasie, you would try the patience of the Mother of God!" Delora took a deep breath, regaining her equanimity, before touching the stopper to Isabelle's temples.

"I'm sure by suppertime Euphrasie will be dressed up pretty as a picture, best manners and all," Isabelle said gently, hoping to dissipate the tension between her aunt and young cousin.

"Oh, spending the day in a state of dishabille is the least of her offenses." With a clink, Delora replaced the stopper in the cologne bottle, then glowered at Euphrasie as the girl shrunk into her shawl. "The altar candles in the prayer alcove are missing—again," she said pointedly.

"No one burns them much," Euphrasie whispered.

"You don't burn them either," said Delora.

Isabelle moved toward the door, longing to be in the parlor hearing news of Forest, not standing in her room listening to an old argument.

"Euphrasie," Delora continued, "you are never going to be able to gather your wits about you if you persist in this—"

"Shall we go down now, Aunt?" Isabelle asked.

"Oh, of course, dear. You go on ahead, and I'll join you shortly when I've finished with Euphrasie.   Mr. Delahoussaye's a well-spoken young man, but leave the hall door open just in case."

Isabelle closed the bedroom door on her cousin's whimpering and soon after quietly entered the parlor. There she found Paul Delahoussaye standing in the middle of the rug, his eyes tightly shut as he held a cup to his lips. He swallowed, grimaced, opened his eyes, and at sight of her, rattled the cup to its saucer, sloshing liquid over the rim.

"My aunt tells me you're suffering from a head cold, sir," said Isabelle.

"Oh, I'm much improved, miss. Riding out here did me a power of good." He shot a desperate glance at the hog's hoof tea.

"I'm glad to hear it. Perhaps you aren't in need of our home remedies after all?"

Paul mumbled his thanks as Isabelle took the cup and saucer from his hand, and poured their contents into a potted fern. While Delora might have sent the vile-tasting brew as a kind of test—a true gentleman would drink it to avoid giving offense—Isabelle saw no reason to press the matter. Her aunt had often told her it was a good thing for both sides if a man felt a little gratitude toward a woman. Setting the cup aside, she motioned for him to sit with her by the fire.

He was quick to join her, maneuvering with an odd combination of agility and awkwardness between the cluster of furnishings by the hearth. Beside her on the low sofa he seemed not to know quite what to do with his long legs, whether to stretch them out in front of him or angle them somehow out of the way. At last he settled for leaning toward Isabelle, his elbows resting on deeply bent knees. His face was close, and she saw the stubble on his chin was almost as pale as his lank hair, and caught a whiff of lye soap. His blue eyes watched her steadily through the smudged glass of wire-rimmed spectacles.

"I understand, Mr. Delahoussaye, that you never actually met my fiancé," Isabelle began.

"No, miss, I never had the honor. Please accept my profound sympathy for your loss."

"Thank you," Isabelle said softly. "I had such hopes that things would be different for Forest and me. Aunt Delora warned me I was too much a romantic. But I have learned to be otherwise. Forest's death was not the shock it might have been because I'd lost him already so many times. Every day without news I lost him."

Paul reached his hand toward her shoulder, then withdrew it without touching her. But he had wanted to, she thought; he had wanted to comfort her.

She was relieved by Paul's willingness, his near eagerness, to tell her his story with little prompting, describing his work during the War and the writing assignment that led to the Yankee major who had found her letters. Throughout, his voice maintained a gentle cadence, rising and falling as his eyes followed the expressions of interest in her face. He closed by drawing the letters from his coat pocket and holding them out to her.

Laying the letters on her lap, Isabelle looked momentarily at her faded, sloping handwriting before her eyes clouded. "During the War," she said, "and since it's been over, we've heard such a jumble of stories. The farm boys coming home tell us their tales; Captain Newell tells us something else. We get a newspaper, and there's another tale and another. How can we know what's true? I'm not like my little cousin, Euphrasie; I can't just choose the story I like best. If I did, I'd still be waiting for Forest." She had kept the sob from her voice, but a tear spilled down her cheek.

"I've told you all I know about your letters, Miss Ross. And it's the truth, even if I am a journalist. I can't add anything to what you've heard about how Colonel Brodie died. I wish I could say something you wanted to hear, and I'm sorry if my coming made you cry."

Isabelle drew a handkerchief from her skirt pocket and pressed it briefly to her eyes. "You're very kind, sir. Kinder than most. Forgive me for carrying on so. As perverse as it sounds, sometimes I've imagined our menfolk didn't go to war, but just abandoned us here in a nightmare where anything could happen—and anything did happen. Then I'm ashamed for being so ungrateful for the sacrifices our men have made."

"You've made sacrifices, too. You've worked harder than a gentleman ever wants his lady to have to work."

"You can't know that. You give me too much credit. Besides, leisure was never mine to sacrifice."

"It should have been," he murmured.

Isabelle, endeavoring to redirect the conversation, clutched the packet of letters. "Mr. Delahoussaye, you've traveled, you're knowledgeable about the War. I know my questions may seem trivial to you, but I must ask them. I can't help wondering: why these letters and not the rest? Were the others lost, left behind—thrown away, for all I know? I wrote so many others since these. Where are they? Only one letter I wrote in May a year and a half ago was returned with his remains. Why that particular letter in his uniform pocket?"

"I wish I could tell you."

Isabelle was struck by his earnestness. "You mean that, don't you?"

"Of course I do. Perhaps, Miss Ross, during my stay, if you'll allow me, we could review some of your correspondence with Colonel Brodie. Possibly I could help you piece together his movements during the War. We might come to a better understanding of what happened to him, and—"

With a rustle of silk, Delora swept through the doorway. Paul jumped to his feet.

"Ah, Mr. Delahoussaye. Langford's on his way even now to fetch your things from town."

"But my bill at Thorpe's," Paul blurted out. "I haven't given you any money."

"I've told him to settle it for you. We can discuss the details later." Delora approached Isabelle. "Are these your letters, dear? How kind Mr. Delahoussaye was to return them. I'll put them away for you." Delora extended her hand.

"Thank you, but I'll do it." Isabelle wanted the letters well hidden from Euphrasie.

"But I insist. I'll put them safely with your handkerchiefs." Delora smiled sweetly, hand opened to receive the letters; Isabelle hesitated, but at last relinquished them. Contradicting her aunt was usually fruitless, and Isabelle would not make a further attempt in front of their guest. "And meanwhile," Delora said pleasantly, "you can take Mr. Delahoussaye out and show him Forest's grave. Best go now before the light fades."

"Yes, aunt."

In the front hall, as Isabelle fastened her cloak, Delora whispered to her in passing, "Keep to the side yard, dear. Lydie Vee and Faye are still out back making sausage."

* * *

Isabelle and Paul followed a muddy path that veered to one side of the pecan orchard. Fallen wet leaves clung to the hem of Isabelle's cloak.

"The ground never seems to dry out in November," she said. "We had a little sun this morning, but no warmth. And now it's come over cloudy again. The only brightness is this little butterweed underfoot."

The path brought them up to a wrought iron fence surrounding the family plot. A single monstrous live oak spread its myriad branches above the graves, and its gnarled roots cut through the earth. The iron gate, hanging crookedly on its hinges, scraped the ground as Paul pushed it open.

"It's like night down here under this tree," said Paul.

"Very nearly. Mind your step. The day we buried Forest, Radley Samson tripped over a root and chipped his tooth on a gravestone."

"This is the second time today I've been warned to watch my footing."

"Oh?"

"Mr. Vasseur stopped by the parlor before you came down. He mentioned a girl died here recently. Falling down the airwell, I think he said."

"Yes. Poor thing. She hadn't been with us long."

"But how did she fall? Is the railing loose or broken?"

Isabelle moved past him into the enclosed graveyard. "We believe Beryl must have been unsteady—from drink," she said. "It happened the night of Forest's wake. Sudden death is very disquieting."

Paul nodded, then asked, "Colonel Brodie never lived at Belle Ombre, did he?"

"No. We were neighbors."

"Yet he's buried here."

"His people lost nearly everything during the War. Most of them have passed over by now. And Halcyon, his family home, was burned to the ground so there was no one there to receive him. I'm glad his remains were sent to me. There's his grave." Isabelle pointed past a row of weathered gravestones to a long, narrow mound of earth. "I don't know when we'll get the stone cut. I'd nothing to mark his grave but pressed flowers and wild ones and dried herbs. After the rains we've had, they look like no more than pulled weeds."

Isabelle bent for a moment over the grave and touched the limp petals.

"Would you tell me about the funeral?" asked Paul.

"We came out early, in the drizzle, of course. Just family mostly. The Thibodeau boys came to help Langford with bringing the coffin in the wagon and lowering it in the ground. Lang had already dug the grave himself—wouldn't let anyone else touch a shovel."

"This Langford's very loyal," Paul commented.

"More than loyal," said Isabelle. "Father Bartholomew came out from town to say the service. Then Auntie Pan fixed us a big dinner and chided me for not eating. But I couldn't get my mind off wishing there had been some way to get Forest home sooner so I could've been the one to nurse him, even if he had to die anyway."

Paul came a step closer to her. "Miss Ross, the opinion of a stranger may not be worth much to you, but though Colonel Brodie's gone, I think he's a lucky man to be honored and mourned by you."

"I appreciate your kind regard, Mr. Delahoussaye." Isabelle retreated to the gate. This young man had put himself to a great deal of trouble for her, traveling such a long way, searching her out to return her letters, treating her with such deference. Isabelle wondered why. "Walking out here," she said slowly, "I've considered what you said about piecing together the information we have about Forest. Perhaps tomorrow we might talk again."

"Yes, certainly. My traveling satchel's stuffed with newspaper stories about the various battles and maneuverings and such. You'll find me well-informed if not well dressed. I have some maps, too."

"Do you? I've always had a fondness for geography. My Uncle Charles Orvin mapped all his lands and the surrounding estates and farms. I used to decorate his maps for him, coloring in the woods and fields and water."

"You must be very artistic," said Paul, following Isabelle back to the path.

She bent to pick a clump of tiny yellow flowers, thinking she'd press them later.

"How far away from here is Halcyon, or what's left of it?" he asked.

"It's clear on the other side of our place, closer to the pike on the way to Verbena. Oh, the ruins of the house are just a couple of miles off, but from here you'd have to go through the holly bog and over Lyre's Creek. The bridge is hidden away among the cypress—the wild woods, we call it."

"Sounds dangerous."

"Sometimes it is, when our hogs are running loose in there. None of them are really vicious, but they can knock a body over when they get stirred up."

"By the favored boar called Priapus?" Paul smiled as he spoke, but didn't look at her.

Isabelle stopped. "How did you know our boar's name?"

Paul stopped beside her. "Oh. . . . Didn't Mr. Vasseur mention him to me?"

"I don't know. I wasn't privy to that conversation."

"Well, he must have said something. Are you ever going to butcher the old fellow?"

"Are you referring, sir, to my Uncle Babcock?"

"Oh, of course I meant—"

"I know." Isabelle smiled, feeling for a moment the pleasure of light conversation as they left the cemetery behind them. "No, we could never butcher Priapus. We had to hide him a few times—not an easy thing, considering his size and temperament—to keep the Yankees from eating him up. Naturally, we can't let ourselves get attached to his offspring, sweet as they are. We've got to eat, and we've got to have something to sell or trade. But old Priapus is different. Some folks say a hog's just a hog—and a man's just a man, for that matter. But somehow we do choose among them, deciding one's a pet and one's produce, one's a friend and one's a mortal enemy."

"One's free and one's chattel," Paul added, as he and Isabelle proceeded again along the path. "When it comes to human beings, how do you make the choice, Miss Ross?"

"For a gentleman who's far too easy to talk to, you ask a hard question."

"I'd still be interested in your answer."

"Well, sometimes the choosing's done for me, and there's little I can do about it. And sometimes. . . Oh, there's Faye coming to fetch us."

Faye Samson trotted toward them, her ashy-colored hair escaping from its net and her sallow face reddened with cold. She wore a soiled butternut cotton apron, and Isabelle assumed she'd come straight from sausage making.

"Miss Isabelle," she cried, "Miss Delora sent me out directly she spied Captain Newell riding up."

While Faye paused to catch her breath, Isabelle introduced the overseer's wife to Paul, then asked, "Is the captain staying for supper?"

"Yes, miss. And he's brought a couple of his men who'll be eating in the kitchen, I reckon." Faye cut her eyes toward Paul, then back to Isabelle. "Miss Delora said you should have a word with Mr. Delahoussaye about . . . about how we keep household troubles private. You understand?"

"Yes. Thank you."

After Faye had hurried off toward the back of the house, Isabelle turned to Paul. "The soldiers have brought us a share of difficulties these last few years," she said. "My aunt prefers we keep what we can private. I know she would appreciate it if we said nothing to the captain about Beryl's accident, for instance."

"I'll watch my tongue, if that's what you wish."

"It's what my aunt wishes," said Isabelle. "Oh, and if you hear some mention of Faye Samson's husband running off, that's something Captain Newell doesn't need to know about, either."

"Oh?" said Paul.

"Well, Mr. Samson just does it from time to time, but he always turns up—wanted or not. And we don't want the Captain thinking we're at a loss for men around here."

* * *

At supper no pork was in evidence. Isabelle's Aunt Delora understood that some of the diners had seen enough of loins and chops for one day. Instead, she planned the meal around fresh fish, "caught just today," she said, "by the Thibodeau boys and poached a second time by Auntie Pan." Mock oysters, some unidentified greens, and a custard pie completed the meal.

Paul made himself pleasant and agreeable, asking questions about the history of Belle Ombre and the grim family portraits on the wall. But though Isabelle had talked on easily enough to him that afternoon, she felt shy of Paul in front of her family and a little anxious as they gathered in the dining room. She was never quite sure what some of her family members might say or do, especially with the Union officer's presence putting everyone on edge.

Delora and Babcock sat at opposite ends of the long oak table. Captain Newell took the seat to Delora's right, and she indicated Paul should sit on her left. Next to him was Lydie Vee whom, Isabelle noted, he turned to repeatedly with a curious expression. Lydie Vee presumably took no notice except to glare once in his direction. Isabelle sat between Newell and Euphrasie.

"Captain, you shouldn't have come tonight," Euphrasie announced.

"Euphrasie," Delora said with a warning tone.

"It's true, Aunt. We have Mr. Delahoussaye here to make it six at table, and Captain Newell's coming makes us odd again. There's nobody across from me, and you know how I hate that."

"Then perhaps we could have a tray sent to your room," Lydie Vee suggested.

Euphrasie frowned and raised her pointed chin defiantly, then suddenly brightened. Using her chair as a step-ladder, she removed the painting of Charles Orvin Raveneaux from above the sideboard. Paul hurried to steady her as she wobbled descending with the heavy gilt frame.

"Much obliged, sir," she said, allowing him to take the picture and instructing him to place it in the chair opposite her. "There now." Euphrasie smiled with satisfaction first at Delora, then at the angular face sneering from its frame. "Now Uncle Charles Orvin can be my supper partner." And she toyed silently and happily with her food for the rest of the meal.

Isabelle observed her aunt carefully guide the conversation among her guests and family. Watching Delora in difficult situations was always instructive. When Newell commented that, unlike Paul, he had never been invited to take up residence at Belle Ombre, Delora replied smoothly, "Well, you understand, Mr. Delahoussaye is a distant cousin, I believe, on the Shreveport side, and my husband would insist I make room for kin. But a worldly man like yourself, with all your retinue—well, I'm sure you and your men have a much more interesting time in town. We're so dull out here."

Ardyce quietly served the supper, and Newell asked crudely of Babcock where that buxom mulatto wench had gotten off to. While Babcock sputtered in the watered-down wine, Delora answered with a shrug, "Beryl's a free woman."

"And are you planning to deed her some land, Miss Delora, same as you've done for others of her kind?" Newell said, arching one brow.

"I just might give her a plot."

The captain turned to Paul. "Our hostess is very generous to the freedpeople—she's that concerned about government confiscation. Don't want the rest of us to know how rich she is."

"I simply follow my husband's written instructions," said Delora. "Of course he's anxious to preserve our home, but he sees the necessity of changing with the times."

"And you are all obedience, I'm sure," said the captain.

"Colonel Raveneaux must take great comfort in knowing you are carrying out his wishes so faithfully," Paul said to Delora.

Babcock coughed loudly before informing Paul that he was the man in charge in the absence of his niece's husband. "And it's not just a household of women I see to, Mr. Delahoussaye. The plantation's on my head now the overseer's abandoned us."

"Elroy Samson ran off?" asked Newell.

"Really, Babcock!" Delora tapped her fingertips impatiently on the table. "We have hardly been abandoned. And the Samsons' domestic difficulties are no particular concern of ours. As to the running of Belle Ombre, Captain Newell—Charles Orvin stays in the closest possible communication with us. And we all abide by his wishes."

Newell sucked his teeth, then asked, "Has he taken the Oath yet?"

Taking the oath of loyalty to the Union would help ensure Colonel Raveneaux's property rights to Belle Ombre, rights Babcock was eager to usurp.

"Well, as a matter of fact, he has."

"Damnation," Babcock muttered.

Delora ignored his exclamation and continued, "Just today, Captain, I received the news. Langford brought me a letter from town when he went to fetch Mr. Delahoussaye's satchel."

"I'd like to see the proof," said Newell.

"So would I, Delora. So would we all," interjected Babcock.

"It will be forthcoming, I'm sure. And of course, I'll be glad to show you his letter, Captain Newell."

"I think we'll retire now, Babcock," said Lydie Vee.

"You go on if you like, woman. We men haven't had our cigars and brandy."

Sometimes he behaved like a willful child, Isabelle thought, confident he wouldn't be denied his treat if he asked for it in front of company.

"I'm afraid we must all retire early tonight," said Delora. "Captain Newell, I beg your understanding. Mr. Delahoussaye needs rest to recover from his head cold. And all our spirits are somewhat low considering recent events." She nodded toward Isabelle.

"As you say, Miss Delora," said Newell. "Though I don't believe I've seen your niece look other than melancholy every time I've been here."

While Delora ushered the captain away, Babcock snatched up the bottle with the remains of the wine and followed his wife from the room. Euphrasie, tossing down the bit of pie crust she had been twirling on her fork, smiled at Paul.

"Shall I show you to your room, Mr. Delahoussaye?'

"We'll all go up together," said Isabelle, offering Paul a lighted candle from the sideboard.

Delora, turning from the front door after locking out the captain, stopped them in the hall. "Girls, you go on ahead. Mr. Delahoussaye, a word with you, please, in the front parlor."

"Yes, ma'am," he said, but he looked at Isabelle a long moment before following her aunt.

* * *

Later, as Isabelle lay down on her bed, her body ached from the day's labor and her head pounded with a confusion of thoughts. Beryl's death and Samson's disappearance both on the night of Forest's wake—if the events were not accident and coincidence, what, as Ardyce had said, would anyone do about it? What would Samson have to say for himself, when and if he returned? And now there was a stranger in the house. Isabelle was accustomed to Delora's smooth handling of rough situations and of men. But this man, Paul Delahoussaye, had sought out Isabelle, and even in the presence of her charming aunt, his gaze was repeatedly drawn to Isabelle. How strange to consider that her letters to Forest Brodie had brought her the attentions of another man.

At last, sleep came, heavy as fog. But within the half hour, she woke abruptly, aware first that a cramp had stiffened her shoulders, next that there was a pressure on the mattress of someone else's body slipping in beside hers.

"Isabelle?"

"Euphrasie! One day you're going to stop my heart."

"Oh, Coz, I nearly stopped my own." Her voice was a breathy whisper against Isabelle's cheek. "I couldn't sleep so I went out on the balcony of the summer parlor."

"On a night like this? You just keep your icy feet to yourself and go back to your room."

"Sorry." Euphrasie pulled her feet away from Isabelle's and drew herself up in a ball. "But I'll never sleep at all if you don't let me stay—not after what I saw."

"What did you see?" asked Isabelle, guessing and dreading the answer.

"Forest!"

"In the dark, in the mist, you saw Forest?" Skepticism and anger rose in her voice.

"I'm telling you I did," Euphrasie insisted. "He haunts the lawn, limping in and out among the live oaks."

"Oh, hush! The only thing that haunts Belle Ombre is you. So if you have to stay, shut your mouth."

Isabelle turned her back on her cousin, and waited with painful slowness for sleep to come again.

CHAPTER SIX

Early the next morning Paul washed and shaved with warm water Ardyce had brought to his door, a luxury not provided at Thorpe's Inn. He put on his next-to-last clean shirt, then opened the curtains for more light—a futile gesture since the sun was still low in the east—and fumbled with his cuff links.

From the window of the small spare room, he could just make out the sloping roof of the back of the house, the outbuildings and kitchen garden, blurred by the receding mist and by Paul's poor distance vision. The figure of a woman in a dark expanse of bell-shaped skirt, discernible by the lighted lantern she carried, crossed the yard toward the smokehouse. Paul's head had cleared during the night, and now he imagined the smells of sausage and bacon frying, biscuits baking, and chicory coffee brewing.

He also savored thoughts of the genteel company he could keep for a few days at least. Soon enough he would be obliged to wire his employer with a report on his activities. For now there were ladies to oblige instead.

Last night in the study, Delora had allowed him to settle the bill she had sent Langford to pay at Thorpe's Inn, maintaining the appearance that she was hardly in need of reimbursement, but didn't want to insult Paul's sense of pride and independence. Then she'd kept him up late, requesting to examine his newspaper clippings and maps, inquiring about the political climate of the various states he'd visited, and catechizing him on the details of significant battles. She had led her source charmingly, but as much as Paul appreciated her charm, he didn't delude himself that he inspired it. This

woman wanted information, and he was intrigued about what
she planned to do with it: perhaps relay certain facts to her
husband, or possibly keep a more assured upper hand with
Captain Newell, and a firmer grip on her property.

Euphrasie and Lydie Vee Vasseur intrigued Paul, too;
Euphrasie because of her fanciful manner, and Lydie Vee
because he had seen her before in very different circumstances.
During supper the night before, he had studied her
distinctively sharp-featured profile. This was indeed the Lydie
Vee whose name he had thought he'd recognized. Now he
recalled where and when: he had heard it whispered by
runaway slaves. And later he had briefly glimpsed her face on
a moonlit night, near the Louisiana and Arkansas border. At
that time, she was turning over a wagon-load of dry goods and
human contraband to a sutler with abolitionist sympathies.
Paul, in his role as a military courier, rode past them with only
a tip of his hat and a shake of his head in the direction toward
which he traveled, a Confederate camp. He wondered how
many in Lydie Vee's family knew of her involvement during
the War with the Underground Railroad.

Isabelle must know. Who would not confide in
Isabelle? Paul had thought her so easy to talk to when they
were alone, and her silence at supper convinced him she could
keep her own counsel or another's confidences. But then,
through her letters, he knew her well—well beyond the hours
of their actual acquaintance, and far beyond how well she
knew him.

His reverie stopped abruptly when an outburst of
repeated, piercing shrieks rose from the yard and rattled the
windowpane. Paul thrust up the sash. Below him the back
door banged, and three women ran outside toward the woman
by the smokehouse, who continued screaming in shrill, forced
blasts.

Paul tore into the hall, then paused, momentarily

confused by his unfamiliarity with the layout of the house. Around a corner he found the narrow, uncarpeted back stairs, scuttled down them, nearly losing his footing, ran through the warming kitchen and out the back door. In the yard the cacophony had subsided, replaced by a low mewling sound. Paul quickly converged with the others before the smokehouse.

There he saw Faye Samson, collapsed in the plump arms of the cook who rocked and crooned to comfort her. Isabelle and Ardyce stood close by.

Isabelle was speaking hurriedly to Ardyce, telling her to run fetch Radley. "If he's not at the pig barn, he may be sleeping in," she said. "Tell him his mama needs him—now!"

Ardyce ran toward the barn.

"Miss Ross, what's happened?" Paul asked in alarm.

"Oh, Mr. Delahoussaye! Faye says her husband's in the smokehouse."

"Has he harmed her?"

"No, sir. She says he's dead!"

Paul shot a glance at the rough wooden door, then looked into Isabelle's pleading eyes.

"Mr. Delahoussaye, would you . . . would you mind very much making sure?" she asked.

Faye wailed anew as Paul bent by her to pick up the lantern with the cracked glass. Slowly, he swung open the door. The first whiff of smokiness was instantly compounded with a sweetish, ghastly stench. Paul held his breath, raised the lantern before him, and entered. For a moment he saw nothing but indistinct shapes in a dim haze. Then his eyes focused, first on the slabs of curing pork hung from the rafters, then on the rotting flesh of a man.

Loops of rope around the body's upper arms had yanked the shoulders grotesquely out and upward, almost above the head that drooped on the chest. Paul thought of a

vulture with its head sunk between its wings—but this form
was food for vultures. The rope ran upward through a block
and tackle with two wooden pulleys, then slanted downward,
stretched taut, and was tied to a stake driven in the earthen
floor. The dead man's boots cleared the floor by several
inches.

Paul took a brief, sickening breath and a second look
at the corpse. The grizzled hair was matted, the face obscured
in shadow. Dark stained clothing hung in torn strips from the
torso, and then Paul realized the abdomen had been gutted.
Backing out of the shed, he jerked the door shut and gulped
the cold, damp outside air. The lantern shook in his hand. He
had run out of the house without a jacket, and now his white
shirt felt clammy against his back. He shivered.

Isabelle touched his sleeve. "Mr. Samson's dead then?"

Paul nodded, then looked toward the others gathering
around the smokehouse: Delora with Langford a step behind
her, Lydie Vee arm in arm with Babcock, Ardyce approaching
from the direction of the barn, followed by Radley.

"Someone. . . someone should cut him down," Paul
said.

"Oh. Is he. . ." Isabelle let the question drop and
turned to her aunt.

"Langford," said Delora, "assist Mr. Delahoussaye."

Inside the smokehouse Langford handed Paul an ax,
then took hold of the corpse's legs, braced himself, and waited
silently while Paul hacked the rope in two. The body fell
forward over Langford's broad shoulders. He staggered under
its weight.

"Here, let me help," Paul said, but Langford refused.

"Just hold the door open, sir."

As they emerged into the daylight, Paul saw the back
of the corpse's head was bashed in and crusted with dried
blood and fragments of bone. As Langford let the body fall

from his shoulders, Paul heard a thud and a crack. The hollowed out torso had nearly snapped in two.

Faye Samson, kneeling on the ground, looked once at the corpse, screamed, then sobbed again into the cook's apron. Maggots had robbed the face of its features. The skin of neck and chest was brown and dry as a chamois. The tattered clothing was damp and darkened with seeping body fluids. Each time Paul had viewed the aftermath of battle, the same prayer had flashed to mind as it did now while he viewed the butchered remains of Elroy Samson: "Lord, please let me die an old man in my sleep."

Radley caught up to the others. "You found Pa?" he asked, then added in an awed tone, "Well, I'll be. His eyes are gone."

Babcock scurried away to the side of the smokehouse and was sick.

"Someone cover it, please," said Lydie Vee before she shook out her handkerchief and went to her husband's aid.

Delora approached Faye and, placing a hand under her elbow, assisted her to rise. Auntie Pan lumbered to her feet also, untied her broad, white apron and offered it to Langford. He spread it over the corpse.

"You must go up to the house now, Faye. Auntie Pan will fix you something for your nerves," said Delora.

Faye stared at her, wild-eyed. "Elroy's dead!" she cried. "And what in hell are y'all going to do about it?"

"You're overwrought, Faye. Understandably so, of course," Delora answered evenly. "Ardyce, help Auntie Pan quiet Mrs. Samson."

Isabelle had been gripping Ardyce's hand and seemed reluctant to let it go. Paul noted how they looked at one another—Isabelle's terrified gray eyes searching Ardyce's impenetrable brown eyes. Ardyce patted Isabelle's hand as she freed her own, then setting her jaw as if in anticipation of pain, she turned away.

Whimpering, the overseer's widow moved toward the house, supported on either side by Ardyce and Auntie Pan. Paul looked to the others. Radley Samson shuffled backwards a few steps from his father's body, no tears in his dull eyes, but his nose was running. Lydie Vee, returning with her blotchy-faced husband, joined Isabelle and Delora and Langford, who stood beside his mistress, not a pace behind her. The five of them formed a half-circle before the corpse, and Paul was struck by the impression that they were closing ranks.

"Where you want me to take him, Miss Delora?" Langford asked softly.

"Oh, I can't have him in the house, I just can't. Let me think now. You fetch a tarpaulin, Langford, and wrap him in that. Then lay him out in one of the empty cabins down in the quarters. And you guard the door and don't let anybody in, you hear?"

"Yes, ma'am."

Langford loped away to begin carrying out Delora's orders.

Radley sniffed loudly and said, "You want I should ride into town and let folks know Pa's killed?"

"Why, Radley," Delora replied, "I'm not used to you showing so much initiative." Paul caught the sarcasm that flew past the tow-headed boy. Then, with the flicker of a smile, Delora added, "Poor child. You just leave all the arrangements to me. Hurry on up to the kitchen now. Your mama needs you."

Radley shambled off as Langford returned with the tarpaulin. Delora linked arms with Paul and nodded to Isabelle who took his other arm. Isabelle was trembling, and he pressed her hand close to his side.

"This is a shocking occurrence, Mr. Delahoussaye, truly shocking," said Delora. "We must discuss what's to be done."

The three of them, followed by Lydie Vee and Babcock, returned to the house, all breathing a little easier for having left the corpse behind.

As they entered through the back door, Delora sent the others on ahead, but Paul caught her hurried words as she paused in the kitchen. "Auntie Pan, don't stint on the pacification remedies for Faye. Never mind about our breakfast. Just send some strong coffee to the parlor. We'll have liver and lights for dinner. Oh, and Ardyce, make sure Euphrasie's locked in her room."

While Paul, along with the others, still reeled with the horror of murder, Delora seemed empowered with determined energy. She dispatched her Uncle Babcock, Lydie Vee, and Isabelle to the front parlor, then settled Paul in an armchair in the book-lined study.

"Please, Mr. Delahoussaye, do make yourself at home. Read, if you like. My family and I just need a few private moments to gather our thoughts. I'll send Isabelle for you soon as coffee's ready." Delora patted his hand solicitously. "This is all so very distressing and embarrassing. I assure you we all regret inflicting such a situation upon you, a guest in our home."

She swirled out, leaving Paul to wonder if the regrets she expressed were shared by the killer.

Alone, Paul was unable to sit still. He rose from the armchair and paced the study as far as its limited confines allowed; a massive, intricately carved oak desk and a small round table and chairs made striding from end to end impossible. Two tall, narrow windows with open slatted shutters barred the walls with sun and shadow and furthered Paul's impression of having been left in a cell.

He glanced over book titles and restlessly pulled a volume here and there from the shelves to examine more closely. He found a wide variety of subjects represented in the little library: books on history, mathematics, and economics, almanacs and manuals on farming and estate management, classical works, the complete plays of William Shakespeare, collections of poetry, and novels in French and English. Returning *The Last Days of Pompeii* to its place, Paul shook his head in slight amazement thinking of Delora's suggestion he might wish to read to pass the time after his recent encounter with a corpse.

He circled the table on which was spread a large map of Belle Ombre. The original outlines were neatly done in black ink and enhanced with watercolors, Isabelle's artistry, he surmised.   But numerous changes had been made with charcoal and wax pencils. Sketches of cabins Paul assumed represented slave quarters were marked damaged or burned down. Borders of cultivated land were redrawn and labeled with names of tenants or buyers. Where one edge of the map curled a clutter of letters and papers was visible beneath; Paul tentatively extended a hand to shift the map, then looked up guiltily.

On the wall above the desk hung a portrait of Delora Raveneaux with amber eyes as deep and perceptive as they were in life. Paul tucked his hands in his pockets and stared at her likeness. Six wide tiers of creamy lace covered Delora's vast crinoline, and yet another tier fell from her powder white shoulders. She was bejeweled like a queen. The artist had caught the glint of gold rings on pale hands, the sparkle of sapphires and diamonds encircling her wrists and throat, dangling from her earlobes and crowning her burnished auburn hair. Belle Ombre mansion in splendid repair was depicted in the background. Paul guessed the picture was done years ago, perhaps when Delora was a bride.

He heard the rustle of a skirt and turned to see Isabelle standing in the doorway. "Oh, Miss Ross. I was just admiring your aunt's portrait.   Her likeness sure has a way of dominating a room."

Isabelle nodded. "Captain Newell covets that picture," she said. "We hid it from his predecessors during the War. But then we hid a lot of things in those days."

"Including Mrs. Raveneaux's jewels?" Paul asked.

Isabelle looked at him strangely, her eyes slightly narrowed. "I was thinking of other things, Mr. Delahoussaye, such as a few hogs and horses—and our personal feelings. I remember my aunt sold her sapphire tiara in '64 to get us through the year."

"Pardon me.   At times I'm too inquisitive even for a journalist."

"Well, sir, your profession is one of the things my aunt wishes to discuss with you. And perhaps she can answer a few of your questions, too. Will you join us in the parlor?"

"Of course."

Isabelle remained in the doorway as Paul came to stand before her. She looked up at him, searching his face. Then her lips parted as if she were on the verge of saying something that was difficult for her.

"Miss Ross, what is it?   Do you want to tell me something about Mr. Samson?"

She shook her head.

"What then?"

"I was wondering why you went to so much trouble for me, bringing my letters here yourself when you didn't know me at all," she said. "And I wonder how much more trouble I'll be to you before you go."

"I'm at your service, Miss Ross."

"Indeed I hope you are, Mr. Delahoussaye, whatever your reasons."

She turned and led the way to the front parlor. There Delora, Babcock, and Lydie Vee clustered on the sofa, whispering and sipping coffee. Isabelle prepared a cup for Paul, then retreated to the piano stool, while Paul was urged forward by Delora.

"Come and take a chair by the hearth, Mr. Delahoussaye." He complied, and Delora set her coffee cup aside and leaned slightly toward him before speaking again in a confidential tone. "Now then, my dear sir, though you came here on a mission of kindness, and you've only been with us a day . . . well, this shocking occurrence has forced a sort of intimacy upon us all. You must recognize that, sir."

"Yes, ma'am."

"We," she continued, "that is, Mr. and Mrs. Vasseur, Isabelle, myself, our entire household hope we can rely on your discretion."

Paul surveyed his companions. Babcock and Lydie Vee were intent on their coffee, Isabelle was veiled by a shadow, and Delora was unreadable.

"Mrs. Raveneaux," Paul began, "am I to understand we won't be notifying the authorities about Mr. Samson? You do realize the man was obviously murdered?"

"Oh, dear me." Delora folded her hands. "What some folks think is obvious is not always true, Mr. Delahoussaye. And what's true is not always obvious. We have to be on guard because there is so much narrow-mindedness in this world."

"But ma'am, your overseer wasn't just accidentally bashed over the head and strung up," Paul protested.

Babcock groaned, and Lydie Vee patted his knee.

"Now I know that, sir," said Delora, evenly. "But what Captain Newell might make of it is one thing. What some folks in Verbena would make of it is another. And then there's our tenants to consider. And the departed's wife and son, of course. As we all know, violence can beget violence."

"Mr. Delahoussaye," said Lydie Vee, fixing him with

narrowed eyes, "you must realize we are concerned about the possibility of a lynching. It's not uncommon in these parts. Elroy Samson was not especially well liked, if you take my meaning, but folks can get up in arms and pick a scapegoat, guilty or not, just because they want to see things settled and done with."

"He was a drunken womanizer," muttered Babcock with pious disapproval.

"But he was a white man—so somebody's going to want retribution," Lydie Vee added.

"A very different situation from the one involving your servant who fell to her death?" Paul wondered if any of them would answer to the irony in his tone.

Delora blinked once and replied, "Why, yes, sir. A very different situation entirely."

"Mrs. Raveneaux," said Paul, "what do you plan to do, besides bury the man?"

"My family and I have a proposition for you, Mr. Delahoussaye. Your being a journalist—well, we reckoned you've had experience interviewing folks and questioning to get at the truth. So, we want you to find out who killed Elroy Samson."

"Me?"

Delora nodded. "What we're asking for, Mr. Delahoussaye, is a week's grace. You spend this week finding out what happened to Mr. Samson, and then you can take your story to the authorities and any newspaper that wants to print it with our blessing."

"Won't the authorities wonder why we delayed? Won't Captain Newell?" asked Paul.

"Blame me," Delora answered simply. "You are my guest here, in my keeping, shall we say? Tell the Captain you only wanted to oblige your hostess."

She fixed him with her gaze and was still, except for

the fingers of her left hand steadily smoothing a bit of lace at her throat. Paul fastened on the rhythmic gesture, recalling a hypnotist he'd once seen in a traveling show. Delay a week, he thought, spend a week at Belle Ombre with Isabelle and her family. Then Paul shook his head to clear his mind. "What if I can't do it in a week?"

Lydie Vee and Babcock looked to Delora as questioningly as did Paul.

"We'll cross that bridge if we reach it," Delora replied. "Til then, we are at your mercy, sir."

"But, ma'am, what does Mrs. Samson think of this arrangement?" Paul asked.

"She'll come 'round. Which reminds me, I must go and see how the widow's bearing up." Delora swept toward the door. "Uncle Babcock, Lydie Vee, shall we leave Mr. Delahoussaye to talk with Isabelle first? I believe she was the last one of us to see Mr. Samson alive."

After the others had gone, Delora shutting the parlor door, Isabelle remained seated in the shadows. Paul approached her, and she rose, the light falling on her face.

"Miss Ross, have you been weeping all this time? Please come and sit by the fire." Paul led her to the hearth and joined her on the sofa. "Tell me what troubles you."

Isabelle brushed a tear away with her handkerchief. "Do you accept my aunt's terms, Mr. Delahoussaye? Do you give us a week?"

"Well, it looks as if I do. Does anyone ever say no to your Aunt Delora?"

"Some folks have."

"But not me—not if this is what you want, too. I'll do what I can."

"Thank you."

Paul thought he would prefer to talk with Isabelle about any number of things other than Elroy Samson's murder, but he had obligated himself. "Those tears weren't for Mr. Samson, were they?" he began.

"No."

"Who then?"

"Someone I love very much . . ." Paul felt an involuntary pang and then relief as she finished her sentence: "someone I love as a sister."

"Euphrasie?"

"Ardyce."

"She was your slave?"

"That's what she was called. But we've been together since we were girls, since I lost my parents. She understood my loss better than anyone."

"And is Ardyce involved in Samson's murder?" Paul asked.

"Of course not! But it's like Lydie Vee said—people want retribution. Ardyce would make an easy scapegoat."

"Why?"

"Really, Mr. Delahoussaye, is this how you conduct interviews? 'Why?' is a very blunt question," said Isabelle. "I thought journalists were supposed to know how to get around folks."

"Well, sometimes I know. But with you, I thought I could just ask directly."

"Why?"

Paul smiled. "Because after our talk yesterday at the cemetery I thought you were willing to put some trust in me. Mrs. Raveneaux's given me a week to find out the truth, and I'd be obliged for all the help you can give me. Why would Ardyce make an easy scapegoat?"

"Well, it's as you said. She was a slave here. Mr. Samson was the overseer."

"That's the only reason?" persisted Paul.

Isabelle sighed impatiently. "You've never lived on a

plantation, have you, sir?"

"Only a small Missouri farm," Paul said, shaking his head at his own obtuseness; of course, to some white men, likely to Samson, Ardyce would be no more than a pretty piece of chattel, to be taken, not asked.

Paul began his questioning again. "So, would you tell me about the last time you saw Elroy Samson alive?"

Then Isabelle recounted Samson's unwelcome appearance in the back parlor on the night of Forest's wake. "The man was full of liquor and vile ideas."

"He attacked you?" Paul asked, alarmed.

"No, no. But he threatened me. He suffered from some ridiculous delusion that there's a second map of Belle Ombre—other than the one in the study—that shows the location of buried treasure. He thought I could get him that map."

"Is there buried treasure?"

"Of course not," said Isabelle. "The only thing buried on this land is our dead. But Mr. Samson had himself convinced Aunt Delora was holding out on him. Oh, that man! He even wanted to pry open Forest's coffin to see if she had hidden valuables in it."

"How did he threaten you?"

"He said if I didn't find him the map, my horse, Morning Glory, the sweetest old gelding that ever was, might go lame. Or Ardyce might. . ." Her voice broke.

Paul lightly touched her hands folded in her lap. She didn't recoil from his touch, and, encouraged, Paul applied a little more pressure. "Go on, please," he said.

"Samson told me Ardyce might fall in the creek. Well, he knew as well as anyone around here that Ardyce fears drowning above all else. That's how her papa died. Some overseer before Samson's time pushed his face in a trough over and over again for a punishment, 'til his lungs were so full of water nothing could bring him back. Ardyce saw it happen."

Paul felt his breath quicken. "I'm beginning to think, Miss Ross, that if I discover who killed Elroy Samson, I'll want to pin a medal on the fellow."

Paul thought Isabelle nodded in agreement as she lowered her gaze and slipped her hands from his. For a moment his fingertips felt the soft, worn cashmere spread over her hoop skirt. Then he straightened his back and his tie.

"It's unusual for a woman to wield as much authority as Mrs. Raveneaux does here at Belle Ombre," said Paul. "Was that a sore spot with Elroy Samson?"

"What's unusual, Mr. Delahoussaye, is that my aunt, unlike many women, doesn't shy away from taking credit for what she does. She can hardly rely on the judgment of her nearest male relative."

"Babcock Vasseur."

"Precisely. But you're right about Mr. Samson not liking the situation. Just before the War, Uncle Charles Orvin and his overseer pretty much ran the place. And for a time after he left, my uncle corresponded with Samson and gave instructions through him. Then, luckily for all of us who hoped to eat in the winter of '63, Uncle Charles Orvin began to place more confidence in Aunt Delora and allow her a free hand to manage the estate properly. Samson was hopping mad, but he stayed on—anything to avoid facing the enemy."

"Somehow I didn't picture him as a man who'd avoid a fight," said Paul.

"Bullying women and children and displaying physical courage in battle are hardly the same thing, sir. He never picked a fair fight."

"Yet someone fought with him—and won."

"Or took him off guard," said Isabelle.

Paul nodded, remembering the shattered back of Samson's head. "Tell me, Miss Ross, what happened that night after Samson left you in the back parlor."

Isabelle answered evenly: "Mr. Samson left the door ajar. I distinctly heard him climb the back stairs that lead to the servants' rooms. Euphrasie slipped in and sat with me by the fire. We talked, and I think we fell asleep for a little while. Then we heard a scream, and I went to see what was wrong. Beryl had fallen through the airwell to her death. When the household gathered 'round her body, Mr. Samson was nowhere to be seen."

"You think there may be some connection between Beryl's death and Samson's?"

"I think there may have been something between them when they were alive, Mr. Delahoussaye."

"And who else thinks this?"

"I don't know. Ardyce told me."

"Then Ardyce may have had something to do with Samson's murder."

"No! I told you, Ardyce had nothing to do with it."

"But you are afraid for her. You've said as much."

Isabelle rose from the sofa, and Paul jumped to his feet, knowing he'd pressed the point too hard.

"I'm afraid of false accusations, sir. Now you must excuse me." She fled the room.

Paul stared at the open door, considering if he should go after her. Then he heard a creak of hinges behind him and turned, expecting to see Babcock sneaking in from the dining room for a shot of brandy. Instead, he beheld Euphrasie, crawling out from behind a section of stenciled paneling below the chair rail molding. She straightened up, coughed, and fanned one hand before her face.

"My, but these hidey-holes do get dusty," she said. "'Course nobody uses them since the War, 'cept me." She brushed a cobweb from the flannel smock that didn't quite cover her pantalets, then looked sideways at Paul, and added petulantly, "They're always trying to leave me out of things around here, Mr. Delahoussaye. It's so unfair."

Recovering from his surprise, Paul asked, "How long have you been in the . . . the wall, Miss Euphrasie?"

"Oh, ever since Ardyce thought she'd locked me in my room. I left a pillow bolster in my bed so she'd think I was asleep."

Euphrasie scurried barefoot across the rug and curled herself on the floor before the fire. "You're so terribly tall, Mr. Delahoussaye. Please sit down, or I'll surely get a crick in my neck from looking up at you."

Paul resumed his place on the sofa.

"There, that's better," she said, with a satisfied smile. "Now I can tell you why Isabelle is so worried for Ardyce. That's what you're curious about, isn't it?"

Paul thought if this girl spent much time in the woodwork she could tell him a great many curious things.

"I'm obliged to you for any assistance in my investigation, Miss Euphrasie."

She beamed importantly and began her ingenuous and uninhibited recitation: "Elroy Samson thought all the slave girls were for his use, you know what I mean? He'd get to them 'fore Uncle Charles Orvin ever had a chance. They were two of a kind about that sort of thing, I heard Aunt Delora tell Langford."

Paul thought that was an odd piece of information for the mistress of the plantation to confide to her slave, but he let it pass as Euphrasie continued chattering.

"Years ago—I disremember how long—Ardyce had a baby by Mr. Samson. I heard her and Isabelle talking about how it happened. It was awful, the way he went about it! Gives me the shivers, just thinking of it. First he—"

"What happened to the baby?" Paul interrupted.

"Oh, poor thing didn't live a minute. Died without

baptism, right here in this house. And you know what that means. That little *couchmal* has been flitting around here ever since, causing no end of trouble."

"So Ardyce holds a justifiable grudge against Samson?"

"She holds more than that. She sleeps with a knife under her pillow and her fist clenched 'round the handle."

Paul had no need to ask how Euphrasie obtained her information; he imagined she was the true restless spirit that flitted through the house.

"You've been very helpful," he said.

"Oh, but I'm not finished." Euphrasie raised herself to her knees and leaned close to him. "Don't you want to know about the other map?"

"But Miss Ross told me there was no other map."

Euphrasie shrugged, heedless of her loose smock as it slipped, exposing one frail shoulder. "Well, there's a mystery for you! Not a week ago she had that map spread out on her bed. And she was running her fingers over it and whispering to herself—I couldn't hear what."

"And you're sure it wasn't the map from the study?"

"Oh, no. I'd just been down there getting a talking to from Aunt Delora, and her map was on the table. I don't know where Isabelle hides the other map—I didn't do more than peek at her that night, since she'd been fussing at me earlier. But maybe I could find out." She pushed a lock of yellow hair from her brow and smiled up at Paul.

"Oh, no, Miss Euphrasie. I wouldn't have you going through your cousin's things."

"But I'd be pleased to do it for you."

With a quick tug at her smock, he covered her bare shoulder, then sprang from the sofa. He was backing away from the girl when Lydie Vee Vasseur entered the parlor.

"Aha," she said, and paused, holding a rigid pose until

Euphrasie, clutching at her smock, dashed from the room.

"It's time Langford nailed this thing shut," said Lydie Vee, crossing to the open panel and pushing it to. "You know, Mr. Delahoussaye, that girl's not right. But none of us should take advantage of her simplicity."

"Of course not, Mrs. Vasseur."

"I've brought you your hat." She thrust the battered article at him. "And your coat." She held it out stiffly, and Paul stuffed his arms in the sleeves. "Now," she said, "I'll accompany you to visit some of the tenants before dinner. I often call on them to see how they're getting on, and perhaps you and I can find answers to a few questions as we go our rounds."

"Yes, ma'am."

She led him outside to a mule and wagon and proceeded to take the reins. As they drove under the live oaks, Lydie Vee grilled Paul on his part in the War, his current employment, his reason for coming to Belle Ombre, asking if he'd ever met Colonel Brodie or Colonel Raveneaux. Paul answered as simply as he could, all the while sensing Lydie Vee was not satisfied with his explanations.

Then, out of sight of the house, Lydie Vee broke the uncomfortable silence that had fallen between them. "Why did you stare so at me last night at supper, Mr. Delahoussaye? There were certainly comelier faces at the table."

"I believe I've seen you before, ma'am," said Paul, "during the War, on a moonlit night."

Lydie Vee scoffed. "Are you sure, sir, you don't have me confused with another lady?"

"No, ma'am. It was near the Louisiana and Arkansas border. You were turning goods over to a sutler, headed north."

She cut her eyes toward him suddenly, with a look of alarm. "You saw me there?"

"I was the corporal, traveling the other way. I tipped my hat to you," said Paul. "I tip my hat to you still, Mrs. Vasseur."

"You've said nothing to anyone at Belle Ombre about recognizing me? Nothing to my husband?"

"No, ma'am."

She took a deep breath, and Paul thought her stiff shoulders relaxed slightly.

"But doesn't Miss Ross share your sympathies, Mrs. Vasseur? I got the impression . . ."

"Rightly so," she replied. "And do call me Lydie Vee. Much as you seem to know about me, I see no sense in formality."

"Thank you for your confidence, ma'am."

"Well, please understand, sir," she continued. "I have tried to be a moderating influence on Isabelle, fearing under Delora Raveneaux's tutelage, the girl might learn nothing except how to outmaneuver mankind. But I'll say this for Delora—she is an ardent lover of books and encourages study in others. Fortunately, Isabelle is both intelligent and fair-minded."

"And how did you come to be so fair-minded yourself, Miss Lydie Vee, if you don't mind my asking? You're a rarity in this part of the country."

Lydie Vee shrugged, then clucked to urge the mule forward, toward a tumbled-down cabin. "Well, sir, I married late and I married Babcock, so I've had time in my life to think. The South didn't invent slavery or the subjugation of women—it just offered fertile ground for those notions to grow. As for myself, I believe in the Golden Rule, Mr. Delahoussaye—always have, always will."

"But am I to understand that Mr. Vasseur doesn't share your ideal?"

"We didn't marry for what we had in common; like

many couples, we married for what we lacked. I'm not saying it's right, sir, but any practical woman knows, marriage allows her a certain status and freedom to move about—particularly if her husband lacks curiosity. As for Mr. Vasseur, well, he needed looking after."

With that, Lydie Vee closed the subject of her personal philosophy and began her interviews with various tenants. No one admitted to seeing Elroy Samson in recent days, and no one confessed to missing him. Only Arthur and Gerard Thibodeau showed a particular interest, asking if Lydie Vee were sure the overseer had left the vicinity and requesting she tell them as soon as he reappeared. Paul recalled the poached fish at last night's supper, credited to the Thibodeau brothers, and surmised the brothers wouldn't want to meet Samson unexpectedly on one of their midnight hunting and fishing expeditions. Or perhaps they had met him, Paul considered, and Samson had not survived the encounter.

CHAPTER SEVEN

Isabelle quietly climbed the back stairs to the third floor. She hardly wanted to contemplate what Paul Delahoussaye must think of her—pouring out her bitterness against Samson and locking in her sympathy for Ardyce. Better not to think of him, better to do something practical, she resolved, entering what had been Beryl's room, intent upon searching it for some trace of Samson's last visit there, some evidence perhaps that his and Beryl's deaths were related. Then, with one look at the cramped cell, she knew hers was not an original idea.

The cot had been stripped of bedding, its mattress ticking slashed and the straw contents strewn over the floor. Isabelle expected the chiffonier to be gone; Langford had sawed it up to make Beryl's coffin. But she remembered Delora told Ardyce to put the clothes and personal items it had once contained in a wicker basket. The basket was now overturned in a corner, the spilled clothing in shreds. And among the shreds were slivers of glass and pottery. Isabelle could only just perceive the sweet, musty residue of whiskey before a gust of November wind blew across the room from the open window and cleared the air.

"Lord have mercy!" Ardyce cried from the doorway, then quickly apologized for startling Isabelle.

"Oh, never you mind," said Isabelle. "I'm all nerves today. Does Aunt Delora know about this hooraw's nest?"

"Don't know, miss. She sent me up to get the room ready for Radley."

"Radley? Up here?"

"Sure 'nough. She wants him and his mama under her roof. Miss Faye is pacified in the room nearest hers, and she wants Radley in here."

Isabelle was taken aback. "You mean Faye Samson's in Colonel Raveneaux's bedroom? What does my aunt mean by this?"

"She means to have her own way," said Ardyce. "She means to have Miss Faye stop hollering about going to town with Radley and bringing all Verbena and the Yankees down on our heads."

"Oh, I see. I hope this arrangement won't be for too long." Isabelle reflected for a moment on her aunt's curious ways of dealing with Samson's widow and son and the repercussions of murder; like so many of Delora's solutions to problems during the War, her current tactics seemed fragile and temporary—yet Delora remained in control of Belle Ombre. "Well," she said, taking another glance around the room, "I'll help you sort out this mess."

Ardyce looked at her shrewdly. "You think you and me might find what somebody else was looking for in here when he tore up this place?"

"Maybe. Though it looks as if whoever did this was thorough, if rushed. I wonder when this was done."

"Hard to say, Miss Isabelle. I ain't been in here since before Beryl died. And Auntie Pan would have said something to me if she'd seen this jumble."

Isabelle stepped carefully through the debris to the window. "There's a scrape on the sill. Somebody could have shinnied up a live oak and come through the window."

"Or gone out the window after coming through the door," said Ardyce.

Then Isabelle wondered if the same person who'd destroyed Beryl's things had also pushed her over the airwell railing. Shutting the window, she said, "Ardyce, you and Auntie Pan sleep in together tonight, you hear, and bolt the door."

"You bolt yourself in, too, Miss Isabelle. And don't forget to lock up Miss Euphrasie."

Together they sorted the torn garments, all now good for nothing but cleaning rags, and they swept up fragments of a glass bottle and a wash basin. Then they restuffed the mattress tick, and Isabelle began sewing up the tear in it, while Ardyce fetched fresh bed covers.

When Ardyce returned she took up one of the rags to clean the windowsill, but stopped suddenly and stared at the cloth in her hand.

Finishing her sewing, Isabelle looked up. "What is it?"

"I reckon, Miss Isabelle, it's a scrap of a man's under drawers. A front piece with buttons."

Isabelle thought of Elroy Samson and of how Beryl got her liquor.

Then Nettie, one of the servant girls who was hired by the day, came running up the back stairs, calling to Ardyce. "Miz Raveneaux wants you right this minute, Ardyce. Something 'bout getting some pork ready for Captain Newell."

"Tell her I'm coming." Ardyce looked at Isabelle. "You come on down, too. Radley can make his own bed." She tossed the sheets and blanket on the cot.

* * *

It was well past noon. Isabelle went to the kitchen and found Auntie Pan bent over the oven door, checking the biscuits.

"I knows, I knows I'm running late with dinner, miss." With a groan, the cook straightened her back. "You can tell Miss Delora I'm doing the best I knows how, but she heaped a bale of trouble on me this morning. Why, I done brewed everything I knows how to brew and poured everything but poison down Miss Faye's gullet. I thought that woman was *never* gonna leave off."

"Oh, Auntie Pan, I didn't come down here to hurry you or scold you. I came to help," said Isabelle. "What can I do?"

"Well, bless your soul, child."

Auntie Pan set her to seasoning the greens, then filling the serving dishes, and they talked as they worked.

"Aunt Delora says someone's been getting into the pantry," said Isabelle.

"That's right. Every few nights looks like something's been messed with in there, and a bit of this and that goes missing."

"Well, Aunt Delora doesn't hold the horn of plenty, but she does try to be sure folks get fed. Who could be taking extra when there's so little to go 'round?"

"Some's just greedy, I guess."

"Maybe it's somebody who ran off during the War and has come back looking for family," Isabelle suggested.

The cook lightly dropped hot biscuits into a cloth lined dish, then covered them to keep them warm.

"Auntie Pan, why have you stayed on with us after the War changed things? Of course, we want you to stay. But so many did leave here. Don't you wonder about your kin?"

Auntie Pan wiped her hands on her apron before answering. "You know good and well I was born in the Vasseur family. All my children was born in the Vasseur family or the Raveneaux family when Miss Delora married against her better judgment."

Isabelle remembered the talk about how Auntie Pan took umbrage when Charles Orvin Raveneaux became her master. After gambling away his own estate, Raveneaux arranged with old Mr. Vasseur to marry Delora and take control of Belle Ombre when his father-in-law died.

"Anywhichway," Auntie Pan continued, "where'd I go

if I left Belle Ombre? No, miss, I'm staying put. That way my children, whether they run off or sold off, knows where to find me."

"Has one found you?"

"Humph! I'm surprised at you, Miss Isabelle. You accusing one of my kin of stealing from our pantry? Who's to say it ain't rats in the house?"

"Oh, I'm sorry, Auntie Pan. I didn't mean it that way."

"Never you mind then. I just get a little riled up when some folks have a hissy about a little pilfering, and then they're so hush-mouthed about murder being done."

Isabelle nodded. "I don't suppose any of us will miss him, but it was shocking the way Samson died."

"Shocking—fiddlesticks! He's gone where he belongs. But who's going to answer for Beryl? And who's going to be next? You can't tell me these things don't come in threes."

"But wasn't Forest's death the first of the three?"

"Well, I'm thinking he may not rightly count in this bunch of three 'cause he died somewhere else, and he died natural. He weren't done in."

"But you think Beryl was? You think her fall wasn't accidental?"

"I thinks I weren't born yesterday, Miss Isabelle. And I'm telling you, we better be wary." Auntie Pan patted Isabelle's shoulder. "Go on now, honey. Make yourself presentable. I'll get Nettie to lay the table."

* * *

Dinner was brief with little conversation to prolong the ritual. Isabelle observed that Uncle Babcock, slurring his speech and spilling his soup, was well on his way to a drunken stupor. Lydie Vee, the color high in her face after her outing, looked appraisingly at the others and said little. Aunt Delora seemed preoccupied with her own thoughts and directed only a few inconsequential pleasantries to Paul. Paul looked pale and ill, as if his cold were reasserting itself, but he struggled to respond politely and do justice to a plate of liver and lights. Euphrasie did not appear and left their number odd, but this time no one evened the table with Colonel Raveneaux's portrait.

As Ardyce cleared the dishes, Delora announced, "Captain Newell, I regret to say, plans to call on us before nightfall. I have it from Gerard Thibodeau that the captain can't wait to carry off some pork and perhaps some horseflesh. Seems his favorite mount has gone lame, and he's looking for a replacement."

"Oh, no, Aunt," Isabelle cried. "We only have the two horses and the mule."

"Let's not forget Mr. Delahoussaye's horse," said Delora.

Paul looked startled. "You mean to say, ma'am, that Captain Newell might confiscate Pickwick? Of all the high-handed, imperious—" Paul stopped himself.

Delora smiled. "Who knows? He might not even care so much about riding after he gets his fill of pork. Besides, he can't demand what isn't here. Langford can find a place elsewhere for some of our livestock. And Isabelle, I suggest you and Mr. Delahoussaye might enjoy an evening ride. You could show our guest the wild woods at sunset."

"You think that's wise, Delora?" said Lydie Vee, sternly.

"I surely do," Delora replied. "The sky's lowering and the rains may start again anytime. Before we're all cooped up for another week going stir crazy, the young people should take some exercise out of doors. You, yourself, look the better for having had an outing today."

Delora and Lydie Vee faced one another across the table, each with one arched brow. Then Babcock's snoring drew away Lydie Vee's attention. She shook her husband half-conscious and escorted him from the dining room.

At Delora's suggestion, Isabelle and Paul spent what remained of the afternoon in the study. Isabelle found it a little strange that her aunt allowed her so much time alone with Paul Delahoussaye. Delora had been so vigilant during her courtship with Forest that Isabelle had sometimes resorted to small deceptions in order to have some private time with him. But, of course, she was much younger then. During the War, she felt Delora had come to rely on her level-headedness and maturing judgment when Yankees or jayhawkers threatened the peace at Belle Ombre. More than once Isabelle had whisked herself and Euphrasie from sight and harm when strangers entered the house. But Delora seemed quite easy in her mind about Paul, putting him forward as a suitable companion for Isabelle.

Perhaps, thought Isabelle, Delora hoped to distract Paul from serious inquiries into family matters and possibly guide the murder investigation toward a conclusion of which she could approve. Through the years, Isabelle had grown accustomed to her aunt's receiving and deflecting the attentions of men. But in this one instance Delora had chosen to offer her niece as a distraction rather than herself. Delora, with her quick perceptions and singular practicality, must have seen what Isabelle felt from the first moment Paul's blue eyes focused upon her; Isabelle was the reason Paul had come to Belle Ombre, and because of her he would stay and make himself useful to her aunt.

Paul was certainly polite, even pleasant, while faced with difficult circumstances and some difficult people. He was earnest, serious, considerate, apparently trustworthy. But that morning in the parlor, even while they spoke of murder, he had looked at her with an unexpected familiarity. Now in the study, she clasped her hands in her lap and recalled how he had touched her hands and more than comforted her. No, she wasn't repelled by him—quite the contrary—but she was repelled by the guilty thought of how quickly a living man might supplant a dead one. And Isabelle was disconcerted by the persistent feeling that Paul knew her better than she knew him.

She poured him a cup of weak tea. "You look poorly, Mr. Delahoussaye. I hope your cold isn't worse."

"Oh, no," he responded quickly. "I'm on the mend, thank you." Paul pulled his chair near hers at the study table, as near as her crinoline allowed.

"Then drink up," she said. "Don't worry, it's only ordinary tea, not hog's hoof."

With a flicker of a smile he accepted the cup."You must be worn out after traipsing around with Lydie Vee and not being properly fed. I am sorry you had to go without breakfast, and then dinner was so late."

"Miss Ross, you and Mrs. Raveneaux amaze me with your concern for my health and welfare at a time like this. I'm inclined to think you two put more store in being good hostesses than in discovering who's done murder around here."

"Well, I take after my aunt in believing that attending to a few niceties helps keep the ugliness from taking over. But I'm certainly concerned about wrongdoing. And I have a strong feeling that what's gone wrong is far from finished."

"Why do you say that?" Paul asked.

"You tell me what you found out today first, and then I'll see if I can explain my feeling."

"If you wish." Paul took a swallow of tea and began. "Working for the *Laurel Dispatch*, I've investigated and uncovered a scandal or two—mostly financial and political shenanigans—but never anything like this." He pulled a small notebook from his breast pocket and thumbed the pages. "I went back in the smokehouse, and I took a second look at the body after Langford laid it out in the cabin. My best guess is that Elroy Samson was killed by a blow to the head, maybe from a shovel or the flat side of an ax, and then, well, gutted somewhere other than the smokehouse, where he was later hoisted with a pulley. He's been dead for three or four days. I base my assumptions partly on things I observed during the War."

Isabelle winced.

"Oh, Miss Ross, forgive me. I don't mean to offend you with these details, but—"

"It's quite all right, really," Isabelle interjected. "I want to know everything about the situation that you know. And I'm not offended. But you see, three or four days ago would be about the time of Forest's funeral and of Beryl's death. I really must have been the last person to see Samson alive—besides the killer."

"Just so, miss. I think we have to look hard at this association between Samson and Beryl. Suppose he did push her down the airwell, and someone saw him do it, confronted him, and killed him?"

"Someone in this house?" asked Isabelle.

"Not necessarily living here. You have hired help coming in and out. But just to keep my facts straight, who actually does live in this house?"

"Family—Aunt Delora, Great-Uncle Babcock and Lydie Vee Vasseur, Cousin Euphrasie, and me. Then our cook, Auntie Pan, and Ardyce and Langford."

"Langford lives here in the big house? Has he always?"

"No, just ever since he came back. He left shortly after the War broke out. When he returned, Aunt Delora gave him what used to be a little withdrawing room on the first floor. She knew she couldn't rely on Samson, but she could always depend on Langford."

"Even though he ran off for a while?" Paul looked at

her quizzically.

"He came back," she said. "Aunt Delora said she'd sooner hold a grudge against Samson for staying than against Langford for leaving. I think his going had something to do with his kinfolk who'd been sold away sometime ago."

"So he's been in the house going on two years?"

"Something like that. How did you know how long he was gone?"

"Well, I . . . I heard he'd left for a couple of years. One of the tenants must have said. That would put him back here sometime in '63?"

Isabelle nodded.

"Where did he get a name like Langford?"

"It was the maiden name of Aunt Delora's mother. Langford belonged to my aunt's family and came with her when she married. It's odd, isn't it? Talking about one person belonging to another. We were brought up with it, but it is truly a peculiar institution."

"Can I take it you share Mrs. Vasseur's sympathies?" Paul asked.

"Her sympathies?" Isabelle repeated cautiously.

"I saw Lydie Vee Vasseur at work during the War. One night, near the Louisiana and Arkansas border. She was helping a slave family find their way North."

"And you approved of what she was doing?"

Paul nodded.

"Yes," said Isabelle. "I share her ideals. How could I not after she gave me a copy of *Uncle Tom's Cabin*? I hope I don't offend you, Mr. Delahoussaye, but I am in full agreement with Lydie Vee that white is not necessarily better than black. And," she added a little testily, "man is not necessarily more intelligent or more capable than woman."

Paul smiled. "I can't argue with you there."

"I'm proud of Lydie Vee for her courage, though I can't

say that to most people. Careful as she tried to be, there were suspicions about her in Shreveport. That's why her home was burned down and she and Uncle Babcock came here," said Isabelle. "Lydie Vee confides certain things to me in the hope, she says, of broadening my own views. But please say you haven't told anyone else what you and I know about her."

"I haven't. But now I think you'd understand that I. . . I wasn't completely forthright with your Aunt Delora. You see, I did act as a reporter and courier for the Confederacy. And I fought a little, mostly in skirmishes, not the grand battles I wrote about for the Dispatch. But I also, like Mrs. Vasseur—" Paul stopped suddenly and looked around the small room, then asked. "Are there any of those wall panels in here like the one that opens in the parlor?"

"Oh, no, not here in the study." Even so, Isabelle dropped her voice to a whisper when she said, "I hope you weren't a spy, were you, Mr. Delahoussaye?"

"No, miss, nothing so dashing and dangerous."

"Helping runaways was dangerous enough. Why did you?

"Many reasons. Like you, I'd read Mrs. Stowe's book. I grew up in Missouri, a breeding ground for divided loyalties, if ever there were. And in '62 I was running away myself, from my grandparents' farm. My grandfather had a small place, and he never owned a slave, but he couldn't tolerate the notion that someone would tell him that he couldn't. If I'd walked off that farm in anything but a gray uniform, Grandfather would have shot me in the back. So, I did what he told me to do, leastwise 'til I was out of his sight. Do you think that was cowardly, Miss Ross?"

"You were very young when the War broke out. We all were." Isabelle considered her own divided loyalties. "By joining the Confederacy, you were one less man taking aim at my loved ones," she added.

"Well, my aim was a little out of focus," said Paul. "Some say it's a liability for a soldier to see good and bad on both sides, and within the same men."

"But it could be an asset for a writer," said Isabelle.

"I hope so. I never fancied myself a farmer or a soldier, to my grandfather's everlasting grief. As a boy I learned to use the telegraph in town—pestered the clerk at the post office until he taught me—and all I wanted to do was write stories and relay news. Still, you get an uneasy feeling when folks expect one thing of you, and you're longing to do something else."

Isabelle smiled. "That feeling gave you something in common with slaves and with women. Perhaps that accounts for your sympathies."

"Do you think Mrs. Raveneaux would be so understanding of me?" Paul asked.

"I'm not sure. She's always had a strong feeling about property. And family. I think she'd just as soon not know some things about you."

"If it's unsaid, then she doesn't have to do anything about it," said Paul.

"Something like that. I don't think she and Lydie Vee ever discuss the Underground Railroad. And Uncle Babcock is still in the dark about why their neighbors turned on them and ran them off." Isabelle suppressed a smile. "Lydie Vee has given him the impression that it was because he committed a social error while under the influence." And, Isabelle thought, Babcock was far more curious about what scandalous act he might have enjoyed and forgotten than about the actual activities of his wife.

Paul cleared his throat and asked, "Loyalty to one's homeland—one's home state—and abhorrence of slavery don't have to exclude one another. You've witnessed that in your family, and in yourself. Did your fiancé share your compassion for other races?"

Isabelle was surprised by the question, but answered truthfully, "No. He told me before he went to War that he'd long outgrown childish affections for Negro playfriends and nurses. And he was unwavering in his devotion to the Cause. I suppose a man would have to be when he's charging into battle. But I was full of doubts. I think. . . ."

"What, Miss Ross?" Paul prompted.

"Well, Forest and I might not have got on so well after the War as we did before."

Isabelle, busying herself with refilling the teacups, felt a blush of shame for her confession of disloyalty. She could claim she was only being honest with Paul, but wasn't she also currying his favor? He had admitted to her misrepresenting himself to Delora, who generously excused his lack of battle experience while approving his allegiance. Now Isabelle had offered him in exchange knowledge about herself, which she withheld from Delora—or which Delora chose to ignore.

"You didn't feel you owned Ardyce, did you?" said Paul. "You didn't think of her as your property."

Again, the sensation washed over Isabelle that Paul knew her too well. "Ardyce is a good person. I've always loved her. And I felt responsible for her, but things happened that I couldn't stop and I couldn't change."

Paul slowly removed his spectacles and rubbed the lenses on his sleeve. He didn't look at Isabelle when he spoke again. "Did Elroy Samson have his way with Ardyce?"

Isabelle's throat tightened and she couldn't answer. Paul must have heard some gossip from the tenants, or perhaps someone in the house had told him.

Paul didn't pursue the question, but replaced his spectacles and consulted his notes again. "When I accompanied Miss Lydie Vee to see some of the tenant families, neither of us said anything about Samson's murder.

She sort of led the conversations, mentioning he was missing, and then let folks talk while I listened. No one volunteered seeing or hearing anything out of the ordinary—whatever ordinary is around here. But I got the impression Elroy Samson won't be missed."

"No, he won't."

"But your Aunt Delora seems to be much admired," said Paul.

"Yes. She has a way about her, a way of getting what she wants done without being cruel. It's something I wish Uncle Charles Orvin could learn from her when he returns. I'm afraid he's not much better liked than Samson was."

"But it seems Colonel Raveneaux has given your aunt a free hand in his absence."

"She carries out his instructions as she receives them."

"Of course. In those letters Langford brings her from town. Tell me something, does Langford know how to read?"

"A little. I know we weren't supposed to teach them, but Aunt Delora thought it would be useful if Langford could read almanacs and manuals and such since he helps her so much with running Belle Ombre. And," Isabelle added, "I taught Ardyce because I thought she might enjoy it."

"Does she?"

"Yes, when she gets a moment to pick up a book. Some evenings we share a novel."

Paul's chair creaked as he leaned forward, pencil and notebook ready in hand. "Now, Miss Ross, will you tell me about this feeling you have that the trouble here isn't finished?"

Isabelle pushed her teacup away and folded her hands. "Well, you know about Beryl's sudden death," she said, "but today I discovered her old room had been ransacked, clothes torn to bits, pottery broken. There's an oak near the house someone could have climbed to reach a second story gable, and from there her window on the third story. There were scrapes on the windowsill, perhaps made by boots."

"You're very observant," said Paul, jotting down a few words. "You'd make a good reporter."

Isabelle was pleased by his remark, especially since he had not qualified it by adding "if you were a man."

"We've been troubled recently with someone stealing from the pantry," she continued, "and I'm wondering if the same person searched the maid's room."

"Searching for what?" Paul asked.

"I don't know. But I want you to look at something."

Isabelle rose, and Paul was quick to follow her to the heavy oak desk below Delora's portrait.

"Langford made this desk for Aunt Delora's father, and it still seems more hers than Uncle Charles Orvin's, though he takes over the study when he's home."

"Fine workmanship," Paul commented.

"Langford's a marvel at woodworking. He even made secret panels and hidey-holes for us when the War broke out."

"So he knows where you ladies hide your valuables?" Paul arched his brows above the rim of his spectacles.

Isabelle nodded as she knelt before the desk and touched the pattern of oak leaves and acorns carved across the drawers. "So he'd have no reason to do this," she said, and pointed to deep scratches in the wood and around the brass keyholes. "Someone's tried to force open this desk, someone who obviously cares nothing about fine workmanship."

"Or someone in a hurry," said Paul, bending close to see the damage. "When did you first notice this?"

"This morning, before Mr. Samson's body was discovered, I'd come in here to put a book away and noticed then. The papers on the desk and table were scattered very much as you see them now, but Aunt Delora often leaves them that way."

"What did your aunt say about the scratches?"

"She said she'd seen them several days ago. We both thought Elroy Samson must have been snooping again. As I told you before, he was obsessed with the idea that Aunt Delora had a cache of jewels hidden somewhere around. But now I don't know. Someone else, an outsider, may have been in the house."

Paul took Isabelle's hand and helped her rise from the rug. Standing before him, her fingertips still curved over his, catching a whiff of starch and bay rum, she was momentarily reminded of how she had missed the proximity of a gentleman. Through so many years of hard times and distressing events, Isabelle had become inured to grimness, and it was the stray pleasant thought that took her by surprise. She looked away from him, down to the floor and saw that the hem of her skirt covered the toes of his boots.

"Mr. Delahoussaye," she said, withdrawing her hand and taking a step back, "when did you arrive in Verbena? Wasn't it several days before you returned my letters?"

"Only a day, Miss Ross. I was trying to get over a cold."

"And all you knew about Belle Ombre was that a girl living here had written to a soldier?"

"Mrs. Vasseur already asked me such questions today and quite a few more," said Paul. "When and why did I come here? Did I know Colonel Brodie or Colonel Raveneaux during the War? What exactly did I do in the War? Where did I go? Who did I work for? I think for a little while Mrs. Vasseur had it in her head that I'd come here to rob Belle Ombre, kill the men, and carry off a woman or two."

"She can be outspoken," said Isabelle.

"We made our peace," Paul assured her.

"But, if any of us seem a little cautious or even suspicious of you. . . well, you are new to our midst, Mr.

Delahoussaye."

"An outsider?"

Isabelle's breath quickened as she spoke. "When we talk, sir, at times I find I have trouble remembering that you are a stranger here."

"Then you don't want me to give up and go?" asked Paul good-naturedly.

"You made a promise to my aunt. And you want to see justice done. Or at least have a story to sell."

"Miss Ross, I wish you never felt the need to be evasive with me, or cynical. I give you my word, I can pursue my livelihood without forgetting justice. And without forgetting my promise to a lady."

Isabelle let her right hand rest lightly on the front of her skirt, not far from his left, on the chance he might wish to clasp her hand to further emphasize the sincerity already evident in his voice and steady gaze.

But in a moment the house reverberated with slamming doors, shouts, and clattering footsteps. Paul looked bewildered and Isabelle dismayed as Ardyce rushed in from the hall. She thrust Paul's coat and hat into his hands and a wool mantle into Isabelle's.

"Captain Newell's coming up the drive," she said breathlessly. "Miss Delora wants you out the back right away. The horses are ready behind the spring house."

Paul tossed on his hat and coat, then hurried to assist Isabelle with her mantle. But she shooed him away, telling him she would join him outside.

Alone with Ardyce, Isabelle pulled the door to and demanded, "How am I to mount a horse in these hoops! I thought I'd have time to change. And what in blazes is going on upstairs?"

"Faye's having convulsions, and Euphrasie's hiding out somewhere," Ardyce replied, gathering Isabelle's skirt up in back and swiftly untying her hoops. "I'll tell you more when I know it. Please your aunt and ride off now. And stay gone a while." Ardyce threw the mantle around Isabelle's shoulders.

Isabelle glanced at her crinoline standing by itself on the rug. "Suppose the Captain comes in here?"

"We don't owe him no explanations. Now get on out of here."

Isabelle hitched her deflated skirts above her ankles and dashed from the house, catching up with Paul in the yard and passing him. Running was all the more exhilarating to her for being rarely permissible. She rounded the kitchen garden and zigzagged between the stable and spring house, where at back the horses were tethered. Filling her lungs with chilling air, tasting the damp, she waited for Paul, with his long, quick walking strides, to reach her and lift her into the side-saddle.

"Dusk comes so quickly this time of year," Isabelle said, taking the reins of her blue roan. "When we reach the woods, there's a narrow path. You'll need to follow me."

"Anywhere you say," she heard him mumble as he mounted his horse.

They rode away, not at a gallop, but a steady, quiet walk, through a ground covering of hoof-deep, crisp, newly fallen sycamore leaves. Angling down the slope behind the spring house, Isabelle knew they could not be easily seen from the big house, but she felt safer still as they entered, single-file, into the dense stand of oak and pine. If Captain Newell was determined to take Morning Glory or anything else from Belle Ombre, he might eventually get it, though better later than sooner; Isabelle thought Aunt Delora had been remarkably successful so far with what she called her "delaying tactics."

The woods were dark, hardly penetrated by the waning light, and the horses' hooves were muted on the spongy forest floor. Isabelle shivered. Her hands were cold and she wished for a pair of gloves.

Paul was silent, and his docile horse followed without so much as a whicker. For a moment Isabelle imagined herself alone, riding down to the bridge of Lyre's Creek to meet the man she loved. Then Morning Glory stopped short, and Isabelle felt a sudden jolt as Pickwick's muzzle collided with her horse's rump.

Paul hurriedly whispered, "I beg your pardon," and reined in his horse.

"Oh, you're not to blame. Morning Glory hates to get his feet wet, and this ground ahead is all puddles," Isabelle answered softly. "We'll turn off here to the left. Then we can tether the horses in the holly bog."

In near darkness, they dismounted. Morning Glory's breath warmed Isabelle's hands as she tied his reins to a sapling. Then she assisted Paul in tethering his horse.

"My sight's not too sharp in the daylight, but I'm blind as a cave fish in these shadows," said Paul.

"Have you ever been in a cave?" Isabelle asked.

"A time or two."

Isabelle wondered if he had hidden runaways in caves during the War, but she didn't ask. She didn't want to think about the War just now.

"Do we wait here with the horses, Miss Ross? Or walk a ways?" said Paul. "I'm at your disposal."

"The horses are well hidden. Let's walk to the bridge," Isabelle replied.

She clutched bunches of skirt, trying not to drag her hem through pools of standing water. Paul followed her closely down a narrow, convoluted footpath overhung with low branches and tendrils of Spanish moss. From the ground the warmth and scent of rotting vegetation rose, a blend of pungency and spice, even as the cold and dark descended through the trees. Isabelle heard the rippling of Lyre's Creek just ahead, then the grunting sounds and rank odor of hogs reached her.

"Wait," she whispered, reaching a hand back to stop Paul. He stepped on her hem, unbalancing her, and caught her hand before she fell.

"Forgive me, Miss Ross. But what's the matter?"

"It's old Priapus and the sows rooting around the giant cypress." Isabelle pointed, and Paul peered ahead. "We—Forest and I—used to call that tree Atlas 'cause it looked to us big enough to hold up the world."

"Looks like they've dug some mighty deep pits, or am I just seeing shadows?"

Isabelle came a step closer to the hogs, but retreated when an especially fierce looking sow met her gaze. "Oh, I suppose this is more of Elroy Samson's handiwork. We've all had to watch our footing after he started digging for treasure."

"Why would he think the Raveneauxs would bury valuables so close to the water's edge?" asked Paul.

"I've no idea. Aunt Delora says he dug everywhere just to aggravate her. We'd best veer this way to the bridge." Giving the hogs a wide berth as the animals trotted away into the woods, Isabelle led Paul by the hand along the creek bank. "You wouldn't think it now, but in the warm weather it's a treasure trove of flowers down here. Not the big, showy field flowers, but delicate little blooms. You have to look for them."

Halfway across the wooden bridge, Isabelle stopped, releasing Paul's hand. His own fingers lingered over hers a moment, prolonging the touch. She hadn't really needed to lead him by the hand; he could have followed her well enough. But she had wanted this connection with him, with this kind man who showed her courtesies, respected her ideas, and who left a scent of bay rum in her palm.

Isabelle gripped the railing. Paul stood just behind her, looking out at the same view, she thought—the ribbon of black water and the sky darkening until the black outlines of trees were lost against it.

Paul asked her questions about her life before the War, and she spoke sadly and fondly of beloved parents lost to fever, her elder sister, Louise, who died in childbirth, her brother-in-law killed at Shiloh. Then she told him of Louise's young daughter now living with paternal grandparents in Galveston.

"I wish someday I could make a home for Phoebe just as my aunt has made a home for me," Isabelle said, then fell silent.

"Is Halcyon across the bridge?" Paul asked.

"What remains of it—three chimneys and a cellar."

"Miss Ross, you don't have to answer," Paul said slowly, "but I was wondering if you and Forest Brodie fell in love at first sight."

"Oh, my." For a moment, Isabelle smiled in the dark. "Have you more romantic illusions than Aunt Delora fears I do? No, not at first sight. We met as children, played together when I visited Belle Ombre. Then when my parents passed over and I came to live here, Forest and I saw more of each other, saw each other in a different way—and love grew."

"And now that he's gone. . . well, I know it's only been a little while. But do you think you might someday have feelings for someone else?"

"I really don't know, Mr. Delahoussaye," she said, trying to shake off the sensation that any feelings were stirring in her now. "I know my life didn't stop when he died. And that's the cold-hearted truth. You see, I understand quite well what Aunt Delora and Lydie Vee have taught me in their different ways: that men are not women's protectors, even when they want to be. No one—not even the strongest, bravest man—is immune to infirmity and death."

"A chilling thought," Paul murmured.

"It's a chilling night," Isabelle replied.

She felt he had moved closer behind her, his body shielding hers a little from the cold. She shut her eyes as if the lids were heavy with the weight of years of loneliness, and leaned her back against his chest.

She heard his quick intake of breath and felt his hands cover her shoulders. "Isabelle"—he called her by her given name, as if he had spoken it many times before.

She tilted back her head and whispered, "I want to cross the bridge."

CHAPTER EIGHT

As Paul caught his breath, the sharp air cut into his lungs. Isabelle turned and linked one arm with his to cross the bridge, and the headache that had plagued him most of the day vanished.

On the other side of Lyre's Creek the woods thinned, and the bank rose steeply to meet the roll of a hill. Clouds that hid the stars slipped briefly from the surface of a half moon; on the slope ahead Paul discerned a solitary dead tree, rising like a column of whitened ash, its upper reaches split, perhaps long ago by lightning. Beyond, on the crest of another, higher hill, towered the silhouettes of three chimneys.

As they reached the dead tree, Isabelle let go of Paul's arm. "My hem's all wet and tangled 'round my... well, I'll trip for sure if I don't straighten it out."

Paul thought brisk walking was only one of many activities impeded by women's fashions.

Isabelle leaned against the broad trunk, one hand tugging at the dark swirl of fabric, the other pressed against bleached wood. As clouds crossed the moon, light and shadow rippled over her, and Paul, watching her, imagined Daphne transformed into a laurel tree. Then, like a penitent Apollo, he dropped to one knee, the damp soaking into his trouser leg, and awkwardly attempted to smooth her sodden skirt and free it from the gnarled roots that broke the ground.

Bending forward, she caught his hands as they moved over the folds of cloth. She brought his hands to her waist and held them there. He rose to his feet. She released his hands, and he slipped them under her mantle, encircling her in his arms. He wouldn't speak for fear she might suddenly realize a need to protest their intimacy. Darkness obscured her face, but he could hear her breathing, quick and fitful, and feel her fingers slip over his collar and link at the back of his neck. He pressed her against the tree trunk, pressing himself against the layers of cloth that hid her body from him. Her crown of hair brushed his open mouth, and he inhaled the woodsy scent that clung to it. He moved his lips over her temple, across her cheek, to her unprotesting mouth. Incredulous, Paul kissed her, and kissed her again. Tomorrow he would think; tonight he'd do whatever she would let him do.

The rim of his spectacles bumped her nose, and he mumbled an apology. He was unsure if a sob or a laugh escaped her lips before she kissed him back. Her hair had fallen free of its combs, and he buried his face in the mass of it that covered one of her shoulders. He lifted her from the ground, one arm wrapped around her back, the other around her hips, and crushed her against him as if he might enter her through the myriad layers of wool and flannel that divided them.

She clung to him and gasped. Fearing he'd hurt her, he loosened his embrace and set her back to earth. She leaned against the tree trunk, and he bent over her, kissing the rough fabric of the mantle that lay across her breast. She gasped again and, for a moment, dug her fingers into his shoulders. He knelt, eyes shut, arms around her waist, willing her to slip to the ground with him under a blanket of gathering fog. "Darling Isabelle," he whispered, "I want to be as near to you as body is to soul."

Her hands slid from his shoulders, and her arms fell limp at her sides. He heard her panting breath that shook her body, but not with passion. Was it with fear? Paul opened his eyes, rocked back on his heels, and looked up at her face, momentarily washed in moonlight. She was staring ahead, not looking down at him. He jerked his head to look in the same direction, up the hill to the ruins of Halcyon, squinting through smeared lenses and cloying mist. Clouds moved across the moon, and Paul saw nothing.

Stumbling hurriedly to his feet, he caught at her icy hands.

"We must go," she whispered.

"But are you all right? Believe me, I wouldn't hurt you for the world. Please forgive me." Paul brushed a lock of damp hair from her cheek, vainly trying to put things to rights between them.

"We must go," she repeated, her voice devoid of emotion. "The horses will be anxious."

She bundled up her skirt and ran for the bridge, Paul stumbling and sliding down the slope after her. On the other side of Lyre's Creek she stopped and faced him as he caught up to her, panting, the cold stinging his throat.

He reached toward her, not quite daring to touch her again. "Isabelle." He took a gulp of air and exhaled with a sigh. "Miss Ross, I meant no disrespect."

"I know. It's nothing to do with you," she said.

"What? What do you mean? I don't understand."

"I heard the horses neigh."

She turned, and he followed her to where the animals were tethered. As he lifted her into her saddle, her hair fell across his hat brim and brushed his face.

"Your combs," he said, suddenly. "Shall I go back for them?" He imagined her walking into the house, facing her family, her skirt muddied, her hair wild about her shoulders.

"No. Leave them," she said, briefly touching his hand as he gave her the reins. "You'd never find them in the dark."

As they neared the house, Langford came forward to take their horses and tell them Captain Newell and his men had gone.

At the back door, Paul tried once more to apologize. "Please tell me, Miss Ross, is there anything I can do to make amends?"

"Don't speak of it," she said, and left him for her room.

He was perplexed by her sudden withdrawal, especially as he sensed no anger directed toward him for having taken liberties. It was as if while he held her, she had suddenly become preoccupied with something else, something that frightened her and drove away all other feelings.

* * *

Later that night, Paul picked at a cold supper and drank a fair amount of musty-tasting port in the company of Babcock Vasseur. None of the women joined them in the dining room.

Babcock, with a piece of fatty ham pocketed in one cheek and a wedge of cheese in the other, held forth on various topics—man to man—for Paul's edification. Paul listened to what was said and what was implied, but often chose to look away from the speaker, whose words and supper were sloshed together with mouthfuls of wine.

"You can count yourself fortunate, young man, that you were out of the house today as much as you were. The womenfolk have been in a mortal tizzy 'round here since daybreak. First this mess about Elroy Samson's murder, and next thing I know, Delora installs the caterwauling widow in this house. Then Captain Newell shows up with men and wagon ready to haul off a side of pork. Meanwhile he's in the front parlor, smiling at Delora, while she pours my second best brandy down his throat."

"Your brandy, sir?" Paul asked, baiting the old bore just a little.

"Damn right, mine! It should all be mine, long as Charles Orvin's been gone." A crumb of cheese flew from Babcock's lips and landed in his glass. Heedlessly, he swigged it down with the wine and continued. "Belle Ombre belonged to my elder brother, Delora's father. His will provided she could live out her life here, but the plantation is hers only as long as her husband is alive to run it. When he's gone for good, Belle Ombre is mine, to run and rule as I see fit—the way my brother and our father before us did."

"Won't that be a little difficult to do without slave labor?'

"You quibble like a Yankee."

Paul surmised that, if Babcock Vasseur did outlive Charles Orvin Raveneaux, the management of Belle Ombre would in fact pass from Delora to Lydie Vee.

After a resounding belch, Babcock continued his remarks, doubtless designing them to show his moral superiority over Delora's absent husband. "What business can be so pressing in Washington that Charles Orvin can't be here to rein in my niece? Delora's been a cunning one ever since she was a lap baby. That gal needs a white man—right here on the premises—wearing her out so she don't have the strength to get uppity."

Paul thought there must be a number of men, other than Colonel Raveneaux, who would vie for the privilege.

With thick fingers, Babcock stroked the stem of his wine glass. His head drooped for a moment, then he lifted his bleary gaze to Paul. "Euphrasie finally reappeared this evening, thank the Lord."

"I didn't know she was missing," said Paul.

"Since late afternoon no one had seen her. So to add to the hullabaloo already going on, we had to turn the house inside out looking for the little imp."

"Was she in the woodwork?"

Babcock slapped a hand on the table and leaned heavily toward Paul. "That's just it." He slurred the words together in a rank-smelling whisper. "She wasn't anywhere to be found. That sweet child was out of this house—with a vicious murderer on the loose."

"Is she all right?" Paul asked.

"Right as she ever is. Just walked into the parlor at sunset, pretty as you please, curtsied to Delora, and said she'd been for a stroll."

Babcock rested his cheek on the tabletop and closed his eyes.

"Shall I ask Langford to help you to bed, Mr. Vasseur?"

"You do that," he muttered, "if Lang's not too busy helping Delora to the same."

Paul was saved making the decision of whether or not to seek out Langford. In the hall outside the dining room, he found him already waiting to assist Babcock upstairs.

Paul returned to the table and finished off another glass of port before Ardyce entered the room to clear away the dishes and bring him a message. Isabelle wanted to see him in the back parlor, Ardyce said, to look over his newspaper clippings about the War. Suddenly, Paul regretted the quantity of wine he had consumed, wishing he were more sure of himself and his sobriety.

He hurried up to his room, splashed his face with cold water, combed his hair, collected his satchel, and sped to the back parlor. There Isabelle sat straight-backed on the bench before the low-burning fire. At sight of him, she rose and turned up the wick of the oil lamp on the mantel. Her recently tousled hair was neatly pinned again, and the dress she'd muddied in the holly bog had been exchanged for a fresh white, high-collared blouse and a dark green skirt over a crinoline barrier. Paul approached her slowly, sensing she had not asked him into the parlor to cross a metaphorical bridge.

"Where shall we begin, Miss Isabelle?" he asked, with an effort to mask his disappointment.

"Oh, I don't know. If you're very tired, sir, you could simply leave the articles with me, and I'll return them to you in the morning."

"I'd rather stay up with you," said Paul, hoping his words did not sound as slurred as they had felt in his mouth.

Isabelle returned to the bench, and Paul dropped awkwardly to his knees on the hearth rug, opening his satchel and extracting a handful of newspaper clippings. She took them from him and began to read, while he spread more pages over the rug. Many of the sheets were yellowed and brittle with age, many were faded or stained with rain water and bad coffee. At the time Paul had collected and saved each story or picture, he considered each as documentation of a momentous event in a grand drama. Now weary and slightly drunk, he viewed the news accounts, the sketches and photographs, his own maps and notes in a different way—as scraps randomly torn from a horrifying tableau.

"This one's about Shiloh," said Isabelle, holding out a column cut from the *Daily Appeal*, "where my sister's husband perished. But Forest survived and went on."

"And received a promotion, no doubt."

Isabelle nodded, then shook her head over another account of violence. "Mr. Delahoussaye, how can men have the courage to face battle? Oh, I understand the momentary ability to fight when directly threatened, but this is something else—this planning and calculating to kill, and then lining up and doing it. It's beyond anything."

She dropped from the bench and knelt, surrounded by her billowing skirt and the spread of newspapers, scanning one article after another. Paul stretched on his side on the rug and propped himself on one elbow; how comfortable it was to be with her at a fireside, even if she were unaware of the pleasure he felt. Then, he watched her gentle eyes reflect the pain of what she read and glisten with tears.

"Vicksburg," she whispered. "I went there as a little girl. It was a beautiful town. My mother had friends there. Oh, but this story, this picture—people lived in holes they dug during the siege, eating rats or starving."

"I should put all this away," said Paul, reaching for his satchel.

"No, don't." She bent toward him and touched his sleeve.

Paul's lips felt dry, and when he moistened them with the tip of his tongue, he imagined the taste of Isabelle's mouth. His thoughts were muddled with wine and the longing of the moment, and he wanted to throw every shred of newspaper on the fire.

"Let's burn the past," he murmured.

Isabelle drew back, her brow furrowed. "Mr. Delahoussaye?"

"If they upset you . . . these articles . . . we could burn them," Paul struggled to explain himself. Had nothing happened between them, he wondered, when they had crossed over to Halcyon? Would she not reach for him again and invite his touch? Cruel as he knew his thoughts to be, he felt impatient for the specter of Forest Brodie to be gone.

"But I don't want to destroy the past," said Isabelle, cutting into his thoughts. "I want to understand it. The last letter I had from Forest was dated June of 1863. He was somewhere in Pennsylvania."

"The Battle of Gettysburg took place that July," said Paul, sitting up, trying to focus on her concern, shuffling through a stack of articles until he found an account of the battle. "The Union major who had your letters fought there. Maybe that was where your Colonel Brodie was captured."

Paul offered her the article, then, too late, realized it was from a Northern paper, one in which the reporter had taken particular satisfaction in his descriptions of Confederate wounded and dead. "I'm sorry, Miss Isabelle. I have another column here, somewhere, from another newspaper."

"Never mind, sir. I've read enough." Isabelle handed the page back to him, and rose, brushing one cheek with the back of her hand.

Paul pulled himself up after her, catching hold of the mantel edge. "I'm sorry, Miss Isabelle."

"Don't be. I asked to read these things," she said simply. "But perhaps I should have fortified myself beforehand with a little port. Good night, Mr. Delahoussaye. Sleep well."

She left him alone by the hearth.

* * *

At dawn the next day, Paul squinted out his bedroom window over the back of the house at the mist shrouded outbuildings. He recalled the previous morning's grisly drama at the smokehouse and was relieved to see the yard peaceful. Only two women, tenant farmer's wives he had met the day before with Lydie Vee, were at work, one heaping laundry into a cauldron of steaming water, the other stirring it with a pole. Only the orange fire they worked around broke the gray drabness of the scene.

A soft knock sounded at Paul's door, and he opened it to Ardyce, who carried a large china pitcher.

"'Morning, sir." She entered the room and, though Paul was fully dressed in his rumpled brown suit, she kept her eyes averted from him. "Here's hot water for you."

"Thank you, Ardyce," he said, "but I've already shaved and washed with cold." And the shock of it certainly cleared away the cobwebs, he thought, then added, aloud: "I'm not accustomed to the service around here. Perhaps someone else could use the hot water."

Ardyce shrugged. "It's washing day, sir. You want us to do your things?"

"Yes, please. I'm wearing my last clean shirt." Paul rummaged in the bottom of the armoire. "It's a cloudy morning," he said, making conversation. "Hope washing day's not rained out."

Ardyce waited by the doorway. "Won't be the first time we've hung the laundry in the attic to dry, sir," she said.

Paul hesitated as he handed her his dirty clothes. "Ardyce?"

"Yes, sir."

"How is Miss Ross today? I was afraid . . . afraid she might have caught a chill last night."

"Well enough, sir. Breakfast is laid in the dining room, if you've a mind to eat." With that she bundled his laundry under one arm and left without once looking him in the face. Was she being deferential, Paul wondered, or guarded?

He gave his thin hair a last brush stroke, then started down the narrow passage that led from his room. Turning the corner into the broad hallway onto which the family's bedrooms opened, Paul caught a glimpse of Isabelle exiting a room through a pair of double doors, leaving them open, and hurrying toward the main staircase.

As he passed the room she had left, he paused and glanced in at what must have been the master bedroom, furnished with dark oak and draped in burgundy velvet. The bed curtains were pulled aside, revealing a jumble of bolsters and bed clothes in the midst of which a pale figure abruptly sat up. Paul gasped in surprise, and the sallow face swiveled in his direction.

"Is that breakfast coming?" Faye Samson rasped.

"Excuse me, ma'am." Paul took a step into the room. "I was just passing by. I'm sure someone will bring your breakfast soon. May I. . . may I offer my condolences on the loss of your husband?"

"Sir?" she said as if she hadn't quite heard him. Faye dropped back on the pillows. "Come closer."

Paul advanced toward the bed. For all the size of Colonel Raveneaux's bedroom, the air was stale and held a trace of something sickly-sweet. Paul noticed an overturned medicine bottle on the bedside table and on the floor below a syrupy puddle, red as blood.

Faye's narrow eyes cut toward the bottle. "Sloe berries and laudanum. They think that's going to put things right for me and my boy."

"I'm sure Mrs. Raveneaux and her family are only trying to help ease the shock of what has happened." Though Paul was actually far from sure what Delora's motives were for drugging the overseer's widow, he thought his comment innocuous enough, the sort of thing he recalled his grandmother murmuring to bereaved acquaintances. He was taken aback when she followed his statement with a flood of complaints.

"Miss High-and-Mighty never cared about my ease before now. Treated the niggers better than me. Anything that's amiss, anything that's left undone, and I catch the blame. Or Radley. Light of my life, that boy's the only one who's ever done right by me. Them other sons of mine were more like their father, 'cept they went to war, and they ain't no good to me now they're dead. I tell you, that Miss Delora's a barren, cold-hearted schemer."

"But, Mrs. Samson, she's brought you into her home, made you comfortable in Colonel Raveneaux's own room."

"She's holding me prisoner!" Faye reached out one shaking hand and clutched Paul's coat sleeve. "Mister," she said, lowering her voice to a breathy whisper, "you ain't one of them. You can go into town—tell folks what happened."

"What shall I say, Mrs. Samson?"

"You tell 'em Elroy was murdered. Folks'll come out here. They'll string up the guilty nigger." Faye released Paul's sleeve and collapsed against the pillows.

"And who is guilty, ma'am?"

"It don't make me no difference," she muttered, shutting her eyes.

Isabelle entered the room, carrying a tray. With a nod, she acknowledged Paul, then set the tray on Faye Samson's lap. "Here's your breakfast, Faye. Would you like another pillow at your back?"

Faye accepted the pillow, tasted the creamed wheat, and turned down the already hard-lined corners of her mouth. "Not very sweet," she said.

"I put some molasses in it myself," said Isabelle evenly. She took a rag from her apron pocket and began sopping up the spilled medicine.

Faye turned her head toward Paul. "Something to stare at, ain't it, sir? Her waiting on me."

Paul backed away, tripped on the edge of a rug, and caught his balance by grabbing the door frame. Isabelle bunched the red-stained rag in one hand and followed him out to the hall.

"Mr. Delahoussaye," she said softly, glancing back once at Faye, who was intent on her breakfast. "The men are burying Mr. Samson this morning. Aunt Delora says under the circumstances burial shouldn't be delayed any longer."

"The circumstances being murder?" Paul said, with sudden misgivings about ever agreeing to investigate Samson's death.

Isabelle sighed. "The circumstances being a danger to everyone's health. You said yourself the man's been dead for at least three days. If we leave him laid out in that cabin any longer, the place won't be fit for bats to live in."

"Of course. But is your family still determined not to report Samson's death?"

"We came to an arrangement with you yesterday," she replied. "Nothing has changed since then."

"Nothing?" Paul looked searchingly into her face. Where was his common sense, he wondered, and his journalist's instinct? He had agreed to Delora's request in order to prolong his time with Isabelle. Uncovering truth, finding and bringing to justice the murderer of a fellow human being, might spark his curiosity and his public spiritedness. Selling a sensational and exclusive story to the papers could fire up his ambition. But it was Isabelle, tears suddenly welling in her gray eyes, who consumed him.

"I have the highest respect for you," Paul began, and asked himself how many other men had said those words while standing at arms length from a comely woman and feeling only the basest desire. With a dry throat, he continued, "I wanted to say something to you last night, in the back parlor, but then the moment never seemed right. So I'll try now. Miss Ross, something frightened you when we were at Halcyon. If it was my behavior, please say you forgive me."

Isabelle's lips trembled slightly as she replied, "Perhaps it was my behavior that surprised you, Mr. Delahoussaye. I've heard it said it's not uncommon for a man to accept what's offered. I hope you will excuse my. . . my lapse of decorum."

Paul smiled, encouraged by her words as he had been by her touch the night before. "Oh, Miss Isabelle, such a lapse endears you to me all the more. If you've been bold in your affections before, well, I can only hope that you'll be bold again."

Paul wanted to reach for her hand, but the wary look she gave him changed his mind.

"Mr. Delahoussaye," she said sternly, "you make it difficult for me to beg a favor of you on behalf of my family. But I must. My aunt requests that you accompany Uncle Babcock and Radley Samson to the graveyard. Langford's dug the grave, but Radley won't have him there for the burial. Any assistance you could give the boy would be appreciated. I fear my great-uncle is not up to wielding a shovel this morning."

"I'm at your service, Miss Isabelle. Always."

"We are obliged to you," she said, and returned to Faye's bedside.

Paul proceeded downstairs to the dining room to fortify himself with fried grits and bacon. She had not actually rejected him for his admiration of her, he mused, or objected to his use of her given name. But trying events and duty to family must weigh heavily with her and account for her erratic behavior. Paul took heart and breakfasted with a good appetite.

Only Lydie Vee and Babcock were in the dining room, the former filling her plate from the sideboard and the latter confining himself to chicory coffee.

"Isabelle wouldn't eat a bite this morning." Lydie Vee eyed Paul. "I hope she hasn't taken ill after that long ride you two took yesterday evening."

"On my way down, I saw her in the hallway," Paul volunteered, "and she looked lovely—healthy, that is. A little pale, maybe, but she's rather fair to begin with. Deceptively delicate is the term I've seen in magazines. Fragile-looking, but she can certainly sit a horse and. . . "

"And butcher a hog?" Lydie Vee suggested. "Honestly, Mr. Delahoussaye, I don't know when I've heard a sober man babble so."

Paul finished his meal in silence, then joined Babcock and Radley in the mule drawn wagon. It was a tight squeeze for two men and a boy on the wagon seat, but no one offered to move to the back with Elroy Samson's corpse. The body, wrapped in a tarpaulin and securely corded, was to be buried beyond the pecan orchard. On the way out of the house, Babcock had remarked to Paul that he was relieved Samson wouldn't be buried in the family cemetery. "And of course, for the widow's sake, we can't put him in the slave cemetery, though, Lord knows, he lay with enough slaves in life," Babcock mumbled. Instead, Langford had prepared a plot near where soldiers had been interred during the War, soldiers Isabelle had nursed and written about to Forest Brodie.

Radley drove the wagon slowly around the orchard which was here and there pock marked with shallow holes—examples of his father's treasure hunting, Paul surmised. At the burial ground, Radley and Paul heaved the swaddled corpse from the wagon and lay it alongside the open grave site. Babcock made a few ineffectual gestures of assistance, but never actually touched the tarpaulin.

With head bowed and hands clasped, Radley stood by the mound of dirt. Paul looked to Babcock to say a few words, but the man merely shrugged.

Paul spoke gently then. "Radley, would you like me to say a prayer?"

"If you know one," the boy replied, wiping his nose with the back of his hand.

Paul recited the Lord's Prayer with the same jerky rhythm with which he had recited it as a child. Radley repeated the "amen" after him, then knelt beside his father's remains and with one push, rolled the body into the earth.

"Ma'll be sorry she missed this," he said, and moved away to fetch a shovel that leaned against a pecan tree.

When Radley was barely out of ear shot, Babcock muttered, "The devil take him," and kicked a clod of dirt into the hole, the extent of his contribution to the burial.

Paul took turns with Radley, shoveling dirt, and at last they smothered the odor of decaying flesh with that of damp earth and rotting leaves. The air was cold and laden with a threat of rain, but his exertions had made Paul uncomfortably warm. When Paul paused to remove his jacket and roll up his sleeves, Radley took the shovel from him and continued heaping dirt, panting and sweating as he worked.

Paul caught a glimpse of a flask as Babcock restored it to his inside breast pocket and continued leaning against the wagon. The man had obviously no liking for Elroy Samson and little enough regard for the dead man's family. But would anyone so drunken and lazy put forth the effort, Paul wondered, to bash Samson over the head, string him up, and gut him? Paul doubted it.

Some distance away, among the trees, stood a woman in a hooded black cloak. Paul couldn't make out her face, but given her small stature, decided she was not Isabelle, but more likely Delora, making sure the burial had been accomplished according to her instructions.

After Radley finished packing down the earthen mound with the shovel blade, he and Babcock climbed into the wagon.

With a satisfied tone, Radley announced, "I'll make a nice marker for Pa and bring Ma out to see it when she's not feeling so poorly. She'll like that."

"You're a good son," said Paul, hoping the words sounded sincere to this pitiful boy only a mother could love.

Paul saw Radley and Babcock off in the wagon, telling them he would walk back. "Don't break a leg in one of Samson's treasure holes," Babcock had warned him, riding away. "If he'd dug one of 'em any deeper, it could've been his grave." And Paul had shouted after him, "Enough of that talk, Mr. Vasseur. The boy's lost his father."

Looking again toward the orchard, Paul saw that the woman had not moved. He rolled down his sleeves, donned his jacket, and started toward her, just missing a gaping hole as he reached her.

"Good morning, Mrs. Raveneaux," he said, recovering his balance.

"Mr. Delahoussaye." She extended a gloved hand to him. "I declare, sir, you are kindness personified. Now you must come back to the house with me for some refreshment—and an early dinner. We nearly starved you yesterday, didn't we? And after all the trials of that day and the rigors of this morning, you must be famished. We should take better care of our private inquiry agent."

Delora linked her arm with his and guided him past the rows of pecan trees.

From the beginning of their acquaintance, Paul thought Delora had a way about her, a way of flattering him, making him feel indispensable. If no mature woman had ever made him feel that way before, he might have had fewer reservations about her now and simply enjoyed the attention. But he had been flattered once already; some years ago in Laurel Grove, Missouri, where he'd grown up, an attractive widow convinced him she saw past his youthful awkwardness, his less than dashing appearance, to the man he was on the verge of becoming. Paul had welcomed her guidance, both in and out of her bedroom, and reveled in her praise. But learning that she had given the same education, even the same compliments, to many of his friends had made him doubt his singular importance to her.

Unlike the widow back home, Delora had made no personal advances toward Paul on her own behalf. On the contrary, she seemed most sympathetic regarding his interest in her niece. But a little experience had taught Paul that a woman such as Delora rarely created an effect at random. Her words to Paul were always polite, her manners ladylike, yet what gentleman could be immune to her aura of sensuality denied and vulnerability conquered by a sense of duty? Still, even if Paul were a little wary of her charm, he might yet serve the ends of Isabelle's guardian aunt.

Delora pulled Paul sharply to the left to avoid a trench dug across their path.

"Land sakes, Langford's been so busy digging graves, he hasn't had time to fill in these holes," said Delora.

"Did Mr. Samson just dig anywhere for this supposed treasure, or did he have some idea where to look? A map, maybe?" Paul asked.

"Oh, Mr. Delahoussaye, have you been listening to gossip? There is no treasure map. And all that's buried on Belle Ombre land is a lot of dead folks."

When they reached the front parlor, Delora served Paul a glass of Auntie Pan's special strengthening punch, a vast improvement over her hog's hoof tea.

"There's nothing quite like one of our cook's restoratives to clear the head and perk up the appetite," Delora said.

Paul, who was more aware of a humming in his ears than a clarity of mind, agreed he was ready to do justice to dinner. Delora remarked that Ardyce had kindly killed a fat hen early that morning. "Radley will be joining us at table," explained Delora, "so we couldn't possibly serve pork—not given the circumstances of his father's demise." Then she went on to describe the tender and delectable chicken pie awaiting Paul in the dining room.

Paul noted that again there was an odd number of diners: himself, Delora, Babcock and Lydie Vee, Isabelle and Euphrasie, and Radley, sitting at one end of the table, far opposite Delora.

"Shall I take down the colonel's portrait?" Paul whispered to Euphrasie as he held her chair. He had hoped by his comment to lighten her mood, but then he realized she was hardly affected by the gloomy occasion for their feast.

"Never you mind, sir. Seven at table could bring luck today." Euphrasie took her seat, looking exceedingly pleased with herself.

The ladies effectively ignored Radley's crude table manners; they were, of course, accustomed to dining with Babcock Vasseur. And Delora did an admirable job of making small talk with the slow-witted boy with whom she had nothing in common.

"Shortly, we'll all go up, Radley, to see your mother," said Delora. "You can tell her just how things were at the burial, and that'll be such a comfort to her."

"She won't be happy about the tarpaulin," Radley drawled. "She knows Langford made a box for Beryl."

"Now, Radley. You just tell her the things she'll want to hear. Tell her about Mr. Delahoussaye's nice prayer and the spreading pecan tree shading the grave and the respect shown. Comfort her. Faye's in such a state, I don't know when she'll recover, and we don't want to make her worse."

"But what's going to happen when Ma is better?"

Along with everyone else, Paul looked to Delora, waiting for her answer, while she waited for Ardyce to finish serving the dessert.

"I'll write to Colonel Raveneaux this very afternoon and ask his advice," Delora said slowly. "While we await his reply, you and your mother may certainly continue to live and work here at Belle Ombre."

"Ma wants to clear out," said Radley.

"Well, that just might be arranged," Delora replied, "when she's well enough to travel."

During this exchange, Paul had scraped the last of bread pudding and rum sauce from his dish. The extent of his appetite had surprised him, but the meal had been especially flavorful. Euphrasie slid her full dish of pudding across the table to him, sliding halfway there herself.

"Take mine, too," she whispered. "I couldn't hold another bite."

"You're sure?" Paul asked.

"Sure as can be."

Isabelle, who had been silent until now, looked sharply at her cousin and reminded her to get off the table and back into her seat.

Paul took a heaping spoonful of Euphrasie's bread pudding dripping with rum sauce. Perhaps the edge was finally off his appetite, but this second serving seemed to lack the mouth-watering flavor of the first.

Conversation droned on around Paul as he finished dessert. Then he trooped upstairs with the family and Radley to pay respects to Faye Samson. She was propped in the master's bed, looking serene, if sallow, and passively accepted the sympathy offered.

Isabelle slipped away from the room before Paul had a chance to speak to her. Delora must have noticed his forlorn expression because she motioned him aside and suggested he go down to the back parlor. "Isabelle sometimes sits by the fire there to sew or read," she said.

Paul followed her advice, but approaching the open back parlor door, he stopped. Isabelle was there indeed, speaking with Ardyce.

"Everything's so topsy-turvy 'round here—sometimes I think if I don't get away, I'll go out of my mind," said Isabelle. "But Ardyce, if I left Belle Ombre, would you come with me?"

"I might. I still say, you ought to talk it over with Miss Lydie Vee."

Realizing the private nature of their conversation, Paul took a few steps back from the door and coughed loudly. He didn't want Isabelle to think he was eavesdropping. Soon Ardyce came into the hall, carrying an empty wood scuttle. She lowered her gaze as she passed him.

Paul stopped in the back parlor doorway. "Miss Isabelle, may I have a word with you?"

"Yes, come in." She stepped away from the hearth and took a seat on the wooden bench, folding her hands in her lap. "I was going to ask Ardyce to fetch you."

"Oh?" Paul came forward, and she motioned him to sit on the bench, also. Between them was a long roll of heavy, yellowed paper.

"I have something to show you," she said, glancing at the paper, then looking up into Paul's face. "But first I want you to know that I'm sure, in your way, you are a very kind man."

"I hope I can prove myself so to you."

"But, Mr. Delahoussaye, we've none of us been above withholding some truth. When I told you there was no treasure map, no map that would be of interest to Elroy Samson, I spoke truly. But I lied, too. There is a map—other than the one you saw in the study." Isabelle handed the cylinder of paper to Paul. "I show it to you now because there seems little point in hiding it any longer. Besides, I'm fed up with Euphrasie turning my room inside out looking for it to give it to you. I told her I'd satisfy your curiosity myself. Go ahead, take a look."

Carefully, Paul unrolled the second map of Belle Ombre. Unlike the first map he had seen, there were no marked out areas or redrawn borders. This map was exquisitely ornamented with watercolor washes and tiny penciled flowers.

"What does this mean?" Paul asked. "Why do you show me now?"

Isabelle pointed to places on the map marked by flower drawings. "This marks the summer garden where Forest first told me he loved me. And this spot, over here, is in the shelter of a willow tree—that's where we stood the first time he kissed my mouth. And there—that's the bridge over Lyre's Creek where we'd meet after dark and cling to one another without so much as a moonbeam between us. . ."

She fell silent as Paul let the map's edges curl together. He didn't know what to say.

"Mr. Delahoussaye, I've shown you this so you'll know there's no dreadful secret about it. The map's only importance is to me. It's private—as were my letters to Forest."

Paul felt his face grow hot. "Miss Isabelle—"

"Please. Let me finish, sir. From our very first conversation, I had a feeling that you knew me. A feeling you understood too quickly for a stranger what my life here was like. There were little things you said, things you knew about my family, even our boar's name. Uncle Babcock didn't tell you that, did he?"

"No," Paul mumbled.

Isabelle stared ahead into the fire and drew her shawl close around her shoulders. She continued, softly: "Then I was impressed by your insight and moved by your tender manner. 'As near as body is to soul,' you said. 'Bold in my affection,' you said. Are these common expressions where you come from? Or were you quoting?"

Paul bowed his head.

"You read my letters," she said.

"I only meant to read enough so I'd know how to return them and to whom."

"But you read all my letters—every private word."

"I wanted to know you," Paul whispered.

"There are things you'll never know," she said. "But whatever your reason—a journalist's curiosity or something else—you have invaded my privacy, my very self. If you'd just given me the letters and gone away. . . But you didn't. You stayed. You've become tangled up in our troubles. And you know or guess how serious they are." Her voice wavered as she continued. "I don't know what to do with you, Mr. Delahoussaye, I truly don't. And the only thing I can think now to ask of you is this: as quickly as you can, discover who killed Samson—and Beryl, for surely she was murdered, too—and tell Aunt Delora. Then neither she nor I will try to detain you."

Paul looked at her, but she would not turn her face from the fire.

"I'll do what you wish," he said, and left her there.

Paul went to the stable, saddled his horse, and rode to Verbena without asking leave of the mistress of Belle Ombre.

CHAPTER NINE

Isabelle set the map on the fire and knelt near the hearth to watch it burn. All through the War, the map had been a secret comfort to her. Touching it, she had traced the pattern of her courtship, conjured images and remembered words of love. But the War was over, the map only paper and ink. She let it go. When the last of it had turned to ash, Delora entered the room.

"Has Mr. Delahoussaye been in to see you?" Delora asked.

Isabelle nodded.

"Well, now." Delora seated herself on the bench and arranged her skirt. "I've had my share of distractions and difficulties lately, but that's no excuse for me to neglect your welfare. Something is brewing between you and our guest. I feel it sure as I'm sitting here. Tell me, Isabelle, has Mr. Delahoussaye taken liberties?"

"Oh, Aunt Delora, I feel so wretched," Isabelle said. "I never meant anything to happen, but. . ."

"I assure you, I understand these matters a sight better than the parish priest. So make your confession, dear. I may not be able to absolve you, but I can give you some practical advice."

Drawing nearer to her aunt, Isabelle began again. "Last night I just wanted to be held by somebody. Somebody kind and gentle. I wanted to feel—something. I don't know what."

"Did he more than hold you, dear?" Delora arched her brows.

"Not much more. And he knows today that I won't be so foolish again. But how could I have done such a thing only days after burying my fiancé?"

"Hush now, you've been mourning Forest for years. You needn't feel shame before me for your natural longings. Your little transgression was just part of a trick of Nature to get a woman into the arms of a man, to make her surrender. But Nature can be thwarted." Delora patted Isabelle's shoulder. "You did the right thing to discourage further physical demonstrations from Mr. Delahoussaye."

Isabelle debated whether or not to tell Delora that Paul had read her letters, and that his presumptuousness, not his touch, had, in part, made her recoil. Her aunt had little patience with prying in others, and Isabelle didn't wish to turn her completely against Paul; Isabelle herself had not turned completely against Paul. Then Delora might or might not dismiss as morbid fancy Isabelle's other reason for withdrawing from him—the growing, disquieting sense that Forest had kept the promise of his last letter to "hover still in this world and delay eternal rest." Isabelle decided to say nothing. She perceived her aunt was in a mood to offer advice, more because Delora wanted to instruct Isabelle than to address the complexity of Isabelle's feelings.

"My dear girl, Mr. Delahoussaye more than admires you. That much is clear as crystal," said Delora. "But don't give in to him. Once you do you are lost. And you'll spend the rest of your days fighting to recover yourself. When a man desires your favors, he's half-demented. And for that brief moment in time, you have the power over him. He will be grateful for the slightest nod of your head, the merest flicker of your smile in his direction. Brush your fingertips across the back of his hand, and his heart will be inflamed with love for

you. But you ever once give him all you possess, and—"
Delora snapped her fingers—"his gratitude vanishes. He
becomes master, and you become chattel."

"Years ago I felt you had some reservations about my
betrothal to Forest," said Isabelle. "I thought then it was
because I was so young. Then I remember you once said the
War might settle some of our differences for us. Are you
advising me now, Aunt Delora, against marriage altogether,
with anyone?"

"Not necessarily. Whether a woman marries or not, a
man's madness for her will eventually fade, and her power
over him won't last forever. But while you have yours, I
advise you to treasure it. Use it. In the long scheme of life,
what you hold onto in yourself, not what you surrender,
becomes your strength. And I guarantee you, Isabelle, that
will bring you more satisfaction than a momentary tremor of
carnal pleasure which may—or may not—have occurred."

Delora tucked a lock of Isabelle's hair back under its
net and smiled down at her niece, seemingly satisfied she had
put her to rights.

"Oh, aunt," Isabelle said, nestling further into the
depths of her petticoats, "there were so many things I
wondered about when Forest courted me. Then he was up and
gone. And all those wonderings and sensations got mixed up
with memories of the past and longings for the future—and
nothing about our love had any physical shape because we
couldn't touch each other. Do you ever feel that way with
Uncle Charles Orvin gone for so long?"

"You're more romantic than I," said Delora, covering
Isabelle's hand with her own.

"Forest was always tender to me. But you know, Aunt
Delora, I've heard tell about rape." She felt her aunt's hand
tighten over hers. "No, I don't want to talk about that. What
I'm wondering now is this: is life ever like the poems I've

read? Is the earthly pleasure of love ever, ever the envy of the angels?"

"My stars, child, what kind of poetry have you been filling your head with?" Delora sighed. "Well, I suppose it's possible—briefly—to feel that sort of transporting sensation some poets describe. But don't be fool enough to pin your hopes on it. Mostly, in married life, you just get used to certain things, and realize it really doesn't matter what a man does as long as he's not too rough. You just think about something else—gardening, for instance, or a new hat, or one of those poems, if you like—and sure 'nough he finishes, and it's all over. Until the next time."

Isabelle shuddered as a log, burnt through, fell with a crack against the andiron. She and Delora sat quite still for several minutes before Isabelle spoke slowly and deliberately: "Aunt Delora, have you and Uncle Charles Orvin decided not to live together anymore? Is he not planning to return to Belle Ombre? And could you not bring yourself to tell me?"

Delora drew in her breath and held it for a long moment before she answered. "Charles Orvin and I have never discussed a formal separation, or corresponded on the subject. Still, I have considered the possibility that he may wish to remain where he is. Yes, it's certainly possible that we might continue as we are, running Belle Ombre as a separated couple." Delora's straight back relaxed a little. "Of course the situation is made more difficult by Uncle Babcock, champing at the bit to call himself master 'round here. And I've heard Lydie Vee's talk of her outrageous plans for my home."

"A boarding school and academy for girls of all colors?"

"Lord have mercy!" sighed Delora. "I'm all in favor of a good practical education for girls and a few refinements for some, but she talks of teaching highfalutin' things girls can never put to use—not in this world. Not unless we kill off all the men the War missed and live like a band of Amazons."

"We almost have lived like Amazons these last years. We've become more self-reliant, anyway."

"Too true. At your age, Isabelle, I was nothing but a silly flibbertygibbet. It seems strange to see you growing so wise while still so young and virginal. You make me think of the goddess Artemis." Delora rose from the bench and offered a hand to Isabelle who rose from the hearth rug. "Now, my bright girl, will you please go up and look in on your flickering flame of a cousin? I have a few other matters to attend to before the day gets away from me."

* * *

Euphrasie was not in her room, but the connecting door to Isabelle's room was open, and there Isabelle found her cousin. Euphrasie in a dressing gown, her hair wound on rags, lolled on Isabelle's bed, stroking Lydie Vee's cat, whose purr could be heard across the room.

"I think Carlotta's coming into her season again," said Euphrasie. "She just can't get enough petting. She needs to find herself a tomcat."

Isabelle sat on the edge of the bed, rubbed the cat's head, and looked at her cousin. "Euphrasie, you did your hair just fine and dressed up once today. Why are you starting all over again this afternoon?"

"Oh, just because." Euphrasie stretched and nestled back on the pillows. "Isabelle, you don't really care all that much for Mr. Delahoussaye, do you? If he took a fancy to someone else—me, for instance—that wouldn't trouble you none, would it?"

Isabelle hesitated before replying. "I don't really know him very well," she said. "Certainly not well enough to form an attachment to him, or to have a claim on feeling envious if he attached himself to someone else."

"Well, that's all fine then," said Euphrasie, with a satisfied smile. "I wouldn't want a rift between us."

Isabelle dismissed her cousin's intimations regarding Paul as just more of Euphrasie's amorous fantasies. What she wanted the girl to tell her more about were her ghostly sightings of Forest, and she moved the conversation in that direction.

"Have you seen Forest's ghost again? Last night, perhaps?" Isabelle asked.

"No, not last night. But the night before. He was haunting the lawn below your window for a spell, then went limping off, ever so forlorn." Euphrasie sighed heavily. "You didn't want to hear about it."

"I changed my mind," said Isabelle. "And you didn't wake me to see him. Do you think I shouldn't see him? That only you can see him? Is that why?" Isabelle's agitated stroking must have upset the cat, who suddenly nipped her fingers and jumped from the bed to the windowsill.

Euphrasie jutted her lower lip. "You were so cross with me when I told you before. You said it was wickedness, and I shouldn't say no more about it."

"Oh, I'm sorry, coz. I couldn't believe you'd seen him or someone like him. But now . . . now I don't know. Last night, maybe—just maybe—I saw him, too."

"Have you?" Euphrasie brightened and sat up straight. "And did he see you? Did your eyes meet?"

"He was only a shape, a shadowy, spectral form. But he seemed so familiar somehow, something about the way his hat was cocked. I think he looked in my direction, though I can't be sure. And then the clouds covered the moon, and he was gone."

Euphrasie almost panted in her excitement. "Tell me everything, Isabelle. Where were you? At the window or on the lawn? How close did you come to him?"

"Near sunset, Mr. Delahoussaye and I had ridden down to the holly bog. Aunt Delora sent us off when Captain Newell came. Well, there we tethered the horses and walked a piece by Lyre's Creek."

"So you saw Forest in your old meeting place in the bog? Was he standing under Atlas waiting for you? And did Mr. Delahoussaye see him, too?"

"No, I'm sure he didn't." Isabelle thought of Paul's face buried in the folds of her mantle, his hands reaching under the cloth to grip her waist. "Mr. Delahoussaye was looking the other way," she said. "But I didn't see Forest in the holly bog. It was after we crossed the bridge. We stopped a moment by the old dead cottonwood, and I looked up the hill. That's when I saw him, as if he'd just appeared from Halcyon."

"Oh, Isabelle! Next thing you'll be claiming you see June bugs at Christmas time!" Euphrasie threw up her hands. "And y'all go on about me having flights of fancy."

"What do you mean?"

"Just this—you couldn't possibly have seen Forest at Halcyon," Euphrasie said with conviction. "He's buried here at Belle Ombre, and I've seen his ghost here, plain as the full moon. He couldn't haunt the ruins, too."

"But why not?" Isabelle persisted.

"Why not! Why, he'd have to cross the bridge over Lyre's Creek to get there. Everybody knows a ghost can't cross running water. You must've seen somebody else's ghost. Lord knows there's enough dead folks in this world."

Isabelle rose and crossed to her dressing table. Her reflection in the looking glass was pale as milk. I don't believe in ghosts, she thought. I never have. There's some poor soldier in a tattered gray coat, hiding in the ruins—a stranger to us, perhaps a stranger to himself.

"It must have been wishful thinking," Isabelle said softly. "I must have just wanted to see Forest so much. One last time."

"Maybe." Euphrasie sounded doubtful. "But it might've been an evil spirit. So you and Mr. Delahoussaye best not be crossing the creek anymore."

Isabelle rummaged in one of the dressing table drawers and brought forth a length of pink ribbon. Handing it to her cousin, she said, "You can try this in your hair, if you ever take those rags out."

"Why, thank you, coz. I'll try it now." Euphrasie pranced from the room, holding the satiny ribbon up admiringly as she went.

Isabelle closed the door behind her cousin, then yanked off her dress and crinoline as quickly as myriad buttons and ties allowed and pulled on her riding habit and boots. She resolved to get to Halcyon and back before a late afternoon rain stopped her.

*   *   *

While saddling Morning Glory in the stable, Isabelle noticed Paul's horse was not in his stall. She worried that Paul might be out riding the grounds. But he was near-sighted and his horse was slower than hers; she might avoid him if she were alert and careful.

If there were a real man camping across Lyre's Creek, she wanted to get a look at him in daylight. Then she would decide whom to tell and what to do about him. Recalling her conversation with Euphrasie, she realized how absurd she'd been to imagine seeing Forest's ghost. A lone figure, shrouded in mist, seen at a distance across the lawn or on a hillside, might resemble a disembodied spirit to the overly imaginative—and yet be quite real enough to steal food from Auntie Pan's kitchen.

Riding down from the stable and into the woods, Isabelle encountered no one. Since her last ride, a heavy pine bough had split and fallen across the path. Pine resin was still pungent and sweet in the cold air, reminding Isabelle of the scent of fresh cut oranges, something she had not enjoyed since before the War.

Morning Glory stamped a hoof in the mud and side-stepped a puddle. Then the path played out as they entered the holly bog, the blue roan snorting his disapproval of the wet earth and dripping branches. Isabelle stroked his neck, murmuring encouragement as the foliage closed around them.

For a while Isabelle heard nothing but the rustling sounds she and her horse made as they moved through a thicket, saw nothing but the surrounding trees and shrubbery, smelled nothing but horseflesh and leather and damp leaves. Then, as they broke into a clearing, Morning Glory neighed, back-stepped sharply, and refused to proceed. Thrown forward in the saddle, Isabelle gripped the reins and peered ahead. The cause of her horse's alarm assailed her with nauseating potency. Two immense sows, sniffing and grunting, their breath like white steam as they rooted around the base of a huge cypress tree, had unearthed a grisly find. Isabelle brought a gloved hand to her mouth, sickened by the stench of decay. The sows had pulled from its shallow burial ground a length of entrails, dark and wet as a giant earthworm.

Morning Glory shied and Isabelle screamed as something heavy and huge shot forth from behind them, barely missing the horse's flank. It was Priapus, the boar, chasing down his sows. Isabelle gasped and clung to her horse's taut neck until the hogs had thundered away into the woods. Then she and the horse wheeled about as one body and tore out of the holly bog.

Losing her hat somewhere in the woods, Isabelle galloped into the open to be assaulted by a sudden cold rain that stung her face and drenched her tangled hair. Morning Glory ran for the stable to escape the downpour with the same passion with which some horses bolt from the field for their supper oats and corn.

But when they neared the half-open stable door, Isabelle slowed Morning Glory's pace, brought him under the eaves, and slipped from the saddle. She wanted to look in and see who she might face in the stable before entering in disarray. By now, Paul might have returned with Pickwick. Rubbing her horse's muzzle to calm him with one hand and gripping his reins with the other, Isabelle peeked around the door into the dim interior. Delora and Langford were inside.

Delora paced, straw collecting in the hem of her skirt. "You said Morning Glory was still here when you noticed his horse was missing. That means they didn't leave together," said Delora, her voice full of agitation.

"They might've met up by the creek," Langford suggested.

"No. And she wouldn't go chasing after him. Not after what she told me." Delora threw up her hands. "Oh, Lang, he's gone to town. I feel it. He's gone to town. I asked him for one week's grace, and he's breaking his word to me. You know how these journalists are. They stir up trouble just so they can write about it. They don't care whose life they destroy."

"Now then, you don't know that for sure," Langford said gently. "I'll go hunt him down and Miss Isabelle, too. You can't all the time be taking everything on your shoulders." Isabelle watched as Langford placed his strong hands on her aunt's shoulders, and for a moment Delora leaned her cheek against the back of one of his hands. "So off with you," said Langford, letting her go and backing away from her. "Up to the house, Miss Del. And stop your frettin'. We just take what comes."

Morning Glory snorted and pulled his reins from Isabelle's grip. She caught his bridle again and led him forward into the stable.

"I declare!" Delora cried on seeing Isabelle. "What's happened to you, child?" She reached a hand toward Isabelle's scratched cheek, but didn't touch it. "Did Mr. Delahoussaye—"

"No, aunt." Isabelle shook her head. "I haven't seen him."

Langford came forward, took Morning Glory's reins, and led the horse into his stall. "Rain spook him, Miss Isabelle?" asked Langford.

"Yes. And—"

Delora interrupted her. "You saw no sign of Mr. Delahoussaye? You've no idea where he went?"

"No, but—"

"I knew it! He's gone to town. He's broken his word and gone to town." Delora was pacing again. "Of course I wouldn't have you compromise yourself, Isabelle, but I thought you understood how important it is to keep him here, to keep him occupied. Did I have to tell you right out—butter that man up like a biscuit!"

"Aunt Delora," Isabelle answered back, "even if Mr. Delahoussaye has gone to town, that's no guarantee he'll be back here with a lynching party. He may have business we know nothing of."

"A slip of the tongue, a word in the wrong ear—and Mr. Delahoussaye could do harm he never intended," said Delora. "As to his business, if he returns, you make it yours to find out what he's up to—just as soon as you make yourself presentable. But if he's done the worst, as I fear he has, all our efforts will come to nothing. I might as well send Langford and Ardyce away right now to save their necks."

Isabelle sank onto a bale of hay, suddenly wearied by her aunt's ranting. She yanked the gloves from her trembling hands. "Aunt Delora, please listen to me," she said in a low, determined voice.

Delora shut her mouth and stopped pacing. Langford paused while unsaddling Morning Glory. Together they stared at Isabelle.

"Maybe Mr. Delahoussaye went as far as town and maybe he didn't. Time will give us the answer to that." Isabelle looked from Langford to Delora and back again. "I rode down almost to Lyre's Creek, and I saw something in the holly bog. It had been buried there under a cypress, but the sows dug it up."

"What was it, Miss Isabelle?" said Langford.

"Entrails, I think. No body—just entrails."

"Lord have mercy!" cried Delora. "Human entrails?"

"I really couldn't say," Isabelle snapped back in an effort to control a sob. "But we all know Elroy Samson was gutted."

A clap of thunder sounded nearby, and Paul's riderless horse bolted through the stable doorway. As Isabelle came forward to catch his reins, Pickwick shied and shot into a stall. Isabelle closed the stall door behind him. Then she hurried to look out the stable door. There was no sign of Paul.

She turned back to her aunt. "He isn't out there."

"Thrown off and limping home, most likely," said Delora. "He didn't strike me as much of a horseman." She seemed relieved that at least Paul's horse was once again in custody. "Langford, soon as the rain lets up," she said, "I want you to bag those entrails and bring them home. And take a look around for our wayward guest. I won't send Radley to help you."

"That's right, Miss Del. Just keep him up to the big house," said Langford. "He don't need to see his Pa's innards—if that's what they be—and I don't need to see Radley."

Delora nodded.

As clearly as she could remember, Isabelle described

for Langford where to find the entrails. Then, in the light drizzle, she and Delora hurried up to the house, while Langford set off with burlap sack in hand.

Auntie Pan met Delora and Isabelle at the kitchen door and ushered them inside. "What you ladies doing out in this mess? You trying to catch your death?"

"Never mind us," said Delora. "Where's Radley?"

"Holed up in the pantry, stuffing hisself on fatback. I thought Mr. Samson's funeral feast was supposed to be over," said Auntie Pan.

Delora sighed. "I suppose we have to indulge the boy for a spell, much as we can afford. Eating keeps him out of trouble. And his mama's so poorly."

"If she ain't fronting us all," said the cook.

Isabelle left Delora and Auntie Pan discussing supper dishes. It was remarkable how quickly her aunt's composure returned when she was taking action or assigning it to others. Sending Langford off for the entrails and possibly for Mr. Delahoussaye, planning the evening's menu with the cook: it was all of a piece, as long as Delora was in control.

Isabelle, not so quick to regain her equanimity, started for the back parlor, longing to make up the fire, warm herself, and think a bit before facing anyone else. Pickwick's returning without Paul worried her. Someone had already done awful things at Belle Ombre and might well do more.

Then the image came to her mind of Aunt Delora, resting her cheek against Langford's hand. Isabelle had heard the rumors, many of them originating with Uncle Babcock, who saw everything in a prurient light, and had discounted them. Delora was almost always on good terms with her slaves-turned-servants, on far better terms with them than she had ever been with the overseer and his family. What Isabelle had seen in the stable was only a brief touch at an anxious moment, surely an act of kindness, not intimacy.

She had just reached the back parlor door when she heard Ardyce calling for her from the front hall.

"Miss Isabelle! Come quick, Miss Isabelle! Mr. Delahoussaye's out here."

Isabelle gathered up her wet skirt and ran toward the sound of Ardyce's voice. She found her trying to support Paul as he staggered in the front doorway. His suit was muddy and damp, his shirt collar torn open, his hat cocked sideways, and his spectacles slipping down his nose. For a moment she wondered if he were drunk, then a whiff of sickness, not whiskey, reached her.

"Here, Miss Isabelle, catch his other arm. We got to get this man to his bed 'fore he's passed out and passed over."

Quickly, Isabelle complied, and between them, she and Ardyce steadied Paul for the climb upstairs. His upper body lurched and reeled from side to side, but he managed to drag his feet from one step to another. Reaching his room, they brought him to rest on the high, narrow bed. Isabelle held his shoulders while Ardyce pulled off his boots. Then together they removed his coat and shirt. As they did so, his gray woolen undershirt rode up a little over his ribs, revealing a jagged-edged purple scar. He'd never mentioned to her he'd been wounded, Isabelle thought. She pulled down the undershirt and, with help from Ardyce, laid him back on the pillows. His hat fell over his face, and as Isabelle took it and his spectacles away, he winced and moaned.

"Better fetch him the basin, miss," said Ardyce.

When Isabelle returned from the washstand and set the basin at the head of the bed, she saw Ardyce was removing Paul's trousers.

"The rain ain't soaked through to his drawers," Ardyce commented.

"Then he can just keep those on," said Isabelle, "while he sleeps off whatever's ailing him."

She and Ardyce gently rolled him on his side, untucked half the bed clothes, rolled him to the sheet on the other side, then covered him with blanket and counterpane. It was a maneuver they had often performed together when nursing wounded soldiers. Isabelle understood nursing required many personal services, and during the War she had performed those services with all possible regard for the dignity of her patients. Maintaining her own modesty was made less difficult by following Delora's advice: "Simply do not see or hear the things that might embarrass you, and never speak of the unmentionable." But tending to Paul was different from nursing wounded strangers, different because he had already trespassed her own sense of privacy.

"I'd better get fresh water and another blanket," said Isabelle, taking up the empty pitcher.

"I'll do that, Miss Isabelle. You sit by him 'case he perks up and wants to tell you what's come over him."

Left alone with her patient, who seemed adrift in an unpleasant dream, punctuated by spasms of abdominal pain, Isabelle passed the time folding Paul's discarded clothing over a chair back, smoothing his covers, and polishing his spectacles with her handkerchief. Then he began to mumble, and she came close to his bedside.

"Am I dead?" he rasped.

"Oh, no. You're quiet safe in your room at Belle Ombre," Isabelle said encouragingly.

Paul's eyelids flickered and opened.

"Isabelle?"

"I'm right here. Ardyce and I have been looking after you. Pickwick ran into the stable without you. We feared you had been thrown off. And then Ardyce found you ill on the veranda. Can you tell me what happened to you?"

"I've been poisoned," Paul rasped again, following this statement with a low groan and a clutching of his stomach.

"Poisoned!" Isabelle gripped the spectacles in her hand, smearing the glass anew. "Are you sure, Mr. Delahoussaye? How? What did you eat in town?"

"Nothing," he answered, weakly. "I wasn't feeling well by the time I got to town."

"Oh. Well, Aunt Delora expressed some concern about the way you just took off this afternoon. Maybe she sensed you weren't as far over your cold as you thought you were. So you've had a relapse of ill health?"

Paul made an effort to raise up from the pillow, then collapsed back against it. "It wasn't any head cold," he said, "that knocked me out of the saddle, Miss Ross."

"I see." Isabelle made an effort to sound stern. Paul looked pitiful, but hardly on the brink of death, she thought; men wore a different look when they weren't going to recover. But the nature of his illness and her own recent sickening discovery in the holly bog combined to make her feel unsteady. She chose to combat the feeling with a show of brusqueness. "If you were coming over poorly on the way to town, Mr. Delahoussaye, you should have turned back. Why did you go to Verbena, anyway, sir?"

"To do what you asked me to, Miss Isabelle. I was hoping to find out something that might help me discover who's been doing murder around here."

"Did you find anything out—before you were took bad?"

Paul rubbed his forehead, then asked, "Could I have my spectacles, please? You're all a blur."

Isabelle quickly wiped the lenses again and handed them over. As Paul adjusted the spectacles, at the same time smoothing his hair back behind his ears, he stared for a moment at the sleeve of his undershirt, then looked at Isabelle. His ashen face took on the trace of a blush.

Isabelle shrugged. "Ardyce and I did a little nursing during the War—as you know, having read my letters. Undressing patients is nothing to us, and should be nothing to you either. We couldn't leave you in your wet things, chilling you to the bone."

"Were you caught out in the rain, too?" Paul asked. "And your cheek—"

"A little scratch of a twig," said Isabelle. "I was out riding, and my horse shied. Morning Glory can't abide puddles and thunder. Now, let's talk about what you've been doing this afternoon. What did you discover in town that made you come over ill?"

"Nothing."

"You discovered nothing?"

"No. I didn't get sick from my discovery," said Paul, his voice strengthening, with impatience, Isabelle surmised. "I told you I wasn't feeling right when I left here. It must have been something I ate or drank."

"Or the prick of conscience jabbing at your insides," said Isabelle.

Paul shut his eyes for a moment, then opened them and looked at her. "I am sorry, Miss Isabelle. From the bottom of my heart, I'm sorry I read your letters."

From the miserable expression on his face, Isabelle guessed he was sorry he'd ever set eyes on those letters. She rose and paced the room.

"Mr. Delahoussaye, you left here after eating the same dinner as everybody else in this house. You say you ate nothing in town. Well, while you're suffering severe dyspepsia, none of us is sick. The only difference I see is that you indulged yourself a little more than some of us at table. Not more than Uncle Babcock, of course, but his system is accustomed to gluttony. A heavy dinner today, after the wine you drank last night—and here you are."

Paul stared at her. "Did Colonel Brodie know what a tongue you have?"

"Maybe not. This sort of situation never occurred when he was here," said Isabelle. "Now can we put aside for the moment the subject of indigestion—"

"Poisoning," Paul interjected.

"And get on," Isabelle continued, "with what you discovered in town? Where did you go? Whom did you talk to? Did you tell folks things that you swore you wouldn't?" Such direct questioning was not what Delora had advised, but Isabelle felt in no mood to practice cajolery.

"No, Miss Isabelle, I did not break my promise to you," Paul said wearily. "I talked to the postal clerk, no one else. I sent a message to Mr. Caulder of the *Laurel Dispatch*, telling him I'd be staying on here a little longer—no particulars, nothing about murder."

Isabelle sat again by his bedside and offered Paul a sip of water. She hoped he was telling her the truth; she wanted to feel more kindly toward him. It was difficult to remain hostile to someone who looked so wretched and sounded so sincere.

"Thank you," he said as she took the cup away. He hesitated, then spoke again. "I did mention to the clerk that I was staying at Belle Ombre. We made some small talk, and I asked him about how fast the mail was traveling these days. I said Mrs. Raveneaux was getting regular letters from her husband off in Washington. The fellow looked surprised at that. He told me that in the two years he's been postal clerk he's never once seen a letter come through for your aunt from Colonel Raveneaux—not from Washington, not from anywhere."

Isabelle drew in her breath, held it, let it go. "That's ridiculous. Of course Aunt Delora gets letters," she said. "She runs Belle Ombre according to Uncle Charles Orvin's wishes.

She's said so dozens of times.   And I've seen the letters myself."

"Langford brings her those letters.   Doesn't he?"

"He brings them from town," Isabelle insisted.

"He doesn't bring them from the post office," said Paul.

Ardyce tapped once and entered the room with a blanket draped over her arm, a water pitcher in one hand and a teacup in the other.   After setting the pitcher on the washstand, she handed the teacup to Isabelle and spread the blanket over Paul.   Then she motioned for him to sit up while she fluffed the pillows at his back.   Paul murmured his thanks, but Ardyce spoke only to Isabelle.

"Auntie Pan made him that tea, said it would unknot his stomach."

When Ardyce was gone, Paul looked suspiciously at the proffered cup.

"It isn't hog's hoof tea," Isabelle assured him.   "You can smell it's hot spearmint."

Paul pressed his lips together and shook his head.

"For heaven's sake, you look like a little boy refusing his castor oil.   This tea will do you a world of good."

"Or finish me off," said Paul.

"Rubbish.   I'll take a sip myself just to show you." Isabelle did so, then handed the cup to him.   "It's delicious. Auntie Pan even sweetened it up for you."

Paul took the cup, but didn't yet drink from it.   "Mrs. Raveneaux thinks pretty highly of the cook's skill in making concoctions to cure colds, pacify nerves, and clarify brains. Why not a mixture to incapacitate a body—or worse?"

"Mr. Delahoussaye, I may not have proof to your satisfaction, but I have my own good common sense.   And I feel sure Aunt Delora and Auntie Pan have not conspired to poison you.   I'll down that whole cup of spearmint tea to prove it."   Isabelle held out her hand for the cup.

But instead of giving it to her, Paul downed it himself. Setting the empty cup aside, he said, "Better I prove it than you."

Isabelle watched him with a trace of apprehension. "I didn't mean to make light of your discomfort this afternoon. I know things aren't quite right around here," she said slowly. "I want to help put things right, but I don't want to hurt my loved ones."

"I know you don't, Miss Isabelle. Look, what happened to me might have been an accident or the doings of someone other than your aunt and the cook. And I'm not saying Mrs. Raveneaux had anything to do with murder. But doesn't your good common sense tell you your aunt has a storehouse full of secrets?"

Isabelle nodded. "If Uncle Charles Orvin isn't sending letters through the post office, maybe it's because he's close by, holed up somewhere, and Langford hand carries the letters for him."

"But why?"

"Maybe he's . . . he's been horribly disfigured and doesn't want anybody to see him. You saw his portrait. He was so proud and handsome. When he left to fight, he claimed nothing was going to touch him."

Paul was quiet, but he held her gaze steadily. "What is it?" Isabelle asked.

He answered gently. "Maybe Mrs. Raveneaux doesn't know what became of her husband. But if the Colonel is dead, she knows Babcock Vasseur would get Belle Ombre. Maybe your aunt writes the letters herself."

In her mind, Isabelle took his supposition a step further. If Elroy Samson had found out that Colonel Raveneaux's letters of instruction were forgeries and if he threatened Delora with exposure, might she not ask Langford to help her end the threat? But murder was one thing, mutilation of the corpse another, even when the victim was cruelty incarnate.

"Mr. Delahoussaye, I hold my aunt in the highest regard," said Isabelle. "She has given me shelter and protection ever since my parents passed away. I've trusted her all this time. Oh, I know she doesn't always do things the way ordinary women do. But she isn't ordinary. Nor is she evil."

"She's expedient," said Paul.

"You're entitled to your opinion." Isabelle rose from the chair and looked down at him. "But tell me this, if you can, sir: why would any woman ask you to solve a murder if she had committed it herself?"

"So she could keep me here and make it impossible for me to solve anything."

Isabelle caught her breath.

"Oh, I'm not saying Mrs. Raveneaux pushed Beryl over the railing or caved in Mr. Samson's skull," Paul said, "but I am saying, she has an uncanny knack for getting folks to do her bidding."

"I'm not listening to such talk."

But Paul continued. "I'm beginning to wonder—even if I did *think* I'd discovered the murderer among us, might he not just be the suspect of her choosing?"

"I'd appreciate it," said Isabelle, "if we could simply agree to disagree about some things, Mr. Delahoussaye, until your week as an investigator is finished."

"Finished," Paul said, "has an ominous sound to it."

Isabelle moved to the door. "You'd better rest now, Mr. Delahoussaye. I'll look in on you later."

"Thank you, Miss Isabelle."

* * *

Complying with her aunt's wishes, Isabelle set about her other nursing duties that evening, which involved bringing Faye Samson a supper tray and sitting with her until she finished her meal. "Be sure she eats every bite," Delora had instructed Isabelle, "and make some conversation with her. Find out what her plans are."

Faye's plan, for the evening at least, was apparently to run Isabelle ragged. The widow complained of the food, whined for another pillow, another blanket, another glass of water.

"Shall I read to you?" Isabelle suggested, hoping for a chance to sit.

"Read what? Stories, lies? That's nothing to do with me, Miss Isabelle." Faye sniffed. "How 'bout bringing me one of Miss Delora's ladies' magazines. Pictures would help me pass the time."

When Isabelle returned to the master bedroom with an out-of-date fashion magazine, Faye had another request, this time for a hairbrush and hand mirror.

"I'm feeling stronger," Faye said, forcing the brush through her tangles with an unsteady hand. "I want to go to town—tomorrow."

"No need to be in a rush," said Isabelle. "Everything's being taken care of."

"I want to go to town," Faye repeated. "I want Radley to take me to Verbena. That's all I've asked since Elroy died."

"Is there something particular you need from town?" Isabelle asked.

"I just need to get there." Faye answered petulantly, setting down the brush and studying her sallow face in the mirror. "I been worked too hard here. Your people done wore me out."

Isabelle thought of how many tasks Delora had assigned to Faye through the years, tasks many plantation mistresses took on themselves, thus freeing Delora to attend to her husband's duties in his absence. Faye, not Delora, had worked beside Isabelle and Ardyce, preserving fruits and vegetables, making candles and soap, gardening, sewing, housecleaning. Then Faye had to face doing the household chores for her own family. But while Delora expected plenty of work from Faye, she granted her certain benefits, too—extra food, first choice of hand-me-down clothes, and long hours in the big house away from Elroy Samson.

As Faye continued bemoaning her hard life, Isabelle wondered if the woman realized how often the Raveneaux family had sheltered her from the hardest part of her life. Isabelle recalled how Faye had looked on a warm day in early fall, stooping to pull weeds in the garden, her sleeves rolled up and her bare arms darkened with bruises. Faye had shuddered at the distant sound of her husband bellowing at a laborer, and mumbled something about Elroy's supper not setting well with him the night before. Then Delora had kept Faye up at the big house all that night, saying she needed her to work late on the jelly making and start early cleaning the pantry next day if they were ever going to be ready for winter.

"Pity you ain't mistress of Belle Ombre, Miss Isabelle," Faye said, finally winding down her monologue of complaint, "'stead of a poor relation. You might've done right by me and my boy, my only boy the War didn't steal from me." She looked weary and spent, but still managed to reach for the magazine and rifle through its pages. "Someday I'll dress like them ladies," she murmured drowsily, "and Radley—he'll take me driving in a carriage through the streets of. . ."

Faye drifted off to sleep, and Isabelle carried the supper tray from the room. If Delora had wanted to temporarily incapacitate Paul, Isabelle reflected, she would have asked Auntie Pan to cook up something for him as she had for Faye—something to make him sleepy, not sick.

CHAPTER TEN

Paul slept deeply, dreaming of Isabelle without her corset or hoops, unresisting in his embrace. At midnight he woke, ravenously hungry.

After pulling on his trousers and an extra pair of woolen socks, he tiptoed down the back stairs to the kitchen. The house was dark except for a circle of candlelight at the kitchen table, and quiet except for the smacking sounds Radley made at the table where he sat hunched over a loaf of bread and jar of peach preserves.

"Mind if I join you?" asked Paul.

Slowly, Radley looked toward Paul, squinted his eyes a moment, then shrugged and went on chewing.

"For a time this evening I thought I'd never eat again, but I sure am hungry now," Paul said, surveying the dishes on the table. Most of them were empty. He took a heel of bread, but passed on the preserves; Radley was eating directly out of the jar.

Paul tried again to start a conversation. "Well, how've you been, Radley?"

"'Bout the same, sir."

"I guess you're missing your pa?"

"Yeah, maybe I do." Radley dug his spoon into the preserve jar to scrape out the last peach. "I really looked up to Pa about some things."

"What kind of things?"

"Well, Pa believed in bettering hisself—not just settling for what folks was willing to give him."

Paul reflected this attitude must have served as Samson's justification for digging up the plantation, searching for Delora's jewels.

Radley ran his slab of pink tongue down the spoon handle. "And Pa knew women. Boy, howdy, did he know women."

In the biblical sense, no doubt, Paul thought, his appetite lessening even without a bite of bread. But he continued the conversation, hoping a better knowledge of Samson would lead him to his killer. "I guess the women'll be calling you Mr. Samson now, won't they, Radley?"

Radley exhaled a laugh, then shook his head. "Naw. Ardyce won't. And Beryl's dead. And white women is too much trouble, Pa always said."

"But Mrs. Samson—" Paul blurted out, then stopped.

Radley didn't bat an eye. "Oh, that's different. Ma's just Ma. She minded Pa, and she's real good to me—most times." Radley twisted his mouth and seemed to struggle with a thought.

"Something bothering you?" Paul suggested.

"Well, you know." Radley rolled his small eyes toward the ceiling. "A fella don't want his ma watching after him all the time. But she can't get riled about things she don't know."

"I understand," said Paul. "Some things a man has to keep to himself."

Radley nodded and began to chuckle softly.

"Or only tells another man," Paul added.

Radley's chuckle rumbled more loudly in his chest. "Oh, no you don't, sir. You ain't going to get nothing out of me."

"Maybe not. But you've got me wondering about something." Paul stretched and arched his back. Then, as if only casually interested, he asked, "Do you think Langford would agree with you about white women being too much trouble?"

Radley's chuckle became a cough, which he quelled with a swig of milk. With a froth around his mouth, he said, "You thinking about him and Mrs. Raveneaux?"

"They seem pretty close."

"Just what Colonel Raveneaux hisself thought. But that nigger ain't getting up to her no more."

"You're sure?"

"Sure as I'm sitting here." Radley grinned. "Pa gelded him—Master's orders—just 'fore the Colonel left for war."

Paul tried not to cringe visibly.

"Ma reckons Lang ought to swing for Pa's killing. Makes sense, don't it? Pa always said when you whip a dog, you better be afeared someday he'll bite you."

"I guess your pa knew what he was talking about."

In an unexpected gesture of generosity, Radley held a dish out to Paul. "You want this last scrimption of bread pudding?"

"No. You finish it off." Paul jerked back his chair and rose. "I'm heading back to bed."

Paul figured Langford must have run off shortly after what Radley so lightly referred to as gelding. But having gotten away, why would Langford return? Why would he wait another two years to take revenge on Elroy Samson? And how could Radley sit in the Raveneaux's kitchen, stuffing himself full as a tick, indifferent to humanity?

Bread pudding, Paul thought as he reached the top of the back stairs. Euphrasie had given him her bread pudding at dinner. At the time he had assumed the edge was off his appetite and that was why the second serving—her serving—had not tasted as delicious as the first. But suppose her serving had been laced with poison? Did someone in the house feel so threatened by this slip of a girl, who amused herself hiding in the woodwork, that someone would wish her ill? Or had someone gone mad, trying murder first one way and then another? Paul decided he would sleep far better if he knew both Euphrasie and Isabelle were safe for the night.

Passing the door of his own room, he rounded the corridor and pressed his ear to the next door. The sounds of heavy snoring punctuated by loud snorts told him Babcock Vasseur lay within; how Lydie Vee slept beside her husband, Paul could not imagine. He tried the door across the hall and found it locked. But the door just down from it swung open at a touch, on silent hinges.

Paul's eyes had adjusted to the dimness of the corridor, and as he peered around the door, he discerned a rumpled, empty bed. He stepped inside the room, moving toward a glow that shone from a doorway opposite, opening onto an adjoining room. Stopping in the doorway, he saw on a night stand the remains of a lighted candle, sputtering in a pool of white wax. On the bed, Isabelle and Euphrasie lay asleep, swathed in pale gowns and folds of cream white bed linens. Paul stepped closer. Euphrasie's yellow curls spread across the pillow, but her face was hidden against Isabelle's shoulder. One of Isabelle's arms encircled her cousin and the other stretched back over her head, the fingers of her hand laced in a tangle of her golden-brown hair.

Isabelle opened her eyes.

For a moment she said nothing, did nothing, and Paul debated with himself on the value of retreat. Then slowly she slid her arm from around Euphrasie and swung her legs over the side of the bed. As she rose the hem of her gown fell over her bare feet, and she caught up a shawl, tossing it about her shoulders. Isabelle moved away from the candlelight to the doorway between her room and her cousin's. Paul followed.

"What are you doing here?" she asked in a cold whisper.

"I. . . I got to thinking about the bread pudding," said Paul.

"Oh?"

Paul went on hurriedly. "You see, my second dish of pudding was meant for Euphrasie, but she gave it to me. Well, it didn't taste quite right. And then I got to thinking about how she hides in the woodwork and hears things. Maybe someone thought she knew something and tried to poison her. Whatever was in that pudding was strong enough to make me very sick and could have been strong enough to kill her. You know how ill I was all afternoon and evening. Then, tonight it occurred to me that someone—whoever tried to poison her—might have tried to hurt her in some other way. So I. . . I slipped in here to see if she was all right. Is she all right, Miss Isabelle?"

"As you see," Isabelle replied, nodding toward her cousin. "She's sleeping like an angel, though sometimes she has trouble sleeping alone."

"Well, that's a relief."

"Mr. Delahoussaye," Isabelle added gently, "I'm glad to see you've recovered from dessert, but don't worry yourself too much about Euphrasie. No one wishes her ill. Now you best go on out the way you came. I lock my door at night, and in the future, I'll be sure my cousin does the same."

Paul shook his head. "I don't understand how you can just dismiss what I told you.   Murder's been done here—twice—and murder could be done again. You asked me yourself to find the killer. But for your sake, I mustn't find that the killer is Ardyce, and for your aunt's sake, it mustn't be Langford. Next Miss Lydie Vee will ask me to find Babcock innocent. Mrs. Samson will want Radley off the hook, and Auntie Pan will ask me to exonerate the kitchen maid and the tenants down the road."

Isabelle sighed impatiently.

"And there's something else," Paul continued. "A few minutes ago, I talked to Radley down in the kitchen. He let fall that his father, following Colonel Raveneaux's orders, geld . . . well, unmanned Langford. That's a motive for murder if ever I heard one."

"Please keep your voice down." Isabelle glanced toward Euphrasie who stirred in her sleep, hugging her pillow. "Good night, sir."

Paul caught her arm as she turned away from him. "Isabelle?"

She looked him square in the face, but her defiant expression was belied by her tremulous whisper. "Really, Mr. Delahoussaye. You come in here in the middle of the night, talking about poisoning and murder and unmentionable acts, and call me by my given name—when I never said you could."

"But you didn't object before—"

"You just don't know what a day I've had! Fetching and fixing for Faye Samson, worrying over one thing and another, including you. First you're missing, then you're ill at death's door. Then Euphrasie drives me near to distraction. And the worst of it all was those entrails!"

Paul released her trembling arm. "Entrails? Did you say entrails?"

Isabelle moved through the doorway into Euphrasie's room, farther from where the girl slept in Isabelle's bed. "Yes," she said. "The hogs were digging them up in the holly bog. And you and I both know who was missing his insides when his body was found."

Paul almost whistled as he exhaled. "I knew Samson wasn't killed in the smokehouse," he said. "This means he might have been killed by the creek—that last night you saw him, the night of the wake. There might be evidence in the woods—signs of a fight, torn clothing, a weapon. You must show me the exact spot tomorrow. That is," he hesitated, "you can describe the spot to me. I understand if you'd rather not go back there."

"I'll go." Isabelle took a deep breath. "I'm interested, too, in seeing what you find there."

The candle flame sank into its pool of wax and went out. Paul stood very still. "I can't see a thing," he whispered. Then he felt Isabelle's fingertips brush the back of his hand. He turned his hand and gripped hers, palm to palm.

"It's only the dark," she said. "Come, I'll lead you to the door."

Paul stumbled along behind her, grazing his shin on a wooden chest at the foot of the bed, just as she warned him of its existence. Silently, she turned the handle and opened the door. Paul didn't want to go.

"Miss Ross, if this weren't such a troubling time for you. . . Well, I can't help thinking about when we crossed the bridge over Lyre's Creek."

"Don't think about it. Please. Good night, Mr. Delahoussaye."

Paul was shut out in the drafty hallway and realized his feet were freezing. But could they be any colder than Isabelle's chilling dismissal?

* * *

Though he went shivering to bed, Paul woke late the next morning feeling pleasantly warm. A fire had been newly made up in the small grate, and upon rising, Paul found steaming water in the washstand pitcher and his laundered clothes stacked on a chair, smelling of fresh ironing. Ardyce had been busy, he thought.

Downstairs no one was in the dining room and most of the breakfast dishes had been cleared, but Paul found some hot coffee left in the pot, poured himself a cup, and carried it to the back parlor, where he hoped to find Isabelle. Instead, he walked in on Babcock Vasseur and Euphrasie.

The girl, not dressed for the day but still in an embroidered wrap and nightgown, slid from her great-uncle's knee and curtsied to Paul.

"'Morning, Mr. Delahoussaye," she said, sweetly. "I hope you're well."

"Yes, I think I am, thank you. And I hope you are, too." Paul smiled, and Euphrasie's already blushing cheeks darkened even more.

Babcock harumphed from the rocking chair, rolling himself forward to give Euphrasie a light swat from behind. "Upstairs with you, girl. Make yourself presentable."

Euphrasie giggled. "Yes, Uncle." Then she danced from the room, letting her dressing gown fall open and the sides fly around her like fairy wings.

Babcock settled back in the rocker and motioned for Paul to take a seat on the bench by the hearth. "Nothing but an imp," Babcock muttered. "Still, she brightens an hour now and then."

Paul took a large swallow of coffee, letting it warm his insides before he began to converse with Babcock. Although his acquaintance with the man was brief, Paul understood the value of flattery in obtaining information from him. He opened by commenting on how reassuring Babcock's presence must be to the womenfolk of Belle Ombre.

"With you here to advise Mrs. Raveneaux, I'm sure the planting will go well next spring, whether or not her husband gets back. I suppose Colonel Raveneaux corresponds with you regularly on the running of his estate." Paul sipped coffee and waited for Babcock to contradict the statement.

Babcock coughed and shifted his bulk in the rocking chair. "Well now, Mr. Delahoussaye," he drawled, "it's a curious thing. My niece's husband doesn't condescend to write me a line. Never mind that Lydie Vee and I pulled up stakes and high-tailed it down here to help that gal. All his letters are for Delora."

"Have you seen the letters?" Paul asked.

"Oh, she shows them to me. That pair never got on before the War, but he gives her a free hand now." Babcock rocked heavily, the chair creaking with his weight. "'Course if Charles Orvin decides not to come back, I'll insist my niece divorce him. Abandonment, don't you know. Then I can take the reins as I should have done when my elder brother, Delora's father, died. 'T'aint right I should live on here like her poor relation."

"Langford always brings Mrs. Raveneaux her husband's letters, doesn't he?"

"He fetches all the mail from town, and supplies. We, the family, hardly ever set foot in Verbena—crawling with Yankees and riff-raff, you know."

"But I learned yesterday from the mail clerk in Verbena that Colonel Raveneaux's letters have never come through his office, not in the two years he's been working there." Paul paused to note Babcock's startled expression. "Perhaps," Paul said slowly, "the Colonel sends his letters by private courier, though that could get expensive. Or maybe he uses some other method."

Babcock raised his shaggy brows. "What other method are you thinking of?"

Paul rose from the bench and stirred the fire. "Suppose," he said, turning back to Babcock, "that Colonel Raveneaux is nearer to home than you all believe. Suppose Langford hand carries those letters between master and mistress."

"Then why the devil doesn't he show himself? Why play us for fools and watch us dance to Delora's tune?" Babcock blustered.

"Well, now maybe the Colonel's disabled, disfigured, doesn't want to be seen just yet. Maybe Mrs. Raveneaux is innocent of her husband's actual whereabouts."

Babcock's face turned purple as an over-ripe plum. "Delora's innocent of nothing! Nothing that's to her advantage, that is. Charles Orvin could be dead and buried, and she wouldn't tell me."

"Dead men don't write letters," said Paul.

"No, by God, they don't! And they don't own property either."

Babcock rocked and stewed in his chair until Paul wouldn't have been surprised to see steam escape from the man's ears and nostrils.

Then a new idea began to take shape in Paul's mind. "Meaning no disrespect to your niece, Mr. Vasseur, but I have noted some odd goings on here. From what I can gather, only Mrs. Raveneaux and the servant, Beryl, took care of the body of Colonel Brodie. Now Beryl is dead so we can't ask her, but I'm wondering about something. A body is a fragile thing, and changes after death in ways that hardly bear thinking about. Do you think it's possible that Mrs. Raveneaux and her servant were mistaken about which Colonel they were laying out?"

Babcock's mouth trembled before words and spittle exploded from his lips: "Blasted! That's what she did! Buried her husband and called him Forest Brodie."

"And the letters, sir?"

"Wrote 'em herself, the hussy!"

"You think Mrs. Raveneaux capable of forging her husband's handwriting?" Paul asked.

Babcock warmed to the idea. "Damned if I don't! If Moses himself had that woman with him in the wilderness, I bet you, she'd be busy behind the burning bush carving tablets. 'Delora Raveneaux, thou shalt set thyself above thy kinfolk,' she'd write. 'Thou shalt keep all for thy own glorification and make thy uncle come begging.' And she'd smile and nod and fool God into thinking it was His own hand that wrote it."

"You realize this is all conjecture," Paul said, evenly. "We don't know anything for a fact except that Colonel Raveneaux's letters don't come through the post office."

"Then I'll get the facts."

Babcock made an unsuccessful attempt to rise from the rocking chair. Then Paul assisted him by pushing the chair forward so that Babcock could spill himself out of it. Puffing his cheeks and pulling at his waistcoat, Babcock seemed to be preparing for action just as his wife entered the room.

"Lydie Vee," he said excitedly, "we have important matters to discuss."

"Yes, Babbie." Lydie Vee waved a dismissive hand, then turned to Paul. "Delora would like to see you in the study."

Paul hesitated, brought up short by a pang of guilt at the mention of his hostess's name. He had wanted to sound out Babcock, not set the old man on a dangerous course of accusations and recriminations. "This is all conjecture," Paul repeated. But if Babcock's speculations proved true, Paul wondered if the Vassuers would also conclude that Delora had a reason for wanting Beryl out of the way and Elroy Samson, too, if he knew or suspected she was perpetrating a hoax. And wouldn't Langford be just the one to help her with her schemes. Still, the matter of the entrails perplexed him. And the possibility that Isabelle's fiancé still lived brought him no peace of mind.

"Mr. Delahoussaye, Delora's waiting for you," Lydie Vee reminded him.

"Yes, ma'am. I'm on my way."

As he left the back parlor, Paul heard her say to her husband, "All right, Bab, what cockamamie notion has entered your head now?"

* * *

In the study at the heavy carved desk, Delora sat beneath her portrait. Though she was not bejeweled as her image in the painting, Paul thought her equally imposing in her high-necked russet silk, her uncrowned auburn hair center parted and pinned back from her face, her eyes clear as pure amber.

"Take a chair, Mr. Delahoussaye."

"Thank you, ma'am." Paul sat in the armchair opposite her.

"I'm so glad to see you've recovered from yesterday's sudden and distressing illness. Of course Isabelle and Ardyce are the best nurses a man can have."

"I quite agree with you, Mrs. Raveneaux."

Delora folded her dainty hands in the middle of the vast desk blotter. "I understand, sir, that you went to town yesterday afternoon, and it was there that you fell ill. Food poisoning, perhaps?"

"Very likely, ma'am."

"So, were you still able to accomplish the purpose of your trip, or was it cut short by your indisposition?"

Paul thought if she chose to angle as delicately in Lyre's Creek, the fish wouldn't have a chance.

"I was able to send a message to my employer, telling him I'd be staying here a few more days. Then I headed straight back to Belle Ombre, not soon enough, I'm afraid. Pickwick dropped me by the veranda, and you know the rest."

"Do I?" said Delora. "So you went to the post office?"

Paul nodded.

"While in town, did you see Captain Newell or any of his men?"

"No, ma'am. The clerk told me they'd been laying low that day."

"Ah. And you didn't forget the spirit of our agreement?" Delora looked at him steadily, piercingly, and Paul made an effort not to flinch.

"No, ma'am, I didn't forget."

"You said nothing—to anyone—about the. . ."

"I said nothing about the murders, Mrs. Raveneaux."

Delora drew in her breath. "I beg your pardon, did you say murders?"

"Yes, ma'am. It's my belief your servant, Beryl, was pushed over that railing, most likely by the same person who killed Elroy Samson," Paul said, watching carefully for her response.

She met his gaze, then pursed her lips in an indulgent smile. "Mr. Delahoussaye, we both know you are new to this type of investigation. And your enthusiasm does you credit. But let's not confuse a lack of self-discipline with murder. To put it plainly, Beryl was drunk."

"And she didn't live through Colonel Brodie's wake," said Paul, "nor did Samson. He was probably killed that same night or in the early hours of the morning. He'd been dead several days when we found him. Two violent deaths, occurring within hours of each other. There's a connection, Mrs. Raveneaux."

"I do believe you're dancing in the dark, Mr. Delahoussaye. Why would a vicious killer settle for tossing my servant head over heels down an airwell, when he could have disemboweled her as he did my overseer? No, sir, these deaths are separate in their causes."

Paul looked up at the portrait above the woman and toyed with the idea of asking Delora about how Langford came by the letters he brought her. He might even ask if the rumor were true that she was overly fond of her servant and had reason to hate Samson for what he'd done to Langford.

Instead, he said, "Your jewels certainly became you, Mrs. Raveneaux. Do you miss them?"

"I part with what I must." Delora sighed. "Besides, jewels don't make a woman beautiful when her youth is past. They only make her rich. And in the end, they may only buy a little food or seed or labor to start another crop. When the money's no good, you can still find someone willing to take diamonds and gold."

"Do you have much left to barter with?" Paul asked.

"That is none of your concern, Mr. Delahoussaye," Delora replied sweetly.

She rose, and Paul jumped to his feet.

"I beg your pardon, ma'am."

Delora smiled. "Oh, no offense taken. Now I must go and speak with Auntie Pan about dinner. Something light, I think, but fortifying." She glided to the door, then turned back to Paul. "I'll leave you here to cogitate, sir, and look forward to hearing your solution to murder."

Alone, Paul drew a paper and pencil from his coat pocket and began adding notes to his list of suspicious persons with sanguinary motives. But he hadn't gone far with his analysis when Isabelle, in her riding habit, came for him.

"The horses are saddled, Mr. Delahoussaye. I can show you that place now," she said with a practiced serenity no doubt learned from her aunt.

On the way to the holly bog, Isabelle was quiet and, it seemed to Paul, watchful. As they rode deeper into the woods, mist coiling up from the creek wrapped them as it wound among the trees. Water seeped up from the ground to fill their horses' hoof prints. And rain hung in the air above them like dew suspended on a spider's web.

"It's through here," Isabelle called back to Paul, bending low over her saddle to pass under a branch.

At the edge of the clearing, they dismounted and tethered the horses.   Paul wiped the moisture from his spectacles and surveyed the soggy ground. Overlapping boot and hoof prints had churned the earth into a wet, indecipherable muddle. Then Isabelle led Paul along the length of a fallen tree, skirting the worst of the mud and bringing them close to a vast cypress tree. A deep hole gaped between two of its gnarled gray knees.

"Were they buried there?" Paul asked, grabbing the branch of a sapling to keep his balance on the fallen trunk.

"Yes. Langford took them away." Isabelle looked past him into the shrubbery, then added, "but this is where they were yesterday afternoon, the sows gathered 'round the tree."

"The tree you call Atlas?"

Isabelle nodded, stepping down from the log and around the broad trunk of the cypress tree. "The creek's just down here," she said, pointing away from the direction toward which she moved. "You can hear the water sloshing on the bank."

Paul leaned around the trunk and thought he saw Isabelle slip something into her pocket. "Have you found something?" he asked.

She brought her empty hand from her pocket. "No, Mr. Delahoussaye. Have you?"

"Not yet." Paul slowly circled the clearing, studying the tree limbs, bushes and ground. Near where the horses waited, at the place they had entered the clearing, Paul found a cluster of thin branches snapped and dangling from a heavier limb.

"I might have done that when I fled from here yesterday," said Isabelle, coming up behind him.

"Maybe so. I don't know what I'm looking for," Paul said with growing frustration. "If Samson were killed here, as seems likely, and if he weren't taken completely by surprise,

I'd expect to find evidence of a struggle. So here we are, and I find a mess of footprints, hog trotter prints and horse hoof prints, and some broken branches. But they don't tell me anything. What do I really know about Samson's death?"

"You know quite a bit," Isabelle said. "You know Samson was a big man, and he was bashed on the head with something heavy. So you know it's not likely a woman killed him. And you know the corpse was mutilated, a peculiarly vicious act." She looked toward the cypress tree, then let her gaze slowly travel upward. "When we butcher a hog, we hang the carcass from a pole," she said. "Isn't that a rope up in those branches?"

Paul hurried to the tree, peered up among the limbs, then jumped twice, each time sinking deeper in the mud, but on the second try, bringing down the frayed end of a rope. He tugged at it and found the other end still firmly tied to a limb. What kind of person, he wondered, could string up another human being, cut his insides out, and bury them close by where the victim's feet must have swung?

"I want to go back to the house now, Mr. Delahoussaye."

"Yes, of course." Paul released the rope and came to help her into her side saddle. Then, as he untied Pickwick, he noticed a piece of butternut cotton cloth caught on a twig. He took the ragged fabric, stared at it a moment, then held it out to Isabelle. "Do you recognize this material, Miss Ross? Could it be from Samson's clothing or . . . or someone else's?"

Isabelle rubbed the cloth between her fingers. "Yes, I recognize it."

"And?" Paul prompted her. "Who has clothing made of this material?"

"We all do, all the women. Last year Aunt Delora took a bolt of it in trade for something. We made aprons for me, Lydie Vee, Faye, Ardyce, Auntie Pan. Aunt Delora and

Euphrasie have art smocks from it, for when they tried landscape painting. And we made shifts for the tenant farmers' girls."

Disappointed, Paul took back the swatch of cloth, tucked it in his jacket, and mounted Pickwick. "If you happen to notice anyone's apron or smock missing a piece, will you tell me?"

"Certainly," Isabelle replied without looking at him.

"And will you tell me what you hid in your pocket when you went around the cypress tree?"

Isabelle looked startled. Then reluctantly she reached in her skirt pocket and withdrew a small pale blue flower on a broken stem.

"What is it?" asked Paul.

"I'm not sure, though it might be lyre-leaf sage. I press flowers. But you already knew that."

"Because of the flowers you put in your letters to Colonel Brodie," Paul finished for her in case she intended another reminder of his transgression.

Isabelle returned the flower to her pocket.

"Miss Isabelle, there's something else I'm curious about. Do you happen to know what Langford did with the entrails that were buried here?"

"He put them in a bait bucket with a lid on it and buried them this morning beside Elroy Samson."

"Oh. I see." He nodded grimly.

They turned their horses away from the clearing and rode single file out of the holly bog.

At the foot of the hill below the stable, they met Radley, red-faced and winded.

"What is it?" asked Isabelle, and waited for the boy to catch his breath.

"Captain Newell's showed up, miss. And he ain't pleased about something. Lang says I'm supposed to take the horses down to the bridge and wait with 'em."

"I'll go with you, Radley. Mr. Delahoussaye, you'd better walk back to the house."

"But Miss Isabelle, I . . ."

"Please. Just tell Langford. He can fetch us home when the Captain's gone," said Isabelle. "It would ease my mind if you were with my aunt while that man is here."

"But you should come back, too," said Paul.

"No, it's better I help Radley with the horses." She dropped her voice and added, "He doesn't have much of a way with them."

As the boy came forward to take Pickwick's reins, Paul slid from the saddle and was privy to Radley's own muttered opinion of the situation: "Don't know what I hate most—taking orders from Yankees or niggers or women."

* * *

With some misgivings, Paul walked to the house alone. Delora, Captain Newell, the Vasseurs, and Euphrasie were just filing into the dining room when Paul arrived. Euphrasie seemed delighted to be partnered by him, giggling and cooing as he held her chair. Lydie Vee silenced her with a sharp glance.

During the meal of creamed turnip soup, an unidentified baked fish with corn relish, and collard greens seasoned with fatback, Paul wondered if Lydie Vee and Delora had arrived at some tacit agreement on diversionary tactics. With her talent for cutting looks and imperious expressions, Lydie Vee was apparently in charge of controlling Babcock's and Euphrasie's tendencies toward unseemly manners and inane conversation. At the same time, Delora maneuvered the Yankee into a slightly less belligerent mood.

"You can't imagine how distressed I was to hear that you and your men fell ill after eating our pork, Captain. Careful as we try to be, the possibility of corrupted flesh is an ever present danger to us all," said Delora. "Thank the Lord, you have all recovered. And of course, as you say, the meat was right out of our own smokehouse. Such an experience! It must have been terrible for you."

"It could have been fatal," Captain Newell said through narrow lips.

"Oh, I think not. Big men like you don't fall so easily. Now if a little girl like Euphrasie got a hold of a bit of bad pork. . . I shudder to think!" Delora refilled the captain's wine goblet. "You know, Captain Newell, Mr. Delahoussaye came down poorly all of a sudden while he was in town yesterday. Perhaps there's something going around Verbena, some dangerous miasma, and our pork's not to blame at all. Isn't that a possibility, Mr. Delahoussaye?" She turned to Paul for support.

"I couldn't be certain, ma'am." He also couldn't quite put it past Delora not to intentionally give the soldiers tainted meat.

When Newell asked after Isabelle, Delora replied vaguely, to no one in particular, "Oh, didn't I hear she was invited to dine with the Thibodeau family?" Lying came so easily to her.

Over coffee, Captain Newell expressed more than casual interest in Colonel Raveneaux's instructions to his wife. Delora sighed impatiently, remarking that it seemed he'd never tire of that subject, but at last agreed to "put his mind to rest." After the meal, while Lydie Vee guided her husband and Euphrasie toward the back parlor, Delora led the captain and Paul to the study. "Bring us the ordinary brandy," she whispered in passing to Ardyce.

In the study, she talked about the weather, while Ardyce brought a tray of drinks and retreated. "The house is so damp this time of year," said Delora, running a finger along a row of books. "I fear the mildew creeps into everything. Late at night I can almost hear it slithering over the wallpaper and under the rug and curling the pages of a novel I've left open on my coverlet."

Newell would not be distracted by her description of crawling dampness. "Miss Delora, that my requests have turned to demands should come as no surprise to you. You've put me off time and again," he said, more petulant than stern. "I'm growing tired of waiting."

Delora smiled demurely. "Really, Captain, you'll embarrass me in front of Mr. Delahoussaye. He might misunderstand what you're tired of waiting for."

"Then send him out of the room, ma'am, for I mean to see these papers you've talked about, but never yet produced."

Paul didn't move, but looked questioningly at Delora.

"I want Mr. Delahoussaye to stay," she said. "And we'll all have a sociable glass of brandy before we get down to business." Her voice had faltered only slightly, and her hands were steady as she poured the drinks.

Newell was not as easily cajoled as he had been at the first dinner Paul attended at Belle Ombre. His moustache twitched disdainfully as he sniffed at the brandy Delora offered him, but he took it and drank it down before speaking.

"You told me some time ago, ma'am, that your husband had sent you manumission orders during the War." He took a step closer to Delora and literally looked down his nose at her as if trying to intimidate her with his height. "You've said he's written you of his new-found loyalty to the Union and his enthusiasm for dividing up his land to be farmed by a bunch of freedmen and white trash. So, Miss

Delora, it's high time you showed me your"—he paused and winked at Paul—"documents."

Delora lifted her chin and turned to Paul. Suddenly, he heard himself saying what he knew she wanted him to say. "Captain Newell, I must object to your taking such a tone with a lady. I assure you that Mrs. Raveneaux follows her husband's orders in letter and in spirit."

"And just what is your assurance worth, sir?" Newell picked up the brandy decanter and sloshed a greedy portion into his snifter.

While Paul tried to think of an answer, Delora began rummaging through the desk drawers. "I've had so much to manage. Business and paperwork don't come easily to me." She dug deeper into a side drawer and brought forth a stack of letters. "But here they are, Captain. My husband's instructions to me. I'm sure you'll find Mr. Delahoussaye's assurance worth the paper these are written on."

Then Delora proceeded to unfold letter after letter, spreading them on the desk top, smoothing them with her fine hands. She allowed both men to examine the letters, and Paul alternated reading with watching the change in Newell's expression from sneering disbelief to grudging resignation. According to his correspondence, Charles Orvin Raveneaux was a model of humanitarian reform. Manumission orders from the Colonel were dated May 1863, only a few months after Lincoln's Emancipation Proclamation called for freedom of slaves in states not controlled by the Union.

Newell's eyes suddenly narrowed and he cut his glance toward Delora. "So, what happened when you freed your slaves?"

"Well, some ran off, of course, but many stayed and worked—for wages."

The captain snorted. "What sort of wages?"

"What I could afford."

"And if I asked your cook or Langford, they could give me an accounting of their wages?"

"If they chose to do so. But I wouldn't press them, Captain. In this part of the world, discussing finances with outsiders is not considered altogether polite."

"Ah. Well, tell me this, Miss Delora: what did the other planters around here think of you freeing your slaves—with your husband's blessing? Didn't they worry your example might stir up rebellion in their own quarters?"

Delora replied carefully, "Those former slaves who chose to continue at Belle Ombre, and are with us still, agreed to keep quiet about their new status. And then, as the War went on, we were left with few neighbors to object to anything we did."

More letters followed, dated at regular intervals throughout 1864 and 1865. They contained vague references to the hardships of war, a few affectionate words from husband to wife, and clear instructions to sell or lease for a pittance sections of farm land. Some of the letters, Paul noticed, seemed to anticipate changes in federal rules and regulations. Delora, at least on paper, had greatly reduced her wealth and the size of her land holdings, perhaps saving Belle Ombre from confiscation, and increasing the chance her husband might be granted a full pardon by the President.

"I've no doubt," said Delora, "that our divvying up parts of Belle Ombre has disturbed my father's eternal rest. And Uncle Babcock has registered his disapproval. But I . . . my husband and I see the need to change with the times." She turned to Paul. "Clinging only to the past, to the way things were, would leave us nothing to cling to. You understand?"

Paul nodded. The letters, regardless of who had written them and why, had worked some good for those less privileged and resourceful than Delora.

Newell laid the most recent of the Colonel's letters on the desk, then took Delora's right hand and raised it for a moment to his lips. She looked to the ceiling with a uninterested expression, indicating she was simply waiting for the moment to be over.

"I'll call again soon, Miss Delora."

Delora arched her brows. "I'm sure you'll call whenever you like, Captain." When they had entered the study, Paul thought he'd detected a trace of nervousness in her voice and demeanor; that was gone now.

Newell paused in the study doorway. "I gave my men orders to fetch another side of pork from the smokehouse. Shall I invite you to dine with me in town, ma'am, and sample from my plate?"

"Oh, I'm sure there's no need for that, Captain Newell. You can always order some private to sample your dinner, like a royal food taster of yore in the court of an unpopular king."

"You do like to tease, don't you, Miss Delora?"

She smiled. "Where would any of us be without a sense of humor? You know your way out, Captain."

Turning her back on Newell, Delora gathered together the letters and stuffed them in a drawer. Paul watched her in profile, her serene face suddenly slackened with weariness, as if she'd just finished a tiresome performance.

"That importunate man!" she muttered. Then, once again Delora assumed her placid composure and took a seat at the small study table, indicating Paul should do likewise. "But, of course, Mr. Delahoussaye, this isn't the first time my privacy has been invaded by an interloper. I tolerate Captain Newell only because I remember the officer who proceeded him was worse. And because I must. You see, sir, in what a difficult position I find myself."

"Did you show those documents to Captain Newell's predecessor, also?" Paul asked.

"Oh, no. I never had to do that."

"Why not?"

"Well, the man up and died. It's hard to imagine, isn't it? A big, fierce-looking man like him—a real *killer* on the battlefield, I'm sure—suddenly carried off by a touch of dyspepsia, I believe someone said. And to think of all the bad food that was eaten during the War."

Paul felt a sudden internal tightening at her reference to a stomach disorder, and clapped one hand involuntarily over his waistcoat.

She smiled at him. "I'm deeply grateful to you, Mr. Delahoussaye, for coming to my defense and backing me."

"I did nothing."

"Oh, but your very presence in the room was a comfort. Every time Captain Newell comes out here, he looks for something to hang over my head, something amiss that he can report about me to his superiors—the numbers of whom are legion, I'm sure."

Paul smiled back at her, as his cramp eased.

Delora continued, "Captain Newell is zealous in his desire to punish the South and humiliate landed people, robbing them of their property whenever possible. But he also seems to enjoy punishing me in particular with his boorish attentions, perhaps because he realizes under normal circumstances he'd never be allowed in my parlor. It must be something peculiar to northern men, for I can't picture our gentlemen ever treating ladies from the South or North so crudely."

"What would Captain Newell do if he found out something was amiss at Belle Ombre?" asked Paul.

"Oh, he might do anything martial law allowed. Or he might offer to keep it to himself and find out how much his discretion was worth to me, if you take my meaning."

"You really are in a difficult position."

Delora looked thoughtful as she folded her hands on the tabletop. "I wonder," she said. "Captain Newell didn't mention anything to me this time about that oath of loyalty. Isolated as we are at Belle Ombre, and even with the little news from town, I can't always be sure of what the Union wants and what the Captain makes up to threaten me. Perhaps next time you go to Verbena, Mr. Delahoussaye, I'll rally my courage and go with you—and find out for myself just what the Yankees are doing to our community."

"Shall we go tomorrow, ma'am? There might be a letter waiting for you at the post office," said Paul.

Delora shook her head. "No, not tomorrow. I've only recently sent my request for amnesty to President Johnson. On behalf of my husband, of course."

"But can't he petition the President himself? After all, Colonel Raveneaux is in Washington."

"Oh, Charles Orvin is so stubborn and slow to get things done. And he can be so gruff. I remember at the dinner table, he could ask someone to pass the salt and make it sound like a hanging offense that his desire had not been anticipated sooner. Besides, I've heard tell Mr. Johnson hates to be snubbed by the aristocracy, so I thought it best that I write to him and appeal to his better nature."

"You think of everything, Mrs. Raveneaux."

"I do my best." Delora stood, and Paul did likewise. "Now, sir, I must attend to a few domestic duties. Please have another brandy and enjoy our little library."

Left alone, Paul looked out the window, hoping to see Isabelle on her way back to the house. Instead, he saw Captain Newell in conversation with Babcock Vasseur. The two men nodded their heads in unison as if they had just agreed on something. Then Newell mounted his horse and galloped away.

CHAPTER ELEVEN

Isabelle had never felt particularly comfortable with Radley, but until today she had spent precious little time in his exclusive company. As he shuffled his feet and rambled through a monologue on his fishing exploits, occasionally grinning at her for no apparent reason, she was grateful for any distraction offered by the horses. When they were restive, she stroked their necks and murmured to them or took them by the reins and led them a few paces along the creek bank. But Radley tagged after her, his nasal monotone unceasing. She thought Langford would never come to fetch her home.

Isabelle had not previously thought of Radley as talkative and did nothing to encourage his conversation, but today he would not be deterred. "Too bad about Ma feeling so down since Pa died. 'Course, when she's poorly she can't make me do so many fool chores. And I kinda like staying up at the big house."

Nearer the pantry, Isabelle thought.

"Hey, I been wondering, Miss Isabelle," said Radley, "has that new fella figured out who killed Pa?"

"I don't know."

"Well, Mr. Vasseur told me Mr. Delahoussaye was some kinda investigator." Radley spoke slowly, struggling to master each long word as he reached it. "So I reckoned he was sent for when Pa went missing. Am I getting it right?"

Isabelle chose not to answer.

Radley grinned and settled back against the bridge railing. "Take somebody pretty smart to outwit my Pa. Too smart to get caught, don't you think?"

"I have never devoted much time to the contemplation of your father's intellect, but his demise was hardly accomplished with subtlety." Isabelle left Radley to sort out her statement, walking away from him to the far side of the bridge and staring off toward Halcyon.

Forest must be dead, she told herself. The body of a colonel now buried in her family's cemetery had been sent to Belle Ombre with a letter she had written to Forest folded inside the jacket of his uniform. But there was someone at Halcyon —that also must be true. She slipped her hand into her pocket and fingered the combs that had fallen from her hair the night she had clung to Paul under the dead cottonwood. Someone had found them and brought them across Lyre's Creek, leaving them near the big cypress tree. And a sprig of blue wildflowers had been twined in the teeth of one comb.

Isabelle became unpleasantly aware that Radley had pursued her across the bridge, continuing his discourse as if she'd been listening to him. "It was up that-a-way, where the barge turn-around is. I hauled it up and flipped it on the bank with no more than one pull of the line. That there fish was long as your arm . . ."

With a thankful sigh, Isabelle glimpsed Langford striding toward her through the woods.

"Time to come home, Miss Isabelle," he called.

Isabelle took the horses' reins and walked between them, catching up with Langford. Radley straggled behind.

"Captain's gone for now, miss. But I'm getting a bad feeling." Langford looked to Radley as the boy neared them. "Your mama's been asking for you," said Langford. "Better get on up to the house."

Radley shrugged one shoulder and ambled on, distancing himself from Langford as if he couldn't be bothered to acknowledge the man and wouldn't be bothered to hurry to his mother's side.

"Something's got in that boy ever since Mr. Samson died," said Langford.

Isabelle handed him Pickwick's reins. "Let's ride back to the stable. But first, tell me why you've got a bad feeling."

"Oh, Miss Isabelle, you know how Miss Delora likes to take the Captain down a peg. I'm just fearful she's done put him off one too many times."

"With her delaying tactics," said Isabelle, as Langford helped her up on Morning Glory. "Well, maybe if the Colonel knew the difficulty of her situation, he'd come back and keep Captain Newell from making so free at Belle Ombre."

* * *

When Isabelle returned to the house, she stopped in the kitchen for a bite to eat, then went to her room to wash and change from her riding habit to a plain, brown wool dress. Under the dress she wore several petticoats but no hoops. Planning to go out again to the woods at nightfall, she wanted clothing that was old, warm, and inconspicuous.

On her way back downstairs, Isabelle passed the master bedroom and overheard Radley whining to Faye Samson. "But Ma," he drawled, "that weren't my fault. You's the one laid up. And now you're talking about some mighty hard work."

Isabelle had heard quite enough that afternoon of his nasal voice; she shuddered and hurried on back to the kitchen. There she spent the rest of the day, cleaning pewter and glassware with Ardyce, dusting the pantry shelves, then beating egg whites for the light omelets Auntie Pan planned for supper.

"How long's this Mr. Delahoussaye planning to stay?" the cook asked Isabelle.

"About a week, I think."

"Well, half a week's gone. And pretty soon we gonna have to go back to eating plain the way we been doing, taking

it easy on the portions if we're gonna get through winter,"
Auntie Pan said, vigorously chopping ham and cooked
potatoes into hash. "Hard times ain't good times for having
house guests, Miss Isabelle. I tries to stretch the vittles and
make something nice with next to nothing, but I can't keep
doing it forever."

"Don't worry, Auntie Pan. You've always been like
magic at the stove. Anything you cook is good."

"Thank you, miss. Sure 'nough, I can cook, and I can
brew remedies. But I don't claim magic. I leaves that to the
traiteuse little Miss 'Phrasie thinks so much of."

Ever since coming to live at Belle Ombre, Euphrasie
had been fascinated by the Cajun "magic woman" who camped
at the swamp's edge and made her living selling potions and
spells.

"That *traiteuse is* going to poison somebody one of
these days, if she hasn't already," said Isabelle.

"Ain't that the truth! Now let me see here. . ." Auntie
Pan laid out dishes on trays. "Supper in bed for Miss Faye.
Miss Euphrasie's 'posed to eat in her room. I got to feed
Radley in the kitchen, mistress's orders. So how many's left
for the dining room?"

"Five," said Isabelle. "I'll set the table."

In the dining room, Isabelle found Ardyce already
setting out condiments and napkins.

"Ardyce?"

"Yes, Miss Isabelle?"

"I've heard some talk, and I thought you might be able
to tell me if it's true. It's something about orders issued by
Uncle Charles Orvin." Isabelle sorted out the forks and knives
as she spoke. "I heard that Elroy Samson. . . well, that he
castrated Langford."

Ardyce shrugged. "Colonel Raveneaux gave that order
just before he left. We all knew about it."

Isabelle knew the "we" meant the slaves. "So Samson really did it," she said.

"That's not for me to say."

"But do you know? Is it possible Aunt Delora put a stop to it?"

"Might have, if she gave Mr. Samson more whiskey for not doing it than he got for taking the job. But he wanted to do it, orders or no. Mr. Samson wanted to be the only cock in the yard." Ardyce winced as if the thought of him could hurt her, then continued, the bitterness ebbing from her voice. "But you think about it, Miss Isabelle—would Langford take anything off Mr. Samson without a real good reason? Mr. Samson never was one to take on folks he couldn't whip."

Isabelle nodded. "We've shared a lot of secrets, Ardyce," she said, but even before finishing her sentence she doubted its truth. Maybe they had been open with one another in childhood. But as they reached young womanhood, Isabelle realized more often than not she had been the one to pour out her heart, and Ardyce had been the secret-keeper. There was always a difference between them that neither one had chosen.

"Ardyce, I don't want anyone else to know this, but I think it might be well for you to know."

Ardyce stopped folding a napkin and looked up. "What's that, miss?"

"Directly supper's over, I'm going out for a while," said Isabelle. "I have a feeling about something, and I want to find out if I'm right."

"You aren't going back to where you found the entrails, are you?"

"No, Ardyce. Just across the creek a little ways."

"I best come with you."

"No. I need you here in case someone asks for me during the evening. You can go up to my room, then come back and say I've fallen asleep. You know, put them off 'til I've had a chance to get back. Please, Ardyce."

Ardyce nodded. "But you better take care of yourself, Miss Isabelle. You hear?"

They had just laid the last place when Delora, Paul, Babcock, and Lydie Vee entered the dining room. Everyone seemed on edge during the meal. Lydie Vee was particularly stiff and taciturn, while her husband gobbled his meal and half of hers, gnashing his yellowed teeth and eyeing Delora with suspicion.

"Really, Uncle Babcock," Delora remarked, "you remind me of that old hog dog we used to have, looking at me as if you're afraid I'll snatch your plate away. Mr. Delahoussaye may get the impression my kin think I'm ungenerous."

Though his mouth was crammed with greens, Babcock attempted a garbled reply, but was mercifully stopped when Lydie Vee placed a hand on his shoulder.

Then only conversation of the most superficial kind interspersed the long silences. Even Delora, who was usually quite glib with her comments after a visit from Captain Newell, confined herself to weather speculations. Paul looked uneasy, fidgeting with his napkin, picking at his food, and glancing furtively at Isabelle. She pitied his discomfort, but could think of nothing safe to say. Domestic chores were not a social topic, and neither were her recent adventures: allowing Paul to take liberties, glimpsing a stranger at Halcyon, and finding entrails in the woods. The questions Isabelle wished to put to her aunt, such as how much longer they must endure Faye and Radley in the house or why Delora had sent Langford to town for letters that weren't delivered there, must wait for a private moment.

As they all rose to leave the table, Paul moved close to Isabelle. "May we talk?" he asked. "Alone?"

"Not now." She noted his crestfallen expression and added, "Later perhaps. I feel a headache coming on. Please excuse me."

Then Delora took Isabelle aside, whispering, "You look as if you're going to be unwell, and it's about that time." Delora kept careful track of Isabelle's and Euphrasie's cycles. "Don't worry about being sociable. I'll play a few tunes on the piano, and we'll pass the evening somehow."

"Thank you, aunt."

She departed, leaving Delora to charm Paul, and Babcock to grumble at Lydie Vee.

In case anyone might be watching her, Isabelle ascended the main staircase with a languor suggestive of an aching head, but soon after descended the back stairs with a gait to match her racing heart. She paused in the kitchen doorway; Auntie Pan, her broad back to Isabelle, was washing up dishes. Ardyce was scraping leftovers into the slops bucket. A hot skillet hissed loudly as the cook dipped it into the water, and Isabelle slipped past Auntie Pan and out the back door. She stopped again on the steps to survey the yard.

The only one out besides herself was Radley, standing some distance away by the tool shed door, a lantern at his feet, checking the lock, Isabelle assumed. She could circle around the shed, passing on the opposite side, and he wouldn't see her.

"That you, Ardyce?" Isabelle heard the cook call.

"Yes, ma'am," Ardyce replied loudly, "I'm still here. Just going out to make sure I latched the coop."

Ardyce stepped outside, and without a word, pulled Isabelle's folded mantle out from under her apron and thrust it into Isabelle's hands, then walked past to the hen house. Wrapping the dark mantle around her shoulders, Isabelle crossed the yard. She would thank Ardyce later for the warmth and secrecy her friend provided.

Years had passed since Isabelle had stolen away at night to meet Forest on the bridge over Lyre's Creek. Then sweet anticipation had guided her down the shadowy hill and into the black woods. Tonight she stumbled and wished for a lantern, though she didn't dare carry one. Clouds curtained off the stars, and senses other than sight guided her to the bridge.

Passing the spring house, she felt the night breeze and openness around her. She gathered up her skirts and descended the hill. As her feet slipped over the wet, grassy incline, she felt as if she would tumble forward into the dark, and she leaned back from the sensation, leg muscles tightening to brace her. Then the trees closed overhead and the earth turned spongy as she entered the holly bog. A barely perceptible lapping sound drew her to the creek bank. Isabelle was glad for the cold, remembering her terror one summer night when an alligator plopped itself into the water only a few feet from where she'd stood.

Slowly, Isabelle walked along the bank. The water was slate, but the opposite shore was pitch, and she could sense the distance across the creek widening. Realizing she was headed for the turn-around and not the bridge, she back-tracked, finding and gripping the bridge's weathered railing, sighing with relief though a splinter pricked her bare palm.

Isabelle hesitated, wishing now that Ardyce were with her. Then, pulling her mantle close around her, she crossed the bridge, passed the dead cottonwood tree, and climbed the hill to the ruins of Halcyon.

The last time she had come here was in summer to gather wildflowers. The drive and foundations had been overgrown with meadow beauties, and honeysuckle twining up the chimneys had sweetened the warm air. Now Isabelle breathed in the clinging damp and the odor of rotting weeds. But there was something else, too—the scent of wood smoke.

Isabelle drew nearer the ruins, reaching out to feel the cold brick of one towering chimney. Silently, she stepped around it into the place that had once been the dining room and turned in the direction of what had been the warming kitchen. Nothing was there except dark, empty space, but she remembered that just beyond was the cellar. Fire had long ago destroyed the wooden cellar doors, but the gaping entrance remained, and in the blackness of night, an orange glow rose up from it as if it were an open gate to the Underworld.

Flinching each time her shoes caused a rotten board to creak or a worn brick to crumble, shuddering each time her skirts rustled or snagged on debris, she inched forward until she reached the cellar doorway. The smoke rose to her, mingling with fumes of burnt bacon grease and the enduring odor of decay.

Isabelle knelt by the opening and looked down at the damaged cellar steps. She listened for sounds of movement and heard only a soft crackle, like the sound of crisp paper crushed in someone's hand, but she guessed it was the splintering of embers. Waiting for several minutes, Isabelle heard nothing more, except the blood pounding in her temples and her own shallow, fitful breathing. She gripped the remains of the door frame, digging her nails into the pulpy wood, and lowered her head to peer into the cellar.

The fire, burning in a circle of stones on the earthen floor, illuminated the nearby bits and pieces of a camp scene—a skillet of fried bacon, a tin cup, a rumpled bedroll—the things Isabelle had suspected she would find. She leaned down farther. Then, where the firelight barely reached, she discerned the toes of a man's boots. And when the fire briefly flared, she glimpsed the man himself backed against the wall, the whites of his eyes momentarily visible beneath the brim of his slouch hat.

Isabelle sat up, rolling back on her heels, and gulped the cold air. Of course she had expected to find a real man or evidence of the presence of a real man at Halcyon. Euphrasie had said a ghost couldn't cross running water, but Isabelle also knew a ghost had no need to steal food from the pantry at Belle Ombre. Somehow she had thought she'd find the man, see him, perhaps recognize him, and flee home again. That he would also see her had not seemed possible 'til now. Had she lived so long in her imagination that she'd forgotten her body must still walk with her mind and spirit? But now she felt that body suffocating in heavy folds of damp wool, and Isabelle was rooted to the earth with the weight of fear.

There were sounds from below. Step, drag, step, drag, step. He was coming, limping, to the cellar doorway. First his shadow, then his form darkened the entrance as he advanced up the creaking steps. She let go the remnant of door frame and drew back her hand. But he caught it in his own. His face was all shadow. Smoke and tears blinded her. Still, when he spoke, she knew him without seeing him.

"Don't go, Isabelle," he whispered. "Don't go."

Her legs felt weak, but she could move them again. She lowered her body over the edge, onto the steps. Forest Brodie, not his ghost, held tightly to both her wrists, steadying her, perhaps steadying himself, as they descended into the cellar. When they reached the earthen floor, he released her and stepped back.

Isabelle blinked away her tears, and her eyes were stung again by the acrid odors of smoke and decay. Had she entered the grave with him, the atmosphere could not have been more oppressive.

In silence, Isabelle stared at him, trying to comprehend his presence and the ghastly error that had been made. She had believed that if the man at Halcyon were anyone she knew, he must be her uncle, Charles Orvin Raveneaux. And yet finding her hair combs left with a wildflower by the cypress tree had made her tremble with the thought of this other strange possibility.

A body is swiftly and terribly changed after death, she knew; she had seen Elroy Samson's corpse three days after he died. Some other young colonel's body had been sent to Belle Ombre and mistaken for Forest's. Some mix-up in papers and records must have occurred. It must have—because Forest Brodie was here, alive, before her eyes.

Isabelle didn't know what to feel. All her years at Belle Ombre she had practiced controlling her emotions so that she would not become a temperamental burden to the relatives who had taken her in. Isabelle had faced the loss of Forest and quietly dealt with her grief. She had even gone so far as to speculate on plans for building a new life for herself as a governess in a city far from the plantation. But now, suddenly, she faced Forest's return and was caught and pulled down again into the ruins.

Forest took his shabby slouch hat from his head. His black hair, once thick and wavy, hung to his shoulders, greasy and lank. In his cheeks and around his eyes were hollows Isabelle had never seen before, and the wide red line of a scar ran from his left brow to his whiskered chin. His shoulders, though broader than she remembered, were stooped, and his arms hung crookedly as he leaned his weight on one leg. His gray coat and trousers were dirty, tattered, and as far as Isabelle could see, were devoid of any military insignia. Only his six remaining brass coat buttons with their pelican design disclosed that he had been a Louisiana soldier.

A tremor seemed to run through him, and then he spoke. "Good God, I never knew you'd grow up to be so beautiful. You take my breath away."

Forest turned from her toward the fire and brought to his face a scarred hand missing two fingers. Isabelle realized then that he was weeping. She reached out and touched his shoulder.

"Forest, why did you stay away from me? We buried a man, thinking he was you."

"I know," he answered without looking at her. "It could've been me. Should've been."

"No, don't say that. I've waited for you and wanted you home again no matter what." Silently, she recalled her vow made the night of his wake: if it were anything but death—if he were lamed, disfigured, driven mad by the horrors he had endured—she would still take him to her heart.

"You don't know what I've done," he whispered.

"I know you're alive," said Isabelle.

She came to stand close in front of him, near the firelight in the corner of the cellar he had made his camp. In the shadows a few yards away, Isabelle discerned a jumble of beams where part of the ceiling had collapsed, but the far side of the cellar was in utter, boundless darkness, as if it stretched on forever. Creatures must have died down here, she thought. The smoke and chill in the air barely blunted the fetid stench, but Isabelle overcame revulsion and breathed it in. She reached up her arms, encircling his neck. In the early years of the war, she had often imagined their reunion—the fierce embrace, the passionate kiss. She had not thought that when they met again she would pity him even more than she loved him.

"I stopped writing to you," he said softly.

"You had your reasons, I'm sure. You were on the move, you were wounded. Perhaps some of my letters to you went astray and you thought—"

"I ran away."

"Ran away?"

Forest bowed his head. Isabelle had never before seen him ashamed. In her memories of him he was always confident and sure. Now, though he seemed to want to shrink away from her, she kept her hands firmly on his shoulders. "How did it happen?" she asked gently.

"Fighting somewhere in Pennsylvania. I was hurt. Some Yankee laid my face open with his bayonet—and I fell in with a heap of the dead. Maybe I could've gotten up, kept on. I don't know. I just lay there as if I were dead, too. Night came, things quieted down, but I didn't go back to my men. Nobody came looking for me either. That was real peace. That was all I wanted."

"What did you do then? Where did you go?"

"I just got up in the dark and started walking. I reckon I had a fever off and on. I walked all the way to western Virginia. Walked at night, hid out during the day."

"And then?"

"I reached a hollow, and some folks who didn't give a damn about the war took me in. They were good to me, though I wasn't always much good to them." One corner of Forest's mouth lifted in the hint of a smile. "Did you ever picture me hoeing weeds in some dirt farmer's field?"

"And you stayed with them for what—two years?"

Forest nodded.

"You never wrote to me after that," she said, but left the reproach unspoken: two years of days and nights and no word from him.

"I deserted."

"But you're here now. Why did you come back, Forest?"

"Those folks—the ones in West Virginia—they said stay on, forget about home. And I would forget for a while, for days or weeks. But then . . . then I'd dream of you. You were calling me home. So I deserted them, too."

Isabelle came close to Forest and lightly kissed his cracked lips, then pressed her cheek against his breast. She recognized the pungent odor that clung to him; it was gangrene. She had smelled it before when tending wounded soldiers. The tremor again shuddered through his body and seemed to enter hers. In that moment, Isabelle resolved she would not question him further or force caution to prevail over compassion. She would not sob or cry out or recoil from his wounds. Tomorrow he might be under the surgeon's knife. Tomorrow she might mourn him again. But tonight, for some little space of time, she would comfort him and minister to his wounds, if he would let her.

Isabelle unfastened her mantle and dropped it behind her, then took Forest's hands and led him nearer the fire. A spasm of pain crossed his face as he knelt with her on the bedroll. But he acquiesced without a word as she removed first his old gray coat, then his newer handsewn shirt—not one of the shirts she had made for him, perhaps the work of some woman in Virginia. By the firelight, Isabelle looked at his body and with her fingertips touched the thick welts of scars on his shoulders and upper arms and across his rib cage. She remembered shirtless slaves in the fields with such scars not so different from these.

Forest lay back on the bedroll as Isabelle asked him to, but protested when she knelt at his feet to unlace his ill-fitting boots. "Leave them," he said in a harsh whisper.

"But Forest—"

"I don't take my boots off anymore," he said, then chanted: "All that walking home. Walking all the way home. Old wounds open. Boots grow to your feet."

Isabelle shuddered. She wondered how many of his toes he'd already lost and how many now were infected with gangrene, and if he would lose a foot or a leg or both legs.

She moved again to kneel by his head and brushed back the matted dark hair from his brow. She willed herself to become inured to the cold and damp, the smell of decay; she felt it, breathed it in, accepted it so it could no longer repel her. For a long while she looked into his face, and he stared up at her. Then his eyes clouded over and he turned his face to the fire. "I'll never see Isabelle," he murmured, "I'll never see Isabelle as my wife."

Isabelle lay her cheek against his, and he turned his face to kiss her mouth. His tongue tasted of musky brandy. "See me now," she whispered.

Then she lay down beside him, facing him, and touched his scarred cheek. This was as far as she knew, as far as she had let herself imagine. And it would be enough. Now he could see how she cared for him, how she accepted him as he was, how she forgave him his weakness and neglect.

But suddenly, a strangeness came over his face, and she no longer knew him. His damaged hands gripped her arms. The image she had cherished for years of their tender reunion was, in an instant, obliterated. Forest pulled her under him on the bedroll and pressed himself against her. She feared she might suffocate under the weight of his body as his mouth covered hers, seeming to suck the life from her. His boots bruised her shins as he tried to force her legs apart with his knees. This was no gentle holding of one another, no loving closeness—this was never what she had intended. And he never would have behaved in this brutal way, Isabelle told herself, if he had not gone to war.

With her fist against her mouth, stifling a scream, she forced herself to look up at his shadowy, contorted features, forced herself to listen to his rapid, labored breathing, then his sudden agonizing moan. Some awful pain, some injury must have seized him. And Isabelle used that moment to press her hands to his chest and, with all her strength, push him away. He collapsed beside her, shuddering.

Sickened and dizzy, Isabelle struggled to her knees, then to her feet. Forest turned on his side and stared into the fire.

She brought him his shirt and dropped it beside him. "You can't stay on here. You must come back with me to Belle Ombre," she said.

"No." He didn't look at her.

"But you must. Auntie Pan, Ardyce and I—we'll take care of you there."

"No," he repeated flatly.

Isabelle gazed down at him. "Forest."

His eyes widened, still staring into the fire. "Isabelle?" he whispered, then shut his eyes and murmured as though he were talking in his sleep: "Don't go, Isabelle. Don't go."

She spread his gray coat over his chest. "I'll come again in the morning." With Ardyce, she thought. "Rest now. I'll be here in the morning."

Forest remained motionless, and Isabelle left him. On trembling, aching legs, she climbed out of the cellar and stumbled ahead into the cold darkness.

* * *

At the Lyre's Creek bridge, she felt her knees buckle, and she clung to the railing. Then the composure she had regained was nearly lost again as someone ran toward her from the trees. But it was only Ardyce, crossing the bridge to her side and wrapping Isabelle's shoulders with a strong arm.

"You been gone a long time, Miss Isabelle. What in the world happened to you?"

"I've been to Halcyon. I've been in the cellar with Forest Brodie!"

Isabelle's own quavering voice sounded as strange to her as did her words. But perhaps, if she told Ardyce what had happened, the event would become real to her and she would believe it herself.

"Now hold on, miss." Ardyce took a firmer grip on her shoulders. "You telling me somebody dug him up and put him in the cellar?"

Isabelle shook her head. "No, Ardyce. The wrong man's buried in his grave. Forest is alive. Euphrasie hasn't been seeing a ghost on the lawn. It was him—coming up to the house, into the house, for food and drink. I've talked with him, Ardyce. I've touched him."

"Oh, Lord have mercy!"

"He wouldn't come back with me tonight. You can help me fetch him in the morning, after he's rested. He's. . . he's not himself, Ardyce. He's not quite right. And I think his feet are bad. He needs a doctor."

Isabelle suddenly felt light-headed and swayed in Ardyce's steadying arms.

"There now, Miss Isabelle. You scared sick? Did that man hurt you?"

"Oh, Ardyce. Just get me home, please." Isabelle's voice broke with a sob, and they said little more to each other as they covered the long distance home, Ardyce supporting Isabelle, dragging them both forward through the holly bog and woods and up the hill.

The rear of the house was dark, and they crept up the back stairs without being seen. Once in Isabelle's room, Ardyce lit a lamp and closed the door, then spoke: "Miss Isabelle, now you've had time to calm down a little, you still gonna tell me you was with Forest Brodie? You sure?"

"Yes, I'm sure."

"And who's in his grave? And what's he doing there?"

"A mistake was made," Isabelle said, hesitating to assign blame. "A dreadful mistake."

"Maybe. Beryl never saw Mr. Forest in life, but she told me that body was . . . well, it was pretty far gone. And she said when they was laying it out, Miss Delora was real heavy-handed, pouring brandy for them both."   A shiver passed over Isabelle, and Ardyce added, "I'll make up the fire, nice and hot."

Soon Isabelle was huddled in a quilt by the warming grate, while Ardyce moved about the room, laying out fresh garments and turning back the bed clothes, and tiptoed down and up the back stairs twice, bringing towels and buckets of warm water.

"You know, Miss Isabelle," Ardyce said, helping her off with her muddy dress, "you smell like the underside of a swamp, girl. We're going to have to wash your hair for sure, no matter how chilled you are."   Then Ardyce paused and stared at the grimy streaks on Isabelle's petticoat. She shook her head, then spoke sternly, "You better tell me right now what that man done to you."

What had he done? Isabelle asked herself. She couldn't call it love making, and she couldn't call it rape. At last, she answered, "He. . . he tried to . . ."

"Tried is all?"

"Yes."

"Lord have mercy!" Ardyce busied herself gathering up Isabelle's clothes, while Isabelle began washing herself in the tin basin by the fire.

"Since I started growing up," Isabelle said softly, "and with the War coming and all, I haven't been around many women who were happy with their husbands, really happy. I know there's some things folks don't discuss. But Aunt Delora's talked to me a little, and even she, who doesn't give up easily—"

"Amen," murmured Ardyce.

"Even she left me with the feeling that some things women just endure. I imagined it would be different for me. But now—I don't know."

"Being with a man can be all kinds of ways, Miss Isabelle, even with the same man. One day he loves you, one day he don't care, one day he's gone."

Ardyce had never said, but Isabelle guessed she had cared for a young field hand who had been sold off just at the outbreak of the War.

"I'm having pains," said Isabelle, wincing at a sudden tightening inside.

"Well, it's about your time." Ardyce handed her a folded hand towel.

Isabelle dressed in fresh camisole and pantalets, then lay on the hearth rug, leaning her head back over the basin. Ardyce poured a pitcher of water over her hair, then worked up a lather of lye soap.

"If I'd let him, would you disapprove of me, Ardyce?" Isabelle said, squinting as the suds stung her eyes.

"Ain't my place to disapprove. But some things are better put off 'til marriage, if you have any choice. And you know why."

"You could marry someday, Ardyce. Maybe someone you used to know, who's free now."

"First, I'm waiting to see what this so-called freedom means," Ardyce replied. "'Cause if I can't say yes or no to the man, and my babies ain't mine to keep and raise—well, I don't want no part of it."

"I'd miss you, if you married," said Isabelle.

"But I'd stay with you, if you married. Is that what you're still planning—to marry Mr. Forest?"

"Oh, Ardyce, I've wanted to be his wife for so long. Now he's come back, I'll keep my word, whatever else happens."

"Whatever else happens! Gracious, Miss Isabelle, folks been killed around here. You tell me Mr. Forest's not himself, and he's been sneaking 'round and in and out the house. How d'you know he didn't pitch Beryl down the airwell? Would you hitch yourself to a killer?"

"Oh, no." Isabelle shut her eyes tightly against the thought, and kept them closed against the onslaught of tepid water, while Ardyce rinsed her hair, then twisted it in a towel. "Ardyce," Isabelle said, turning to face her as they knelt by the hearth, "is that what you think, that Forest did these things? But *why* would he?"

"Would he need a reason, if he's gone and lost his mind?"

"But maybe he hasn't, Ardyce, at least not completely. Forest promised me in his letters that, if there were any way, he would come back if he could do me good. And he did come back."

"To do you good? Times change, Miss Isabelle. People change. Why didn't you hear from him sooner? Where's he been all this time? Why was some other man mistook for him?"

Isabelle told her the little she had learned from Forest. "I think he was ashamed to show himself, ashamed to face us."

"But not too 'shamed to try to take your maidenhead."

"Oh, Ardyce." Isabelle shivered.

Ardyce brought her a flannel nightgown and dropped it over her head. "Your pains still bad?"

"Yes."

"Get yourself into bed then, and keep your head wrapped. I'll bring you a cordial."

"Thank you, Ardyce."

Alone, Isabelle lay back on her soft mattress, under a heavy quilt. Turning her cheek to the smooth pillow, she inhaled the lingering scent of jasmine sachet. She thought of Forest in that dank cellar, suffering in his body, drifting in his mind, knowing her and not knowing her. What had she told Paul Delahoussaye the day after his arrival at Belle Ombre?

"Forest and I might not have got on so well after the War as we did before." Then on the Lyre's Creek bridge she had said the words: "I know my life didn't stop when he died."

Isabelle thought again of that last letter she had received from Forest. Had he really kept his promise, hovering in this world and delaying eternal rest, to do her good—or to spoil any hopes she might have cherished of a future with anyone else?

Tomorrow Forest must come to Belle Ombre, and what wounds of his that could be treated would be treated. Then Isabelle would keep her promise to marry him, honor it as she would a penance, and Aunt Delora and the rest of the household and Paul Delahoussaye need never know what had happened in the ruins of Halcyon.

But couldn't Delora look once at Isabelle's face and see the change in her? Perhaps not. Perhaps she would see only what she expected to see: her dutiful niece. After all, Delora had mistaken a stranger's corpse for Forest's body. And then—Isabelle's hand flew involuntarily to her throat—Delora had found a letter, written by Isabelle, folded in the dead man's breast pocket.

CHAPTER TWELVE

Late that night Paul sat up in bed, notebook on his knees, tired eyes straining to review his jottings. Between the midday and evening meals, he had interviewed Langford in the stable, but as Paul mulled over that conversation, he was still uncertain what he had learned. At first Langford had respectfully intimated that Paul could mind his own business. Then, when Paul in turn intimated that castration was a strong motive for murder, Langford opened up a little. He said Samson was even greedier than he was mean, and Langford had struck a bargain with him.

The scene gave Paul a cold sensation. Langford, stripped and tied to a tree in the holly bog, awaiting the knife, had somehow persuaded Samson to send his henchmen out of earshot. Then Paul could only imagine how Langford must have donned the mask of groveling humility before the loutish overseer. The result of the bargain, Paul learned from Langford, was that Samson received a double reward—from Colonel Raveneaux for doing the job and from Mrs. Raveneaux for not doing it. Also, Langford promised on pain of death to keep clear of the slave women, and Samson retained full bragging rights about the supposed gelding. Saving face, particularly before his son Radley, must have mattered deeply to Samson. Before he had untied Langford, he sliced the black man's inner thigh and insisted Langford cry out loud enough to be heard all the way to the big house.

Elroy Samson had been a hated man. When so many fine men had died on both sides in the War, what did it matter that a brute like Samson had met a violent end? If, for instance, Samson had surprised Arthur and Gerard Thibodeau while they were poaching, and they had struck him down in the bog—well, it was no more than the man deserved. But Beryl had also died violently, in the house itself. For that reason, and believing the two deaths were related, Paul ruled out the Thibodeau brothers as Samson's killers.

All Paul had heard against Beryl were hints that she drank too much and fornicated with the overseer, hardly shocking vices for a woman raised as chattel. Regardless of how little he knew of Beryl's character and how much he knew of Samson's, Paul could not ignore the brutality of their deaths. By the nature of these vicious acts, someone had set himself apart from humanity. And if that someone had found murder a convenient solution to a problem, might he not continue killing until all his problems were solved? Or until he were stopped?

Paul turned to a fresh page in his notebook. "Why does one person kill another?" he wrote. There was the motive of self-preservation, of course, and the necessity or excuse of following orders in wartime. Patriotism or the will of God were sometimes invoked. There were haphazard killings as when a brawler struck too hard a blow or a surprised thief panicked and silenced his witness. But what Paul sought were the causes of premeditated murder. As images flickered through his mind of the inhabitants of Belle Ombre, he scribbled hurriedly: "Hatred deeper than momentary anger; planned concealment of secrets or crimes; jealousy and greed, supposing the victims had something someone else wanted."

Paul thought of Euphrasie, who eavesdropped and spied and whose poisoned dessert he had consumed. Perhaps Beryl, working about the house all day, had garnered information, also, but took a fall when she tried to turn it to her advantage. Perhaps Samson had dug too deeply in Delora's earth or Delora's desk. Paul thought of Colonel Raveneaux's letters to Delora, letters that never arrived through the mail and always managed somehow to further Delora's position as mistress of the plantation. These letters favored Langford, also, and it seemed Delora depended on him far more than she did on Babcock or ever had on Samson. How many at Belle Ombre danced to her tune, Paul wondered, and how many hoped to see her miss a step?

By himself, when not directly caught in the circle of Delora's influential light, Paul was highly suspicious of her. But Isabelle's loyalty to her aunt frustrated Paul's attempts to cast Delora as Lady Macbeth for he had little or no sense of objectivity about Isabelle, whether in her presence or out of it.

Paul tapped his pencil point on the phrase "planned concealment of secrets or crimes." Perhaps someone had quarreled with Beryl by the airwell, then pushed her a little too hard. Then Samson, the witness, had been deliberately killed. But he had also been deliberately strung up and gutted—acts of a madman.

Thunder sounded like a canon volley over the roof. Paul pulled on his robe and went to the window. Lightning slashed the blue-black clouds and briefly lit the deserted yard. For a while, he watched for and listened to the pattern of swift lightning and ponderous thunder. The storm was putting on a great deal of show, but Paul wondered if there would be any rain behind it. Still, on the chance a downpour might follow, he wedged a hand towel into the cracked window casement.

A white spear of lightning flashed low over the out buildings, and for a moment Paul feared a roof had been struck. He peered out, glimpsing a momentary flicker of yellow light somewhere near the tool shed. Then the yard was dark again, and Paul focused on the reflection of his bedside candle, shivering in a corner of the windowpane. He turned toward the bed.

Euphrasie, in a white gown and shawl, waited there, kneeling on the counterpane, clinging to the bedpost, wavering as if the slightest draught would whisk her from the room. Paul sucked in his breath, but refrained from crying out in surprise just as Euphrasie put a finger to her lips. He looked to the door; she must have shut it behind her when she slipped in.

Taking a step toward her, Paul whispered, "Miss Euphrasie, what are you doing here?"

The girl shrugged. "I came to see how you was feeling, to see if what Isabelle said was true."

"What did Miss Isabelle say?"

"Well, you looked all right to me this morning, but Isabelle told me my bread pudding liked to a killed you yesterday. And I was kinda wondering . . ." Here Euphrasie paused to fidget with the edge of her shawl. "I wondered was sick all you felt after eating my pudding. Or did you have a little twinge of something else?"

Paul looked at her curiously. "Sick was all I remember feeling. Dizzy and sick. I'm glad you didn't eat the pudding."

"Oh, I didn't need to. I already have that . . . that sort of funny feeling you were supposed to get." Euphrasie released the bedpost and curled her legs under her as she sat on the corner of Paul's bed nearest where he stood. She continued, earnestly, "I don't know why it didn't happen, and Isabelle said we shouldn't say no more about it. But I like you so much, Mr. Delahoussaye, and I couldn't sleep without telling you I'm sorry you got sick. I'm sorry 'cause it's all my fault." She bowed her head, yellow hair falling across her face.

"Miss Euphrasie, are you trying to tell me you put something in that bread pudding? Something you meant me to eat?"

She nodded, and without looking up, whispered penitently, "I snuck off the other day to see the *traiteuse*. And I got a potion from her."

"What kind of potion?" Paul asked, fearing he already knew the answer.

Euphrasie sniffed loudly behind the curtain of hair. "Please don't be riled at me, Mr. Delahoussaye. It was a . . . a love potion. But it didn't work, did it?"

She pushed back her hair and looked up at him, hopefully. Paul didn't know what to say.

Euphrasie spoke again, softly, oblivious to the pain she caused him. "From things Isabelle said, I figured she wouldn't much care if you fancied me instead of her. And no matter what anybody says, you're lots better looking than Radley. You're lots better looking than a lot of men, even if there were more of them 'round here. I never had a real beau 'fore the War took the men away. I was too little. I just hid in the shadows and watched older girls like Isabelle dance and court and kiss. Mr. Delahoussaye, is anyone ever going to want me?"

Paul sank down on the edge of the bed beside her. "You're still very young, Miss Euphrasie. The War's over now. There'll be somebody for you one of these days, so don't you dare settle for Radley—or me—just because we're handy."

"I'm still sorry about the potion," she said, half smiling at him. "Sorry it didn't work."

Paul shook his head. "You are something. Here I've been worried somebody had tried to poison you and got me instead."

"Why would anyone poison me? I'm not rich and I'm not mean."

"Of course you're not. But maybe," Paul said gently, "you've heard or seen something that someone didn't want you to see or hear, maybe something on the night Beryl died and

Samson disappeared. What do you remember about that night?" Paul asked, hoping to gain something from their conversation other than Euphrasie's misplaced affection. "What did you do and see?"

"Well now, I disremember what I was doing before I came down to the dining room. But when I walked in, Aunt Delora and Lydie Vee and Uncle Babcock stopped talking and looked gloomy. Then Delora made a fuss 'cause I'd come down in my nightgown. She snatched me and one of the candelabras so fast I thought she was going to set me on fire. But she just yanked me out of the room and told me to go to Isabelle and spell her for a while. I knew what that meant—*sitting with the body*—and I didn't want to. But Aunt Delora dragged me halfway there and said I had to stop being useless."

"So you went in the back parlor?" Paul asked.

Euphrasie hesitated. "Hmmm. I might've straggled a little on the way."

"Did you see your aunt return to the dining room, or head for a staircase, perhaps?"

"I don't know what Aunt Delora did next. I just know I wasn't in any hurry to sit by a coffin."

"So what did you do?"

"First I kinda peeked around the parlor door. And I saw Mr. Samson acting ugly to Isabelle. Then, when he came stomping out, I plastered myself up against the wall like a swatted fly so he wouldn't see me."

"And he went up the back stairs?"

Euphrasie nodded. "To see Beryl, I reckon. Don't know why, exactly." She shrugged and let the shawl drop from her shoulders. "He'd already been with Beryl once that evening in the pantry. Radley knew 'cause he was in there eating some pie and had to crouch behind a shelf 'til they were finished. He told me it gave him the cramp and he was going to tell his mama why he didn't feel like hauling firewood. Aunt Delora says Radley's always got some excuse."

Amid her chatter, Euphrasie interjected her shocking comments with such apparent innocence that Paul wondered if she even understood the import of her words.

"I guess I fell asleep for a while in the back parlor with Isabelle," she continued. "Then I was really scared when she left me there—all alone with Forest's coffin. We'd heard a screaming and a clattering and Isabelle had gone to see what was the matter. Come to think of it, somebody ran past the door just before Isabelle went out."

"Did you see anyone?" Paul asked.

"No, the door was shut then, but it was somebody with heavy feet, like Mr. Samson, I reckon. Isabelle left the door open when she went out 'cause I asked her to. I was scared, like I said, and I hid under the bench by the hearth and shut my eyes. But here's the odd part. After Isabelle had been gone a minute or two, I heard something peculiar, Mr. Delahoussaye. I didn't dare open my eyes, but I heard something."

"What?"

"A whooshing sound." Euphrasie pursed her lips and repeated, "Whooshing! Right past the doorway. It came so fast it could have been that girl's soul blown clean out of her body. That's when I stopped up my ears and started singing." Euphrasie shivered and wriggled a little closer to Paul.

"Thank you for telling me all this, Miss Euphrasie," he said, "but now I think it best you get back to your own room before your great-uncle thinks I lured you in here and has me thrown out of the house."

"Oh, I can get around Uncle Babcock any old day." Euphrasie slid from the bed, her gown gathering up above her knees before falling again over her thin white legs as she stood. "Walk me back?"

"You can take my candle," said Paul.

"Please? I heard that *couchmal* moaning just before I came to you. And sometimes Forest Brodie's ghost roams around here, too." Euphrasie clapped her hands to her mouth, then let them fall to her sides. "I wasn't supposed to say that. Please don't tell Aunt Delora, not about Forest. Isabelle made me promise."

Paul didn't believe in ghosts and wondered if Isabelle really put any store in them. "Has your cousin seen Colonel Brodie's ghost?" he asked.

"Well, I've seen him, and I told Isabelle. At night on the lawn he limps out from between the live oaks and looks up at the house, looking for her."

"But has she seen him?"

Euphrasie giggled nervously. "Well, she thought she did. Thought she saw him one night, standing on the hill at Halcyon. You were there, too, but she said you were looking the wrong way. 'Course I told her it couldn't have been Forest she saw. Forest haunts this side of Lyre's Creek, and Isabelle had forgotten ghosts can't cross running water." Euphrasie paused, then cocked her head and added, "Maybe she saw Forest's third cousin, Waldo. Seems to me he was in the same regiment. Cut up something awful with a saber. He was buried at Halcyon before it burned. What do you think, Mr. Delahoussaye?"

"I think I'm too tired to think. And I will walk you back to your room."

As they proceeded down the hall, Paul tried to steady the candle in its holder while Euphrasie, her arm linked with his, cavorted on tiptoe, pulling him from side to side. Hot wax dripped on the back of his hand as he freed himself of his charge and sent her into her room alone.

On the way back to his own room, Paul heard again the rumble of thunder, this time followed by rain pelting the roof. Then ahead of him, he saw Ardyce starting down the back stairs, a bucket in each hand and a bundle of cloth bunched under one arm. Rather late for someone to be having a bath and a change of linen, mused Paul, wondering if Ardyce's day ever ended.

* * *

Seemingly moments after Paul fell into bed and shut his eyes, morning arrived, and with it Ardyce bearing towels and a pitcher of hot water. She looked tired, and her hands shook a little as she poured water into the basin.

"Is something troubling you, Ardyce?" Paul asked.

"No, sir," she replied without looking at him, and hurried away.

Downstairs in the dining room she was again on duty, silently filling the coffee cups. The family was gathered—Delora, Babcock, Lydie Vee, Isabelle, and Euphrasie—by the sideboard. Paul lined up behind Radley, who looked freshly scrubbed for a change and who, with unexpected graciousness, handed Paul a plate. Delora carried a small serving of fried grits to her place at the table. Babcock, after smothering biscuits and grits with gravy and making everyone else wait, lifted the cover of the bacon dish. In an instant, his plate crashed to the floor, shattering.

In unison, everyone at the sideboard gasped and recoiled, not for fear of being splattered by Babcock's gravy, but in horror at what he had revealed on the sideboard. The bacon platter was alive with a squirming mound of angler worms.

Euphrasie shrieked, and Paul immediately brought a protective arm around her shoulders. Then with his free hand, he grasped Isabelle's elbow and brought the two girls to the table where they dropped into their chairs. Turning again to the sideboard, Paul saw Babcock reel backward as Lydie Vee briskly clapped the cover over the worms.

"Well, I'll be," mumbled Radley. "Must've been a bad batch of pork."

Delora stood and surveyed the scene, with cold anger in her eyes. "Please remove that dish, Radley. And if you have any appetite left, you'd best eat in the kitchen with Auntie Pan."

"Don't mind if I do, ma'am," Radley answered back with a rakish confidence that surprised Paul, and he bore away the covered dish.

"Ardyce," Delora continued, unruffled, "coffee will be all for us this morning. You may go, too."

When the family and Paul were left alone in the dining room, Delora resumed her seat at the head of the table, opposite her sickly-faced uncle. She turned to Paul, who sat on her right. "Once again, Mr. Delahoussaye, we must beg your pardon for another affront to the senses."

"This is a nasty prank," snapped Lydie Vee, "and I'm not begging anyone's pardon until I know who's responsible for it." She shot a glance at Euphrasie, who raised the backs of her little white hands for everyone to see.

"My fingernails are clean," said Euphrasie. "And I'm still hungry."

"Then you may go to the kitchen," said Delora, and waited for her niece to leave before she spoke again. "I will deal later with whoever's taking pleasure in shocking our household. But I will say this: it is a serious mistake for anyone here to assume that all of God's human creatures share the same sensibilities." Delora looked at Paul. "Now, Mr. Delahoussaye, it occurs to me that your week with us will soon draw to a close. I'm sure we all mourn your imminent departure."

Paul looked to Isabelle in hopes she would show a sign of concurring with her aunt's statement. Lifting her wan face, she returned his gaze with sad eyes suffused with unshed tears.

Was this grave look offered for his "imminent departure," he wondered, or for his impending doom? He slipped a finger inside his stiff collar, attempting to alleviate a sudden feeling of constriction.

Delora cleared her throat. "I believe," she said, "that the unpleasantness around here has continued far too long and must be brought to a conclusion. When you've finished your coffee, Mr. Delahoussaye, I would like you, Uncle Babcock, and Lydie Vee to come with me to the study. Isabelle, you and I will talk later. Oh, and Faye Samson will join us, too. I hear tell she's much improved this morning. Then, once and for all, I think we can now resolve this problem of her husband's disappearance."

"Disappearance? But we're talking about murder, Mrs. Raveneaux," said Paul.

"And we're talking about more than Elroy Samson," Lydie Vee added.

Paul was struck with the impression that many things had changed over night. Isabelle looked more distressed than Paul had ever before seen her. Despite Lydie Vee's sharp remarks, Paul noted her furtive, almost anxious glances toward her husband, as if this time he were not under her control. Delora, on the other hand, and though rarely lacking self-assurance, was stronger than ever this morning. Finished with subtle maneuverings, she appeared set for confrontation—but she was not unchallenged.

Babcock, recovered from the sight of the worms, proclaimed loudly, "We are talking, Delora, about mendacity! Deception! Prevarication! We are talking about a white woman and a black man and a pack of trumped-up, farfetched, cock-and-bull lies!"

Delora drew in her breath. "Uncle Babcock, what in tarnation has come over you? Are you forgetting who runs Belle Ombre, forgetting who keeps it from washing away on a tide of musty liquor? Are you forgetting, sir, on which side your bread is buttered—and buttered—and buttered?" With each slathering of butter, Delora rose farther from her chair, as if her indignation would carry her through the ceiling.

"I'm not forgetting nothing! Not how my brother inherited Belle Ombre. Nor how you and your ne'r-do-well husband kept it when your daddy died. Nor how you played me for a fool these many years."

"If you're a fool, Uncle, it's no fault of mine."

"Babcock, calm yourself," Lydie Vee chided. "At this rate, you'll burst a vessel. Besides, Captain Newell and his men should be here any moment."

Babcock released his white-knuckled grip of the table edge, eased back in his chair, and nodded grimly. Paul noted Isabelle's stricken expression and watched Delora sink into her seat.

"What do you mean? Why would you know of his coming, when I was not informed? And what business, pray tell me, does Captain Newell have with us this morning?" Delora spoke softly, her hands clasped over her breast as if to slow a pounding there.

Babcock snorted. "Why, he's coming to perform the exhumation!"

"What!" Delora cried.

"You heard me, woman. If Forest Brodie's buried in that new-made grave—well, I'll be a donkey's ass."

Paul turned to Isabelle, but in that instant she had fled the room. And he heard only the rustle and whoosh of her hoop skirt as she vanished.

CHAPTER THIRTEEN

In the back parlor Isabelle clung to the mantelpiece, gasping for air. She longed for a knife to cut her laces. Before dawn, when the short-lived rainstorm had spent itself, Ardyce had gone to Halcyon with a flask of hot coffee and a blanket for Forest. She had insisted Isabelle stay in bed, saying they would go together later in the morning to fetch him to Belle Ombre. But just before breakfast, Ardyce had returned, bringing Isabelle news that the cellar was empty. Forest was gone.

Isabelle was furious with Uncle Babcock. Why must he interfere on this of all mornings? Forest Brodie could be roaming about anywhere. Perhaps he would even come limping up to his own graveside to witness this loathsome act of exhumation.

Of course Aunt Delora had made a mistake about the body. And if the mistake were intentional, Isabelle wanted to understand her aunt's reasons for it in private, not see her humiliated before a crowd. For Babcock Vasseur to invite Newell's participation in exposing family secrets was despicable.

"Miss Isabelle," Paul said, softly.

She slowed her breathing and brushed her cheek with the back of her hand before turning to face him. If only she could mask her feelings as Ardyce had so often done. Let Paul think the cause of her distress was the exhumation alone and not the certain knowledge that Forest was not dead, though likely dying, while wandering about, confused and ill.

Paul stepped through the doorway, his voice and furrowed brow expressive of concern. But was Isabelle being unfair when she thought she also detected in him an undercurrent of suppressed excitement?

"Captain Newell and his men have arrived. They're going out to the graveyard now with Mrs. Raveneaux. I understand this is all very difficult for you, Miss Isabelle. But when we know the truth, we can put things to rights."

A cramp seized Isabelle's insides, and she sank onto the hearth bench. "Some things can never be put right," she said. "Some things can never be mended."

"Then that's when we cut our losses and start again."

"You wouldn't say that if you knew what the losses were."

Paul dropped to his knees before her. "Miss Isabelle, I think this morning I finally understand how the murders were managed, if not why. Though why may become clear after the exhumation. I want—I need your help to prove it. You're the only one here I trust."

"And I don't know why you do," Isabelle whispered. Then with a voice that hardly seemed her own, she added, "If only the dead could stay dead."

Paul covered her hands with his. "Perhaps we can put them to rest with the truth. I think your Aunt Delora, with her love of playing with words and meanings, may actually have told me the truth when she said Beryl's and Samson's deaths had separate causes. But they aren't unrelated. It's my belief a woman killed the maidservant and a man killed the overseer. A woman and a man working together because they had something to conceal and something to gain."

Isabelle stiffened her back and pulled her hands free of Paul's. He rocked back on his heels and looked into her face, his expression earnest, his voice almost pleading. "We have to forget our prejudices and even suspend our loyalties if we're ever to understand what's happening here."

Isabelle narrowed her eyes at him for it was one way to keep herself from crying in protest.

"Now, just bear with me, Miss Isabelle, please. If Colonel Brodie is not in his grave, then we have to acknowledge that your aunt may have intentionally deceived you and the rest of your family. The servant, Beryl, helped lay out the body and may have known the truth and—given her intimate association with Elroy Samson—may have told him. Samson could also have known or suspected something wrong about those letters Langford brings Mrs. Raveneaux."

"You're accusing my aunt of murdering Beryl," Isabelle said coldly. "I won't believe that."

"Well." Paul rose and paced before the hearth, then stopped abruptly. "Maybe they argued out by the airwell. Beryl was drunk. Maybe your aunt gave her a push—accidentally—and over she went."

Isabelle shook her head. "When I came down the hall and saw Beryl's body, I also saw my aunt holding a candelabrum from the dining room. And all the rest of the household was with her."

"Miss Euphrasie told me Mrs. Raveneaux was carrying that candelabrum when she led your cousin from the dining room and sent her on her way to this back parlor. Who's to say your aunt didn't leave the light in the hall, then go upstairs instead of straight back to the dining room? When Miss Euphrasie was alone in here, she heard a sudden whooshing sound go by the open door. I think it may have been the kind of sound a lady's skirt makes when she's running, running as fast as you did this morning from the dining room."

"You think, you think!" Isabelle snapped. "Where's your proof, Mr. Delahoussaye? Has anyone who was in the dining room that night told you Aunt Delora absented herself long enough to run up two flights of stairs, commit murder, come whooshing back down, pick up a candelabrum, and discover the body?"

"All right, it sounds absurd put like that," said Paul. "But I plan to find out how long she left the dining room."

"Find out from whom? Uncle Babcock? He has more than a passing interest in discrediting Aunt Delora so he can take over Belle Ombre."

"There are other witnesses. And I'm asking for your help to time the running up and down stairs in a hoop skirt."

Isabelle clenched her hands. "And shall we step outside after that so I can bash you on the head with a shovel to see if someone in a crinoline had the strength to do in Mr. Samson?"

Paul looked momentarily surprised, smiled, then said, "Langford could have done that deed. No one saw him in the house the night of the wake. And it's very likely Samson was killed sometime on that same night as was Beryl. Each time I've tried to talk to Langford, I get a stronger feeling he's holding back something important."

"And what ever made you think he'd tell you his secrets?" asked Isabelle. "You're a white man and a stranger to him."

"That's part of it, maybe. But there's something else, too. I think a silence has been imposed on him by a woman," said Paul, "a woman for whom he has very strong feelings."

"Are you quite sure you're a journalist, Mr. Delahoussaye? This story you've concocted sounds like an installment of a romance in a ladies' quarterly."

"And you're the heroine, Miss Isabelle, prejudiced by love, refusing to admit you have been betrayed."

Isabelle thought of the love letter her aunt had returned to her, saying it had lain next to Forest's heart. Had, in fact, this particular letter never been posted, never reached Forest at all? Had Delora purposely kept it hidden among her own things on the chance she might find a use for it someday?

"The worst you know of my aunt is that she may have practiced some kind of deception," Isabelle said, more in an effort to convince herself than Paul.

"*May* have?"

"My Aunt Delora may not always act according to your code of honor, sir. But we are all guilty of one thing or another." Paul flinched as if stung by her words. "Mr. Delahoussaye, did you tell Uncle Babcock what you told me about your discovery in town—about Colonel Raveneaux's letters not passing through the post office?"

"Well, I was trying to sound out Mr. Vasseur on the possibility that Miss Delora's husband was closer to home than she'd led us to believe. But he jumped to the conclusion that Miss Delora writes herself those letters, and that she buried her husband in your fiancé's place. Of course, this may be all wild speculation."

Or it may be the truth, Isabelle thought. "Whatever it is," she said, "Uncle Babcock has obviously shared his ideas with Captain Newell. And now we are to have an exhumation."

"I feel responsible, Miss Isabelle."

"And you are, sir, at least in part."

"I am truly sorry," he said, his face as contrite and earnest as his words.

Forest Brodie had hurt her far more than had Paul Delahoussaye, yet she excused Forest and forgave him, though still unsure how much of his neglect of her was intentional. But then, she loved Forest, didn't she? Forest had attempted to invade her body, maddened by momentary lust, even if he didn't know her afterwards. And she forgave him. Paul had invaded her thoughts, reading her letters, insinuating himself into her confidence, into her life. He wanted to know her, he had said; perhaps he wanted to love her.

Paul's voice broke into her thoughts: "Will you ever forgive me, Miss Isabelle, for the pain I've caused you?"

From a constricted throat she whispered, "I might. If you give me time."

"Thank you."

His fleeting, hopeful smile touched her, and she was relieved that he apparently accepted her terms. When he came to sit beside her on the hearth bench, he maintained a few inches distance between them.

"You said you believe a woman and a man are working together," Isabelle said, returning businesslike to the topic of his investigation. "So you wouldn't consider a woman working her mischief alone?"

"I find it unlikely. Women are limited in taking action and often must rely on persuading men to take some actions for them."

Isabelle felt a flash of annoyance at his courteous tone. "And who limits us, sir, if not those very men who accuse us of manipulating them into action?"

"Begging your pardon, Miss Isabelle, but there are certain aspects of Elroy Samson's murder and mutilation that no lady, not even an exceptionally devious one, could—I mean to say—would choose to accomplish."

"Beyond the lace and frills, I've found ladies are often just as strong—and just as weak—as everyone else. I've been called a lady more than once, yet I know how to disembowel an animal. And I've buried a stillborn piglet and wept over it. We must all live with our contradictions and try to forgive them in others," said Isabelle, reminding herself of her resolve to be more lenient toward Paul, if only he didn't provoke her.

"You could forgive murder?" Paul asked.

"Oh, I don't know," Isabelle cried, a sudden sob catching in her throat. "But need it always be in your mind my Aunt Delora and Langford who did these awful things? Why not suspect someone else, anyone else? Lydie Vee and Uncle Babcock? Euphrasie and Radley? Or perhaps myself and a secret accomplice?"

Paul hesitated a moment, then said, "There could be someone else. Someone nobody's told me about."

Isabelle hid her face behind her hands. All of it—the killings, ransacking, gutting, even the worms—could have been the work of someone else, someone whose mind had been dreadfully altered, someone who haunted Belle Ombre, but was not dead.

"You rest here," Paul said gently. "I'll go to the cemetery. If everything is as Mrs. Raveneaux says, then I can only beg your pardon and try again."

"We'll go there together," said Isabelle.

"Are you sure?"

"Yes. I should be with Aunt Delora."

On the way from the house Paul tried to dissuade her again, but Isabelle reminded him she was not some faint-hearted girl to be locked in her room like Euphrasie.

Approaching the graveyard, Isabelle saw four Union soldiers, wielding shovels, their boots mired in mud. Their work was overseen by Captain Newell and Babcock, both furiously puffing on cigars as if the odor of tobacco could mask the stench of decay. Lydie Vee, Faye Samson and her son gathered by the wrought iron gate. But Delora stood apart from them, just within the rail, silent as a monument, looking at no one, responding to nothing.

Lydie Vee addressed Paul in a low voice, "The graves were a mess this morning after the rain. The gate was left open, and the hogs were in here, rooting all over the place for the last of the acorns."

Radley nodded. "Them hogs is crazy for acorns."

"Fortunately," Lydie Vee continued, "Newell's men just ran the beasts off instead of shooting at them. For a minute or two, I feared for old Priapus. He looked fit to charge at the Captain, but backed down in time."

Isabelle was relieved that Lydie Vee chose to speak to Paul and not herself. She'd never been particularly close to Lydie Vee, but had always admired her for her fairness and her ideals. While it was easy enough for Isabelle to feel anger toward Babcock, she was discomforted to feel it toward his wife, who apparently had known of and approved the exhumation instigated by her meddling husband.

Isabelle turned to Radley, who dutifully held his mother's arm. Faye, in her best black dress and mantle, looking gaunt and hollow-eyed, clung to the boy and watched the proceedings with feverish excitement.

"Radley," said Isabelle, "you shouldn't have brought your mother out in this weather. The cold and damp can only do her harm."

"Harm's what those remedies of Auntie Pan's do me," muttered Faye.

Radley's lip curled over his chipped tooth as he drawled, "Ma's feeling better now, though, and I don't want her to miss the big doings."

Isabelle turned away from them, her eyes searching the surrounding woods for a glimpse of Forest Brodie. With one gloved hand tapping each spear point of the wrought iron fence, Isabelle followed the outside boundary of the little cemetery until she reached the gnarled roots of the live oak and stopped.

Just on the other side of the fence, Newell's men had completed their excavation. The tallest among them, a sergeant, stabbed his shovel into the newly made mound of wet soil and humus. They were ordinary men; Isabelle observed nothing particularly hateful about them. Just ordinary men who had fought beside each other and against other ordinary men. The thinnest and oldest one leaned on his shovel, panting and wheezing, his complexion sickly, perhaps from the after-effects of tainted pork combined with heavy labor. Two were hardly more than boys, one of whom darted a glance toward Newell before offering Isabelle a quick, bold smile. The sergeant with red scarred hands uncoiled a length of rope. He was handsome, Isabelle thought, in a heavy-browed, strong-featured way, and should have been in his prime except that one leg had been replaced by a stump of wood.

"Give us another few minutes, miss, and we'll have you out of mourning for your colonel," Captain Newell called out to Isabelle.

The boy who had smiled at her dropped himself down into the hole to work the ropes under the coffin. Isabelle heard his boots thud on the coffin lid. He called for a spade and toiled out of her sight some time before his head and shoulders reappeared.

"Must the thing be raised?" asked Babcock. "Couldn't you just pry it open down there and see what you find."

"Oh, no," said the captain. "We'll have that box up here where we can all see the contents. I may need your help in making an identification, Mr. Vasseur."

Babcock's eyes bulged as he was suddenly seized with a great fit of snorting and hacking. Lydie Vee came forth to pound his back.

With the ropes in place, the four soldiers began to hoist the coffin from the earth. Paul left Faye and Radley by the gate and moved toward Isabelle, outside the fence. Delora, within the enclosure but apart from the others, cut her eyes from face to face, at last resting her gaze on Isabelle. And Isabelle felt a coldness creep over her, certain that the mind behind those amber eyes was busily spinning and weaving yet another lie.

Clods of mud fell away from the coffin as it rose. Two soldiers, gripping the ropes, stepped forward, two stepped back, and the coffin dropped to the ground just at the edge of the hole. A hollow groan escaped the old man. The two boys rubbed their rope-burned hands. The soldier with the wooden leg bent his back awkwardly as if it pained him and ran the claw end of a hammer under the rim of the coffin lid.

It seemed then to Isabelle that everyone in unison took a deep breath and held it. But they were forced to exhale and breathe again when Captain Newell ordered, "Hold a minute, Sergeant." Isabelle, along with everyone else, turned her eyes to the approaching men who had caught Newell's attention.

Two soldiers advanced through the grove, roughly pulling Langford between them. They stopped near the cemetery fence, released their grip on Langford, and saluted the captain, who then demanded an explanation.

Langford reeked of wood smoke, and Isabelle noted his mahogany face was smeared with black mud and ash. In one hand he clutched a rib bone.

"We were taking a look around like you told us, sir, and found him by the creek, damping down a bonfire," one private reported with the eager tone of the overly ambitious.

The other private, not to be outdone, grabbed Langford's arm and waved it and the rib bone Langford held, saying, "He was stirring the ashes with this, sir. And there's more bones lying in the cinders."

Delora gathered her hem above the muddy ground and swept to Newell's side. "Captain, I'm sure Langford was only burning rubbish, far from the house for safety's sake. Isn't that right, Langford?"

Isabelle watched Delora and Langford exchange a long look before he answered.

"Well, not exactly, Miss Del."

"I should say not exactly," said Newell, snatching the rib bone. "What were you up to, Langford?"

"I'm sure. . ." Delora began, but the captain stopped her, snarling, "You let your nigger man answer for himself."

Delora trembled, but Langford spoke evenly, his face a mask. "I was burning some rubbish, sir, like Miss Delora says. But I was charring and grinding bones, too. Auntie Pan needs 'em for her influenza remedies. Winter's coming on. Influenza gonna be bad."

"And just where do these bones come from?" said Newell, shaking the rib in Langford's face.

Langford didn't blink an eye. "That one there come from the side of a hog, sir."

"You folks got a witch for a cook," Newell muttered, tossing the rib to the ground.

He instructed the two privates to watch Langford, then turned his attention back to the sergeant. "All right. Open it up!"

The claw of the hammer ripped into the pine lid, splintering the edge as the first nail was pried loose. Isabelle felt Paul's arm close around her shoulders, and she didn't resist his offer of support. The wood of the coffin was already darkened and discolored from days in the wet earth. Isabelle had not remembered so many nails, some of them bent and rusty, as well as wooden pegs, and though the sergeant worked quickly, it was many minutes before he finished his task.

Newell instructed the two young soldiers to remove the lid, but even as he snapped the order, they hesitated. Babcock, covering his nose and mouth with a handkerchief, moved closer, followed by Lydie Vee. Radley led his mother in for a clear view. Delora moved a step nearer to Langford. But Isabelle, Paul by her side, stayed where she was, outside the fence and just out of range to see the corpse as it was revealed.

The soldiers lifted the lid and moved aside with it. The smell of death rose up, swirling like a fog around the living gathered in the cemetery. Still, Isabelle would not look in the coffin. Instead, she watched her aunt, who stared into the pine box, then reached a hand toward Langford, but let it fall without touching him. Babcock, eyes bulging, tottered and stumbled back. "God Almighty!" he cried as Lydie Vee braced to keep him from toppling over. By contrast, Radley and Faye Samson behaved with dignified reverence, gazing solemnly at the remains.

Then Radley cleared his throat and said slowly, "Now ain't you 'shamed, Captain Newell—disturbing Colonel Brodie's eternal rest."

Isabelle's heart froze in her breast. Tearing free of Paul's restraining hands, she lunged forward, nearly impaling herself on the spears of the iron fence. She saw the body in a tattered gray uniform, the face waxen and lifeless. Forest lay in the coffin.

Darkness surrounded Isabelle's field of vision until Forest's face was all she could see, like a point of light at the end of a tunnel. His eyes were closed, the lids swollen and purple-veined. The thin line of his lips, the deep scar on his cheek were mauve against ashy whiteness. The point of light contracted and disappeared. Isabelle swayed backward and fell, as if a pit opening in the earth had swallowed her.

CHAPTER FOURTEEN

Paul stumbled forward as Isabelle fell back limp against him. Her head and shoulders struck his chest, and he dropped to his knees, catching her awkwardly in his arms. Regaining his balance, he eased her down, cradling her upper body with one arm and, with his free hand, drawing back the hood of her cloak that half covered her face. She moaned as if she were lost in a nightmare and unable to wake.

Paul looked up, holding Isabelle more tightly to shield her, unconscious though she was, from those closing in about them. The soldiers rushed to the fence, one young private eagerly offering Paul his folding knife and suggesting Isabelle be cut free of her corset laces. The Samsons, mother and son, came to peer at the latest source of excitement, Radley gallantly offering to help Paul carry Isabelle to the house. "I'll take her feet," he said, but his mother continued to grip his arm for her own support.

Paul didn't move, but looked to Delora, standing now by the captain, speaking to him as if she were the commanding officer.

"Naturally, Isabelle fainted, sir. What did you expect her to do? You have exhumed the body of her beloved and callously exposed his remains to her innocent eyes. Were not your acts of war brutal enough for you, but you must come here to our peaceful home and torment us still? You are heartless, Captain Newell. You stand here before me, living and breathing, and yet you have no heart!"

Newell, only slightly daunted, called out to Babcock, "All right, Mr. Vasseur, what's the meaning of this? Is Colonel Raveneaux in that box or isn't he?"

"Charles Orvin!" Delora cried with incredulous indignation. "Why, you've seen my husband's portrait in the dining room, Captain. This is obviously not Charles Orvin."

Babcock took a hesitant step forward, a second look in the coffin, and spoke into his handkerchief. "It's Forest Brodie, sir. I don't know how or why, but it's Forest Brodie, sure 'nough."

"So that's settled, Uncle Babcock," said Delora. "Now, Captain, kindly have your men put the body back where it belongs."

Isabelle, regaining consciousness, turned her face against Paul's chest and wept. He rocked her gently, stroking her hair, but kept a watch on her aunt.

"Just hold on a minute, Miss Delora," said Newell, grasping her arm and forcing her to turn with him toward the open coffin. "You told me Brodie had been dead for weeks when his corpse was transported here. And you people buried him a week ago. Look at him, ma'am. Take a good, long look. Then you tell me—how come anybody can recognize him after he's been dead that long?"

Isabelle's sobs were muffled in the folds of Paul's coat, and for a long moment not another sound was heard in the graveyard.

Then Delora wrenched her arm free of Newell's grip, lifted her chin, and replied in a clear voice for all to hear: "Captain, what you see here is a miracle of science. The generous folk who sent Colonel Brodie's remains back to his homeland for burial saw to it first that he was properly prepared for the journey. His pure and beautiful visage is brought to us through the wonders of the embalmer's art."

At this, Radley whistled and was shushed by his mother.

Babcock spluttered into his handkerchief, and Lydie Vee admonished him, "Oh, pull yourself together, Babbie," before abandoning him to Newell's glare. "And will someone please put the lid back on that coffin before we all succumb?" she added, then left the enclosure of the graveyard and approached Paul, urging him to take Isabelle away.

When Paul lifted Isabelle from the ground, she wrapped her arms around his shoulders, and he could feel the warmth of her uneven breath on his neck. Taking swift, long strides, he carried her toward the big house without ever having seen for himself the remains in the coffin.

Ardyce, who was sweeping the steps of the veranda, tossed aside her broom and ran to meet Paul. Together they helped Isabelle to the front parlor. Then Ardyce busied herself removing Isabelle's cloak, arranging cushions, settling Isabelle on the green brocade sofa, and making up the fire. Paul stood by, staring down at his muddy boots that had tracked the moss-colored carpet.

"My suspicions were wrong, Miss Isabelle," he began. "I beg you to forgive me."

Ardyce stared at Paul and asked sharply. "What happened out yonder?"

"Miss Isabelle fainted—quite naturally—after seeing the remains of her fiancé. I'm responsible. If I'd never mentioned my doubts about who was buried there to Mr. Vasseur, none of this would have happened."

Ardyce knelt by the sofa and looked to Isabelle. "What is he going on about, miss?"

"Forest was in the coffin," Isabelle whispered. "I saw him."

"Dead?"

"Yes."

"But Miss Isabelle, what was in that coffin couldn't have been more than a rack of bones."

Paul was bewildered by their exchange of words.

"I saw him, Ardyce. Everyone saw him."

"You, too, sir?" Ardyce asked Paul.

"No. No, actually I didn't. But everyone else did. Mrs. Raveneaux, the Vasseurs, Mrs. Samson and her son—all agreed they saw Colonel Brodie's remains."

Ardyce straightened up and stood before Paul. "When Miss Isabelle tells me something is so, it's so. I'm not doubting her word, you understand. But something ain't right here. Sir, I think you better get back to the cemetery now and take a good look at that body."

"Is that what you want me to do, Miss Isabelle?"

She nodded. "Yes. I want to know how Forest got there. You see, Mr. Delahoussaye, I fainted not because I saw him, but because I was not expecting to see him."

"What!"

"I'll explain later. You must hurry—the soldiers might already be lowering the coffin back into the ground. Go with him, Ardyce. Both of you go."

"Only if you promise to stay put on this here sofa."

"Yes, Ardyce."

Paul and Ardyce ran toward the family cemetery, abandoning the path and veering among the pecan trees, leaping rain filled holes left from Elroy Samson's treasure hunting. Breathless and panting, they arrived just as the one-legged soldier had finished driving the last nail into the coffin lid.

Captain Newell and Delora faced each other in stony silence. Babcock and Lydie Vee were walking away toward the house, Babcock quivering like a mound of aspic. Langford stood between the two soldiers who had brought him to the graveyard, and his face was no longer quite such an impassive mask. He looked with some interest at Radley, who yawned and shuffled at his mother's side.

Paul caught his breath and spoke. "Captain Newell, sir, I've not yet seen the corpse."

"Well, ain't that a pity," said Newell. "But I'm sure this lady can tell you all about what you missed. Damned if I'm not right, Miss Delora."

She turned her face away.

"I must see the body," Paul insisted.

The sergeant sighed impatiently and set the hammer on the coffin lid with a defiant thud. "Didn't you see enough dead men during the War?" he said to Paul.

Newell sneered. "No, I'm afraid he didn't, Sergeant. Mr. Delahoussaye wasn't much of a fighter. He preferred to record other men's brave deeds."

"With your permission, sir, and Mrs. Raveneaux's, I could open the lid myself and nail it shut. I don't wish to inconvenience anyone, but I must look inside the coffin," said Paul. "Miss Ross was so overcome, she could hardly believe her eyes. She asked me and Ardyce to confirm what she saw."

Newell smoothed his mustache as he spoke. "And she trusts your report over her kinfolks' word? Now that's interesting. 'Specially considering you never saw her fiancé when he was alive."

Ardyce briefly touched Paul's sleeve as if to encourage him to persist.

"As a disinterested observer," Paul said, "I can describe the body to her and let Miss Ross draw her own conclusions."

The captain glanced around at the assembly. His soldiers shifted restlessly.

"I think we're about through here today, men. Let the reporter have his peek and then get this box in the ground. I'm going up to the house for a word with Mr. Vasseur and," Newell took Delora's arm, "for whatever my hostess may offer me."

Paul picked up the hammer and began work prying the lid open as Newell instructed his men to let Langford go about his business. "For now," the captain emphasized, moving away with an unusually silent Delora in tow. Langford didn't move. Radley and Faye stood on the sidelines while Paul worked, but Ardyce was near him, ready to assist in lifting the lid.

"This pulpy wood's going to pieces after all the hammering and prying," Ardyce said, holding a split corner together as Paul dug the hammer claw under its edge.

"I wonder what good's this embalming when there's still such an odor," said Paul.

"Whew-whee! Something's ripe," put in Radley.

"Hush up," Faye snapped.

Together, Paul and Ardyce lifted the lid, Paul holding his breath. The body inside was that of a young man, close in age to Paul, scarred in battle and shrunken in death so that his shabby, dirty uniform seemed to swallow his remains. A wave of black hair lay across the stark white brow, and Paul was struck by the fineness of the skin on the once handsome face.

Ardyce knelt by the coffin and rubbed a fallen leaf between her palms.

"What's that girl up to?" asked the sergeant.

"Ardyce?" said Paul.

"It's a charm, sir. We done disturbed his rest, and we don't want him disturbing ours."

Carefully, she unbuttoned Forest's coat, barely opening it, moving her hands under the cloth and arranging the bits of leaf. She leaned far over the corpse, murmuring something incomprehensible, then rolled back on her heels. "Colonel Brodie's ready to go back to earth," she announced.

Langford approached Paul beside the grave. "I'll nail the box shut, sir. You go on back to the house."

Gratefully, Paul nodded and walked away, followed by Ardyce. When he had outdistanced the stench and could no longer hear the grumbling of the soldiers, Ardyce caught up beside him.

"Was the body really Colonel Brodie's?" he asked her.

"Yes, sir," she said, then dropped her voice to a whisper. "Slow up, sir. Let Miss Faye and her boy pass us up."

Paul glanced over his shoulder to see Faye and Radley coming down the path from the cemetery. He slowed his pace as they came abreast and nodded to Faye.

"It's been a trying morning, Mrs. Samson," he said. "I hope your son will see you safely out of this damp weather."

Faye cut her eyes toward him. "My son will see me safely out of this rotten pit in God's earth."

Radley sucked his broken tooth as he and his mother moved past Paul and Ardyce.

Ardyce shook her head in disgust. "Auntie Pan always says if she fried Radley for a fool, she'd be wasting the fat."

Paul smiled at her, hopeful that her recent actions and remarks signaled her willingness to put some trust in him. "What was all that about the dead disturbing our rest, Ardyce? Do you believe in ghosts?"

"I don't know, sir. Nothing I can do about 'em."

"But back there you worked some sort of charm over the corpse."

"Oh, that." Ardyce shrugged and kept walking. "I just wanted a close look at the body."

"Why?" Paul asked.

"No offense, sir, but I don't want to say no more 'til we reach Miss Isabelle."

"Ardyce, does this mean you'll trust me to help your mistress—and you?"

"You're straighter than some 'round here, sir."

They entered the house through the front door, Paul stopping to wipe his boots on the mat before going on to the front parlor. Ardyce said she would fetch a hot drink for Isabelle and join them soon.

But Isabelle was not in the front parlor. Captain Newell sat on the brocade sofa, Delora at his side refilling his brandy snifter.

"Oh, I beg your pardon," said Paul.

"Not at all, Mr. Delahoussaye. Do come in and join us," urged Delora.

Newell was not so welcoming. "If you're looking to file your report with the melancholy Miss Isabelle, she said she was retiring to the back parlor."

"Thank you, sir."

"But don't rush off, Mr. Delahoussaye," said Delora, rising from the sofa and thus forcing the captain reluctantly to his feet. Delora slipped around him and advanced toward Paul. "I was just telling Captain Newell about how unfortunate family differences were at the heart of today's spectacle. He understands that my uncle has long coveted my husband's estate, and envy alone led to these wild accusations." Delora glided to the doorway.

"But, Miss Delora," said Newell, "I don't believe we've quite concluded our discussion."

"We simply must resume at another time, sir," she replied with the carefully controlled smile Paul had seen her offer Newell on other occasions. She continued walking and speaking, Newell trailing after her into the front hall. "I feel in such a dither after the goings-on this morning. And I must have a word with Radley about bringing his mama out to the cemetery. She's been poorly, but now she looks at death's door." An exaggeration, Paul wondered, or a prediction? "I'll just go see if she's collapsed," Delora continued, ascending the stairs, then called down, "Of course you'll come again, Captain Newell, under happier circumstances," before she disappeared.

Newell replaced his hat on his sleek black hair, glowered at Paul, and left the house. Paul hurried toward the back parlor, meeting Ardyce in the hallway. She carried a steaming cup of something dark and sweet-scented, and he opened the door for her.

Inside, Isabelle paced the frayed, faded blue rug before the hearth.

"Here, Miss Isabelle," said Ardyce. "I fixed you some sloe cordial tea."

"Thank you, Ardyce."

The two young women sat together on the bench, and Paul drew up a ladder-back chair. Isabelle sipped the tea as Ardyce spoke.

"Your eyes weren't fooling you, Miss Isabelle. Colonel Forest Brodie's remains is in that coffin."

Isabelle set the cup in the saucer with a sharp clink. "But I saw him alive last night at the ruins of Halcyon," she said. "I more than saw him, Ardyce. You believe that?"

"I believes you, miss. But the body I saw in the coffin was the image of Mr. Forest, and it ain't been long dead."

Despite the chill in the room, Paul felt a strange heat suffuse his face and neck as he stared at Isabelle and Ardyce.

"Euphrasie claimed she saw Forest's ghost haunting the lawn," said Isabelle. "But it wasn't his spirit that came at night to take food from the pantry and the smokehouse. He was living in the old cellar at Halcyon." She looked at Paul. "I suspected someone was holed up there when I saw the silhouette of a man on the hill the night you and I crossed Lyre's Creek. Then, that day in the clearing, when you asked me to show you what I'd picked up and put in my pocket, I showed you the flower. But I didn't show you my hair combs—the ones I'd lost. He must have left them for me to find by our old meeting place."

"How can this be so?" murmured Paul.

"It just is," she said wearily, as if her emotions were spent. "I realize now your suspicions were well-founded, Mr. Delahoussaye. Aunt Delora was deceiving me, deceiving us all. After she and Beryl, in secret, laid out the body sent here, she handed me a letter I'd written to Forest in May of '64. She must never have posted it, but kept it by, one day to make such a use of it."

Isabelle drained her cup, and Ardyce took it from her, setting it aside.

"Last night," continued Isabelle, with a slight catch in her voice, "I learned from Forest that he'd deserted and lived in hiding in western Virginia the last part of the War. He was sadly broken down, and so ill. If only I'd brought him here last night, if only I hadn't left him."

Ardyce took Isabelle's hands in hers. "I thank the Lord you were safe home without him," said Ardyce. "I don't know how his body got in that coffin, Miss Isabelle. But I do know this—Colonel Brodie didn't die of no old war wounds or sickness. Last night he was murdered."

"How do you know?" Paul and Isabelle asked in unison.

"Mr. Delahoussaye saw me bending over the body, pretending to do some charm for the dead. Some white folks are only too willing to believe we're up to some voodoo," said Ardyce. "But what I really did was look under that gray coat. And what I saw—well, I'll swear he was done in."

"Tell me everything, Ardyce. I need to know," said Isabelle.

"You sure?"

"Yes. Paul and I both need to know."

It was the first time Isabelle had referred to him by his given name, and Paul noted it, even as he waited anxiously for Ardyce to answer her mistress.

"Under his coat, just below his ribs," Ardyce said, placing her hands upon her waist, "he was all stove in. Near cut in two."

Isabelle winced.

"By a sword, do you think?" asked Paul.

"No, sir. By something broad, sure 'nough, but more blunt somehow than a sword or a cleaver. His coat must've been open or he wasn't wearing it when he was hit. I'm thinking it might've been the broad blade of a shovel driven straight in under his ribs—bringing part of his shirt into the wound without necessarily cutting the cloth all the way through."

Paul looked at Isabelle; she was pale, but composed.

"Perhaps," she said, "Forest surprised a grave robber."

"Who then killed him and put his body in the coffin that we've already been told he was buried in," said Paul. "That still leaves the questions: who killed Forest Brodie, whose body was buried at Belle Ombre a week ago, and where is that body now?"

"Uncle Babcock and Lydie Vee knew before any of us that the soldiers were coming today for the exhumation," said Isabelle. "And I think they were genuinely expecting Uncle Charles Orvin's body to be revealed. I think I was expecting it, too."

"Even your Aunt Delora seemed taken aback when the lid came off," Paul said. "Of course, she quickly recovered with that story about embalming."

"Miss Delora sure didn't say nothing about embalming when Langford brought that other body from town."

"That's right, Ardyce. Aunt Delora said the body was horribly changed and I shouldn't look on it. And Auntie Pan said Beryl deserved to get drunk after helping with that laying out," said Isabelle. "But why would someone dig that body up and where is it now?"

Paul leaned forward in his chair. "Suppose, and this is just a possibility, suppose that Forest Brodie was killed before the grave was disturbed. Then the murderer dug up the coffin and switched the bodies. That, of course, would mean the murderer knew who he was killing and knew an impostor lay in Colonel Brodie's grave."

"It's a dreadful thought, but I've wondered if Forest could have killed Beryl and Elroy Samson. Somehow, it seems less likely now. . . now that Forest is a victim of murder himself. Unless. . . ." Isabelle let her sentence trail away.

"Well, there's this mystery about the other body," said Paul. "Given how busy the killer must have been last night, digging and burying, chances are he couldn't have taken the corpse very far. It might be in a shallow grave somewhere in the woods."

"Then the hogs'll sniff it out," put in Ardyce.

"The hogs, yes. Lydie Vee told me they were loose in the cemetery this morning, trampling the graves." Paul remembered how Isabelle had discovered the entrails in the holly bog when the hogs rooted them up. Then a thought struck him of hog bones and human ones and something he'd learned as boy on his grandparent's farm. His grandfather was fond of saying: "Lay a hog carcass on its back, and you'll find its innards arranged just like a man's—hard to tell the difference." Man's oneness with Nature, Paul mused; and a piece of a man's rib might pass for a hog's.

Paul jumped up, nearly overturning his chair. Catching the ladder-back and gripping it, he stared at Ardyce. "You said you played on white folks' notions about voodoo. Couldn't Langford have done the same? He told Captain Newell he was burning rubbish and grinding hog bones for Auntie Pan's influenza remedies. Does she use ground bone? And even if she does, who's to say he wasn't burning a man's corpse at dawn and grinding human bones?"

Ardyce and Isabelle exchanged a guarded look. "Auntie Pan uses powdered bone in some remedies," Ardyce said noncommittally.

"I. . . I have trouble thinking it's even remotely possible that Langford killed Forest," said Isabelle. She shut her eyes a moment, as if to shut out that painful thought, then opened them and continued shakily, "Aunt Delora and Langford have always been good to me. I realize now my aunt has deceived me in many ways, and yet I still love her. I'm suspicious of her and Langford—how could I not be now? I'm hurt and angry. But more than anything, I'm grieved."

Paul nodded sympathetically, but couldn't help thinking how finer feelings and sensibilities could impede a murder investigation. Steering the conversation away from feelings and towards facts, he questioned Ardyce closely about the circumstances of Beryl's death. That night Ardyce had been going back and forth from the dining room to the warming kitchen, helping serve and helping Auntie Pan prepare the courses.

"I was in the dining room when little Miss Euphrasie skipped in barefoot in her nightgown," said Ardyce. "Well, Miss Delora snatched up one of the big candelabra right off the table, took Euphrasie by the arm, and got her out of there quick."

"That's when Miss Euphrasie said her aunt sent her to Miss Isabelle in the back parlor. But did Mrs. Raveneaux come right back to the dining room?" Paul asked.

"No, not right away that I know of. I'd gone to the kitchen and stopped for maybe ten minutes to swallow my own supper, then come back with a tray for the clearing up. That took me through the back hall, and I didn't hear or see anybody about then. But I'd just set foot back in the dining room when I heard the scream and the clattering."

"And Miss Delora wasn't in the dining room?"

"No, sir. Mr. and Mrs. Vasseur and me—we started for the door leading out to the hall, and Miss Delora met us there with her candles blazing. Auntie Pan trotted out from the kitchen, a little groggy since she'd been dozing in her chair. We all met up in the back hall around the body under the airwell," said Ardyce. "I remember craning my neck around and looking up, too, and not seeing anyone near the airwell railings. Second floor was all dark, but there must've been a lamp lit on the third floor 'cause I saw a little flickering light."

"Did you think then that Beryl had been pushed?" asked Paul. "Is that why you looked up?'

"I thought the rail might be broken," said Ardyce.

"What happened next?"

"Miss Isabelle came 'round the corner from the back parlor. And pretty soon Faye Samson showed up."

"From which room?"

"I don't know, sir. Just coming from the front hall, I reckon."

"Paul," said Isabelle, "it occurs to me that Euphrasie didn't come straight into the back parlor when Aunt Delora sent her there, and my aunt must not have led her all the way to the parlor door to make sure she'd go in. Euphrasie said she was listening outside the door when Elroy Samson was going on at me. She didn't come in until he'd stomped out."

"So your aunt wasn't in the back hall and she wasn't in the dining room," said Paul. "But she could have run up the main staircase."

"Which only goes to the second floor. To reach the servants' rooms she would need to run down the corridor to the back stairs. That's a lot of running," said Isabelle thoughtfully. Then she added, "We must bear in mind how unreliable Euphrasie is—and how indiscreet. I suppose she heard Mr. Samson going on about what might be in Forest's coffin besides a body, and she could have mentioned what she heard to anyone, including the *traiteuse* she recently visited. Samson was suspicious of Aunt Delora. He thought she was burying treasure with the corpse, that she'd already buried valuables all over the plantation. And like some greedy pirate, he demanded I find him the treasure map."

Paul decided not to pursue the topic of the map, but brought out his pocket watch and asked Isabelle and Ardyce to help him gauge the time needed to run up to the third floor and back in a hoop skirt. Isabelle, dressed for the part, was to do the running. Ardyce protested, but Isabelle assured her she was up to it. Ardyce would then repeat her movements of the night Beryl died, and Paul would wait below the airwell with his watch.

On Paul's signaling nod, Isabelle pretended to shoo Euphrasie off toward the back parlor, then disappeared toward the front of the house. Ardyce walked to the kitchen, waited ten minutes, and returned to the dining room. Paul stomped on the floorboards to indicate the body had fallen. Moments later, Isabelle descended the back stairs, whooshed past the back parlor door, dashed by Paul, and reached the dining room door to then proceed with Ardyce back to the spot below the airwell.

Still panting, she told Paul, "Perhaps it can be done as you imagine. But it's a lot of running." She caught her breath. "The time Ardyce was in the kitchen and Euphrasie and I drifted off to sleep hardly seems long enough to confront Beryl, argue with her, have some reason to push her over, and then drag her out to the third floor hall and do it."

"If the killer already had her reason, she may only have been in need of an opportunity," said Paul.

"But, sir," Ardyce said, "Miss Delora wasn't out of breath when she got back to the dining room."

Someone above cleared her throat, and they looked up to see Lydie Vee leaning over the second floor railing of the airwell. In a harsh whisper she called down, "What is all this running and stomping about? I just got Babcock quieted after the conniption he had leaving the cemetery."

"I beg your pardon, Mrs. Vasseur," Paul called up.

"Quite." Lydie Vee peered down in particular at Isabelle. "Oh, Isabelle, don't move. I'll be right there." She disappeared from view, then some moments later reappeared, advancing toward them from the front hallway. Lydie Vee reached out and grasped Isabelle's hands. "My dear girl, are you all right?" Isabelle nodded, and Lydie Vee continued in a hurried, hushed tone: "What a morning! I never would have given my consent to the proceedings, if the suspicions presented were not so strong, so convincing."

Here she glanced at Paul, who protested, "But, Miss Lydie Vee, I never intended—"

"It's done, sir. Babcock would not be persuaded to wait or discuss the matter or hear any other explanation. He went straight to Captain Newell, and we all know the rest. I apologize to you, Isabelle, for my husband's precipitous behavior. Babbie may be worse than useless sometimes, but he's mine and I'm responsible for him—more so than ever now that he's apparently gone 'round the bend."

"I don't blame you for anything, Lydie Vee," said Isabelle.

"Dear girl." Lydie Vee patted Isabelle's hands and released them. "Now, while Babcock rests, I'll just take a calming turn around the lawn. Will you join me?"

"Thank you, but you go on without us," Isabelle replied.

"Join me later, if you change your mind," said Lydie Vee, and left them in the hall.

At Isabelle's suggestion, Paul and Ardyce retreated with her to the front parlor. There, she shut the doors and dropped down on the sofa.

"Miss Isabelle," Paul began, "Forgive me for asking you to run through the house. But you do see it proves Miss

Delora had time to go upstairs and down before the others gathered around Beryl's body."

"But it doesn't prove to me that she did it, Mr. Delahoussaye," said Isabelle, returning to the use of his surname.

Paul looked to Ardyce, hoping for some affirmation. "What do you think?" he asked.

"I think what I always thought, sir."

Isabelle nodded. "Tell him what you said to me, Ardyce."

"Well, Miss Isabelle's pretty sure she heard Mr. Samson stomp off upstairs that night. I think he'd had all he wanted of Beryl, and he pitched her over the railing like a forkful of dirty straw," said Ardyce.

"He was that cruel?" Paul said, regretting his comment even before he finished it.

"Sometimes, sir, Mr. Samson remembered he was a married man and a father. So he'd up and blame a colored woman for tempting him from the path of righteousness, and he'd punish her."

Paul started to speak, but Isabelle stopped him. "You've no need to ask how Ardyce knows, but she's telling you the truth about the kind of man he was."

"But even if she's right about his killing Beryl," said Paul, "Samson didn't kill himself or Colonel Brodie."

"Before we do anything else," Isabelle said softly, "I want to talk with Aunt Delora."

Paul shook his head with frustration. "Well, she's had all morning to concoct a story for you."

Isabelle sat up straighter and fixed Paul with a steady gaze. "Mr. Delahoussaye, I wanted us to come to this room because I have a plan—a somewhat devious, but necessary plan. There are some things I want my aunt to explain at least as much as you do. Unlike you, I don't see her as a cold-blooded murderess, but if she confesses that she is, I suppose I must accept it."

"Confesses? You think we should simply ask her?" said Paul.

"Not exactly," Isabelle replied. "Aunt Delora would never be as open with you as she might be with me. But you could hear our conversation." Isabelle looked toward the stenciled panel in the wall from which Paul had once seen Euphrasie emerge. "I'd never want my aunt to know I arranged this," she added.

"I'll do my best to see she never does," said Paul.

He went to the panel and felt beneath the chair rail molding for a way to open the secret door. Ardyce came forward and showed him the tiny latch hidden in a carved curlicue. "These here are little air holes, sir, worked into the design."

"Thank you, Ardyce."

Carefully, Paul pulled open the panel, and from out of the black recess a dainty white hand dropped into view. "What the—!" Paul stopped himself, fell to his knees, and peered inside.

"What is it?' said Isabelle, hurrying to join Ardyce and Paul near the opening.

"Why, it's Euphrasie," Paul answered, gently reaching into the darkness and drawing her out in his arms. She was a soft, warm, drowsy bundle—not a corpse, as he first feared. Paul smiled as Euphrasie stirred in his embrace. "She must have crawled in there and fallen asleep."

Isabelle knelt beside Paul and rubbed Euphrasie's hands. "It's so close in there. It's a wonder she didn't suffocate."

Paul knew he must have looked alarmed because Isabelle added, "Oh, it's safe enough for a short time, say the time it took for foragers to go through the house. My cousin and I both hid in here together sometimes. But if Euphrasie fell asleep too long ago—well, we must try to bring her back."

Ardyce brought a drop of brandy and held it to the young girl's pallid lips. Euphrasie wrinkled her nose and sneezed, sending the brandy down her chin. She sat up suddenly, and Paul caught her shoulders to hold her steady. She looked at him sideways and smiled.

"Euphrasie," said Isabelle, "how long have you been behind the panel?"

Euphrasie yawned and arched back against Paul's steadying hands. "Oh, I don't know, Coz. Since before Aunt Delora and Captain Newell came in, anyway. He was getting real close to her when Mr. Delahoussaye here came in." The girl shrugged one shoulder. "I got kinda sleepy after that."

"Ardyce, please take Miss Euphrasie to her room," said Isabelle. "And would you tell Aunt Delora I'd like to see her here?"

Ardyce nodded and held a hand out to help Euphrasie from the floor. But the girl dropped back against Paul, causing him to hit his head on the corner of the panel door. He almost cursed, then scrambled to his feet, pulling Euphrasie with him.

"Oh, I am so weak," sighed Euphrasie. "Couldn't Mr. Delahoussaye just carry me upstairs?"

"No!" said Isabelle and Ardyce in unison, the latter taking a firm hold on Euphrasie and guiding her to the door. Euphrasie dragged her stockinged feet, but at last she was gone, the door shut behind her.

Paul and Isabelle were alone.

Tentatively, Paul touched her sleeve. "Miss Isabelle, I'm deeply sorry about Colonel Brodie. With all that's been happening, I— "

Isabelle turned away from him. "Aunt Delora may come in any moment," she said. "You'd best get in your hiding place."

"As you wish."

Paul stretched once while he still could, then bent down. He seated himself with his back against one side of the boxed-in space, his knees drawn up almost to his chest. The ceiling was low, and he was forced to keep his neck arched slightly forward. Isabelle knelt and looked at him for a moment with her unfathomable gray eyes, then closed and latched the panel door.

CHAPTER FIFTEEN

Isabelle ached in body and mind. Uncharacteristically, she poured herself a short glass of brandy and downed it in two gulps, then circled the room, hugging her sides. Should she wheedle and coax her aunt for information, she wondered, like a little girl, or demand outright an explanation? How could her aunt love her and yet tell her so many lies? And was Paul Delahoussaye anyone to put her trust in, or just some stranger who'd come to Belle Ombre wanting what most men wanted—and some of them took? What made him any different except his gentle manners and his schoolboy willingness to please her? Isabelle shivered because her feelings were cold and her heart was hard with anger.

"What has come over you, dear?" said Delora.

Isabelle spun around to face her aunt. Her head pounded so that she hadn't even heard Delora enter from the hall and shut the door.

"But how can I ask that?" Delora's voice was sweet with concern. "After what you've seen today, it's no wonder you're all nerves. Ardyce told me you needed me here, and I can see you surely do. Now just sit yourself down on the sofa and I'll fix your hair. It's tumbling loose."

Isabelle obeyed silently, searching her mind for a way to begin the necessary conversation. Her aunt stood behind her, cool, deft fingers lifting the locks of fair hair from Isabelle's neck, coiling and tucking them under the snood.

"You do have lovely hair," said Delora. "The color of a walnut shell was Mr. Delahoussaye's apt observation."

Isabelle thought of Paul doubled up in the hiding place, unable to see anything now except a few pin pricks of light.

"He admires you very much, dear," Delora continued. "I had so hoped his attentions would be a pleasant diversion for you during his brief stay. But it seems around Belle Ombre it's just as the Bard said: 'Chaos is come again!'" Delora finished with Isabelle's hair and took a seat beside her. "Still, our comfortable old routine will return one day. And perhaps, after he's gone, you can correspond with Mr. Delahoussaye."

Isabelle looked steadily at her aunt. "But will he ever receive my letters, Aunt Delora? Or would I do as well to write to a dead man?"

"Sugar, this morbid turn of phrase is unbecoming."

"Oh, Aunt Delora!"

"What, dear?"

The flood of words came. "Aunt Delora, I don't know whether to cry or scream, but I must know what your part is in three deaths." Delora drew back slightly, and Isabelle continued, her voice gathering strength. "You told me the body you and Beryl laid out was horribly changed and I shouldn't look on it. You didn't say a word then about embalming. Then Beryl, the only other person here to see the body besides yourself and Langford, fell to her death the night of the wake. And Samson disappeared. But before he did, he told me he was suspicious about what was in the coffin. I might well have been, too, if I'd known then that Forest was alive, holed up in the cellar at Halcyon."

Delora gasped, but said nothing.

"Forest raided our pantry for food and wandered the grounds of Belle Ombre—his mind wandering in a world of its own. He was scarred with old wounds. His boots were worn out, and gangrene had started in his feet. I know this, Aunt, because I saw him last night. I talked to him. I touched him.

I know he was alive at midnight, and this morning he was in his grave!"

Delora clapped her hands to her mouth and shut her eyes.

"The body you laid out was not Forest's body—and you knew it from the beginning. When Forest was exhumed, he was recognizable because he'd only been dead a few hours. And I'm asking you: did you kill him, or did you order him killed so you could continue your hoax?"

Delora opened her eyes wide. "Oh, Isabelle, darling! Neither one. Nothing of the sort, I swear to you." She rose and took a turn around the carpet in front of the hearth, wringing her hands with an air of desperation Isabelle had never before witnessed.

"At least one of my letters to Forest—one I know for certain—was never posted to him. You kept it, Aunt Delora, and you told me it was in his pocket next to his heart when his body arrived here. But of course, it wasn't his body. Whose body was it, Aunt? And why, in heaven's name, did you tell me my fiancé was dead?" Isabelle persisted.

Delora seemed to struggle a moment for her composure, then resumed her place on the sofa. She covered Isabelle's hands with her own. "Dear girl, I hoped to spare you all of this. But I will confess to you now because I wouldn't for the world have you believe I deliberately set out to hurt you. You see, not long before you wrote that letter to Forest, the one I said was in his pocket, his cousin Clara Ann wrote to me from Shreveport. You know how you hadn't heard from him for ever so long, and we were all afraid for him."

Isabelle nodded; she remembered the uncertainty more clearly than anything else about the War.

"Well, Clara Ann's husband, who was in Virginia at the time, heard some rumors and made some inquires," said Delora. "It seems Forest Brodie went missing after

Gettysburg, but he was later recognized by someone who'd served with him and was on leave after being wounded. Honey, Forest stopped writing to you because he'd deserted."

"He told me that," Isabelle said softly. She thought of Paul, hearing every word.

"But there's more," said Delora. "He was living in a hollow somewhere in western Virginia—with some woman!"

Isabelle's heart pounded, as if it would bruise itself within her breast.

"So you must understand," Delora continued gently, "when I learned about the situation, I figured the sooner he was dead in your mind, the better for you. He deserted his men and he deserted you. I never dreamed he'd show his face around here again."

"I think he got homesick," Isabelle whispered to herself, then spoke more clearly to her aunt. "Why didn't you tell me this when you learned of it? Why let me go on writing letters and hoping?"

"I prayed for time to soften the blow," said Delora. "And then I saw an opportunity to put his memory honorably to rest."

Isabelle's vision was suddenly blurred with tears.

"Now, now," murmured Delora, dabbing Isabelle's cheek with her lace handkerchief. "No sense puddling up for that boy. Let that other woman cry her eyes out for him."

Isabelle thought of the beautifully made shirt that woman must have sewn for Forest. He might have stayed on in Virginia, safely hidden away. But he had come back—walked all the way back to Belle Ombre—to gaze at Isabelle's window, to put a flower in her combs, to drift in and out of love with her, as a dying man drifts in and out of consciousness. Isabelle swallowed the tightness in her throat and spoke clearly, for her aunt and for Paul: "Sometimes I think we expect too much of men. We expect them to fight with strength and daring, while, in truth, what they may feel is utter exhaustion and terror. How can I judge Forest harshly when I have kept my heartache and my loneliness safe at home, while he carried his with him into one hellish battle after another? I might have been as weak as he, and with less justification."

Delora forced a smile. "You put me to shame, Isabelle. Such a charitable attitude was never mine towards Charles Orvin."

"Who did you bury in Forest's place?" asked Isabelle.

Delora seemed momentarily surprised by the directness of the question. She answered, as Isabelle expected, with evasion. "Well, now. That's hard to say."

"Who, Aunt?"

"Just some poor creature with a colonel's stripes on his sleeve."

"Sent to Verbena for you."

"Or for some tenant farmer's wife. Who can really say?"

"And that story you told about Forest's being a prisoner in the North, then released and taken in by a kind family in Mississippi, who then sent his body here?"

Delora shrugged. "It happened to someone."

"I wonder," Isabelle said, staring fixedly at her aunt. "I can try to accept that you lied to me about Forest's death to spare my feelings. But how do you explain his actual death? And why was his body conveniently in that coffin when Captain Newell's men exhumed it this morning?"

"Someone put it there," replied Delora primly. "Someone I can't answer for. Someone out of my control."

Isabelle wondered whom that might be at Belle Ombre.

"Now, dear, I understand why the shock of seeing Forest's remains brought on your faint," Delora added. "It gave me quite a turn as well."

"But you recover so quickly, Aunt Delora. After Beryl broke her neck, after Elroy Samson was strung up in the smokehouse, and after Forest was near run through with a shovel and put in another man's coffin. Every time you've recovered and covered your tracks," Isabelle challenged her aunt.

Delora sprang to her feet. "I won't stand for this! Yes, you have a grievance against me, but I am still your aunt and guardian and you are my niece. And you will hear me out in respectful silence, young lady." Delora arranged her burgundy skirt and lifted her chin as if in preparation for a dramatic recital. "Samson and his latest trollop were plotting against me, spreading stories to Captain Newell that Charles Orvin was never coming back. Samson wasn't going to let it rest 'til I gave him all my jewels and valuables, treasures that had been in my family for generations. Oh, Samson promised to leave here peaceably if I did, but he said he had to go in style. Well, someone saw to it that he did. And I thank them for it."

Delora continued more softly. "The night of the wake, after I sent Euphrasie to you, I went up to my room for a fresh handkerchief. I'd spoiled one stopping the flow of Babcock's spilled wine across the tabletop. That was when I found that someone had discovered the hiding place for my jewels—a hollow bedpost Langford fashioned for me years ago. Of course, I had my suspicions about who'd gotten into the post. And I was near certain it wasn't Euphrasie just getting carried away with her little snooping games. I'd already caught Beryl nosing around my desk and poking through my armoire. Samson had put that minx up to going through everything in the house. But back to that night. Next thing, I heard stomping around on the floor above and went out in the hall. I could hear Samson and Beryl having a few words—slurred, drunken words. Then there was a scream, a clatter, and a thud. He killed her, Isabelle, sure as I'm standing here."

"Maybe he did," said Isabelle. "But who killed him and disemboweled him? And why?"

"Seems Elroy Samson did have a taste for the high life. But he swallowed something somebody else wanted, somebody besides me," said Delora.

"What?"

"What Beryl stole for him, thinking she'd share in the loot. All my loose diamonds and sapphires and a few rubies. I'd sold the silver and gold mountings last year. Anyway, I'll always be grateful you found those entrails before the hogs ate them, so Langford could recover my property."

"Samson *swallowed* your jewels?"

"Washed them down with rot-gut whiskey, no doubt. I reckon he laughed about it in that crude way of his, maybe taunted Beryl that now she couldn't get at his jewels."

"You heard him?"

"Not exactly. But I can well imagine. I know the thought's disgusting, Isabelle, but that's what he was—disgusting. And he must have figured he'd hit on a sure way to take the jewels with him. Even if I discovered the theft and raised the alarm before he got out of Verbena, no one would find my property on his person."

"Why didn't you raise the alarm, Aunt Delora?"

"And have Captain Newell out here nosing around? No, thank you." Delora resumed her place on the sofa. "Besides, that night I thought there was still a chance my jewels hadn't yet left Belle Ombre, that Samson was still hanging 'round, meaning to take his wife and son off with him. He didn't treat them well, but they belonged to him. So that meant there was still a chance that Langford might get my jewels back for me."

"And he tore apart everything in Beryl's room looking for them?" Isabelle asked.

Delora nodded. "With my blessing."

"And that was the night before Samson's body was found in the smokehouse?"

Delora nodded again.

"When Langford didn't find the jewels in Beryl's room, did he then tear apart Samson looking them?"

"No, certainly not. We'd no idea Samson had swallowed them until . . . 'til later. As I said before, I'm beholden to you for that discovery. By the time Lang reached the spot in the holly bog where you said you'd seen the hogs rooting out those entrails, the beasts had already torn into them. Langford recovered most of the jewels, but he'll be checking the hog manure for the ones still missing."

"Oh, Aunt Delora, it's all so coarse!"

"Well, it's just the two of us talking about it. Right now we don't have to impress some gentleman with how dainty we are. Really, Isabelle, I'm trying to help you understand some things and put your mind to rest. But I don't feel I owe you an explanation for every move I make."

Isabelle rose, walked toward the panel, then turned back to face her aunt. "Would you help Mr. Delahoussaye try to understand some things, too?"

"I don't see why I should," Delora replied. "If he leaves here confused, well, so be it. He isn't family."

"But Langford, who isn't family, knows where you hide your jewels and your important papers. He knows all about your correspondence with Uncle Charles Orvin. He searched Beryl's room for you. He extracted your jewels from Samson's peculiar hiding place and returned them to you. Why does he do all this for you, Aunt Delora? He ran off once, but he came back—back into slavery. He's not your slave anymore. And yet, here he is, living in your house, doing anything for you. Why is that, Aunt Delora? Are things between you and him the way Uncle Babcock hints they are?

Why does Langford know more about you and your doings than anybody else at Belle Ombre? He isn't family."

"Oh, but he is, honey," Delora said softly. "He's the closest family I've got."

Isabelle's lips parted, but she couldn't speak.

"Langford is my half-brother. Oh, I know what folks like Babcock would say, if they knew—why am I so attached to one of my father's bastards? Didn't a lot of planters breed a little extra stock off their slave women? But Langford was always different—and he wasn't my father's offspring. He was my mother's love child when she was just a foolish, passionate girl. A slave woman who'd just lost her baby took Langford to raise. You know, he might have gone free if my mother had claimed him—a white woman's black baby didn't necessarily have to be a slave. But she just couldn't admit what she'd done, and her daddy wouldn't have let her, anyway. So, everything was hushed up—now that you know, you must never tell a soul, Isabelle—and Mother was eventually married off to Father. But she kept Langford near her, and he kept her family name. When she was old, she gave him to me and took my promise never to sell him or mistreat him.

"During the War, when everyone around here thought Langford had run off, he'd really gone with my blessing to his father's deathbed, all the way to East Texas. Lydie Vee helped him cross the state line going and coming home again."

Delora smiled and held out a hand to Isabelle, who came to her and knelt before her aunt. "Sweet child, it feels so good to say it out loud: Langford is my half-brother, and I love him dearly. He's always been his own man, even when he was called a slave, and I don't ask where he goes or who he sees when he's not with me. But through the years, Langford's looked after me at least as much as I've looked after him. And don't you know it would kill my soul if Babcock Vasseur, or any other popinjay claiming to be my nearest male relative, stepped up and took Belle Ombre away from me—and thus from Langford."

"But suppose," Isabelle said soberly, "he's done something wrong. Suppose he killed Forest and buried him. Even if he thought he was doing it to protect you, it would still be wrong. Has he told you what he did last night and what he was burning this morning?"

"Well . . . you know, with all the haranguing going on this morning, I've hardly exchanged a word with him," said Delora.

The door flew open, and Lydie Vee entered from the hall. "Delora, I am beside myself! I must speak with you." Lydie Vee sailed into the room and dropped onto the sofa. "Oh, Isabelle, you'll have to excuse us. Go have a lie down. You look done in."

Isabelle shot a glance at the panel behind which Paul was hidden.

"Yes, get some rest, dear," Delora agreed. "We'll talk again later."

Isabelle retreated to the hall, Delora shutting the door after her, but she didn't go upstairs. Her mind whirled with Delora's explanations and revelations. Lydie Vee's voice droned on maddeningly behind the door, rising and falling and rising again. Paul must be nearly sick of the cramped closeness of his hiding place. Isabelle racked her brain for a way to clear the parlor and let him out.

Then she heard a rustle and a footfall on the front staircase. Faye Samson, in her best black and crinoline, leaning on Radley's arm, slowly descended.

Reaching the last step, Faye asked, "Is your aunt in the parlor, Miss Isabelle? I'll have a word with her."

"She's in there with Lydie Vee. Perhaps you could wait for her in the back parlor, and I'll ask her to come to you soon," said Isabelle.

"I'll see her in the front parlor now," Faye announced haughtily, her hand already on the doorknob. "I've finished with being pacified and hidden away. I won't be long, Radley."

"Whatever you say, Ma."

Isabelle looked from mother to son. Then Faye entered the parlor, closing the door after her, and Radley stood facing Isabelle.

"What's come over your mother?" she asked.

"I reckon she's just perked up today 'cause of something I did and something I give her."

"And what was that?"

Radley looked very pleased with himself. Isabelle wondered if she were in for a speech as dull and self-congratulatory as one of his fishing stories.

"I found a ring," he said.

No, Isabelle realized, this time he wouldn't ramble; he would let her work to extract every morsel of information. "What sort of ring did you find, Radley?'

"Weddin' ring."

"And where did you find it?"

He grinned before he answered. "On a dead man's finger."

Isabelle caught her breath. "Forest? But I don't recall a ring."

Radley shook his head. "Naw."

"Who then? Where's the body?" Isabelle felt her pulse quicken.

Radley's lusterless eyes almost brightened. "A soldier—mostly bones and a gray coat. I could show you, Miss Isabelle. But we'd have to walk out a piece, past the pecan grove."

Isabelle wondered how much longer Paul could tolerate being confined in the wall before he'd burst out, regardless of who was in the room. Perhaps if she just ran out to the grove and back, she would have news that would bring the women in the front parlor running to the hall, and Paul could slip out of hiding and through to the dining room. Or perhaps she would return with knowledge she wouldn't choose to share.

"Is it very far, Radley? I don't want to be gone long," said Isabelle.

"Fine by me. I can trot if you can."

Isabelle nodded and hurried for the front door, snatching her mantle from the coat rack as she passed it. Outside, the cold air revived her energy, and faintness and aching disappeared before an impatient drive to know what remains the boy had discovered in the orchard. She gathered up her hem and dashed down the path toward the pecan trees, Radley wheezing, but keeping pace with her.

In the midst of the grove, they slowed their steps, impeded by mud, scattered branches broken off in thunderstorms, and shallow holes dug by Elroy Samson.

Radley looked puzzled. "Must be farther on," he said.

"Near the family cemetery?"

"Maybe just past it." He rubbed his spotty chin. "Yeah, that's it over there."

They ran on beyond the graveyard, past the edge of the pecan grove to where a mix of pine, oak, and sweet gum grew.

"This isn't in the orchard at all," said Isabelle.

"It ain't too far off."

"What do you mean?" Stopping to catch her breath, Isabelle realized how very far they had come. "A few more yards and we'll be coming into the holly bog, Radley."

"Yeah, that's where it must be, the holly bog. Not far."

Isabelle followed him a little farther, and Radley pointed ahead to a bank of dark wet leaves against the broad trunk of a water oak.

"The corpse is right under here." He picked up a stick and poked it into the pile of leaves. "You gonna faint for sure when you see what I got, Miss Isabelle," he said proudly, jabbing further with the stick. "But don't worry none. I'll catch you 'fore you hit the ground."

Isabelle took a step back, noting a shovel with a muddy blade leaned against the tree near where the boy searched. "How did you come upon this body, Radley? Did you see someone concealing it here? Langford?"

Radley was on his knees, pawing through the rotten foliage, throwing aside handfuls, stirring the rank air, and still no corpse was exposed beneath the leaves, only the solid earth. He rocked back on his heels and twisted his head to look at Isabelle. "Langford," he said, and spat. "That old barrow! He musta took it and burnt it, tarpaulin and all. Ma was right—all his talk about hog bones was hog shit."

"Radley," Isabelle said, "please tell me: did you see Langford, maybe late last night or early this morning, put the body here after he put another in its place, in the coffin that was dug up today?"

Radley's eyes narrowed. "Is that what you think? You think Langford did all that work?"

"Is that what you saw?" Isabelle repeated.

"You think Langford killed your man?"

"Did he, Radley? I know for a fact Forest was alive last night, and he isn't now. Did you see Langford kill him?"

Radley exhaled with a whistling sound. "Jesus H. Christ!" he said, pulling a rusty serrated kitchen knife from his coat pocket and testing its point with his thumb. "You want I should kill him for you, Miss Isabelle? Got a reward for me if I do?"

"Oh, no, Radley, no. No killing. I just want to hear the truth."

The boy twisted his mouth, and he scratched behind his ear with the knife point, as if he were contemplating a reply. Then slowly, absently, he drew an oddly shaped piece of butternut cloth from his inside coat pocket and ran it over the knife blade. The cut edges of the cloth were frayed, but one side of it was folded over and neatly sewn with a narrow length of material hanging down from it. It was a piece of apron, Isabelle realized, with apron string still attached.

"Is that your mother's?" asked Isabelle.

"Yeah," Radley answered with a shrug. "She done snagged it bad and cut it up for rags."

Isabelle looked down at his pale head, his doughy face. She heard his stomach growling; hardly anyone in the house had had a proper meal since the platter of worms had been revealed at breakfast. He went on slowly rubbing the blade as if he could bring a shine to that old knife, as if it were important to him. Radley was so limited, so dim, so easy to despise. But when Isabelle thought of his deficiencies and his burdens—a brutal father, an embittered mother, brothers all lost in the War—she felt less contempt and more pity.

"Radley," she said, almost gently, "on the night Beryl died, was your mother upstairs on the third floor? Is it possible she knows what happened?"

"She knows all right. Ma's knowed all along. Miss Delora knows, too. But Ma ain't the one pushed Beryl over."

"Of course not. We've always said around here Faye Samson couldn't stand killing anything." But, Isabelle also recalled it said, once an animal was strung up, Faye Samson sure could butcher.

Isabelle took another step back, putting a little more distance between herself and the boy. "Radley," she said, "I guess you'd do anything for your mother."

He glanced up at her from where he squatted on the ground. "Most anything," he said.

Isabelle remembered the words she'd overheard him whine to Faye: "But Ma, you're talking about some mighty hard work." Digging graves was mighty hard work, whether to bury a body or exhume one.

Isabelle heard a soft rustling, but Radley didn't seem to notice. Then, a few yards away behind Radley, Langford appeared between the trees, hunting rifle in hand.

"It's a shame about that body being missing," said Isabelle, watching Radley for his response. "Maybe some animals got to it."

"Or one skunk in particular," he said sullenly.

"So did you think like your pa did that there was some treasure hidden in Forest's coffin? And then all you found was a corpse with a wedding ring."

Radley shuffled to his feet. "Weren't just any weddin' ring, Miss Isabelle. It were a big braided gold band with writin' inside." He wadded up the butternut cloth and pocketed it and the knife, then continued importantly, "Ma says I did real good bringing her that ring. She says with that ring she can get all the diamonds and sapphires and rubies Pa ever planned on shittin' in Texas. Oh, he was chucklin' about that 'fore he tossed that gal over, but he ain't laughing now. Ma says she can get anything she asks for from Miss Delora 'cause—thanks to me—Ma's got Colonel Raveneaux's weddin' ring!"

Isabelle darted a glance past Radley to see Langford, who raised the rifle to his shoulder. With a dry mouth, she whispered, "Oh, Radley, to please your mother, did you kill your pa? Did you murder Forest Brodie?"

Radley stuffed his hands in his coat pockets and chewed his lip before he answered. "Ma says I ain't murdered nobody. You can't go telling folks I did. I was just trying to slow Pa down. That's all. So's he wouldn't run off from us." Radley reached for the shovel propped against the tree, then took two steps toward Isabelle. "And Colonel Brodie—well, I didn't kill him. I laid a ghost is what I did. And it was Langford put him in the ground."

Isabelle stared at Radley, then slowly shifted the focus of her eyes to the rifle barrel Langford raised some yards behind him. She felt herself enveloped in a cold vapor, moisture oozing up from the earth, dripping from branches, seeping into her garments, and trickling down her cheeks in place of tears. But even as the chill penetrated her flesh, Isabelle was aware also of an encroaching, steaming, fetid heat.

CHAPTER SIXTEEN

Sweat beaded Paul's forehead and meandered down his temples, his cheeks, his neck, slipping at last under his starched shirt collar. Stifling in his hiding place behind the wall panel, Paul thought back to the runaway slaves who had coiled themselves into barrels, flattened themselves under planks of buckboards, buried themselves alive in bales of hay or cotton, all hoping for a safe secret passage from bondage.

But despite Paul's discomfort, he found eavesdropping fascinating and effective. No wonder it was one of Euphrasie's favorite pastimes. In the space of minutes Paul was gathering facts and nuances of meaning he might never have gleaned from direct questioning. Delora had been evasive with Isabelle, but at times the emotion in her voice rang truer than her words, and Paul was forced to revise his opinion of just how devious she could be. And Isabelle, Paul imagined, must have sometimes forgotten he was listening—how open she had sounded, as if she had nothing to lose.

Then the tenor of Delora's interview with Lydie Vee had surprised him. His previous experience of the two women had led him to believe in a long-standing animosity between them. But perhaps the ill feeling was more between Delora and Babcock. Lydie Vee seemed willing enough to compromise, accepting that Forest Brodie's embalmed body might have lain all along in its coffin and that Colonel Raveneaux might still communicate by secret courier through Langford, who brought the messages to Delora. In fact, Lydie Vee was ready to overlook and accept a great deal if Delora were willing to do the same and adopt some of Lydie Vee's priorities for her own.

"There's no going back to Shreveport for us," Lydie Vee had said. "No matter how many fits Babbie has, he's still not going to be master of a house there or here. I can live with the situation, and I'll make damn sure Babbie lives with it, if you'll just let us stay on, Delora."

"I've never turned away kin," Delora said evenly, "and I don't intend to start now. With your assurance that you'll keep your husband under control, I don't see why we can't go on as we are a little longer. I have a deal of respect for you, Lydie Vee. But Uncle Babcock has to understand that Langford and I—and the Colonel—will decide how we're going to make a living out of this played-out soil and how we'll go about paying the taxes. I don't want any more scandalous rumors. Babcock has thrown filth my way, but I won't catch it—and it won't cling to me. Is that clear?"

Apparently, it was. The conversation proceeded in lower tones to the subject of Lydie Vee's starting some sort of girls' academy at Belle Ombre, an idea Delora agreed to think on. "I haven't forgotten your kindness to Langford when his father was dying," she said. "I might consider a school here, as a sort of auxiliary operation."

"You wouldn't be sorry," said Lydie Vee. "All the time I've been here I've envied you Belle Ombre, seeing how land can help dispel the sense of one's own barrenness. But for myself, I understand it's work with human beings, not land, that completes me and always has. It's a difference between us we might put to good use. I've worried ever since we left Shreveport that circumstances would force me 'to rust unburnished, not to shine in use!'"

"As I recall, Tennyson has a good deal to say in that poem about striving and not yielding," said Delora. "Certainly, we both have a void to fill, even while maintaining the status of married women. I'd be the pot calling the kettle black if I said you might have made a wiser choice of husband. But I'm confident you can work around Bab—"

Delora broke off suddenly, and Paul heard the parlor door open. A few moments of silence followed. He wondered if Isabelle had returned to call her aunt and Lydie Vee from the room, but then doubted it. Rather stiffly, Lydie Vee announced she'd be going to the kitchen to see if a meal could be arranged for sometime that afternoon. In a strangely flat voice, Delora offered a few menu suggestions, then was silent. The parlor door opened and shut again.

A kind of unease settled over the room. Paul sensed it and wished he could see as well as hear from his hiding place. Two skirts rustled and swished, throats cleared, and he pictured a pair of women circling one another, closing in on one another as the walls seemed to close in on Paul.

If he had Delora's hubris or Euphrasie's ingenuousness, he wouldn't wait to suffocate in hiding; he'd simply make an entrance from the panel and explain nothing. But Paul determined to hold on a little longer, hoping Isabelle would find a way to clear the room and allow his escape.

As he waited, wondering what had become of Isabelle and listening for a new conversation to begin in the parlor, Paul took solace in being right about a few things. The whooshing sound Euphrasie had described was made by a woman's skirts as she ran down the hall, the woman, Paul felt sure, who had seen Samson push Beryl over the railing and who didn't wish to make her appearance from the back stairs when the household gathered to view the body.

Delora had had good reason to keep an eye on Beryl, suspecting her as she did of taking the jewels from the hollowed-out bedpost. But the night of Beryl's death, Delora, while going to her room for a fresh handkerchief, had only just made the discovery that her jewels were missing. She told

Isabelle she'd no idea Samson had swallowed the stones until his entrails were found. As Paul reasoned, it was unlikely that Delora, on the night of Forest's wake, would choose to run to the third floor alone and confront Samson and Beryl, involving herself in their drunken altercation. Her refined sensibilities would rebel at the thought.

But there was another woman who had reason to keep an eye on Samson and eavesdrop on him; a woman who could have heard Samson's entire conversation with Beryl, learning that night that Samson had swallowed the jewels; a woman whose sensibilities were not refined. And this woman had a son, a son who would brag and play pranks and do anything to shine for his ma and be one up on his pa—even do murder and mutilation.

Paul flinched at the first sharp sound of Faye Samson's voice.

"I have his ring. Inside the band it says, 'Delora to Charles Orvin' and it matches yours, 'Charles Orvin to Delora.' My boy took it off his boney finger."

"Well?" Delora said archly.

"Well, nobody ever need know about my having the ring if you do what I say," Faye replied. "You give me all those jewels—every one of them your nigger took back for you—and me and my son will ride out of here and never come back. Refuse, and we ride to Captain Newell with that wedding ring and tell him all about you and your schemes."

"It'll be difficult for you, Faye, to tell him all about things you don't even understand. Besides, you'll drive out of here," Delora said, "in my wagon, drawn by my horse, over my dead body. If anybody's going to tell Captain Newell anything, it'll be me telling him about your boy bashing his father's head in and murdering a noble soldier."

Faye snorted. "Just two more Southerners dead as far as the Captain's concerned. He'll be just as willing as everybody else in Verbena to say Langford did murder for you. And I'm willing to chance he'll be mighty interested in Colonel Raveneaux's ring."

"It's only Radley's word that he took the ring from the Colonel's finger. In truth, my husband left his ring behind when he went to war. He had a horror of losing it in the surgeon's tent. Newell will believe me over you any day."

"Fiddlesticks! You'd have to be his whore for sure to get him to swallow any more of your lies."

"In this War, Faye Samson, far better women than you played the whore just to put food on the table for their children. So you put this thought in your coddled brains: I'm keeping Belle Ombre, and I'm keeping my jewels, until I decide when to part with them. You ought to know by now there's next to nothing I wouldn't do for my home."

"Next to nobody you wouldn't use and step on. You'll see what it's like when Captain Newell wears you out and grinds you under his heel."

"You listen here," Delora shot back, "before my daddy died, I married Charles Orvin so as not to lose my land to some fool of a male heir. And if taking Charles Orvin to my bed wasn't a whore's work, I don't know what is. Anyone else, including Newell, would be a picnic after that man."

Delora must have been pacing as she spoke, for Paul heard her taffeta rustle, her voice rise and fall as she crossed to and fro, and he caught a barely perceptible whiff of gardenia toilet water.

"Oh, I pitied you, woman," Delora said, "for being saddled with Elroy Samson because I understood what it was like to be chattel for some beast. I tried to protect you when I could, despite our differences. I've tried to protect others, even when I couldn't protect myself. Because we are all one in our suffering; we are all sisters at someone else's mercy—until—and you listen to me, Faye Samson—until we take an innocent life." Delora had stopped on the other side of the panel, and Paul heard her words distinctly. "Your precious Radley murdered Forest Brodie. Langford saw him do it."

"Langford!" Faye snapped. "Always Langford and his word against my boy's."

"Let me remind you, Faye, I let it go by that he'd killed his pa. That man killed my thieving maid and could have done the same to you any night of your life. Samson was no loss to you. All your outrage was show. Although I've no doubt it did give you quite a shock to see his body swinging in the smokehouse—not where you'd left it swinging, I'm sure—but another of your son's tasteless pranks. The rest of your fits were just stalling, 'til Radley could dig up the entrails and you all could be gone with my jewels."

"That boy!" Faye exclaimed with less than maternal pride.

"Yes, that boy of yours," said Delora. "Couldn't finish the job that night, could he? Apparently, he just knocked the life out of his pa, then headed back to the kitchen for a little something. I've heard tell, murder makes a man powerful hungry. Was it later that night you sent Radley out to the bog to string up his old man—to keep the animals from devouring the body before you two could gut it at your leisure?"

"I've had no leisure 'round here," Faye shot back.

"Oh, did we keep you so busy? Still, you did find time to butcher your husband's body, before you were taken so poorly."

"You poisoned me, Delora Raveneaux! But I stopped eating and I purged myself."

"Now then, I only tried to pacify you, Faye. I needed time, time for you to see reason, time for me to get my own back."

"Time to get your jewels back!"

A silent moment passed before Delora spoke again. "Well, I must say I am perplexed, Faye Samson. Whatever made you think in the first place that you were entitled to my jewels—or anything else of mine? You scorn me for using those near to me for my own benefit, as if my supposed meanness gave you a right. But all the time, you, yourself, have used your own pitiful son. You incited that boy to murder—sent him out, didn't you, to lay in wait for his drunken old man and bash him on the head? And not to save you from a brute of a husband, but for gain—to set yourselves up in style at my expense."

"Radley only knocked him out that night," Faye interjected.

"And finished him off later with your help and encouragement. You scheming woman! Well, Faye, there's nothing I can do to save you now. You've made your choice to act like white trash."

"White trash!" shrieked Faye. "You got more gall than a hog's liver."

Paul heard a crashing sound, perhaps made by a piece of furniture toppling over. Then a moment of quiet followed before Delora spoke with an uncanny calmness. "Your mention of hog organs reminds me, Faye: I was telling Langford just a short while ago that everybody in the house is about sick to death of eating pork. And no one even wanted to sample the delicacy your son surprised us with at breakfast. So I sent Langford out with the Colonel's hunting rifle to see if he could shoot us a little wild game or whatever. I asked him to take Radley with him."

Even Paul behind the panel couldn't miss the menacing tone Delora gave her last words. Faye must have been incensed. He heard her screams from the direction of the hearth and a great clattering, perhaps of fire irons. Delora shouted at her to drop something, Paul couldn't understand what, but feared it might be the poker. Scuffling and thuds followed. Secrecy be damned, he thought, and kicked open the wall panel.

Free from his hiding place, Paul sucked in a lungful of air and shook his head to clear it. On stiff, aching legs he lurched toward the two woman who had fallen together before the hearth, Delora swatting wildly at Faye. Paul grabbed Delora around her waist and lifted her off of Faye, depositing her on the sofa. Faye sat up, scowling, and beat a few times at the folds of her black dress. Paul, surveying the scattered fire irons, the fallen fire screen, and breathing in the odor of singed wool, realized Faye's skirt had caught fire. Could the two women only have been beating out the flames?

Recovering from her share of the exertions, Delora leaned against the sofa cushions, looking first at Paul, then the open wall panel, then back to Paul. She arched her fine brows. "Well, I declare, Mr. Delahoussaye. What a fortuitous time you've chosen to arrive. Mrs. Samson and I might have been reduced to cinders on the hearth if you'd delayed a moment longer."

"I b—beg your pardon, Mrs. Raveneaux," Paul stammered, feeling much as he had as a boy when the schoolmaster rapped his knuckles. "I thought you were in danger."

"Then, sir, your gallantry is appreciated," said Delora.

Faye, refusing Paul's offered hand, pulled herself to her feet, shook out her sooty skirt, and ran across the room to throw open the door to the hall. Then she spun around, glowering at Delora. "Radley's gone. Where'd Langford take him?" she demanded.

"I don't know that Langford's taken him anywhere yet," Delora replied calmly. "So you might first try looking in the pantry."

Faye responded with a hiss and vanished from the room like escaping steam.

Delora shut her eyes a moment and sighed, then looked up at Paul. "Well, Mr. Delahoussaye?"

She must be anxious, Paul thought, to know what he planned to do with all his overheard information. He wasn't sure of the answer, but remembering his promise to Isabelle, he sought a way to explain his presence without implicating her. "Well, ma'am," he began, "I learned about this hiding place from Miss Euphrasie. I only thought to try it out."

"An extraordinary inspiration on such a day," said Delora.

"Yes. . . But Miss Isabelle and then you came in, and I couldn't. . . well, that is, I hesitated. . ."

"I quite understand, Mr. Delahoussaye," said Delora, in a way that made Paul feel she was reassuring him and not the other way around. "It's my opinion that when a person has been discovered doing something unmentionable, then that same something is unspeakable. So there's nothing more to be said—or written—about any of it. Nothing. Not a single, solitary word. Isn't that right, Mr. Delahoussaye?"

As Delora smiled and nodded, Paul felt his own head bob involuntarily in agreement. But the spell was broken when Ardyce rushed into the room.

"Miss Delora, I been looking for Miss Isabelle and can't find her nowhere," she cried. "Something's wrong. Nobody's upstairs. Nor the stable neither. Morning Glory's gone. I was coming in the back, and Faye tore past me 'cross the yard, screaming for Radley. And Auntie Pan's wailing in the kitchen, fit to be tied, saying we're all going to be bashed and buried with the Devil's spade."

Delora's response to Ardyce was lost to Paul as he sped from the house to the stable. What could have possessed Isabelle to go riding off on Morning Glory, leaving Paul holed up in the parlor? He bridled Pickwick, threw a leg over the sorrel's bare back, and, ducking the top of the door, galloped from the stable. Had Isabelle dashed off to town on some pressing business, or had she ridden into the woods or across the creek to Halcyon? Had someone persuaded her to go? Or forced her? Paul determined to start for the wild woods and Lyre's Creek. Then, if she were not there, he'd circle back by the family graveyard and through the pecan orchard.

Galloping down the hillside toward the thicket of oak and pine that hid Lyre's Creek from view, from far off to Paul's left beyond where he gauged the bridge to be, he heard a shot ring out. Pickwick shied and swerved, trying to turn himself back toward the stable, but Paul reined him in and turned his nose instead toward the holly bog. The horse obeyed and lumbered as swiftly as he could over uneven terrain, but on the outskirts of the bog he reared in panic and threw Paul from his bare back. Pickwick neighed his concern, prodding Paul's shoulder with his muzzle before tossing his head in a "follow me" gesture and retreating. Paul gained his footing and looked after his horse running for the safety of the stable. Was it the smell of blood that drove Pickwick away or the rank odor of another animal he had no wish to meet?

Paul stood still a moment. Even if his spectacles had not been smeared and fogged over, he doubted he could see anything beyond the dense screen of bay, holly, and fern. But he heard something: crackling twigs and branches, the sucking sounds of hooves pulled from thick mud, and breathing that seemed to boil up from bestial lungs. Slowly, Paul moved around the vicinity from which the sounds came and entered the holly bog through a break in the foliage. The earth was like sponge cushioning his steps. Leaving behind the cold open air, surrounding himself with the humid heat of decay, Paul edged nearer the scene he had heard and smelled and felt. He wiped a sleeve across his spectacles and parted the drapery of Spanish moss, peering ahead, at last bringing the tableau into focus.

Across a shadowy clearing Isabelle stood, her back pressed against the trunk of a broad cypress tree. Radley, at the center of the clearing, wielded a rusty shovel, jabbing the air with its blade within inches of Isabelle's face. On the ground, a few feet to Paul's right, Langford sprawled on his back, eyes closed, blood oozing from his brow. And near him Priapus and two huge sows snuffled and pawed over a hunting rifle.

Radley's back was to Paul, and Paul was sure he hadn't noticed him yet. The boy was too intent on terrorizing Isabelle.

"You was going to kill me, wasn't you? You and Langford. You lured me out here to kill me."

"You brought me here, Radley, to see a body. Remember?" Isabelle said in a strangled voice.

"You was so eager to come. I should've known. I can just hear you now, plotting with Lang." Here Radley broke into a grotesque falsetto: "Slow, stupid Radley—I'll just get him to follow me into the woods, and you can blow his head clean off." He poked at Isabelle's waist with the point of the shovel until she winced, then added, "But slow, stupid Radley was too fast and too smart for the both of you."

Isabelle looked toward Langford lying motionless. Then, slowly her gaze traveled round a half-circle of the clearing and fixed on Paul.

"We could've been long gone, me and Ma," said Radley. "But Miss Delora kept on drugging Ma. And I couldn't bring the loot to the house or have it on me with her looking to get her jewels back. Then you and Langford beat me to Pa's guts. It ain't fair after all the work I done."

"If I hadn't come on those entrails, Radley, they would've been eaten up by the *hogs*." Isabelle laid particular stress on her last word and shot a desperate look past Radley to Paul.

What could he do? Paul wondered. The hogs surrounded the rifle, taking turns, it seemed, lifting the barrel from the mire with their snouts, exhaling great clouds of hot breath over it and slathering it with saliva. If Paul could reach the weapon and wrest it from Priapus and his sows, would it even fire, coated as it was with hog spittle and mud?

Radley waved the shovel blade to and fro, chuckling softly. "You're gonna be real sorry you messed with me," he said. "I ran that ghost-man through. And I can do the same to you. But I ain't doing any more diggin' graves, that's for sure. I'll just toss you in the creek, and the nigger, too."

Radley brought the shovel back in preparation for a lunge. Isabelle recoiled, scrambling up one knee of the cypress, but still not out of Radley's reach. And Paul did the only thing then in his power to do: with all his strength he threw himself, bellowing like a demon from hell, forward into Priapus's broad haunches and drove the furious hog like a battering ram into Radley.

Radley whirled to face his attacker, and, though no sound escaped, his mouth dropped open just as Priapus's great bulk slammed into him. Radley fell back, still clutching the shovel handle, and the hog trampled over his body.

Paul saw no more as he toppled forward, mud splattering his spectacles. With his arms he covered his head as the sows thundered past close on either side of him, pursuing their boar.

As the sound of hogs tearing through underbrush died away, Paul raised himself on his elbows and strained his eyes to peer over the top of his glasses. Isabelle, a blurry shape of gray skirt at this distance, slipped down from the knees of the cypress and ran to Langford. Quickly, Paul wiped his lenses on one of the few remaining clean spots on the shoulder of his jacket. Replacing his spectacles on his nose and shoving back his lank hair, Paul stood and looked about him. Radley's trampled body lay motionless, but Langford was making an effort to rise. Isabelle assisted him, pulling her handkerchief from her sleeve and pressing it to his head wound. He staggered backward and came to rest on a fallen tree trunk. Isabelle looked to Paul.

"Langford was talking to Radley, trying to get him to put the shovel down and come back to the house. But Radley was all nerves. When Langford got too close, Radley swung at his head with the shovel and knocked him down, and the rifle discharged," said Isabelle, shakily. "Oh, I don't know what I would have done, Paul, if you hadn't come when you did. Radley was so scared to be caught out—he was ready to do anything."

Paul stepped closer to her and saw her pale face was streaked with grime and tears. He wanted to hold her, but even as she trembled, he saw she was so busy being kind to someone who needed her, and he dared not interfere. She stood by Langford as he sat on the trunk and held the compress to his wounded brow, letting his head rest against her body and his blood darken the front of her dress. Her mantle had fallen to one side over her shoulder, and with one hand she unfastened the clasp and held out the garment to Paul.

"You can put this over Radley," she said.

"Aren't you cold?" Paul asked.

"No, not anymore. I'm numb."

Paul took the mantle and approached Radley. Cloven hooves had torn and muddied his clothing. One foot lay skewed at an odd angle to his leg, the ankle snapped, Paul assumed. As he'd fallen, Radley must have brought the shovel back, blade behind his head, for now he lay with arm crooked, fingers gripping the shovel handle, and his head dropped back against the blade as if it were his pillow. What there was of his chin jutted skyward, and his mouth still gaped. Paul bent slightly to spread the mantle over the boy's body and was just pulling an edge up to cover the contorted features and vacant eyes when he heard something—a low strangling gurgle issued from Radley's throat, then ceased. The death rattle, Paul thought, and covered the face.

Returning to Isabelle's side, he saw that Langford had rallied and stood, tying his own blue bandanna around his head and over the lacerated brow already covered by Isabelle's handkerchief. In a low voice, Langford offered Isabelle an explanation and apology.

"I was trying to keep track of Radley, keep him out of more trouble, but he snuck off late last night. I didn't get to him 'til after he'd opened the grave. Miss Faye sent him to find more treasure, since they'd lost Samson's entrails. Well, your Mr. Forest had already met up with Radley and his shovel. That boy was a-shaking and a-blubbering, talking nothing but ghosts. So I told him I'd fix things. Then he perked right up, full of hisself, and I knew I'd have my hands full today. I never meant you no harm, Miss Isabelle, never in this world. But young colonel was dead, and you already thought he was buried there."

"Until yesterday," said Isabelle, softly, "when I saw and spoke to Forest at Halcyon."

"I'm real sorry, Miss Isabelle. I just wanted to put things right for you and for Miss Del."

"I know you did, Langford. And I forgive you."

Between them, Paul and Langford carried Radley from the holly bog, past the woods and up the hill toward the stable yard, Paul holding the shoulders and Langford the feet. Radley's hand would not unclench from the shovel handle so Isabelle was obliged to walk alongside, helping to support the shovel and prevent it from dragging the ground.

Paul's horse peeked from a stall window, then withdrew from sight as they approached. Delora, Ardyce, and Auntie Pan advanced toward them across the yard. And from the orchard Faye came running, hair loose, eyes wild, braying Radley's name.

Paul and Langford laid him down, and his mother immediately tore the mantle from him, screaming, "Murder, murder!" and glaring accusingly from Delora to Langford to Paul.

"The hogs ran him down," Paul tried to explain over the din Faye created. "He'd struck Langford and was about to hurt Miss Isabelle when the hogs trampled him."

"Murder, murder!" Faye continued to shriek.

Delora stepped closer, staring imperiously down at Faye and her son. "Woman, if you don't shut your mouth and open your eyes there will be murder done on this spot. Your boy's as alive as any of us." Faye was silenced by Delora's words. "Well, just look at him, all of you," said Delora. "Look at his chest. He's breathing, sure 'nough. Just knocked senseless, is all."

Faye gasped her relief and kissed Radley's bruised, swollen cheek, then fell to sobbing over him.

Delora cast a distressed look toward Langford, and Paul heard him murmur, "Everything gonna to be all right, Miss Del."

Delora almost smiled, then set new plans in motion. Langford was to hitch the mule to the wagon and take Radley to Verbena to see a doctor. His mother was welcome to ride along. "I know how anxious you've been, Faye, to get to town," Delora commented. When Faye objected to the journey, Delora pointed out that following her plan would bring Radley to treatment much sooner than would fetching the doctor out to Belle Ombre; or, thought Paul, the bumpy ride to town would finish him off more speedily.

Delora asked that Paul ride alongside on Pickwick in case Langford needed his assistance. "I'm worried about Lang's head injury. And, of course, Radley's precarious condition." Her aunt entrusted Isabelle to Ardyce's care and the salubrious effects of Auntie Pan's remedies. Delora announced she would watch over the Samsons until all was ready for their departure.

"And when you get to town, Mr. Delahoussaye," Delora added, "I trust you to explain to whoever might be curious—Captain Newell, for instance—about Radley's unfortunate *accident.*"

"Yes, ma'am," said Paul.

Paul hoped for a private word with Isabelle before he left for Verbena in his mud-caked suit. But, for the moment, the best he could manage was to catch her up on the way to the house with Ardyce and Auntie Pan. They did stand back a little, though not out of earshot, as Paul spoke to Isabelle.

"Will you be all right?" he asked.

"I'll be fine," she said. "I'll never forget your bravery, sir."

"Bravery?" he said modestly. "It was all Priapus's doing."

"He'd have done nothing without encouragement."

Then she turned away, and flanked by Ardyce and Auntie Pan, retreated toward the house, as Paul stared after them. Isabelle and Ardyce walked arm in arm, their heads together for a moment. Suddenly, Isabelle stopped. Ardyce and Auntie Pan glanced back at Paul, and he thought the cook made a sort of shooing gesture with her hand at Isabelle Then she and Ardyce proceeded without Isabelle, who turned, just as Paul had wished and willed her to do, and advanced toward him.

Reaching him, she spoke, and Paul heard a kind of weary relief and mellowness in her voice. "Oh, let them all do what they must up there." She nodded toward the house. "Walk with me, Paul."

What pleasure it was to hear her speak his given name. He offered her his arm, and she accepted.

"Where shall we go?" he asked.

"Oh, anywhere. Anywhere, but a graveyard."

Paul strolled with her then, past the kitchen garden.

"I'm glad I was wrong about my earlier suspicions of your aunt," he said. "At least about her involvement in the murders. Of course, there are other things . . ."

"That are none of your concern," Isabelle finished for him, but gently, with no hint of reprimand. "When did you manage to get out of the hidey-hole?"

"After Miss Lydie Vee had left and Faye Samson had come to the parlor."

"So you heard their conversation?"

"And their scuffling by the hearth. Mrs. Samson's skirt caught fire. I made my entrance just in time to see Miss Delora beating down the flames."

"For Heaven's sake!" Isabelle stopped by the spring house and faced him. "Aunt Delora knows you heard everything."

"She already has my assurance I won't repeat a word. And she knows nothing about your part in my eavesdropping, and never will."

"You'd lie for me?"

"She won't ask," Paul replied confidently. "If she has a suspicion, she doesn't want to know. Besides, she has more pressing concerns."

"Such as what's to be done about Radley."

Paul nodded. "What he did to Elroy Samson—well, that could be considered execution more than murder."

"Though he didn't do it to avenge Beryl's death," said Isabelle.

"And what he did to Colonel Brodie was murder indeed," Paul added.

Isabelle looked away, yet her gray eyes seemed not to focus on anything in the distance. "The boy thought he saw a ghost," she said softly, "so he lashed out with what he had at hand—a shovel—and brought down a man."

Paul covered her cold hands with his, not knowing what to say to her, and she met his gaze.

"Forest had ruined his feet, walking all the way home in ill-fitting boots. He had gangrene. And his mind was half gone. He knew me, and then he didn't know me. As I told you the first day you came here, I lost my fiancé a long time ago."

Paul brought her hands to his breast to warm them.

"I've been thinking," she said a little shakily, lacing her fingers with his, "after all that's happened—well, my holding a grudge against you about my packet of letters—it's petty somehow. If those letters were what brought you here . . . well, sir, I'm not sorry you came to Belle Ombre."

"Nor am I," Paul breathed. "Miss Isabelle, I swear to you, I will never again trespass upon your privacy. And I will never come near you without your permission."

"Mr. Delahoussaye!" Delora's voice carried from the veranda and over the lawn. "Time to depart!"

In an instant, before Paul could comprehend the full pleasure of it, Isabelle's lips brushed his fingertips. Then her hands slipped from his, and she was away from him, beyond arm's length.

"Mr. Delahoussaye!" Delora called again.

"Will you come back to the house and see me off?" asked Paul.

Isabelle shook her head. "No. You go on without me. I'll say goodbye here."

"But I'll see you again?"

Isabelle smiled. "You see me now."

Paul stared at her, fixing the image of her in his mind as she was now, as she had been the first time he saw her: in a blood-spattered dress with muddied hem, tangles in her fair hair, and grime streaked across her ivory cheek.

Paul thought the words would catch in his throat, but he uttered them anyway: "First time I laid eyes on you, Miss Isabelle, I wanted to offer you my handkerchief."

He reached into the inside breast pocket of his coat, withdrew a rumpled but clean cotton handkerchief, and held it out to her. Isabelle accepted it, touched it to her cheek, then took it away again, a curious expression coming over her face. Holding the handkerchief before her in one hand, she unfolded it with the fingers of the other. There, on the white cotton, lay a lock of hair the color of a walnut shell.

Paul sucked in his breath and held it, while slowly Isabelle refolded the handkerchief. Stepping closer to Paul, she tucked the handkerchief back in his breast pocket. "You'd better keep it," she said.

Then Isabelle walked away from him, down the hill, in the direction of Lyre's Creek. Only after she was out of sight could Paul make himself turn toward the house. When he reached the front drive, he found his skittish horse, saddled and waiting, held at short rein by Langford. He gripped Pickwick's reins and mounted, the horse all the while stepping sideways from the mule-drawn wagon, where Radley was settled, his mother hovering over him. Then, Langford swung himself up onto the wagon seat and waited.

Delora descended the front steps. She handed Faye a blanket, and Faye, in turn, handed Delora a small object; Paul thought he caught a glint of gold before Delora's hand closed in a fist and disappeared for a moment into her skirt pocket.

Langford, after accepting a packet of papers and some money from Delora, leaned his ear close to her mouth, listening and nodding as she whispered. Paul looked past them to the veranda where Lydie Vee sat rocking and cradling what appeared to be a small chest with the lid thrown back. Her cat, Carlotta, sat nearby, whipping her tail to the rhythm of the rocking chair.

Breaking away from Langford, Delora came nearer Paul, laying a soothing hand on his horse's neck as she spoke. "Mr. Delahoussaye, Lydie Vee has had a terrible shock. I was just explaining to Langford. Sometime this morning, after the exhumation, Babcock took Morning Glory and all the valuables he and Lydie Vee had in the world, salvaged from their dry goods business, and rode off. She's been sitting on the veranda ever since, in a state of shock, holding that empty cash box."

"Did he leave a note? Any explanation?" asked Paul.

"He didn't, but Euphrasie did. Babcock and Euphrasie have run away together! In her note—badly spelt as it is—she calls it a lark just to cheer up her old uncle." Here Delora dropped her voice to a whisper. "Fortunately, as Lydie Vee assures me, Babcock is not *capable* of doing a body much harm." Then she spoke up again. "I've told Langford, if you all see them in town, don't try to reason with them, just haul them home with whatever they haven't spent. And please bring back the horse."

"You can rely on me, Miss Delora." Paul tipped his battered hat.

Radley groaned from the rear of the wagon, and Faye cast an anxious look toward Delora. Delora nodded and moved aside to let the wagon pass. "Remember what I told you, Faye," she called, then turned her back and ascended the steps of Belle Ombre.

* * *

Paul passed three days in Verbena before riding back to Belle Ombre.

First he conferred with the town doctor, who stitched Langford's forehead and assessed Radley's condition. The boy's cuts and bruises were superficial, but one ankle was broken and required setting. "Won't need to tell the boy to stay off his feet," the doctor quipped. Radley's fall, with the resulting blow to his head, had left him semiconscious at best. "Young Samson," the doctor continued, "may survive any number of years in this stupor, given good nursing and a fortifying gruel I will prescribe. But I'm afraid the boy's reason is damaged beyond repair." Radley had little enough to begin with, thought Paul.

Then Langford drove Faye Samson and her insensible son back to the plantation. Tied to the rear of the wagon was Morning Glory, who had been left at the livery stable in favor of a coach and four. Babcock and Euphrasie had certainly gone somewhere in style. Just where, Paul mused, was a mystery for another time.

At the post office, wires and letters awaited Paul from Mr. Caulder, who demanded his itinerant journalist produce some stories immediately for the *Laurel Dispatch* or lose his position and expense account. Thus, Paul returned to a room at Thorpe's Inn, sent his suit and shirt out to be laundered, wrapped himself in a blanket, and, with newly purchased paper and pencil, wrote. But his stories were not, as he had originally planned, about war widows and their grief, though he did write about women, women who strove and survived in a beleaguered South.

While explaining recent events at Belle Ombre to Captain Newell, Paul thought Delora would be pleased with him. A week in her company had taught him something about the value of noncommittal remarks and about the art of evasion. Paul described Radley's accidental encounter with the hogs, saying: "I recall Miss Isabelle's telling me on the day I arrived at Belle Ombre that the hogs weren't vicious, but they could sure knock a man off his feet." Then Newell brought up the exhumation; "Something odd was going on there, and I still wouldn't be surprised to learn Miss Delora has her husband's body stashed somewhere on the premises." "Oh, I feel certain there's no evidence of that," Paul had replied, and changed the subject with an offer to write a glowing piece about the captain for the *Laurel Dispatch*. Newell, in a celebratory mood, having just received orders for a transfer, invited Paul to a farewell banquet.

The morning after the festivities, a rare clear day, Paul, a little bleary-eyed but in a clean suit, rode back to see Isabelle. He was met at the door by a maid he'd not seen before and ushered to the front parlor. Perhaps the room had been recently aired, for it seemed not nearly so musty as it had the first time he entered it.

Soon Delora joined him, gliding in with a welcoming smile.

"Mr. Delahoussaye, how delightful to see you! How kind of you to stop by before you leave our vicinity entirely," she said, and urged him to join her on the faded green brocade sofa.

At her prompting, Paul described the goings-on in town, then asked how things were at Belle Ombre.

"Oh, law! We're in a whirl of activity. Langford and I have spent the whole morning planning how we'll bring the land back to life next spring. And Lydie Vee is busy working up her curriculum, as she calls it, for a girls' academy. She plans to hold classes in the back parlor. And the boarding students can occupy the spare rooms and make themselves useful doing some of the housework—as part of their education."

"Any word of Mr. Vasseur and Miss Euphrasie?" asked Paul.

"Not a whisper. I've enlisted the aid of a man who used to track runaways. But at least Lydie Vee is occupied and not brooding. Some things are just out of our hands." Delora opened her palms heavenward. "Take Radley," she said. "What in the world would we have done had we been forced to bring that boy to justice? But now he's in a prison of his own, beyond any of us."

"And Faye Samson?" said Paul. "The day we left here, did she really give you Colonel Raveneaux's wedding ring in exchange for a blanket for Radley?"

Delora looked a little wary, then half-smiled. "Is that what you thought, Mr. Delahoussaye? Lord, no. She did give me the ring—which Beryl had taken from the bedpost, where I'd hidden it when my husband left here and which had somehow been found by Radley. But in exchange for a blanket—hardly. She gave me that ring in exchange for sanctuary."

"Sanctuary? They're still here then?"

"Not in the big house. Faye Samson will never set foot in here again. But I've allowed her to stay on in her cabin, where she can nurse her boy and do a little laundry and mending for us as need be. Where else could they go? Who else would take them in?"

"You're very kind-hearted, Miss Delora."

"Not at all, Mr. Delahoussaye. Faye lost all her sons but Radley in the War. I had no sons to send. So there you are. Maybe she's entitled to something from me after all."

"Miss Delora, there's a question I've been mulling over, while I was in Verbena. Could I be so bold as to ask—did you ever really need my assistance?"

"Why, certainly. You've been invaluable, particularly in dealing with that dreadful Captain Newell."

"But," Paul persisted, "did you ever intend me to discover Elroy Samson's killer?"

"Well you did, didn't you? And you kept occupied and gave us a little time. And everything worked out, now didn't it?"

"I hope so." Paul heard a light footstep pass in the hall and looked hopefully toward the parlor door. "With your permission, ma'am, might I see Miss Isabelle before I leave?"

"Of course you'd have my permission—my blessing, in fact," Delora replied. "But Isabelle isn't here. She and Ardyce left yesterday morning for New Orleans. Isabelle has accepted a position there as a governess. Her employer, Mr. William Pascal, is a very respectable widower. Lives quietly as one can in such a city. Lydie Vee knew his late wife when they were girls, so he comes recommended. He's an undertaker with a nice clientele, I believe, and father of two adorable children. I hated to part with her, but Isabelle needed a change. And what could I do? These young women nowadays! So eager to have their independence."

"She left yesterday?" Paul was stricken.

"Yes, you see, the Thibodeau brothers and their grandmother were making the trip, and it was a golden opportunity for Isabelle to travel with them, well escorted to her destination. But don't be too downcast, Mr. Delahoussaye. Before you leave today, I shall be sure to give you Isabelle's new address. You do get about so, traveling on business and such. Perhaps you would be so kind as to look in on her, if the opportunity presents itself."

"I hope it will, ma'am. If not, I'll make an opportunity," Paul said with conviction.

"You are the most reassuring of gentlemen. Of course I worry about her. Anything can happen in New Orleans."

"Or on a plantation?"

"Oh, I guarantee we've never had more excitement here than the week of your stay," Delora replied. "But New

Orleans was an occupied city for most of the War. The
Yankees are still there, aren't they?"

"Yes, ma'am, and showing no signs of leaving, so I've
heard."

"Well, there you are then. You simply must go—soon
as you can persuade your employer to send you."

Paul smiled and nodded, thinking what an excellent
tutor Delora had been in the art of persuasion.

"Oh, and before another minute passes us by, I have
something for you, sir." Here Delora swirled to the mantel,
took down a folded paper, and presented it to Paul. "Isabelle
left a letter for you."

Paul took it eagerly, then hesitated to open it, fingering
the wax seal.

"Shall I give you a few moment's privacy, sir?" asked
Delora.

"I'd be obliged." Then Paul reached into his breast
pocket and extracted a letter, which he handed to Delora.
"And I have something for you, too, I brought from the post
office," he said. "Something you may wish to read in the
privacy of your study."

"Oh?" Delora gazed at the neatly printed return
address on her letter and brightened. "From Washington,
District of Columbia. Why, how kind of you to bring me a
letter from Colonel Raveneaux!"

"It was my pleasure, ma'am."

Delora started for the door, then turned back. "You
know, Mr. Delahoussaye, I thought to myself the first day I
met you, now here's someone who possesses the quality I
admire most in a gentleman."

"What quality is that, ma'am?"

"Why, discretion, of course. Now I'll leave you to your
letter." She was as good as her word.

Alone, Paul slipped a finger under the flap of paper and broke the seal."Dear Mr. Delahoussaye," Isabelle wrote in that familiar, gently sloping hand, "my hasty departure has made it impossible for me to thank you in person for your many kindnesses to my family and myself. For the present, may this note suffice. Perhaps one day, when our recent difficulties are no more than shadowy memories, we may meet again in happier circumstances. Until then, please know that I wish you well. With gratitude and friendship, Isabelle Ross."

Gratitude and friendship—they were a beginning, thought Paul. But what truly gave him hope was a tiny yellow wildflower Isabelle had pressed within the folded page.